Praise for Curtiss Ann Matlock's
THE LOVES OF RUBY DEE

"A superb story that hooked me right at the beginning and didn't let go until every emotion had been rung dry. This is one of those stories that will stay with you, in your heart and in your mind, for a long time to come."

Rendezvous

"A wonderful antidote to glitz romance . . . these are just real folks. Ruby Dee is so sweet, so loving, so wise that you know she'll get it right in the end, and you stay with her all the way."

Detroit Free Press

"Matlock's world is filled with warm, wonderful characters who grab your heart and won't let go. I laughed and cried with them, and will do it again and again."

Dixie Browning

"Beautiful and touching . . . THE LOVES OF RUBY DEE is a wonderfully crafted and thoroughly heartwarming tale of misfits and loners learning to share and love one another. This is a book guaranteed to touch your heart."

Romantic Times

Other Avon Contemporary Romances by
Curtiss Ann Matlock

THE LOVES OF RUBY DEE

CURTISS ANN MATLOCK

LOVE IN A SMALL TOWN

AVON BOOKS ◆ NEW YORK

LOVE IN A SMALL TOWN is an original publication of Avon Books.
This work has never before appeared in book form. This work is a novel.
Any similarity to actual persons or events is purely coincidental.

AVON BOOKS
A division of
The Hearst Corporation
1350 Avenue of the Americas
New York, New York 10019

Copyright © 1997 by Curtiss Ann Matlock
Inside cover author photo by Glamour Shots
Published by arrangement with the author
Library of Congress Catalog Card Number: 96-96874
ISBN: 0-380-78107-7

First Avon Books Printing: February 1997

AVON TRADEMARK REG. U.S. PAT. OFF. AND IN OTHER COUNTRIES, MARCA
REGISTRADA, HECHO EN U.S.A.

Printed in the U.S.A.

RA   10 9 8 7 6 5 4 3 2 1

Author's Note

I'm asked repeatedly where my stories come from. I have to admit that they come from my own life, from the lives of family and friends and their friends, and from the lives heard about while waiting in grocery store checkout lanes.

The story of Molly and Tommy Lee is the universal story of love and marriage and family. In this way it is my story and that of at least 85 percent of the married couples in the world, in one way or another.

With that in mind, let me put in here, lest there be mistaken supposition: I have no sisters, and I adore my lovely mother-in-law, who has a lot of color in her life, not to mention all of us making a mess of her life at numerous holidays. My own dear mother can be wonderfully eccentric, but she drives a Toyota and never goes out for breakfast.

This book is for those two grand ladies, who have taught me much of what I know about loving, and for dear friends Karen, Dixie, Machelle, Carolyn, and Mary, and to all of you out there who have walked the valleys and the hilltops of the familiar road and continue to walk on.

Most of all I dedicate this story to James David Matlock, my husband, the bravest man I know.

—Curtiss Ann Matlock

1

You Don't Even Know Who I Am

When Molly awoke, she knew right away that Tommy Lee hadn't come to bed all night. She knew, without opening her eyes, because she could feel the emptiness beside her. She had been married to Tommy Lee Hayes for almost twenty-five years. She knew what the bed felt like with him in it or him not in it.

She stretched out her arm and felt with the flat of her hand the cool smoothness of the sheet beside her. Testing at first, seeking a sign of lingering heat, and then simply rubbing her palm across the taut sheet and wishing.

Molly was a quiet sleeper, didn't hardly mess up a bed at all, whereas Tommy Lee always left the covers looking like he'd wrestled them all night. He couldn't stand his feet to be cramped, so he tugged the sheet out at the bottom, and he shifted his body so hard that he got the fitted sheet all bunched up. Sometimes he got so rambunctious he would throw his pillow on the floor and then snatch Molly's right out from beneath her head, and the whole time he never woke from a sound sleep.

Cracking an eye, Molly peered at the red numerals of the digital clock. It read 6:47.

"Oh, Lord," she mumbled and pulled the pillow over her head.

A moment later she came up from beneath the pillow, her hair a wild nest and her cotton gown hanging off her shoulder. She looked down at the pillow and saw streaks of black—the telltale evidence of a woman who has fallen into the poor habit of not removing her makeup before bed, and then cries off her mascara. She looked at the bedcovers, all neat at the bottom. And then she sat there, listening to the music floating up from the stereo down in the shop. The music was the tip-off that Tommy Lee was out there. He couldn't do a lick of work without his music blasting.

Not even seven o'clock on a Saturday morning, and Tommy Lee was already working. Molly could count on both hands the number of times in their marriage that her husband had managed to sleep past five. A man with his own successful business kept long hours, and a man who had a passion for what he did kept them even more so.

Tommy Lee certainly had a passion, all right—for engines and cars. He was known for building and rebuilding racing engines, and he was so good at it that people came from Arkansas and Texas all the way to his small shop in Oklahoma, which sat right there on the other side of the driveway from their house and therefore allowed him to be over there any time day or night. One thing about it, Molly always knew where Tommy Lee was. She didn't have to worry about him being out with another woman.

Sometimes Molly thought she would stand a better chance against another woman. She had never managed to compete well against six-hundred-plus horses harnessed in a hunk of metal.

Thinking about Tommy Lee already up and productive and herself sitting aimlessly on the bed and brooding made her feel guilty, so she dragged herself up and headed for the shower, by way of the double open windows. The first thing Molly always did each morning was to go look out the window.

Their house, which was the house Tommy Lee had grown up in, was one of those big old farmhouses. Eight years ago, when they had moved in, Molly had pretty near hated this house. It had been so stark, everything in it painted white and with white blinds at the windows. But then Molly had looked out their bedroom window and been totally captivated.

At the moment, the spring breeze fluttered her thin cotton gown and caressed her skin. May was at an end and June coming next week. Blue sky stretching forever, a hawk soaring high, the windowsill beneath her fingers covered with fine grit.

To the southwest she could see the town of Valentine: the tall trees, the co-op elevator, the Baptist church spire, the big old silver water tower. Valentine was where she'd grown up, where her mother and eldest sister lived, where she and Tommy Lee shopped and had Mexican food on Friday nights.

Directly south the land rolled away in grass and canyons and patches of trees. In the near pasture she saw her gelding, Marker, swishing his tail, and farther out she could see Mr. Gil's registered longhorns grazing happily.

Tommy Lee had inherited two thousand acres at his daddy's death, but he had quit trying to farm it five years ago and rented most of it out to Mr. Gil. Tommy Lee'd had to let his daddy be dead and buried nearly four years before he could bring himself to do it. There never was a thought of selling the land, though, and Molly was glad. Molly was a hoarder of land. Not that she really considered this land hers. She couldn't somehow; she was of Collier blood, not Hayes. But she did think of it as Tommy Lee's and their children's land, and she hoarded it for them.

Turning from the view, Molly went on into the bathroom and into the shower, without glancing at the mirror as she passed. Lately she had felt a strange tightness across her chest whenever she happened to look into a mirror. It seemed like confusing questions leaped out at her from the glass and demanded answers. Molly not only had no answers, she didn't understand the questions.

But a mirror is not an easy thing to avoid. After Molly had showered and dressed in a soft denim shirt and faded Wranglers and slipped on Keds, she went to brush her teeth and was confronted by the mirror that took up the entire wall above the cultured marble sink.

She stared at herself, and then, slowly, she leaned forward and studied her eyes. The circles beneath them were dark—like she had two black eyes.

Oh, Lord.

Molly swallowed. Lately she had been feeling as if she were holding a ball of tears down inside. Just then the ball was growing and swelling and trying to push its way out. It had done so several times in the past weeks, and each time the tears had come with such force they frightened her. Molly was about the ugliest crier on earth. Even Rennie said so.

Mostly no one had seen Molly's eruptions of tears, but last Wednesday afternoon, when she had gone to the movies with her mother and her sister Kaye—which was a trying experience in itself, but it had been hers and Mama's little birthday present to Kaye—she had started crying for the heroine, who'd had a fight with her lover, wrecked her car, and then lost her dog. The movie had had forty-five minutes still to go, and it was a romantic comedy, and Molly had known good and well everything would turn around for a happy ending, but she'd just sat there and boo-hooed uncontrollably into the only tissue she could find, which was a used ragged one from the bottom of her purse.

Kaye had been embarrassed as all get-out. "Good Lord, you need to get some hormones or somethin'," she said. Kaye could be like that, tactless as wallpaper falling down.

Undoubledly Kaye would have much more to say if she knew the shocking fact that the F-word had crept into Molly's thoughts. A couple of times the statement, *"I don't give a fucking damn,"* came clearly across her mind.

Well, Molly had been brought up better than that. She had never used the F-word in her life; the idea appalled her. Aside from several times telling Kaye to "kiss my ass" in a fit of fury, the strongest curses Molly used were "sugar" or "spit" or "dang."

Then, on top of that, the past Thursday she had been barreling by Eulalee Harris's place, and Eulalee's chickens had been all over the dusty, rutted road, like they always were, and Molly had not tried to swerve at all. What she thought was, "Get out of my way, you f—— chickens."

Not that she could hurt chickens. It was nearly impossible to run over a chicken on purpose. But that was not the point. The point was that she hadn't cared one whit if she mowed them down.

Her image in the mirror started in with those silent, demanding questions again, and the best answer Molly could come up with was that if Tommy Lee would quit falling asleep down in his BarcaLounger in front of the television, she would do a lot better.

Then she straightened herself up, breathed deeply and blinked her burning eyes. She did not intend to do something as stupid as start the day out crying. Lord knew the circles beneath her eyes were bad enough.

She combed her hair up into a ponytail and dabbed on a bit of makeup from the Estée Lauder kit Rennie had given her last Christmas. Rennie would spend $120 like that, whereas Molly would have had to wait for half price—not that she couldn't afford it, but she was darned near incapable of buying anything when not on sale price. She put on her favorite dangling pewter earrings and her silver-and-turquoise cuff bracelet and decided she felt a lot better, more in her skin where she belonged.

Downstairs in the living room she straightened the cotton throw that was all askew over Tommy Lee's BarcaLounger and picked up his dirty socks thrown right there beside it, just like it was his bed, and an empty Coca-Cola can from the end table and took the things on into the kitchen. Socks on the washer, Coke can in the recycling bin. She paused at the sink; the window above it was opened and Tommy Lee's music came loudly through it.

Tommy Lee liked all sorts of music, but his favorite was country, just like Molly's. He said within the country sound were mixed the seeds of all other music, from classical to blues to rock. Tommy Lee's mind clicked with details like that. He could tell the artist and the song title of every country song recorded from the early fifties until today, and in the same manner he could glance at any car and tell the make and model and year it was produced, going all the way back to the first assembly line models. He liked his cars fast and his music loud, and Molly was of the opinion that both had pretty much ruined his hearing, which was why he kept the stereo volume up. He also shut people out with the sound of his music and his engines; he'd told her this once.

Through the window she could see across to the shop, could see Tommy Lee in his dark shirt and jeans beneath the fluorescent lights. She watched him a moment and then closed the window and turned on the little black radio on the counter. The sultry country voice of Patty Loveless came out the speaker, and Molly sang along while she made a fresh pot of coffee.

The coffeemaker gave up that final steamy gurgle, and Molly got two mugs out of the cabinet, filled them—sugar for her, black for Tommy Lee—and carried them out the back door and across to the shop. Tommy Lee was working on an engine perched on a stand, working it over with his strong, greasy hands and his biceps veined and bulging and stretching his T-shirt sleeves.

In all truth, Tommy Lee had not changed in looks a whole lot since he was sixteen years old, except to fill out, cut his velvety mahogany hair shorter and have it come in silver on the sides and have crow's-feet grow out from the corner of his summer blue eyes.

Molly thought he was a lot more handsome these days than when they first had married. He was every inch a man and no doubt about it. He was in her opinion the most attractive man in Valentine, despite his never having kept up with fashion. He still favored T-shirts with hot rods emblazoned across the front and Levi's that rode low on his lean hips. Women looked at him in those Levi's, too. Molly had seen that, and she couldn't blame them. Tommy Lee wasn't a man to look back, though, at least not so anyone would tell. Tommy Lee was quite proper about things like that. And he was shy. He would blush deep red at the least thing.

He didn't hear her step or hello, because of the music drowning everything out. Juggling the two cups, Molly went over to turn down the volume. Tommy Lee saw her then.

"Well, good mornin'," he said. "Sleep well?" He was frowning in deep concentration at the engine before he even finished speaking.

She said, "I brought you a cup of coffee," and he didn't notice that she didn't answer his question.

He said thanks. "You can just set it there. . . ." He motioned to the tall red toolbox.

She set his cup where he said and stood there, sipping from her own, watching his hands and forearms.

Molly had always liked to watch Tommy Lee work on anything. There were few things in this world that Tommy Lee couldn't build or repair, and she had always been amazed at how he could be so strong and gentle at the same time. She kept on staring, watching his strong, grease-stained hands feel all in and around the smooth cylinders. Memories and feelings tugged at her. A desperate longing and a crazy anger all swirled around inside her. The anger embarrassed and scared her.

Quite suddenly Tommy Lee went to wiping his hands on a rag, reached for his cup and looked directly at her.

"It's an awfully nice mornin'," he said.

He cast her a grin, but it didn't reach his eyes. He looked hesitant. That look made Molly mad and sad at the same time, and she got that tight feeling in her chest.

She said, "Did you sleep okay in your chair?"

Tommy Lee looked down at his cup. "I'm gonna have to quit that, I guess. It's makin' me real stiff." He drank deeply from his mug, then looked back at the engine. "I meant to come up, but I got to watchin' that racing movie with Paul Newman, and the next thing I just fell asleep." He looked sorry, and that made Molly feel worse.

She thought how he'd rather be down there watching a movie than up with her, but she didn't think it would improve anything at all to say it. She didn't think she could say it, because then it would be thrown out there like the bald truth and they'd both have to face it.

She said, "Would you like to sit on the porch for a few minutes? There's a couple of cinnamon rolls left. I'll pop them in the microwave."

She watched his face, watched his gaze dart back down into his coffee cup. Hiding there.

With a shake of his head, he said, "I'm already greasy. I might as well finish here first. I'm a week behind on this engine for Cormac."

Hurt sliced through Molly, so strong it brought an actual pain across her shoulders and a knot beneath her breastbone. She felt rather like she was shriveling and at any moment she would be no more than a tiny dried lump on the floor, where she could be swept up with the bits of greasy dirt and engine carbon and thrown away with all the other stuff Tommy Lee had no use for.

Tommy Lee said, "I'll be up for lunch," but that didn't make her feel a lot better. She told herself to quit being an overly sensitive child and that she, too, had a lot of things to do. Saturday was housecleaning day, and she was always behind on the business accounts.

Turning, she looked around for dirty dishes to take back to the house. Tommy Lee, and Woody Wilson, his part-time helper, were forever bringing their drinks and snacks out and leaving their dishes. She found three empty ice tea glasses, a plate of crumbs, and a fat glass half filled with milk. The milk was still cool, obviously left from that morning.

Molly went to the door and called, "Kitty, kitty." The fat gray tabby, Ace, came at a quick waddle. The dog, Jake, rose from beneath the workbench and came over, too. He appeared more stiff than usual. He had been shot two years ago by Mr. Gil for chasing Mr. Gil's longhorns, and the shot had creased his backbone. After the vet bill, Tommy Lee said Jake was the most expensive free stray dog they'd ever had. At least Jake couldn't chase cattle any longer.

Molly tipped the glass first for the cat and then let Jake have a couple of licks.

"Geez, Molly, do you have to do that?"

"What?" She looked up to see Tommy Lee frowning. She'd forgotten that Tommy Lee never liked for her to feed the animals out of the house dishes. Usually she made certain he didn't see. She said now, "I've fed them from the house dishes for years."

"I know that, Molly," he said, his blue eyes sharp. "But plates are one thing and a glass is another. We put our mouths on the glasses."

"I do wash them, Tommy Lee, same as the plates. I put them in the dishwasher and that sterilizes them."

By now Ace had quit sticking his head in the glass and had gone to wetting his paw in the bit of milk and licking it. Jake had lain back down.

"It's still not a sanitary practice. I just don't like the thought, okay?" Tommy Lee said, as if his word was to be obeyed.

Molly lifted the glass and straightened, and she said, "When you eat at a restaurant, you put the fork all the way into your mouth—a fork that you know not in whose mouth it has been or even if it has been properly cleaned. I should think if you're willing to do that, you'd have very little problem with drinking out of a glass you can be certain has been through the dishwasher after an animal has licked it."

Tommy Lee shook his head and looked down at the part he was wiping with a rag.

Molly clamped her mouth shut and took the dishes and went back to the house. As she opened the porch screen door, she heard the music start up again, with a blast, as if to smack her back into the house. Like an invisible door slammed against her.

In retaliation, she marched over and turned up the

volume of the little radio on the kitchen counter. Then she stared at all the dirty dishes, in the sink and out of it, and heard her mother-in-law's voice: *"I've always believed that a woman should get her kitchen straight before bed."*

That was a good idea that Molly had let slide a number of years ago, when she started keeping the books for Tommy Lee's shop and then somehow had found herself with her own full-fledged business. She simply had never been able to keep the house as orderly as her mother-in-law had, as orderly as Tommy Lee would like.

With resignation she began rinsing the dishes in the sink and putting them into the dishwasher. A dark line on one of the plates caught her eye, and she paused, gazing at it. The plate was one of the set her mother had bought for them up at the old TG&Y store in Oklahoma City when she and Tommy Lee had gotten married. The plates were cream colored, with a black-and-yellow line and a single spray of yellow daisies around the rim of each plate and cup. There were only three of them left, and the dark line on this one was where it had been broken and glued back together. Staring at that line, Molly counted back the years and thought maybe she should send a letter of testimony to the makers of Super Glue.

She thought, too, how the plate was a reflection of her marriage.

The next instant, she lifted that plate and smacked it on the divider of the white enamel sink.

Sounded like a ball going through a window. Molly scrunched her eyes as tiny pieces of china peppered her face and flew into the air and out across the counter and down on the floor. The bigger pieces clattered into the sink.

Molly was shocked. She stared at the shards.

Goodness! *What had she done?*

Mortification crept in. It simply wasn't done,

breaking an innocent plate, no matter that it had a glue line. It certainly wasn't done by Molly Jean Hayes, mother of three grown children, certified public accountant, and upstanding member of both the chamber of commerce and Methodist church. The action was destructive, wasteful . . . and possibly a little deranged.

But by golly the reckless act felt so darn good that she did it twice more with the two yellow daisy plates remaining in the sink. Lifted the plate and brought it down, felt the impact and the disintegration, and heard all the shattering, then did it again.

There. She supposed she could break a few dishes in her lifetime if she wanted to.

Breathing as hard as if she'd run a mile, Molly stared at the broken china. Tears filled her eyes and rolled down her cheeks. Turning, she went to the pantry, brought back a broom and dust pan and began to clean the slivers off the floor. She cried silently, feeling totally lost and confused and alone.

Tommy Lee came in as Molly got to cleaning the bigger pieces out of the sink. She heard the familiar thump of his Wolverines cross the back porch and enter the laundry room behind the kitchen. Quickly she sniffed back her tears and tried to gulp down her shaky sobs.

She knew before he said a word that he was going to ask her where something was, and sure enough, he said, "Molly, have you seen my box knife?"

"In by your chair."

She heard him go through to the living room and then come back again and stop on the far side of the breakfast bar. She felt him looking at her, but she didn't look at him. She didn't want him to see her face. Very carefully, she kept picking the big pieces out of the sink and putting them into the plastic trash basket.

"What happened?" Tommy Lee asked.

She thought for a moment, then said, "I broke some plates."

Quite possibly she should have offered him some explanation, but she refused to do so. A piece of the china bit into her finger. She pressed harder against it.

"Is it because of what I said about lettin' the cat eat out of the glass? Are you mad about that?"

Molly said, "I'm not mad about that. You have a right not to like the animals eating out of your dishes if you want . . . even if it is a stupid opinion."

She didn't look at him, but she could feel him looking at her, could feel his anger hitting like darts. And then he had to go and ask a really dumb question.

"What's the *matter* with you?"

It was the tone of his voice, not the question that sent smoke coming out Molly's ears. Tommy Lee could ask the silliest questions. So many times, when Molly got up in the night to go to the bathroom, he asked, "Where you goin'?"

For the first ten years or so, Molly had actually answered, "To the bathroom," and then one time she finally said, "Dancing." He still asked sometimes, and she went to saying things like "To the dentist" or "To the movies."

Then there were the times when she would be lying in bed, under the covers, with the pillow over her head, and he would come over and lean down close, lift up the pillow, and say, "Are you asleep?"

Lord, men could be so stupid. Molly had a private theory that the reason many women like her stayed married was that they were convinced their man needed them—like Tammy Wynette sang in "Stand by Your Man."

Molly at last lifted her eyes to meet his. His eyes were cool as a winter sky and slapped her the same as if he'd reached out with his hand.

She said, "We haven't made love in over three

months, and you're askin' me what's wrong?" She threw a shard of china into the trash. "I guess you askin' that question pretty much shows just how wrong things are."

He did that rolling his eyes thing, and Molly wanted to smack his face. Then he said acidly, "So you're gonna break all our dishes? Is that gonna explain things to me?"

Tommy Lee always managed to make her feel stupid. Well, what she thought right then was *You can take your f—— ridicule and stuff it.*

She pulled up straight and tall and said quietly, "It made me feel better. And I guess I can break half the dishes in this cabinet if I want. Half of them are mine."

Pure shock crossed his face, and the next instant his pale blue eyes shot fire, and he came flying around the breakfast bar, saying, "By God . . ."

Molly stepped backward and bumped against the counter, automatically putting her hands up in front of her. Tommy Lee had never laid a hand on her—he never physically fought with anyone—but he sure looked like he was going to kill her at that moment.

Then he stopped and pain crossed his features, pain so strong it went right across and sliced Molly's heart.

"I don't want us to fight, Molly." He looked away, and his shoulders slumped.

It made her ache to reach out to him, but she just stood there, feeling like her arms had turned to wood, and he stood far away from her. It was as if she were speeding back from him, watching him as she got farther and farther away.

Half turning, hardly aware of what she was doing, she reached for the blue checked dishtowel. "I don't, either," she said, her voice a raspy whisper. She felt like she couldn't breathe and that loneliness was swallowing her whole.

"Tommy Lee, I'm not happy with the way things

are between us, and I can't go on pretending everything's just hunky-dory when it isn't. Not for me, anyway."

He just stared at the countertop.

"Are they for you?" she asked, prodding him, wanting him to say something for her to take hold of. She was willing to settle for him saying just about anything at all.

He shook his head. "No," he said tightly, which was a whole lot less than anything at all. Then he rubbed the back of his neck and looked tired of living.

Molly said, "We just don't have anything in common anymore, Tommy Lee. We don't even *know* each other anymore."

But Tommy Lee said nothing to that, either, just kept on looking tired.

So damn tired, as if life with her was just one big trial.

That's when she said it, tossing down the blue checked cloth and stating, "I think I'll go live at Aunt Hestie's for a while."

At that his head swiveled up, and he stared at her, his blue eyes going wide. Her pronouncement had struck him, and she would have had to admit that she was glad to see it.

Then he said, real tight, "If that's what you want," and his blue eyes got small and shot fire.

What I want? Molly thought, every muscle rigid. He wanted to see it that way, to put it on her like that. Fine! There was just nothing she could say to that. And as if she knew what she was doing, she walked swiftly to the stairway and up the stairs.

From the big closet, she dragged out the tapestry luggage—the set she had bought for the planned trip to Mexico City last year after they'd gotten Colter, their last, settled in college, a trip that they had never taken because Tommy Lee had bought that '65 Corvette instead, for which they'd had to drive to California and spend four days with a car club there. Tommy Lee had always wanted a classic Corvette, and Molly hadn't wanted to begrudge him his precious dream. But she guessed she still did.

She jerked clothes from the closet and pulled them from dresser drawers and stuffed the bags. Suddenly she sat down on the bed, her legs gone weak.

Yanking a tissue from the box, she blew her nose. She tried to pray, asking God to help her get control of her anger. God . . . oh Lord, help me. . . .

Her attention veered away because she was listening for Tommy Lee's footsteps. She listened so hard that she heard the trees rustle outside the window and the drip of the toilet.

Oh, God, what am I doin'? I don't know, but I do know I just can't go on livin' like this anymore. It hurts too bad.

When she heard the back door slam, she jumped up and ran across to the window. There was Tommy Lee down below, sauntering over to his shop. Sauntering in that way he had of resting down in his lean hips, all those hard muscles moving along in his hell-with-you stride, swinging a can of Coca-Cola in his hand.

Molly jerked back, dropped the blind and began singing loud and full, "You don't even know who I am. . . ." Her tears stopped. Like turning off a faucet. By heaven, she didn't need to stay where she wasn't wanted.

Moving coolly, feeling her earrings sway, she pulled off her Keds and tugged on her boots. She gave her hair a few swipes with the brush and let it go, hanging straight back past her collar. In the bathroom, she scooped up her Estée Lauder kit and toiletries and dumped them into the cosmetic case. When it wouldn't close, she left it halfway unzipped. The entire time she was singing, went from all verses of "You Don't Even Know Who I Am" into "These Boots Were Made for Walkin'," just that chorus, because she couldn't recall the rest of it, and that was all that pertained to her heart at the moment.

Back in the bedroom, she snatched up pictures of Savannah, Boone, and Colter, grown now but her babies always, and tucked them in the big bag between jeans. She turned the picture of her and Tommy Lee, taken five years ago at their twentieth anniversary, downward with a hard bang. She grabbed up her daddy's old Bible and her blue dumbells and threw them into the overnight bag.

She stopped, looked at her wedding band. It was simple carved yellow gold, all they could afford when they were first married. Tommy Lee had talked of buying her a more expensive one, but she didn't really care for diamonds or other jewels, and any ring other than the one Tommy Lee had put on her finger when they made their vows just wouldn't be the same at all.

She tugged furiously at the band but couldn't budge it over her knuckle. "Oh . . . dang!"

Giving up, she dragged the bags down the stairs, grabbed up her purse and briefcase, with her notebook computer, and in two trips hauled it all out to her El Camino and threw it into the truck bed. She went back inside, got the pet carrier, caught Ace, and put him in it.

She set Ace in beside the bags, slipped behind the wheel, jabbed on her sunglasses, and backed, weaving from side to side, down the drive to where her two-horse trailer sat. She had never before hooked it up alone, but she managed to get the job done. Just went to show that she could. One more thing she didn't need Tommy Lee for.

Still moving like an oil pumper going at full speed, she got Marker from the pasture and loaded him up, and threw a bucket of grain in beside Ace. Then, breathing hard and with sweat trickling between her breasts, Molly headed back up the drive.

Tommy Lee, with the Coca-Cola in his hand, stood

leaning in the big open doorway of his shop, watching her come. She stopped the El Camino and lowered the window. He sauntered forward. Molly's heart was beating so hard, it was about to come out of her chest.

Tommy Lee said, "If anyone calls, you want me to give them Odessa's phone number?" Cold and hard as frozen steel.

Molly said, "Yes."

For an instant something shone in his eyes, something mean as she'd ever seen. Then he just stared at her, and it was as if a thick plate of glass had come down between them.

Molly shifted into gear and drove away, a lot more slowly than she wished because she had to think of Marker back there in the horse trailer—and because she was listening hard for Tommy Lee to stop her.

But he didn't.

And then she was sobbing and driving along. The chickens were clucking around in the road when she passed Eulalee Harris's place, but they had plenty of time to get out of the way, and Molly absolutely refused to think the F-word. Her life was falling to pieces, and she had to grasp control somewhere.

2

Fallin' Apart

Tommy Lee never had believed that Molly would really leave. As he stood there, gazing through the shop window, watching the dust cloud she raised on the road, he thought, *She took the dang horse.*

Then he turned and flung his can of Coca-Cola at the wall. "Goddamn her!"

The can was still full enough to hit with a hard thunk right below the Pennzoil sign. It sprayed Coke on the wall, then landed, all dented, and dribbled the rest of its contents across the workbench. Tommy Lee grabbed a box and flung it on the floor. But it was only a box containing gaskets and didn't give much satisfaction at all.

He stood there, breathing hard, wishing to tear the shop apart, looking around for something to punch and at the same time telling himself to calm down and not be an idiot. Besides, there wasn't a thing to let go on that wouldn't break his hand, and his hands were his livelihood. That he could think so rationally in the midst of his fury made him even madder. Made him feel like life had overtaken him and worn him down.

After another second of inner struggling, he

grabbed up a steel mallet and smacked it through the wall. The act gave him a measure of satisfaction, although he immediately regretted the hole in the wall. Doing that was wasteful nonsense.

He tossed aside the mallet and jerked up shop towels and spray cleaner and started to clean up the Coke. He sure didn't want it drying sticky and drawing flies and sweat bees. And he was particular about his shop and tools. A well-kept shop was the mark of a man's quality work. Just because Molly had gone crazy was no reason for him to follow.

He should have called after her, he thought, scrubbing hard and breathing heavy. He should have stopped her.

He looked down to see Jake looking accusingly at him. "She's gonna come back," Tommy Lee said.

He threw the soiled paper towels into the trash, then jerked the *Hot Rod* calendar from its place on the wall and went to tack it up over the hole he'd made with the mallet.

Then he stalked back to the house. In the middle of the driveway, he stopped and stared at the entry, listened but didn't hear the El Camino. It ran awfully quiet, though. He'd rebuilt the engine himself.

Jake had gone on ahead and was looking back. "You think you know so much," Tommy Lee told the dog as he passed and went up the steps. He wiped his boots good on the bristly mat. He realized he was doing it and stalked on into the kitchen.

Molly's kitchen radio was still playing. His gaze went over the room—the dirty dishes on the counter, a pile of damp dish towels, the dishwasher setting open, and the trash can with the broom propped against it. All of it left there when Molly had stormed out.

Just like Molly, he thought. She was forever getting right in the middle of something, then going off and leaving it. She had more than once left the vacuum at the end of the stairway, where everyone could stumble over it.

Feeling an odd apprehension, he stepped over and looked in the sink. There were half a dozen big pieces of china—the remains of the yellow daisy plates.

Something sharp sliced across his chest. Clear out of nowhere, for an instant, he recalled Molly bringing those dishes home.

"We got them on sale, fifty percent off!" Green eyes all bright and shining, as if she'd just brought home the world. Molly never could pass up a sale sign, and the bigger the savings, the more excited she got, as if she'd won a prize. Tommy Lee sometimes thought she could sale them right into debt.

And then he remembered how Molly had looked at him when she'd said she had broken the plates. How her eyes had been cold and blaming, saying as clearly as spoken words, *Our marriage is in the toilet and it's all your fault.*

The anger came churning and boiling up his chest like a storm out of the southwest, making him so mad that he couldn't think. He stepped backward and jerked open the refrigerator, only to discover that there were no more Coca-Colas in there. There were two cans of cream soda and a bottle of vegetable juice, both of which he hated. One of the cans of cream soda was half full, and there was half a slice of peach pie, both Molly's doing. Molly had the habit of eating half of things: half a cookie, half a doughnut, half a steak.

She's coming back. She will get halfway to Hestie's and turn around and come back.

He slammed the refrigerator door and stalked over to the pantry. There were two six-packs of Cokes sitting right in front, but he ignored those and bent down, reached far back, way back behind paper towels and extra bottles of vinegar, where his mother wouldn't see it when she came to visit, and drew out a bottle of tequila. He unscrewed the cap, tipped the bottle to his lips and took a deep swig. It burned like fire going down and landed in his stomach like a bomb, even made him blow out a breath. He wasn't much of a drinking man.

He took another good swig and then looked at the bottle. There was something about holding a bottle of Mexican liquor by the neck that made him feel tough and in control of the world.

The next instant the telephone there on the counter rang.

Tommy Lee froze and stared at the phone. It rang again.

His arm kind of pumped of its own accord, as he thought, *Answer it. . . . no, don't answer it.* It might be Molly calling on her cellular . . . but it could be one of the kids. He didn't want to talk to one of the kids. He couldn't quite hear himself saying "Your mother has left me."

The answering machine clicked on and made him jump. After a few seconds, a voice said, "Mama, it's me." Savannah, their eldest, calling from Arkansas and sounding like she was right next door.

A cold chill cut down Tommy Lee's back. He had the strange feeling that his daughter could see him standing there holding a bottle of tequila by its neck.

Savanna was saying, "Stephen found out yesterday for sure that he can get off, so we'll be able to spend a few days there for yours and Daddy's anniversary party. The doctor said it's okay, as long as I get out and walk regular and . . ."

Tommy Lee capped the tequila bottle, slammed it down on the shelf, right in the front where anyone could see it, snatched up one of the six-packs of Coca-Colas, and walked out of the kitchen. Savannah's voice trailed after him—Savannah had a carrying sort of high-pitched voice— "Because the baby's so close, though, we're comin' early and will have to leave right after the party. We'll probably be there on Thursday. . . . 'Course I know you'll call me. . . ."

The screen door slammed behind him, and he left his daughter's voice and Molly's country music back there in the kitchen.

He tossed the five remaining Cokes into the shop refrigerator, popped the lid on the one in his hand, no matter that it was warm, and turned the volume on his stereo back up. He threw himself back into working on the engine. It was something he could understand. It was his world.

But he couldn't stop his mind. It kept spinning like a fly wheel. His hand slipped with the wrench and he scraped his knuckles bloody. He grabbed a rag and dabbed at the torn skin and cursed Molly. It occurred to him to wonder what he was most mad at—the argument with her, or all the things he hadn't gotten said to her.

Tommy Lee didn't know how it had come about between them, how they got to where they could hardly say a civil word to each other, how they couldn't even look at each other, much less touch each other.

Molly seemed like she put up a wall around herself, and whenever he tried to reach through that wall, all he felt was cold. Most nights he would watch television until he couldn't hold his eyes open, until he couldn't think, because he didn't want to think. Sometimes he'd lie there beside her and hear her soft breathing and feel her warmth, smell the woman scent of her. Molly had a certain scent all her own, a mixture of lavender and powder and woman scent, that could almost make him feel drugged. He'd know she wanted him, and he'd want her, but he'd be torn between wanting her and wanting to get the hell out of there, get up and drive off and be free from everything.

When he really thought about it, he thought that for most of his marriage he had been torn between wanting Molly and wanting to be free. The shadow of long-held guilt seeped over him. Lately he had been thinking more and more about being off by himself. Wondering and imagining what it would be like if he was on his own. He hadn't wished to be on his own . . . but he had thought of it.

And now it had gone and happened.

The CD player stopped, and he went over and started it again, turned it up even louder until the music filled his ears, and he stood there recalling how he had once been a young, hotshot mechanic on Johnny Kemp's racing team and he and Molly had been running on fire and dreams.

Lord, he said into the silence inside himself, where did all the fire and dreams go? Where in the world did eighteen turn into forty-three?

3

❖ ❖

Standing On The Edge Of Good-bye

Molly circled north, avoiding the town. She kept thinking that she couldn't believe she had left Tommy Lee, that here she was just driving along, towing Marker, and her heart still beating and the sun still shining. She felt as if something had taken hold of her, some dark force, and was leading her down the highway, down her mother's long, crushed gravel driveway and straight to her mother's house.

When she caught sight of Aunt Hestie's cottage sitting off to the right, a pain shot in her eyes and down to her chest. She averted her gaze and pulled around back of the big brown Collier home. She jumped out of the El Camino and raced up the steps and in the back door.

"I need to use your phone, Mama."

She breezed past her mother, who stood at the kitchen sink in her fuchsia robe, her mouth open in surprise, and went to use the phone in the downstairs bathroom. Her mother had a phone in every single room of the house.

Molly had four sisters, but it was Rennie she called and Rennie she babbled to, certainly not making much sense. She knew she had awakened her sister, and she thought she heard whispering in the background, a man, which was a little embarrassing but not unusual. The more lonesome a man looked, the more susceptible Rennie was.

Rennie said, "I'll be right down," just as Molly had known she would. "I have to shower and get dressed. No more than an hour." Rennie lived up in Lawton, was an economics teacher at the junior college there.

Molly hung up and sat there with her hand on the telephone, thinking of how she was going to have to call her children. The thought made her sick. Whatever in this world was she going to say to them? Whatever in the world was she *doing?*

A scent caught her attention then, and she noticed the small bottle of Lysol sitting on the side of the sink with the cap off. Her mother did that sometimes because the room was an eighty-year-old converted closet with no window.

Suddenly, staring at that bottle and smelling that scent, Molly was remembering the first time she had ever seen the woman who was to be her mother-in-law. She had been about five and her daddy had taken her with him to the Hayeses' farm to ask permission to fish in their pond. It had been at bare first light, and Virginia Hayes had been down on her knees and scrubbing her front porch with a brush and Lysol water. There was no mistaking that scent, and the little brown bottle sat right on the steps. Molly had thought that the strangest thing, someone scrubbing a wooden porch with Lysol, and by the front porch light, because the sun wasn't up yet.

She had also thought that the woman resembled the wicked witch in *The Wizard of Oz*—coarse dark hair pulled back into a bun, dark print dress and stout shoes and an expression that sent Molly hiding behind her daddy's pants leg, something that she had never, ever told Tommy Lee. She didn't think it would be a nice thing to say to him about his mother.

Later Molly had come to learn that Tommy Lee's parents revered getting up and going to work hours before the sun, as if they would get points in heaven and the rest of humanity were slackers on the road to hell.

Molly's mother was of a different mind. "Only activities to relax the spirit—prayer, fishing, sex, things of that sort—should be done before eight o'clock. Anything else is extremely unhealthy" was her proclamation.

Everyone knew that Odessa Collier, Collier being her maiden name and held through her marriages, was next to a sage. She had studied philosophy for a semester at the University of the South and published articles in New Age thought magazines. Since retiring from her bookshop, she went about lecturing at spiritual retreats up in Colorado and out in California, where such topics were eagerly embraced.

It had been evident right from the start that Molly and Tommy Lee came from vastly contrasting backgrounds. Stand their mothers side by side, and it was like looking at night and day.

Molly got up and went out to the kitchen and told her mother, "I've left Tommy Lee." Then she laid her head in her arms on the kitchen table and cried.

When she finally lifted her head, her mother set a box of tissues and a cup of sweet Darjeeling tea in front of her.

"How about a bite to eat?" her mother asked, peering into the refrigerator. "I have some corn flakes . . . and there's always toast and jelly. Oh, here's a couple of Hardee's biscuits. . . . How about one of those?"

No one in their right mind ate out of Mama's refrigerator. Things tended to stay in there for months; in the case of jelly, years. Mama truly believed that refrigeration very nearly suspended spoilage.

Molly was in such a fog, however, that she forgot this and just nodded, and a few minutes later a microwaved Hardee's biscuit was set in front of her. She just looked at it. Everything, the tabletop, her mother, the room around her seemed foggy, and she couldn't seem to feel anything.

It wasn't until she'd had two cups of tea that she had the presence of mind to remember Marker and Ace and hurried outside to take care of them. She put Marker in the wooden fenced corral, where he could stick his neck through and nibble from the adjacent alfalfa field but not gorge himself on it. She took Ace in his carrier back to her mother's kitchen.

At no time did she allow her gaze to stray to Aunt Hestie's cottage, and she made no move to go over there, either. She kept wondering if maybe she wouldn't get back in her truck and go back home, but deep inside she knew she wasn't going to do that.

Deep inside Molly had the sense of being atop a wild runaway horse, and the best she could do was hang on until the end of the ride.

Rennie announced her arrival with several honks on the horn of her new candy-apple-red Mustang and came through the door in her lithe, long-legged stride. Mama was dressed and ready with her basket of cleaning supplies and no sooner had Rennie come in and hugged and kissed Molly than Mama was breezing out the door, heading for the cottage.

"You two stay here and hash things over," she said. "I'll start on the cottage. I haven't been over in a while. . . . It'll need airing and who knows what all."

What she was really doing was getting away from Molly's crying. Tears put Mama on edge.

Rennie lit a cigarette and poured herself a cup of tea and said, "Okay, so what's goin' on, Sissy?"

Molly gazed into Rennie's golden green eyes a moment, looked out the window for another moment, then said, "I can't talk about it. Let's go help Mama."

Rennie looked somewhat startled. Molly scooped up Ace and slipped on her sunglasses and waited for Rennie to go first out the door. She kept her eyes averted from the cottage. Each time she caught it in full view, her eyes squinted and ached, even though the cottage sat in the deep shade of tall elms.

Mama was fiddling at the electric fuse box. Rennie waltzed around, looking into the living room for an ashtray and then opening cabinet doors, checking out the contents.

"You know, I read of a man who found a painting by Monet—or one of those famous painters—in his family's old barn. Has anyone ever really checked this place out?"

Molly, still wearing her sunglasses, stood in the middle of the tiny kitchen, until Mama nudged her and told her to start opening windows. She went on wearing her sunglasses until she had to select fresh sheets out of the linen trunk. She removed them in order to see well enough to make certain there were no spiders in the trunk.

The cottage was old, an institution in the Collier family, something of a shrine to womanhood. It had belonged to Mama's aunt Hestie Collier, built for Hestie by her father on the occasion of her separation from her husband because her father had not wanted Hestie, or any of her three sisters, to return home once they'd left. Aunt Hestie had gone through with her divorce and never remarried but had lived in the cottage until her death, sharing it whenever need be with one or the other of her sisters or their daughters. Thus it had remained all the years since, specifically stipulated in Aunt Hestie's will as the place of refuge for Collier women made destitute by separation, divorce, or widowhood.

So far in all those years Mama had been the only widow in need of the cottage, and there was debate on whether her brief episode could truly be counted as widowhood, because Mama had been separated from Al Moss at the time he got run over by his own car.

There was no air-conditioning, but in the shade of the tall elms and with the blinds and drapes pulled, the temperature wasn't too bad at the end of May. Molly didn't know how anyone stood it later in the summer, when it was common in southwestern Oklahoma for the temperature to soar beyond one hundred. She and her sisters had lived with Mama in this house in the summer, but she couldn't recall how they had stood the heat.

"We went up to town a lot, to Blaine's soda fountain," Mama said. "And then I broke down and went back with Stirling that last time. It got to be July, and we were dyin' here. Stirling had a brand-new air-conditioned travel trailer. He was a roughneck in the oil patch then."

Molly remembered that, remembered them all staying in the tiny trailer. Sometimes Mama and Stirling would spend the night in Mama's Impala station wagon. Mama lined the back windows of the Impala with aluminum foil for privacy. Molly thought it said an awful lot about her mother that the last man she had married had been ten years her junior and named Stirling Stirling.

Mama held the record for use of Aunt Hestie's cottage. She had been married four times to three different men, having married and divorced Molly and Rennie's daddy twice. With these three men, Mama had had five daughters: Kaye, the eldest, and then Molly and Rennie, Lillybeth and Season. Each of these daughters, even the first, had been conceived during the reconciliation after a fierce argument. If Al Moss hadn't been killed before he and Mama had had a chance to make up that time, no doubt there would have been at least six daughters.

At the moment, Mama sat on the floor of the cottage living room trying to get the little television, a fan, a radio, and two lamps to work off one electrical outlet. Rennie was in the kitchen, wiping dishes.

Molly, holding a rag and the cleaner she'd been using to wipe the bathroom, stood in the doorway of the small hall and gazed at her mother. Suddenly she wanted to run away. She had the strong urge to go out to her El Camino and get in it and drive west and just keep on going. Away from everything that she was.

She said, "Mama, I don't need to use all those things at once. I'll just plug and unplug as I want to use things."

Mama was pushing the electric plugs into a plastic multiple outlet. Built in 1922, the old cottage had only a single outlet in each room, and even those had been added long after the cottage had been built.

"It'll be fine," Mama said. "I've done this before. It's just that you have to get these plugs pushed in just right."

She would push a plug into the adapter on one side, and the plug on the other side would slide out. Ace sat beside her, watching, blinking his slit eyes, as if pained by the procedure.

"Well, that adapter's cracked," Molly pointed out. Then she added, "It could let off sparks and right there's the rug. It could start a fire, Mama."

"The rug's real wool. Wool is naturally fire retardant."

Molly gazed at her mama, who sat on the floor as easily as a teenager, one leg drawn up and the other spread out.

Mama was a Collier, a family with a propensity for producing girls and retaining youthfulness. Everyone said the Collier girls never looked their ages—and

included in this group was not only Mama but her
daughters, all Colliers, too, no matter their maiden or
married names. Molly had always suspected that the
reason her mother had never stayed married was
because being a Collier had been so important to her.

Mama was beautiful still, with snow white hair
worn in an elegant bun and pale, pale skin that
seemed to glow. Of course, she wasn't the age she
declared—she was sixty-three but claimed fifty-seven.
She had shaved off the six years back in her forties
and refused to own up to it even today. She easily
passed for fifty-seven, except when Kaye admitted to
forty-four, and she insisted on doing this grandly,
which made Mama first giving birth at thirteen. That
really looked tawdry.

Sweat trickled between Molly's breasts and dotted
her upper lip. Her mind ran a picture of herself
screaming at her mother to stop it. To just get out and
leave her alone.

She set the rag and cleaner on the table, turned
around, went into the back bedroom, and stopped just
inside the door.

Thin slices of late afternoon sun slanted through
the wide metal blinds of the west windows and
illuminated dust particles in the air. Flower-sprigged
wallpaper, double oak spool bed, lady's vanity with a
big rounded mirror, growing smoky now with age.
And the scent—it seemed to permeate the cottage—
that of old wood and paint and perfume and tobacco.
Pleasant but heavy, like the scent of an old widow
woman freshly dressed for church. Each time Molly
moved a curtain, opened a drawer, lifted a bed sheet,
the scent wafted up around her.

She had developed a headache and was certain it
was caused by the scent. And by battling the thoughts
and memories of Tommy Lee and herself that kept
pushing and shoving at the edges of her mind. The

struggle against the memories was so arduous that it made her feel dizzy and light-headed.

Feeling dizzy right then, she stepped over and switched on the old black metal fan setting on the steamer trunk. It rattled for two seconds and then, to Molly's faint surprise, it went to whirring smoothly and oscillating back and forth. Blowing away the lonely scent and Molly's dizziness.

Tugging her denim shirt out of her jeans, she unbuttoned it, held it wide, allowing the fan to blow on her sweat-dampened lacy bra and breasts. Turning, she went to the mirror and looked at herself standing there, with her shirt hanging open and her lavender bra showing.

Rennie, her cheeks flushed and tendrils of hair damp around her face, came to lean against the doorjamb and gave a flop of a dish towel. "Well, the kitchen is clean enough. Probably won't matter much, after Mama starts an electrical fire and burns the place down."

She threw the dish towel over her shoulder and brought a cigarette to her lips, took a deep draw and blew out gray smoke. Her movement was graceful and feminine, despite the cigarette. Rennie was by mutual agreement the prettiest of the Collier women. She had wonderfully high cheekbones and a figure that allowed clothes to flow right over her with nice curves but no sharp angles. Her hair was an auburn blond, without a strand of gray. She may or may not have dyed it, only Miss Clairol knew, which drove Kaye wild.

At first glance a person would take Rennie for as young as twenty-five. She always had kept up with the latest styles and looked great in tight jeans and midriff tops. Once you got a close look at her face, however, you could tell she was much older. Smoking gave her lines around her lips, and there was a certain sad knowledge of the world in her golden green eyes. Most men thought this was really sexy. Molly thought Rennie was about the saddest-looking person she knew.

"Remember Kaye and you and me sleepin' in that bed," Rennie said, gesturing toward the bed, "and Lillybeth in the dresser drawer?"

Molly said, "I remember you wetting the bed every other night. I got to where I slept on the rug. Can you spare a cigarette?"

Rennie disappeared and came back with a pack and lighter she tossed to Molly. Molly sat on the vanity bench, drew up one leg, lit the cigarette and inhaled deeply, then coughed. Rennie's lips twitched. Molly shook her head and inhaled again, with more satisfaction. Although she had given up smoking when she had carried Colter, she had retained the habit to use in emergencies, such as when Boone had been in that car wreck last year, and when Rennie had suffered that miscarriage and about bled to death on the bathroom floor.

Molly caught herself in the mirror, her pale hair hanging around her face, her shirt hanging open, showing the creamy swells of her breasts and lace of her bra, the smoking cigarette between her fingers. She thought she looked a little dangerous, which was really a silly thing to think. But she would have liked to look a little dangerous right then.

"A few months ago," she said, looking up at Rennie, "when Savannah was home, she said to me, 'Mama, you're just like Grama. . . . You're just like her.'" Her voice dropped to a ragged whisper. "She thought it was amusing. So cute. And then she pointed this out to Tommy Lee, and he agreed. I went off by myself and cried.

"Oh, it isn't that I don't love Mama," she said quickly, feeling disloyal. "I do . . . and I admire her, too. She's the kindest spirit, and she isn't afraid of hardly anything, and no matter what someone might say about how she's lived, she's a survivor. I admire that the most, and I want to be like that. But I don't want to have her thighs, and I don't want to sit like her, and I do that, and sometimes I rest my head in my hand like she does, and Lord, Rennie, I've started to play my tongue over my teeth like she does."

Rennie kind of laughed and shook her head sadly. "We're all just like her," she said. "I see myself making her facial expressions, and I have her hands. Look."

She came over, sat beside Molly on the bench, and they each held out their hands. "Oh, Lordy," they said in unison.

"It's Collier blood, Molly, and there's nothing to be done about it. Mama gets more and more like Grama used to be, and the older we get, the more like Mama we get. Kaye is almost her spittin' image." Rennie drew deeply on her cigarette and blew out a stream of smoke. "Except on Kaye it doesn't come off as well. Mama has such flair, but on Kaye it tends to come out ridiculous."

Molly thought that was true. It made her sad for Kaye. Made her just want to cry, and now she was looking at her wedding band and having a very hard struggle with tears.

"You know," she said, lifting her eyes to look at herself and Rennie in the mirror, "when Shirley down at the IGA found out I was about to be married twenty-five years, she was so surprised. People are always surprised to find out I've been married so long. Sometimes I find a way to mention it, just to see their reaction." Rennie was the only person on earth Molly would admit that to.

"But what do they think—that I'm supposed to have my hair cut and curled and be wearing elasto-band slacks? Lord, Rennie, twenty-five years sounds so long, but it really isn't. Sometimes it seems like just yesterday Tommy Lee and I were in that little apartment over Montgomery's garage and spending all Saturday night tanglin' the sheets."

She remembered that more clearly than she would have thought possible. And she yearned for something from those times, not only the passions but the sense of hope and expectation.

After a minute Rennie said, "I've told you before, Sissy, what you need is a red-hot affair. There is nothin' like an affair to give a woman new life . . . and to fire up a marriage."

"And what do you know about marriage?" Molly countered.

At thirty-nine, Rennie had never been married. She'd had more than one offer, and she had lost one man she wasn't likely to ever get over, but she was terrified of commitment, just as all of them were.

"I may not have marriage experience, but I do have affair experience," Rennie said, making Molly chuckle. "Besides, I don't have to fly like a bird to know the dynamics of it, and I know enough about men to know they have a pure idiotic need for competition to stir them up sometimes. Just look how they are about football."

Rennie could always make Molly laugh. Then she sighed and shook her head. "Try havin' an affair in Valentine. Everyone would know of it within twenty-four hours."

"Well, I know one man who'd be perfect for you," Rennie said, raising her eyebrow. "Sam Ketchum."

"Good grief," Molly said.

"He would. . . . You know he would. You like him, and he looks at you."

Molly shook her head. "Sam doesn't live here, remember? He only visits. And I wouldn't know how to have an affair."

"Oh, Sissy—you learn how to have an affair by having one."

Molly didn't reply. She'd only taken a few puffs of
the cigarette, and it had a long ash now. She put it out
in the crystal ash tray, got up, went to the window and
pulled back the curtain to peer through the blinds. As
she moved the curtain, the sweet musky scent fluttered up to her again.

Her gaze went far out at the back of the sweeping
lawn to the wooden fenced corral, touched on Marker,
and then moved on to the small horse barn with a
rusty running horse weather vane tilting on the top of
it. Memories came rushing back to her again, filling
her and flowing over with such a force that some had
to leak right out.

"The first time Tommy Lee and I did it was out
there in the horse barn," she said.

Turning, she pressed herself back against the faded
flowers of the wall, gazed at the cracked ceiling, and
fingered her wedding band. The scene kept rolling on
inside of her, making her heart beat rapidly—the
fresh scent of the hay and the hot scent of Tommy
Lee, the pricks of hay through the clothes they spread
out, and the sweet pain that took hold of her body and
wouldn't let go.

"And I was like Mama then, too," she said, her
voice scratchy, "because it was after we'd had an
awful fight, and I got pregnant right then and there."

She looked at her sister. "The whole rest of our lives
has been because of that."

Rennie's gaze shifted downward. Molly smelled the
faint sweet musky scent of the cottage and wondered
if it had been doubts about their lives that had
brought all the women before her to this house.

Then Rennie came over and put her arm around
Molly's shoulders and squeezed her. Molly laid her
head against Rennie's.

"Oh, Sissy," Rennie said after a second, speaking
very seriously, "come on up to Lawton, with me. You
can have an affair there."

Half laughing, half crying, Molly turned her face into Rennie's neck.

Suddenly a loud pop sounded from the living room, and beside them the old black fan quit humming. "Shimmy!" they heard Mama say.

Tommy Lee simmered all day long and into full dark. He felt like an engine running hot, the oil burning and the metal beginning to warp.

He worked in his shop until dark and the june bugs and moths were fluttering around beneath the lights. Instead of turning on the air-conditioning, he had left the doors wide and used the big fan. He'd wanted to keep an eye out the door for Molly, should she come. But she never did, and finally he turned off the fan and switched off the lights, pulled down the garage door, and clicked the handle into the locked position.

He stood there a moment under the Milky Way and looked toward the driveway entry. He could hardly believe that Molly hadn't returned.

Jake was lying at the foot of the back porch stairs, his nose pointing at his empty feed bowl. Tommy Lee took the bowl up onto the porch, switched on the light, and looked around until he found the dog food. He felt awkward; it was Molly who always fed the animals.

When he brought the filled bowl and sat it in on the walkway, the dog sniffed at it, as if it wasn't to be trusted, coming from Tommy Lee's hand. Tommy Lee felt so annoyed that he almost kicked the bowl.

Leaving the dog, he went back up the stairs and into the house. The kitchen was dark. He wasn't used to that. It seemed so strange that for an instant he even felt he was in the wrong house. Molly's radio played out into the dark, and now the blinking green light on the telephone answering machine showed there had been three calls.

He switched on the overhead lights and went over, around the trash can still in the middle of the floor, and shut off the radio. Then he pressed the button on the answering machine. He kind of held his breath. Maybe one of the calls had been from Molly. He cursed himself for not coming in to check earlier.

He listened to Savannah's entire message about coming home and how the baby was due in six weeks, and then the second call, which had been Colter, just calling to say hello.

"Just wanted to let you know I'm alive and well," Colter said. "Could use a twenty, like always," he teased.

Tommy Lee thought of Molly and how she'd cried after leaving Colter down at the university in Austin last fall. She'd cried so hard that she'd made herself sick, and he'd had to pull the car over to let her vomit on the side of the road. He'd been real worried about her then. Colter was her baby, the one she'd almost lost.

Rubbing his forehead, he waited to hear the third caller. It was Lillybeth, Molly's sister, calling from Oklahoma City, saying she had bought plastic plates that looked like crystal for the anniversary party.

The reminders about the anniversary party made him get all tight. He switched off the answering machine. Then, his steps heavy, he went up the stairs.

The bed had some of Molly's clothes strewn on it. In the bathroom a drawer was partially open, and there were empty spaces around the sink where Molly's various lotions and things usually sat. Tommy Lee turned his back on the sink and the mirror and began shedding his clothes.

He showered and dressed in clean jeans and T-shirt and slipped his feet into his comfortable canvas boaters and went back downstairs without letting his gaze settle again on the empty places in the rooms.

Moving around the trash can and slivers of china, he got slices of ham and cheese from the refrigerator, threw them on a plate along with some bread, and poured a glass of milk. He took up his meager supper and went out to sit on the front porch steps. The only light was what filtered through the house from back in the kitchen, and from the bright stars above. The night air stirred lightly and brought with it the sweet scents of new-mown hay and moisture off the leaves. Jake came padding up and lay down at a respectful distance.

Tommy Lee felt a little foolish because in that moment he was sure glad for the company. He tore off a piece of the ham and fed it to the dog. He was glad to see the dog take it.

Looking down at the porch floor, Tommy Lee thought how different life at this house had been from life at Molly's house—at any of the houses Molly lived in, because she was always moving around. Dogs and cats had always been coming and going at Molly's house. Molly had been allowed to sleep with them even. Things had been so noisy at Molly's house, smoky with cigarettes and ringing with laughter and radio music and bright with colors.

Suddenly he realized he was smelling the scent of the boxwoods that grew around the porch, and he remembered a day, back when they were kids, that Molly had sat in this very spot with him, at the edge of the porch with their feet on the steps. He remembered she had ridden all the way from town on her bike. His mother had forbidden him to ride to and from town on his bike, because of the danger along the county highway, but Tommy Lee occasionally used to do it anyway. His life had been so filled with don'ts; he'd been envious of Molly, whose life seemed to have no rules at all. He remembered Molly's hair had been in pigtails that day; she'd had on a shirt and jeans and boots, like always, just in case they got to go riding the old mare.

He'd been nervous, as he always was when she was here, wondering what she would think of his house, clean as a hospital, and worried that his mother might tell her to go on along, like she sometimes did his friends.

He probably could have counted on one hand the number of times Molly had come to the house before they were married. Back then he hardly ever had friends over. His mother said she didn't like the mess they tracked in, and his dad never liked kids around.

His parents had been nearing forty when Tommy Lee was born. They'd had their lives set and went on living them in a perfectly orderly and quiet fashion. The drawers in their house were all arranged with little boxes to hold various objects, and the furniture was arranged squarely with the walls. His mother wiped over the windowsills and floors daily. His father had a hook and bin for every single tool in the barn, and every morning at six o'clock, after downing three cups of black coffee, he put on his work boots that sat on the back porch and headed out to the barn. He would only return at noon and again at six in the evening, each day, except Sunday, when the routine included morning services at the Valentine Baptist church.

When his dad had spoken, it was in one- or two-word sentences, "Yes," "No," "Chores first." Once, when a calf Tommy Lee had been raising had gotten cut up in wire and his dad had brought it into the kitchen to tend, his mother had started berating them both. His father had said sternly, "Leave off," and his mother had shut up like she'd had a cork put in her mouth. His parents would sit in the living room for evenings on end, his mother reading and his dad reading and neither ever talking to each other. They might make a comment to Tommy Lee or to the air, but not to each other. Though they slept in the same room, it was in twin beds.

Tommy Lee had known his parents loved him fiercely, although he didn't believe either one of them had loved the other, and that had always made him sad. He had loved them, respected them, but he certainly hadn't understood them, and he'd been a little embarrassed by the way they were, so regulated and stern and standoffish.

That particular day when Molly had come, rather than tell her to get along, his mother brought them out two little bottles of Coca-Cola.

"You need some boxwood bushes around this porch, Mrs. Hayes," Molly said. "They have a nice smell in the summer, and it's really nice to sit out on a porch at night with boxwoods smelling."

His mother answered, "Bushes give critters somewhere to hide and draw bugs." Then she went back in the house.

For the years afterward, the front porch had remained just as bare and unrelenting as it always had been, until Molly and Tommy Lee moved in to make the house their own. That very first week, Molly planted boxwoods around the porch. Then she had gone on to paint the porch bright blue and the house yellow and inside a number of different colors, none of them white. There were times now when Tommy Lee didn't recognize the house as the one he'd grown up in, and mostly he was glad.

He tilted up his glass and drank his milk. He didn't want to do any more thinking about him and Molly.

He considered going inside, sitting in his Barca-Lounger and watching television and falling asleep. But the thought made him sick. It made him suddenly feel like he would burn up if he tried to do that. He'd managed to swallow half a sandwich, and it seemed to lodge in a hard ball at the top of his stomach. He took the plate of food and plunked it in front of the dog.

"Here, buddy. Help yourself on my plate."

As if the dog had understood the argument Tommy Lee had had with Molly that morning, he gingerly picked up the food and moved it over to the porch floor, then ate it.

The next moment, Tommy Lee was on his feet and going back through the house. He grabbed his keys from the hook and went on out and across to the shop, where he backed the red-and-white Corvette out of the third bay and took off with tires throwing gravel.

The night wind buffeted his hair and shoulders but didn't cool him. Tommy Lee felt like he was on fire. He was mad, as mad as he could ever remember being.

Dim yellow light shone through the windows of the little cottage. The Corvette's headlights flitted over the rear of the El Camino. Tommy Lee came to a crunching stop and called, "Molly!" as he leaped out, slammed the car door, and strode toward the cottage. *"Molly!"*

As he jerked open the screen door of the front porch, the inside door came open and Molly appeared with the yellow light. She wore her blue robe, and her pale hair was piled atop her head and tumbling down all soft and glowing. Her green eyes were wide and fearful, and she put her hand up to the door frame, as if to brace herself.

Tommy Lee burst out with, "I have a few things to say to you, and you're gonna listen," and then he let it all out, all that had been running through his mind since that morning, when he'd held himself in.

"You put the blame on me, but there are two people in this marriage. You put me off plenty of times, going off up to the bedroom to pout any time things don't suit you." He poked his finger at her. "And I waited for you the other night, but you had to spend a damn hour with Savannah on the phone."

"She was worried about her delivery," she said in a breathless protest. "I had to talk with her."

"Fine . . . but when do I get your time?" He jabbed his chest with his finger. "You've always put the kids before me, Molly Jean, all the years of our marriage. The kids and your sisters. And you're the one who had to have her own damn office in town and a private checking account after twenty-four years of havin' a joint one. That's certainly not a step toward togetherness."

"Quit jabbin' that finger at me!" she yelled at him.

Only then realizing how he was pointing, he dropped his hand, but he didn't give ground, continuing to stare at her, demanding an answer.

She crossed her arms and said evenly, "You have a place for your work, I want a place for mine."

"You had a room at the house. What more do you need?"

"It's not the same. Would it be the same for you to work in the garage?"

He hated it when she talked to him as if he were a child, and he hated it even more that he couldn't think of an answer for that, just like he couldn't back in February, when she'd taken the office in town.

But he could throw at her, "I didn't require my own damn separate checking account. Sharin' with you like we always have was fine for me." Every time he thought about that private account he got so mad he could hardly see.

"We still share it," she said. "My havin' my own doesn't change that."

"Then why do you have it?"

"To have my own money, Tommy Lee. I want my own."

She jabbed at her chest, and her robe slipped off one

shoulder, seeming to shake there with her fury, a fury he only just then saw and that startled him. He gazed at her, and she gazed at him, her chin lifted.

He said, "I've always taken care of you, Molly."

No matter what else, he'd always made certain to take care of her, and he couldn't understand how she could think he wouldn't.

"I know you have always taken care of me, Tommy Lee."

The flat way she said it and the sudden slump of her shoulders confused him. A roaring went off in his head, and he went to poking his finger at her again.

"You think you're the only one who has complaints? Well, let me tell you that I've got plenty of my own. I've done my best to make you happy, Molly Jean. But I'm done tryin'."

Those final words came spewing out before he even realized they were coming. They came out and sat there while he and Molly stared at each other, Molly with tears flowing down her cheeks.

Then Tommy Lee turned around and jerked the screen door so hard it ripped off its hinges. He held it for an instant, his mind not comprehending what had happened. Then he tossed it aside with a clatter, stalked out into the blackness, and vaulted over into the Corvette seat. He was out of there with engine roaring and gravel flying, and when he hit the blacktop, his tires squealed and smoked. He shifted gears, letting the power of the machine flow into him.

When he found himself in the middle of town, he wondered where in the hell he was going. He pulled into the Texaco, came to a screeching halt, hopped out, and strode inside. He bought a pack of Marlboros and came right back outside. He felt as if everything was crowding in on him and he needed air. He stopped on the cooling concrete, the night soft and cooling around him. He felt as if he were steaming in it. He tapped the pack and opened it, shook out a cigarette and tucked it in his mouth. He'd stopped smoking for eight years, but he couldn't tell it.

He stood there, smoking his cigarette and looking at a group of teens gathered beneath the light on the far side of the street. A gleaming Camaro drove by with young arms waving out the windows and shouts of, "Hey, buddy . . . cool, man!" at his Corvette.

Flicking his cigarette into the big sand catcher, Tommy Lee walked rapidly to the pay phone attached to the end of the brick building, plugged in a coin and dialed.

There was a bit of confusion when both Odessa and Molly answered, and then he heard a click and Molly said, "It's just me now. Tommy Lee?" she added when he didn't say anything.

He thought of her sad green eyes.

He swallowed. God, he hated telephones. His tongue didn't seem to want to work. Finally he got out, "Savannah called today, left a message on the machine. She and Stephen are plannin' on comin' down the Thursday before the anniversary party." He had to clear his throat.

She said something, and he couldn't catch it.

"What?"

"I said . . . I'll call her. I'll call each of them."

He breathed deeply. "Well . . . Colter called, too, just to say he was doin' fine."

"I'll call him. Tomorrow."

The line hummed between them. Tommy Lee leaned close to the phone and gripped the receiver. "What happened to us, Molly?"

"I don't . . . I can't . . . maybe . . . we got . . . we never . . ."

"Molly . . . I can't understand you. Don't . . ." She was sobbing good now, and he knew she couldn't hear him. Molly didn't cry often, but when she did, she could cry louder and harder than anyone he knew. He felt the sinking feeling of loss.

Then she said, clearly enough to be understood, "Thank you, Tommy Lee," and hung up, leaving him standing in the Texaco parking lot, holding the phone, wondering why she told him thank you and why her saying that was worse than her blaming him.

4

❖ ❖ ❖

Time Passes By

With Tommy Lee's words, *"What's happened to us?"* ringing in her ears, Molly hung up the phone and threw herself on the sofa, sobbing so loudly that she frightened herself and Ace went scurrying out of the room. She was certainly glad Tommy Lee wasn't there to see her. She was glad no one could see her. . . . It was embarrassing even to think that God could see her. Once Rennie had told her, "Sissy, for such a pretty girl, you sure do go downhill when you cry."

Pressing her face into one of the big old throw pillows, she strove to quell her sobs and muffle her voice, which was nearly screaming with fury and pain. But then she was gulping air and shaking and so full of emotion that she thought she might shatter into a million pieces.

Gradually her sobs dropped to shudders. It was almost surprising to find herself alive and still in one piece. She sat there, in a strange place between exhaustion and fear.

If she had died from crying, she thought, no one would know until God knew when. She had told Rennie she didn't need her, that she wanted to be alone, and Mama would be over in her living room with her books until the early hours of the morning and probably wouldn't think a thing about not seeing Molly for a day or maybe two. It was a new and disturbing situation she found herself in. Getting off on her own did have certain drawbacks.

Moving on instinct, she forced herself up and into the bathroom to rinse her face and brush her teeth. The next instant, she spit out the toothpaste and dropped the brush into the sink, threw up the window, freed the screen and tossed it aside, and poked herself clean outside, gulping in the fresh night air. She stayed there, half hanging out the window, asking herself exactly what Tommy Lee had asked: "What happened to us?"

Molly thought that she could have answered, "It was the toothbrush."

She was fairly certain the toothbrush had something to do with it, although she wouldn't have told anyone she thought that, because they would think her crazy. And the mistake with the toothbrush wasn't the whole of it. It all began much earlier than the toothbrush. It could have begun many lifetimes ago, according to her mother. Molly was inclined to feel that starting with her childhood this time around would be enough for anyone to digest.

Molly recalled clearly the first time she had seen Tommy Lee. He had come riding up on his own horse to the pond where she and her daddy were fishing. It was about the second or third time she and her daddy had been fishing on the Hayeses' farm.

Daddy had greeted Tommy Lee with his usual charm. "Well, by golly, young man, we're pleased to make your acquaintance." Daddy had a way of making everyone feel special, and in minutes he had the boy down off the horse and fishing with them.

Although Tommy Lee had only been one year older

than Molly, which made him only six, he had been
tall for his age and the best-looking boy she had ever
seen, and riding his own horse—which had really
been a pinto pony but seemed so big because of Molly
being so small—made him very mature in Molly's
eyes.

Sensing his power over her, Tommy Lee had very
shortly taken charge.

"You haf'ta watch out for copperheads around
here," he told her. And, "Keep your shoes on when
you wade into that water. You better not go out too
far. Here, let me help you with baitin' that hook."

Pretty soon Daddy had just gone over, stretched
out beneath a cottonwood, took secretive nips from
the bottle he always brought with him, put his hat
over his face, and gone to sleep. Thereafter, whenever
Daddy took her fishing, he did a whole lot more
sleeping than fishing. Tommy Lee always watched
Daddy's line, too.

Oh, yes, it was true: From the very beginning
Tommy Lee had taken care of her. And she'd wel-
comed it as only a little girl who at the age of five was
already in charge of a household could.

Her mother had not been a bad mother, simply a
preoccupied one. Her mind had been divided between
her "endeavors at growth," as she called each job she
took on, her philosophy books, and her husbands.
When each new baby came, Mama doted on it for six
months, when she believed babies should be breast-
fed, but after that the baby was given over to the care
of her sisters and whatever young girl Mama had
coming in to help at the time.

It was Mama's belief that everyone had to do their
own growing. She had seen to it that her daughters
had a roof over their heads and healthful food in the
kitchen, but the details of everyday living were left to
the girls themselves.

By the age of three, Molly was setting cereal on the

table for herself and Kaye and had virtually taken over Rennie, diapers and all. When Lillybeth and then Season came along, it was Molly who rocked the croup out of them and fixed their peanut-butter-and-jelly sandwiches. She was even the one to sign their school absence excuses.

By rights it should have been Kaye, as the oldest, who looked out for them all, but Kaye was preoccupied, too, with books as Mama was, but mostly with herself.

"I'm goin' somewhere out of here," Kaye said often. "I'm gonna study and be somebody."

Kaye truly had been a scholar, achieving the highest grades of anyone before or since at Valentine High School. She received a full scholarship to the University of Oklahoma, but she came home sick after four weeks and never went back. She couldn't bear to leave her home, although she never had admitted this. She liked to see it as circumstances conspiring against her.

On occasion Molly's daddy, Lloyd Bennett, and later Stirling made stabs at being responsible fathers.

Molly's daddy had been a charmer. He used to call himself a stockbroker. He bought and sold—brokered—cattle, horses, hogs, sheep, when he worked. Mostly, though, he drank. His efforts at parenting primarily consisted of cooking breakfast—his favorite being omelets stuffed with sausage and mushrooms and hot peppers—and taking his girls fishing. Kaye never would go, though, and Rennie had been only a toddler. The first and only time Daddy took Rennie fishing, she had gotten a sunburn so bad that Mama had had to take her to the hospital. After that Daddy wasn't allowed to take Rennie anywhere for a long time.

Stirling, who had looked like a California body-builder, had focused his fatherly attention on their clothes. He'd had something of a passion for washing clothes, and he even could sew quite well. He had never cared where his daughters went in their clothes, or what they did, but he wanted them to be dressed nice at all times.

As the years had gone on, it had been Tommy Lee who got the fishing hook out of Molly's head when her daddy had cast his line and caught her instead; Tommy Lee who took her to Doc Nordstrom's office when she'd gotten bumped off a horse and broken her wrist; Tommy Lee who had taught her how to put out a fire in a pan of grease, and saved the house from burning, and taught her how to ride a bicycle and a horse, and how to drive a car with a stick shift.

It had been Tommy Lee who taught her to kiss, right out there in the horse barn, and it had been Tommy Lee who had taught her how to have satisfaction without going all the way, thus keeping her a virgin, when she wanted to give herself to him. And when they finally had succumbed to their long-denied passions, it had been Tommy Lee who had married her because he'd gotten her pregnant, as he saw it.

Molly couldn't say for certain, but she suspected that she had been determined to get Tommy Lee to make love to her and get her pregnant. She had been frightened and ashamed right from the first that this could possibly be true, and she had told Tommy Lee straight away that he didn't have to marry her.

But he'd said, "Of course I'm marryin' you, Molly. Don't be stupid."

She had known he would say that, and truth be told she had counted on it. She had no idea what she would have done if Tommy Lee hadn't married her. She had been seventeen and pregnant and with no job skills of any kind and no one but Tommy Lee to turn to.

They had gotten married at the Free Methodist Church, by Pastor Howell, who had christened Molly as a little girl. She had felt so guilty about being pregnant that she'd had to tell the pastor, but he only smiled and said it made no difference. Of course that wasn't true at all. In those days, people still raised eyebrows at being pregnant, at least in little towns like Valentine, Middle America. Molly's being pregnant certainly made a great deal of difference to Virginia Hayes, who could hardly say a word to her, and to Kaye, who said Molly should most definitely *not* wear white.

Molly did wear white, partly to annoy Kaye but mostly because she didn't want to embarrass Tommy Lee or disappoint her sisters and Mama, who was so proud of having found a bolt of antique lace to use for the dress.

"Molly . . ." Her mama was so excited that she had shone like a star. "Molly, I found this lace for your dress. It's Irish lace, antique, honey." She had the lace and a dress pattern, too. "I never had a real wedding dress," Mama said, "not even that first time, when I married Al." There were tears in Mama's eyes then, and a look that Molly had never seen before, a look that reflected longings and dreams Molly had never associated with her mother.

Rennie and Stirling helped Molly sew up the dress in three days. Stirling, who was still married to Mama at the time, not only hand embroidered the button-holes on the wedding dress, but he took care of many of the wedding preparations, such as getting the flowers and the refreshments for the reception. Mama hadn't been able to do any of that because she had been busy with the opening weeks of her bookstore up in Lawton at the time. In defense of Mama, the bookstore had been her lifelong dream. She had even been late getting to the wedding and hadn't been there to keep the whiskey away from Molly's daddy, who managed to get Virginia Hayes, who never had touched a drop of liquor in her life, drunk.

Because it was rainy and hot, and the church had central air-conditioning, those in the wedding party got dressed at the church, using the Sunday school rooms. This was the best way to keep all the women's hair-dos from falling. While he was dressing, Molly's daddy managed to rip the zipper of his pants. While Stirling sewed up his pants, Daddy, wearing his shirt, coat, tie, socks and shoes, and boxers shorts, wandered off where he could sneak snorts out of the bottle hid in his coat pocket.

This was when he found Tommy Lee's mother sitting alone. When she said she had a sick headache—she seemed to get a sick headache whenever around a lot of people—he offered her a drink from his bottle. Daddy had about the softest heart anyone could ever have and was always eager to be helpful. One time, when he'd still been married to Mama, he'd gotten up in the middle of the night and had gone down and made Mr. Blaine open the drugstore and sell him a jar of Vicks Vapo Rub and bottle of aspirin for Mama's cold. He did things like that all the time, as if he couldn't get enough of helping people.

Molly could imagine how Virginia Hayes had probably rebuked her daddy in a huff. Virginia had not approved of liquor or Daddy, and certainly not Daddy in boxer shorts. But insults just went over Daddy's fuzzy head. He went into the fellowship hall and kindly brought her back a glass of punch.

"She told me that was the best punch she ever drank," Daddy said later, and quite proudly.

Daddy had spiked it, of course, with "the smoothest bourbon Kentucky has to offer," he said. Not knowing what liquor tasted like, Virginia hadn't known—or else she simply liked bourbon and punch.

She had liked it so much that Daddy had gone back and gotten her another. Three glasses of punch in all and Virginia felt much better. By the time the guests started arriving, Virginia didn't have her headache anymore, and she didn't have her hat, either, and she was waltzing around the fellowship hall with Daddy, with the front of her dress unbuttoned near to her waist, exposing her voluptuous slip-covered breasts.

"That woman was corked in too tight," had been Daddy's defense. "She needed air."

Stirling called Daddy to put his pants back on, and Pastor Howell's wife got Virginia put back together to go down the aisle on the arm of the usher, although everyone noticed something strange about her. Her hat kept trying to slide off, and she unbuttoned the top buttons of her dress again and was fanning herself. Tommy Lee's father, Thomas, sat beside her rigid as a statue, while Virginia turned and waved her handkerchief at Daddy, as he escorted Molly down the isle.

Molly stumbled when she saw Virginia, her iron gray hair poking wildly, fluttering her hanky. As it was, Molly was sort of weaving because she was shaking so hard, and Daddy wasn't much help in steadying her. Just before they started down the aisle, he'd offered her a drink from his bottle, and she'd been sorely tempted, but she'd been more afraid that everyone would smell the liquor on her breath and that she might throw up.

It turned out that it was Tommy Lee who threw up.

He stood there at the front of the sanctuary, looking so strange in his dark suit. So skinny, and so somber. Molly had never before seen Tommy Lee in a suit. She had the startling thought that he looked as if he should be laid out in a casket. She got so tickled over this thought that she started shaking harder.

Then, just when she reached his side, Tommy Lee mumbled something that sounded like "Oh shit," right there in God's house, and bolted back down the aisle.

Sam Ketchum, the best man, was the first to make a move, running after Tommy Lee, and then Molly and Pastor Howell went hard on his heels. Molly's dress was tea length, with no train to hold her back, so she quickly passed the portly pastor. She caught sight of Sam running into the ladies room. Tommy Lee had gone in there, rather than going all the way on the other side of the church to the men's.

Molly burst into the ladies room and stopped at the sight of Sam's wide shoulders blocking the stall door and the sound of Tommy Lee retching. In that same instant, she caught the faint scent of whiskey and figured her daddy had been trying to be helpful to Tommy Lee.

Then Pastor Howell was coming through the door and others were trying to crowd after him. The pastor pushed them out. "You, too, Virginia. . . . Let Sam and Molly handle it for now." And he firmly closed the door and locked it.

"Are you okay, buddy?" Sam said.

"How is he?" Molly asked, pressing up to Sam. "Tommy Lee?"

"I need a drink of water," Tommy Lee mumbled, and Molly jumped to get it, only there weren't any cups.

"There aren't any cups." Oh, Lord, she didn't know what to do.

Pastor Howell rolled down a length of brown paper towel and soaked it under the faucet; then he gently eased around Molly and squeezed Sam out of the way. Pastor Howell was a rotund man and used to squeezing around people.

"How are you now, son?" he asked Tommy Lee.

Molly heard Tommy Lee mumble, "Better."

She was thinking that maybe she should leave, that she should never have come busting in here in the first place, and Sam was looking at her as if he was thinking all of the same things. But then she thought of all those people ready to pounce on her when she opened the door and lost courage. Besides, Tommy Lee might need her.

Oh, Lord, here she was pregnant and scared to death and in the ladies room with three men.

"Okay . . ." Pastor Howell gave Sam a nudge. "You go on out of here, Sam." Sam left as fast as he could, and Molly prepared to follow, but the pastor said, "Molly, you stay here. Tommy Lee, you come on to the sink and wash your face and rinse your mouth."

Tommy Lee came out of the stall, but he kept his eyes cast downward. Molly stepped back to give him space. It was getting hot in the room now, and she could feel herself starting to perspire between her breasts and getting sticky under her arms. She began to think of how she would soak her wedding dress, but how that wouldn't matter because Tommy Lee was probably going to say the whole thing was off. She'd have to go live with her mother to have the baby, and it would grow up in the same crazy household she herself had. She had sinned, and she was going to have to pay for it and so was her baby, that was all. *Oh, Lord . . . oh, please, Lord . . .*

Her stomach started churning and she burned with shame, thinking of Virginia Hayes with her hat all askew, and Thomas Hayes with his granite face, and the knowing looks on all the women's faces every time they eyed her. She looked at Tommy Lee and knew his condition was all her fault. She felt as if she might throw up, too, but she thought she would choke before she threw up right there in front of Tommy Lee and the pastor.

Pastor Howell said, "I imagine Tommy Lee would feel a lot better if he could brush his teeth, Molly. Would you have a toothbrush in all that paraphernalia there?" He gestured at the array of cosmetic bags stacked on the edge of the counter.

After a second of surprise, of watching Tommy Lee splash water on his face and mouth, Molly nodded.

She quickly moved to find it. Only then did she realize she was still holding her bouquet, had it clutched in a death grip. She set it aside in order to dig into the bags; she and her sisters had just thrown everything together when they'd been putting on their makeup.

She found her toothbrush and the little tube of Crest right with it. "Here." She held them toward Tommy Lee.

He took them, and she noticed his calloused hands were shaking. He did a swift job of brushing his teeth and then straightened, and Molly braced herself to hear him say that the whole thing was off.

Just then Pastor Howell said, "I think I can pronounce you man and wife right now."

Molly saw he was beaming at them and wondered what in the world had suddenly made him so happy and why he would say such a thing. Tommy Lee looked as puzzled as Molly felt.

Pastor Howell said, "Molly, you never hesitated to lend Tommy Lee your toothbrush, and Tommy Lee, you never hesitated to use it. That is as good a test of two people being able to share their lives as any there is. If you both can use the same toothbrush, you are both capable of sharing any other intimate and messy parts of life."

Molly slowly looked at Tommy Lee. His gaze came hesitantly to hers, and as they looked at each other, his blue eyes warmed. He didn't look like he was going to call it off.

"I don't care to say my vows in the bathroom," Molly said to Pastor Howell because she thought maybe that was what he intended.

They went out and faced everyone and got married in the chapel, as they were supposed to do, but to this day, Molly didn't remember a thing about it. She didn't remember a word of her vows, or anything anybody said at all. She couldn't recall anything that happened after Pastor Howell pronounced them man and wife in the church ladies room.

And what she had never told Tommy Lee or anyone was that she had thrown that toothbrush away after Tommy Lee had used it. All she'd been able to think of was Tommy Lee vomiting and then using it, and she just couldn't brush with it.

She had quickly grown worried, however, about throwing that toothbrush away. It occurred to her that she simply could have washed it in hot water and dunked it in peroxide. The more she had thought of having thrown it away, the more worried she had become, as if maybe she had jinxed their marriage, not that she believed in jinxing or anything, but it seemed like Pastor Howell had put such stock in their sharing the toothbrush and that she had possibly done a very unwise thing, possibly a disloyal thing in throwing it away.

So on the second night of their honeymoon down in that old New Orleans hotel, which Mama had paid for, she had made certain to brush her teeth with Tommy Lee's toothbrush. To try to make things right again, she had done it every night for a week, as well as a number of times throughout the years since.

Now here she was, her marriage in pieces, and it could all be because she had thrown away that toothbrush. It seemed a silly supposition, but she couldn't quite dismiss it.

Maybe what had happened to her and Tommy Lee had been that they had had a very poor beginning, Molly thought. In all truth she had gotten exactly what she wanted, because she had never wanted anything but to marry Tommy Lee Hayes and have his children. She had needed his responsibility and dependability, and more than anything in this world she had wanted Tommy Lee to love her best of anything in his.

But Tommy Lee had wanted other things, besides Molly.

Tommy Lee had wanted to design and build and

run race cars for top drivers on the stock car circuit. He had been on his way to doing just that, too. Right after high school graduation, he had gotten a job as a mechanic on the team of a small-time racer and was looking ahead to moving on up to the big leagues.

He would have done it, too. Molly knew this without a doubt. If it hadn't been that he'd had to leave it all and marry her and take on a child, he would have made himself a major name in racing.

Maybe he could have gone back to it, and once he did try, but again he had been caught by Molly and another child coming along. Molly honestly hadn't planned that to happen, had been as surprised as Tommy Lee about it. Each of their children had been a surprise, although much loved ones.

Through all the years, Molly had held inside of her the suspicion that Tommy Lee was married to her because he was caught by his sense of responsibility. And of late she had come to think that twenty-five years was long enough for either herself or Tommy Lee to live on false pretenses. She thought that she could not live another day feeling beholden to him, or guilty for holding him where he didn't want to be.

5

Hold Me

At dawn Molly went into the kitchen and made a cup of instant coffee. The coffee was a cheap generic brand that came from her mother's refrigerator and had an expiration date of the year before, but it was coffee and obviously not lethal because Molly drank six cups and kept breathing.

The sun rose higher and filtered through the trees, but Molly continued to sit at the tiny maple table in the kitchen with a cup of instant coffee and the warming summer breeze wafting through the back door screen. She had put on her sunglasses again, which made the room dim and seeing the numbers on the telephone dial a little difficult. The telephone was an old black rotary model, connected to the wall plug by a fifty-foot line, so it could go anywhere in the cottage and even out the back door. A number of times Molly reached out and took hold of the receiver, but she never lifted it.

She had told Tommy Lee that she would call their children. What was she going to say to them? How could she tell them that she had left their daddy? She couldn't even stand to think the words: "left Tommy Lee."

The sound of a car startled her, and she jumped to look out the window, thinking immediately of Tommy Lee. What would she *say* to him?

But then she saw it was Kaye's Buick. Molly was so disappointed that it wasn't Tommy Lee—angry, even. She didn't want to speak to him, and it wouldn't help either of them, but she really would have liked for him to try to initiate contact again.

She was sick that it was Kaye. *Why did it have to be Kaye?* The fact that it was Sunday cut through her hazy brain. Every Sunday morning Kaye stopped by Mama's on her way to church, to have a cup of coffee and to try to talk Mama into going to church with her. Mama had given up church after Season had moved out; she said she didn't need to go to a special building to have church. She preferred to have church in her own house.

"The Lord wants me as I am," she always said. "I can be myself in my robe in my own home. When I start thinking of church, I start thinking of what will I wear and that's not thinking of the Lord."

"The Bible tells us to go to church," Kaye argued. "Where two or three are gathered—that's where the Lord is. That's what it says in the Bible."

"It also says when you pray to go into your closet." Mama took that literally. When she did heavy-duty praying, she went into the big closet she'd had made when the house was remodeled. "I'll go to church, but only in my robe," Mama sometimes said.

Kaye never responded to that threat; she knew, just as everyone did, that Mama would get a kick out of doing something so outrageous.

It was Molly's opinion that church had little to do with bringing Kaye to Mama's every Sunday. She believed Kaye came to escape her dull husband and to indulge in verbal sparring with someone who was her equal in intelligence. Of the five of them, Kaye was the closest to their mother. Those two had the most in common—both having keen minds, if a little screwy, and a passion for books. Also, Mama always tried to give Kaye extra attention, trying to make up for not producing a sister-companion for her eldest.

Not having a full-blood sister was a bitter pill for Kaye. "Molly and Rennie have each other, and Lilly-beth and Season have each other, but I'm just out there on my own," she would say, and she always gave this little wave when she said "out there on my own," as if she were a cast-off orphan.

Kaye seemed to have been born with a great need for special attention. This inordinate need had led her to marry Walter Upchurch, a meek and rich man who bored her to death but who worshiped the ground she walked on. It was Molly's private opinion that Kaye's need for attention had led her to decide not to have children, with whom she would have to compete for Walter's and everyone else's attention. It helped that Walter had been in line to be mayor of Valentine after his daddy, thus making Kaye the wife of the mayor and a woman of some importance worthy of attention.

Still, Molly guessed all the attention in the world would not be enough for Kaye, who could never be given the one thing she really and truly wanted, a blood sister. This disappointment was probably why Kaye was so annoying much of the time. Since she had taken on the exalted position of sales representative for Country Interior Designs she had become even more annoying than usual; she kept pressuring everyone to have Country Interior parties.

Through the window, Molly watched as Kaye got out of her car, looked from Molly's El Camino to the cottage, and then came striding across the lawn, not giving way to the pointy heels of her pumps that sunk into the soft ground.

Molly squeezed her eyes closed and sat back down.

"Well!" Kaye said, standing there staring in through the screen door. She stood there for a long moment before jerking open the door and striding inside. "Well . . . I knew the day you and Tommy Lee got married that this was bound to happen sooner or later."

Molly said, "Thank you for that comment, Kaye. It was real helpful."

Kaye's heels clicked across the linoleum. She gave a breast-heaving sigh and plopped her patent leather purse on the table.

"Why are you wearing sunglasses? Oh, Lord, did Tommy Lee beat you up?" She brought her hand to her heart.

Molly took off the sunglasses.

"Oh. Well, you look awful enough to wear the glasses," Kaye said, with a little dismissing wave.

Molly put the sunglasses back on. Kaye had already turned and was looking around the room. She went over and looked into the sink, touched a cabinet. "I haven't been in here for years," she said absently. She went and peeked into the living room. "God, this place always gave me the creeps. I hated living here."

Hidden hurts vibrated in her voice, and Molly didn't care to hear them. She had enough hidden hurts of her own to deal with at the moment. She got up and turned on the flame beneath the kettle.

Kaye said she would take a cup of coffee, too. She pulled out the opposite chair; Ace was curled there, and she unceremoniously dumped him on the floor. He gave a hiss and streaked from the room.

Kaye picked up the jar of instant coffee and looked at the date. "Oh, Lord, you've been drinking this? Yes . . . I still want some."

She let Molly make it for her and frowned when told there was no cream or milk. Kaye could get more mileage out of a frown than anyone Molly knew. Then they were sitting across from each other, sipping the coffee.

"I don't think you are sitting here because you came over for a vacation," Kaye said. She carefully set her cup down and leaned forward. "I don't believe, either, that Tommy Lee tossed you out. He isn't the sort to do that. So that means that you got into a snit and left."

"You certainly do save me the trouble of tellin' you anything," Molly said. "And why would you think he beat me up, if you don't think he would throw me out?"

"You in those glasses jangled me for a second. It is pretty strange, you sitting inside a dim kitchen in dark glasses."

Molly said, "I imagine you would be a good judge as to what was strange, Kaye."

Kaye gave her a patronizing smile and then arched her left eyebrow, which she had expertly penciled on. "So—is it serious? It certainly must be if you're here. The only place you've ever gone without Tommy Lee is on a trail ride. What happened—did you catch him runnin' around?" The eyebrow went higher.

"No, of course not."

The idea somewhat startled Molly. It hadn't really been presented before. Of course, the wife is the last to know. She didn't see where Tommy Lee would have the time for another woman, though, between his engines and his BarcaLounger.

Kaye looked disappointed, and she gazed at Molly for a long minute, waiting for an explanation. Molly thought she might should explain things to her sister, but she couldn't say a coherent word. There were no words inside her, only tangled feelings, which she didn't understand but which didn't seem very nice because the way Kaye was looking at her made Molly have the faint urge to knock Kaye right off the chair.

Kaye inclined her head to the telephone. "So . . . are you waiting for him to call?"

Molly remembered then what she had been doing. She looked down at the phone and swallowed. "I need to call the children . . . to tell them." Her words came out a hoarse whisper, and she kept staring at the phone.

After a moment, Kaye said, "Do you want me to call them?" The gentleness of her tone surprised Molly. She lifted her eyes to see her sister's face all filled with pity. "It may even be better for me to tell them."

Molly grasped at that idea for an instant, then let it go. With a shake of her head, she said, "No. I need to do it."

"Well, in that case," Kaye said practically, "you should take a shower first and get yourself dressed. You'll feel more like you can handle it if you're put together. Come on, honey," she put her arm around Molly.

With Kaye urging her, even going on in and starting the water warming, Molly went to take a shower. She seemed to have no will of her own. She felt adrift and unable to focus and was even grateful to Kaye for giving direction.

One thing about Kaye, she always did have a clear head. Except for when she had run home from college, Molly couldn't think of a time she had seen Kaye make an emotional decision. Kaye seemed so devoid of passion. Molly thought this sad, but yet, despite herself, she harbored a secret admiration of her sister's strong self-discipline.

When Molly came out of the shower, Kaye was just hanging up the phone. Molly got a terribly sinking feeling as Kaye told her that she had called Lillybeth and Season up in Oklahoma City. "They are comin' right down," she said.

"What for?" Molly stood there, again wearing the

sunglasses and her blue robe, which had a propensity
for hanging off one shoulder or the other, and with her
wet hair wrapped in a towel.

"Well, to be with you, of course. I know Rennie
must already know about everything, but I did go
ahead and call her. She wasn't home, so I left a
message on her machine that we were all gatherin'
here. Lord only knows when she'll come in. . . . You
know she's with some man."

Kaye wrinkled her nose when she said the word
"man." She was clearing the table of wadded-up
tissues and dirty cups and the ashtray with three half-
smoked cigarettes, walking back and forth between
the sink and table and saying, "You'd better not start
smoking again, Molly. That will be no help at all.
Mama's gonna bring over that big coffee maker she
has—the one she got for Aunt Lulu's seventieth
birthday party—and when she gets here and can stay
with you, I'll go to the store and get some decent
coffee."

Molly felt confused, as if she had missed something. As if she had suddenly contracted a fatal
disease and her family was gathering to spend the last
hours with her.

Then Kaye said, "I called and told Murlene Swanda
that she would have to go solo at church. We were
supposed to sing a special today, but I told her that I
just couldn't make it because we all need to be
together at this time."

"You told Murlene about me and Tommy Lee?"

"Well, of course. I don't have secrets from Murlene.
She *is* my best friend." She pointed at the phone, at a
slip of paper tucked beneath its foot. "Murlene gave
me the name of her sister's divorce lawyer. Murlene
says he did very good by her sister."

The word "divorce" unnerved Molly and momentarily set her off track. "I never said I was getting a
divorce."

Kaye looked up from the sink. "Well, I know it's all a strain right now. And maybe you and Tommy Lee will get back together"—she rubbed Molly's upper arm—"but right now is when you need to know where you stand, Molly. You don't want to let it wait. A woman always needs to know where she stands."

Molly felt like her head came off. "I appear to be standin' in the path of a blabbermouth who is tellin' my business all around town!"

Then she stretched over, snatched up the phone and stalked out of the room. Kaye came hurrying after, her pumps clicking on the linoleum, then thumping on the living room rug.

"I did not tell Murlene anything she didn't already have an idea of," Kaye declared. "She was already wonderin', after Eugene told her that Rennie had come in the hardware store yesterday to buy fuses for the cottage. He had to choose them for her, even, because Rennie didn't know what kind to get. And she asked him if he thought there was a way to run an air conditioner in the cottage. You think all *that* didn't tell him someone was movin' in here again?"

Molly had to stop in the hallway and untangle the long telephone line.

"Murlene's lived here all her life." Kaye was nearly screaming in Molly's ear. "She knows about Aunt Hestie's cottage, and since you and I are the only two married Collier girls and she knows I'm with Walter, it wasn't hard for her to settle on *whom* to wonder about. She has a right to know, Molly. She is my supervisor for Country Interior Designs, and she is entitled to know anything and everything that may affect my performance as a representative for the company."

"Well, she certainly knows it all now, doesn't she? She has the scoop, and she's tellin' it to all and sundry at church . . . which I guess means that you won't get that satisfaction."

Molly slammed the bedroom door in Kaye's face. She told herself that she had a right to do that. She had almost yelled "Fuck you, Kaye," and that was all Kaye's fault, too, because only Kaye could get her so mad that she would erupt with something so disgusting.

Sitting on the vanity bench, the phone in her lap, she wondered wildly if Kaye had already called the kids, but then she remembered that Kaye wouldn't have the phone numbers and calmed down a little.

Slowly she turned her head and looked at her reflection in the smoky mirror. She didn't look dangerous. She looked, felt, small and confused and lost. Maybe a little crazed—a woman in sunglasses and with a towel wrapped around her head.

The towel tilted at a precarious angle, and she knew her hair was drying beneath it and would be shaped funny around her face. She didn't want to unwrap it, though, because her hair all damp and knotted would not be an improvement. She thought that she certainly couldn't consider herself—in her bathrobe, a towel around her head—being put together enough to make the calls she needed to make, but she wouldn't set the phone down to get dressed because she may not pick it up again. And she had to telephone her children now that Murlene Swanda was on the loose at church. Ruthann Johnson went to the same church, and Ruthann was Savannah's best friend. It was entirely probable that Ruthann would be on the phone to Savannah as soon as church was out. Savannah had let slip that Stephen was angry about the phone bills due to calls to Molly and Ruthann; six months, and Savannah had not adjusted to moving to Arkansas.

Molly wondered what she could possibly say to her children. As easily as she could think the F-word, she couldn't think the word "divorce," much less say it.

Of course she didn't want a divorce, she thought,

now gazing at her wedding band and turning it around on her finger. Who in the world ever wanted a divorce? Any sane person didn't get married simply because they wanted a divorce. Although in this world there were quite a few strange people who might.

She sighed heavily. A divorce wasn't something she wanted, but she didn't want a whole lot of other things that had been going on, either.

She didn't want to continue to see Tommy Lee avoiding looking at her; she didn't want to continue to avoid looking at him. She didn't want to continually feel so angry at him that she wanted to smack him, or to feel guilty that she was keeping him from fully living his life. She didn't want to continue to go to bed so hungry for his touch that she might die without it.

Oh, God . . . after all these years, she still wanted Tommy Lee to love her best of anyone in the world. She still wanted that, and she didn't understand it. She didn't believe it would happen, and yet, she could not throw away the longing.

She supposed she wanted it all: the romance and the passion. She felt a little silly, wanting all that. Wasn't it natural for romance and passion to fade as people grew older and used to each other?

Maybe it was, she thought, but she couldn't seem to accept it. It made her angry at life because it was life that took passion away.

When a couple was young, what did they have to think about but being in love and making love and all their lovely lives ahead? But then day-to-day living seeped up and flooded over before a person even realized it: first the monthly rent and then babies and diapers and mortgages and five o'clock in the morning five days a week and stopped-up toilets and leaky roofs and bills and five o'clock in the morning six days a week. Pretty soon being in love and making love became something two people do in between trying to hold everything else together, and the lovely life they have imagined was only going to happen if Ed McMahon came to their door—which was less likely to happen than snow in July.

All these thoughts made Molly start to feel a sort of panic, and she cast about, looking for some good memories to hold on to. There were some—she and Tommy Lee had shared more than a few moments of romance and passion during their married years together.

Memories flickered like movie scenes through her mind. There had been those times early on, when Tommy Lee would return from the racing circuit and she would run across the little, weedy yard to meet him, and he would grab her and whirl her around in the air, his strong hands holding her easily by the waist—just like in the movies. Their eyes, all full, would caress each other and they would sit side by side in the porch swing and hardly be able to keep their hands off each other until they could get Savannah down to sleep and be alone.

Once, when things had been tough between them, they had packed up all three children and gone on a driving vacation to the panhandle of Texas and into New Mexico. Tommy Lee hadn't wanted to go; he had never wanted to go anywhere once he'd stopped the racing circuit.

"Geez, Molly, it's crazy to spend a week cooped up in a car with three kids under the age of eight."

"It will widen their world. Do you want your children to grow up with no concept of life beyond Valentine?"

"How wide a world do they need at their ages? They can't be crossing the street alone—I don't think we need to press on with seein' America until they can do that."

But Molly had insisted, because she needed to have her own narrow world widened, and because it had irked her that Tommy Lee had gone off for those years but had never been inclined to take her with him. And because she felt their passion slipping away, and she so desperately wanted to have Tommy Lee all to herself.

They'd had a grand time. On the afternoon of the second day, while they were walking the trail through Palo Duro Canyon, Tommy Lee had taken her hand and looked long into her eyes and said, "I'm glad you made me come." Then he'd put his fingertips on her chin, tilted her face to his, and kissed her in that way that seduced her body and soul.

Because they had been spending every night in a motel with the children in the bed right beside them, they had not been able to make love, but they had been driven to the brink of madness by their mounting passions. Finally, on the last night before heading home, they went out to the car—Mama's Oldsmobile, which they had borrowed because they'd possessed only an aging Camaro at the time—and made love in the backseat.

Lord, Molly's face burned just remembering it. Her eyes teared. Their time together in that Oldsmobile had been some of the sweetest love they had ever shared. It had been so wild and pure at the same time, springing from a well of love so deep that for weeks afterward Molly would think of it and cry.

She sat there now, remembering the cool vinyl seat against her back and Tommy Lee's hot mouth on her breasts. Remembering the scent of Brut on Tommy Lee's neck and hair. Remembering how they'd struggled for an accommodating position, and how she'd been afraid someone would walk by and look in, but then hadn't cared about anything but what was happening to her. Remembering how she had come so hard that she had held on and screamed, and Tommy Lee had covered her mouth with his to muffle her voice. And remembering how he had held her as she had cried against his chest.

Suddenly Molly realized she was quivering, aching with longing. She wiped her cheeks and sighed and wished heartily that their problems now could be solved by a trip away. But she couldn't drum up enough enthusiasm to propose a trip . . . and she was too afraid Tommy Lee would say no. She knew perfectly well he would say no, and she had no energy, no belief, to talk him into it. She didn't want to have to talk him into it. She wanted him to sweep her off her feet, a thought that brought her near tears again.

At last, she lifted the receiver and began to dial Savannah's number with a shaking hand.

She called them by birth order, she realized when she had finished. Savannah first, then Boone, then Colter. She told them each that she was staying for a time at Aunt Hestie's—she did not use the term separated—and that unfortunately the anniversary party was off. She spoke calmly, having practiced many times in her years as a mother, a role that required being calm on the outside even though she might be screaming her head off on the inside.

"Oh, God . . . oh, my God," was Savannah's first response, and she sounded as if she couldn't breathe.

"Now, honey, calm down," Molly said, thinking of her pregnant daughter. "It isn't the end of the world, and you cannot afford to get upset."

"Well, if you didn't want me to get upset, you shouldn't be doin' this!" Savannah wailed. "Has Daddy been havin' an affair? Oh, God, he's at that age, but I just never thought . . ."

"Of course not, Savannah. And I'm not certain there's a special age for that sort of thing."

"Then you've found someone else." Her voice rose even higher.

"No, Savannah."

"Then *what* is it? You've been married for twenty-five years. What? Have you just decided to call it quits? Just like that? And now it's all been for *nothing*?"

That jolted Molly. "I don't think so, no."

It hasn't been for nothing. . . . It couldn't have been.

This was racing through her mind, but she had to pay attention to Savannah. She gripped the receiver and listened as Savannah was yelling, demanding, "What is going on, Mama? Have you both gone crazy? I'm comin' down there. I want to know *what* is going on."

"Savannah, this is between your father and I," Molly said, summoning her most firm mother voice. The thought of Savannah racing down, of having to face her daughter, made Molly feel as if she would fly to pieces. "This is a decision we have made right now, and it is between us, not you." An inner censor told her that it was a decision Molly herself had made, but she thought to word it that way would simply add to the confusion.

"Just don't do anything rash, Mama. I really can't come down there right now. Stephen can't just pick up and leave, and he would have a fit if I went without him."

That little remark pricked Molly, but she didn't think she needed to comment on it.

"Oh, Mama, my baby's gonna have divorced grandparents." Savannah began to cry.

Molly calmed Savannah, and when she finally told her good-bye and hung up, she moved down to sit on the floor and rest her back against the vanity and take deep breaths.

She took only enough time to get her breathing even, however, before dialing Boone's number. His voice answered, but it was his answering machine. More often than not, she got his machine when she called. Boone lived down near Fort Worth and worked in partnership with Cyrus Shubert as a promoter for rodeos and performance horse shows.

His work required that he travel a lot, and he loved it. It seemed Boone had been leaving home from the time he was nine years old, when a circus came to town and he ran off with it. He had left home for good the day after he had graduated from high school, early, at the age of sixteen, having skipped a grade, and he had never seemed to look back. Molly couldn't figure out why Boone was this way; he'd never been disciplined harshly, never even been spanked. Molly had never cared for spanking, and Boone hadn't needed it. He'd never done anything wrong, except annoy her and Tommy Lee no end because he'd always seemed off in his own world, which was that of the old cowboy ways.

Once, feeling as if she must have done something to make him feel unwanted at home, Molly had asked Boone about it.

He had shaken his head and cast that half grin of his that was so much like Tommy Lee's. "Aww, Mom. It isn't that I dislike bein' here at home. . . . It's that I really like seein' other places. They just tug at me, Mom."

Molly was so nervous at trying to figure out the message to leave on his machine that she forgot to wait for the beep. When it sounded she was already speaking and went to stumbling all over her words.

"Mom?" Boone cut in.

He was there, groggy from sleep. How did she tell him, when he'd just woke up?

"Boone . . . I'm sorry to wake you."

"That's okay. What's up with my best girl?"

Molly heard whispering in the background—a feminine whisper, and Boone telling the person that it was his mother. It was as embarrassing as could be, catching her son in bed with his lover. She wondered if it was Cheryl, the girl he had brought home the past April when they'd celebrated his birthday. Cheryl had struck Molly as a very sweet girl, well mannered and certainly caring of Boone. But a mere twenty-four hours didn't allow much time to get to know her.

"Sorry, Mom. . . . What's goin' on?"

If he was surprised when she told him, he certainly didn't show it, other than a long pause before saying, "I wasn't sure I could get home for the party, anyway, Mom." As if he needed to say something cold.

"We're still right here, if you need us," Molly told him. "Your daddy's at home, and I'm here at your grandma's number." She gave him the number, and then he was saying that he had another call coming in.

"I need to get it, Mom. . . . This is the business phone, too." And then he was gone, leaving her listening to a dead line.

She squeezed her eyes closed. It hurt more because she had tried all of his life to understand this dear son, and she had never succeeded enough. It would have been easy to believe that Boone had taken it in stride, but Molly had her doubts. Then she thought, *Oh, I don't know anything anymore.*

She stood, still clutching the phone, took deep breaths, and walked around the room. She thought of calling Tommy Lee and asking him to call Colter.

But that would be unfair; she was the one who had left. Besides, Tommy Lee had such a time talking on the telephone. He seemed to consider the phone in the same manner he did a snake—as if it might bite him any moment. He always let Molly make any business calls that didn't specifically require his input. Anytime he had to speak at length on the phone, he would pace back and forth, or doodle heavily on paper, or pace and then doodle and pace and then doodle. If he happened to sit down, one or both of his legs would bounce at an incredible rate. Tommy Lee probably could have handled talking to the children in person but not on the phone.

Finally she went over, opened the small closet door, went inside and sat on the floor. The toe of a boot poked her rear end, and she had to move it. Then she pulled the door closed, but not all the way, because she felt she might suffocate. The scent of the cottage was strong in the closet. She closed her eyes and prayed for words and quieted herself. Then she removed her sunglasses and stuck her face close to the telephone dial in order to make out the numbers.

Colter's warm "Hello, Mom," went like an arrow into her heart.

She couldn't tell him right off; she had to ask him about school. He was enthused. He was pleased to have stayed down to take summer classes and work on campus. Doing that gave him an opportunity to really get to know some professors and a number of other students. One of his engineering classes would be having a competition against another; they were each going to strive to build the best robot.

Molly chatted with him for ten minutes before she finally managed to tell him what she had to say.

"Mom, are you okay?" he asked, his voice anxious.

"Yes, honey." She squeezed her eyes against tears.

"Are you sure?"

"Yes, I'm fine." And that sounded really stupid; she was sitting in a closet, for heavensakes. She cleared her throat. "Your daddy and I simply need this time apart. It isn't his fault, Colter. . . . It isn't anyone's fault. This just happens sometimes, honey." It occurred to her that her explanation sounded like what was happening was the same thing as getting a cold.

When she finally hung up, she sat there, staring at the closet door, suddenly so exhausted. Children grow up, she thought. They grow up and go into their own lives, and they aren't even a part of you anymore and their lives really have no connection to their parents any longer, except at holidays, when they would come for the big supper gatherings and reminiscing. That's what it all came down to.

Sorrow fell all over her, and she felt the almost overwhelming need to call Tommy Lee. She wanted him to hold her.

But if she called him, she'd just be leaning on him, and she didn't want to do that anymore. She didn't want to impose on him. That's how she felt these days, like she was an imposition on him. One more chore for him to see to. She couldn't bear that any longer.

It was all so mixed up. She wished she could just stay in the closet forever and not have to figure anything out. But she had begun to cry and her nose was running, and she just had to get out and get a tissue.

She blew her nose and wiped her eyes and then, again in front of the smoky mirror, she took the towel from her head. Her hair was just as she'd feared; the little wisps had dried around her face and stuck out funny.

6

❖❖

Get Real

To Molly's mind, the gathering at the cottage resembled a funeral visitation, with everyone bringing food.

Mama brought over the big coffeemaker, a jar of sugar, and an unopened can of Folgers; Kaye still checked the expiration date. Lillybeth and Season arrived together from Oklahoma City in Lillybeth's BMW, and they brought a Kentucky Fried Chicken picnic pack.

"We figured you hadn't felt like going shopping, and this would be a lot better than tryin' to make a meal out of Mama's refrigerator," Lillybeth said and hugged Molly.

Season could do nothing but cry when she hugged Molly. Her tears made Molly's own stop up behind her eyes. She wouldn't let herself cry for fear of completely unhinging her little sister.

Since a young teen, Season had suffered periods of deep depression. She had been in and out of therapy and several times had resorted to antidepressant drugs. What had seemed to help her most was viewing comedy shows, a therapy suggested one day by a fellow customer at the prescription counter. The comedy shows did seem to be working, because she hadn't suffered a bad bout of depression for over eight months since she had begun watching at least an hour of comedy a day. Molly certainly didn't want to be the cause of setting Season back.

Rennie came shortly after, and she brought Oreos and cold Coca-Colas and a bag of ice, and even Murlene Swanda stopped by and, for some strange reason, she had brought a pecan pie.

"I just want to give you my condolences," she said, shoving the pie at Molly, "and to tell you I'm prayin' for you and Tommy Lee."

Molly gazed into Murlene's face coated with pancake makeup and filled with sincere compassion and said, "Thank you, Murlene." She was quite confused, feeling she ought to comfort Murlene and assure the woman that she wasn't dying.

As Murlene was driving out, Walter, in his Buick that matched Kaye's, came in. Walter had to drive way over on the grass because Murlene, in the Swanda Hardware van, didn't even attempt to give room on the driveway. Discovering she didn't have any packets of Sweet'n Low in her purse, Kaye had phoned Walter to bring some over. She yelled to him out the window, "I'll come get it, just wait in the car!" and without missing a step, Walter turned right back to his Buick.

Once Kaye got her Sweet'n Low stirred into her coffee, she brought up the subject of what to do about the anniversary party. At mention of the anniversary party, Molly began to get a headache. She put her sunglasses back on.

Mainly Kaye and Lillybeth discussed the situation of the party. Mama was busy trying to repair the kitchen's single electrical outlet—they'd had to plug the coffeemaker into the overloaded outlet in the living room. Rennie was licking the filling out of Oreos, and Season was crying and blowing her nose. Molly sat silently behind her sunglasses, mentally getting in her El Camino and driving away, or perhaps grabbing Season and driving up to a Lawton movie theater and seeing comedy movies. She thought she might really do that, if she could get herself to move. An odd feeling of paralysis had seemed to take hold of her.

"Well, they won't return our deposit for the VFW hall," Kaye said, her lips in a firm line.

"How do you know?" Lillybeth asked. "Did you sign a contract when you reserved it?"

Lillybeth looked soft, with a cherub face and short, curly ash-blond hair, but her eyes were sharp. Many people saw only the softness, and she had learned early to use this perception to her advantage. She was a legal assistant at the moment, but she was studying to become a corporate attorney. She said that legal assistants, especially the women, did all the work but the attorneys got the money and the glory. She didn't much care about the glory, but she wanted to be paid for her work.

What she often said was, "I'd rather work honestly for my money and not marry it the way Kaye did. That is really too darn hard."

Due to money inherited from his father, Big Walter, as he'd been called by everyone, Kaye's Little Walter, as he was sometimes called, was set for life. Big Walter had secured the family fortune in a trust fund because, he had said openly, Little Walter didn't have the sense God gave a turkey, which of course wasn't much at all, since a turkey was known to have the crazy habit of looking up during heavy rainstorms and drowning.

Molly thought people underestimated Walter; he'd had sense enough to marry Kaye, who would always be looking out for Walter because she would always be looking out for herself.

Kaye said now, "No, I didn't sign a contract. As an Upchurch, my word is my contract."

"So what you're sayin' is that you simply won't ask for the money back." Lillybeth looked satisfied in besting Kaye, which seemed her ambition whenever she was around her older sister.

"Stop it!" Season stuck out her hand. "Will you two focus on what is important here. Molly and Tommy Lee are breakin' up . . . and I think that is a whole lot more important than worryin' about the stupid hall."

Season was the peacemaker in the family. She was the soft one, inside and out. She had quit a promising modeling career in Dallas to work for long hours and little pay raising money for animal shelters across the West. People just seemed to open their wallets and turn them upside down for Season; there were few people who could deny her and her beautiful golden eyes anything.

Kaye, unfortunately, was one of the few, and she said, "I realize Molly's situation is a terrible thing, but the world has to go on, Season. And your carrying on isn't helping any of us. Would you please dry up."

Rennie looked up from her bag of Oreos. "Good Lord, Kaye, if she dries up, then she'll be just like you. I don't think you'd like havin' competition."

"Well, we all certainly know you're always wet, don't we, Rennie, and we and half the men in the state know where."

"Jealous?" Rennie asked.

Kaye was puffing up and searching for a good retort, and Molly was thinking she ought to do something to stop the wrangling before Season got further upset, when the telephone rang from in the bedroom. Season jumped up, saying, "I'll get it," and sprinted from the room on her long legs. Season was the designated telephone answerer when they were all gathered. She seemed the expert with the phone from her fund-raising endeavors.

The phone rang again, and Season called out, "Where is it? Oh, I've found it!"

Molly began to quiver inside, wondering if the caller could be Tommy Lee, wanting it to be Tommy Lee and not wanting it to be him at the same time.

"Molly!" Season called in an excited whisper. She appeared, holding the receiver to her breast. "It's Tommy Lee," she said, her eyes round and worried and hopeful all at once.

Molly's heart pounded and a panic rose inside her. "Ask him what he wants," she managed in a hoarse whisper.

Oh, Lord, what if he was going to say he wanted to talk about a divorce? Maybe he was going to give her the name of his lawyer and say that she would be contacted. Isn't that how it was done?

I'm done tryin'. That's what he'd said. Molly saw Season speaking into the phone, but she didn't hear what her sister said because she just kept hearing Tommy Lee's voice inside her head. *I'm done tryin'.*

Suddenly she was on her feet and headed out the back door. The screen door banged behind her and Kaye was calling after her, but Molly kept on going, her heart pounding so loudly it drowned out Kaye's voice.

She couldn't hear him say he wanted a divorce. Not now. Later she could take it, but she wasn't ready now.

Breaking into a run, she went to her horse trailer and yanked open the tack compartment. She swung the bridle onto her shoulder and hoisted the pad and saddle, lugged them over and threw them atop the fence. She caught a reluctant Marker and saddled him. When she was opening the corral gate to the big pasture, Rennie's call stopped her.

Rennie came running across the grass, waving Molly's brown Resistol in the air. "You need your hat!"

Well, goodness! Rennie climbed up on the fence and held out the hat. As Molly took it, she saw Lillybeth and Mama standing just outside the back door.

Then Rennie cast that sad, crooked grin and said, "Ride out where you can really hoot and holler, Sissy."

"Tell them . . . I love them, but right now . . ."

"We know." Rennie waved her away. "Go on."

Molly turned Marker, tapped him with her heels and galloped away from all the pain and uncertainty. She was crying now, though, and had to trust Marker to watch where they went.

Molly didn't return until dusk. She had ridden Marker for miles south of Valentine. She knew where the gates were, and if they had been moved, she would ride along a fence until she found one. Once she and Marker jumped a low-hanging fence. She saw a couple of farmers from a distance but didn't meet face-to-face with anyone, which was her intention. She soaked up the sun and the breeze and the time alone in which she didn't try to understand all the confusion inside her. She was tired, dusty, and sweaty and looking downward and didn't see Tommy Lee until she was only a hundred feet away. Then she looked up and saw him sitting up on the seat back of his Corvette parked just on the other side of the corral fence.

She halted Marker, and sitting on the back of her horse, she stared at Tommy Lee. He stared back at her.

Molly was the one to avert her eyes. She slowly dismounted, stiff and trying to hide it. Tommy Lee came over the fence and without asking began unsaddling Marker.

It wasn't that Tommy Lee didn't know horses and all about riding. When they were kids, he and Molly had ridden a lot on two horses Tommy Lee's daddy always had kept around the farm, but gradually, when he entered his teens, Tommy Lee's passion had shifted to vehicles. Tommy Lee had put a hand in and helped when Boone was interested in high school rodeo, but Boone had graduated and Colter's interest was as wild as Tommy Lee's for engines, so Tommy Lee had given up horses altogether.

Still, he deftly unsaddled Marker and slung the saddle and pad across the top rail of the fence, then led Marker over to the water trough.

Molly looked at him uncertainly, removed her hat and shook out her sweat-dampened hair. It occurred to her that her hair would look awful, so she put the hat back on. Looking downward, she tried to brush some of the dust from her shirt and pants. Tommy Lee had on clean jeans and T-shirt, his hair neatly combed. She watched him work the headstall off Marker and smack him on the hip, sending the horse away. Marker was tired and ambled a short distance and went to eating grass.

Then there was just Molly and Tommy Lee standing together, gazing at his Corvette on the other side of the fence.

"What did you need earlier . . . when you called?" Molly asked.

"Oh . . . I needed to know where you put the salve for my hands." He held them up. "I had to use that cleaning solvent again today."

Molly stared at his hands. At last she said, "It's in the lower right drawer of the bathroom vanity."

He nodded. "Good. I can use it when I get home."

Tommy Lee breathed deeply and rubbed his calloused, chapped hands together. There was a lot he had planned to say, but he couldn't manage to think of any of it now that the opportunity presented itself. This seemed a definite weakness on his part. While he was thinking this, Molly said something, and he had to say, "What?"

"You didn't cut your hands, did you? You might need the Neosporine, if your skin is busted."

"Well, it is . . . on my thumb knuckle." He held his knuckle up, but the light was growing too dim to really see it.

Molly said, "You probably should put the Neosporin on that then. It's right there in that drawer with the salve."

"Okay. I will."

Again they were both silent. Molly thought she could hear him breathing, but then she realized it was herself.

"Mol . . . ," Tommy Lee said, but she started speaking at the same time, so he shut up and waited for her. But she didn't say anything. "You go first."

"No . . . you go."

He said, "Savannah called earlier. She's pretty upset."

"I know."

"You called the boys?"

"Yes. I told you I would," she said defensively.

And Tommy Lee said quickly, "I wasn't criticizin' or anything. I just wondered."

Molly turned, leaned her shoulder against the fence. "They took it okay. . . . You know the boys. They'll think about it. Boone's busy, like always. I told them both they could call you."

"Okay." Tommy Lee nodded, raked his hand through his hair.

Molly swallowed. Her spirit had raised a fraction because he hadn't said anything about a divorce.

"I just need this time, Tommy Lee . . . to think things out." When he didn't respond, she added, "This gives you time to think, too."

Tommy Lee said, "I didn't leave, Molly." He looked at her.

Molly trembled and then let herself say, "There's all kinds of ways to leave, Tommy Lee."

After a second, he said, "Yeah . . . I guess so." He

breathed deeply. "What do you want, Molly? What do you want me to do?"

Molly considered that a stupid question, and it annoyed her. The bit of sarcasm in his tone annoyed her, too. "I don't want you to do anything you don't want to, that's for sure. I don't have any answers, either. I just thought we weren't doin' very well together, so maybe we would do better apart. I just want time alone to think."

"And just what am I supposed to do while you're doin' this *thinkin'*?"

Molly's first thought was that he ought to try thinking a little so he might come up with an answer to that.

She said, "I guess you can go on doin' what you've been doin' for months . . . anything you want to do."

That led to another long silence, and Molly thought that she was not doing well at all in holding her tongue. She was so tired of measuring words. She was tired, period.

"I'm really tired, Tommy Lee. I can't talk about this anymore." She climbed over the fence, turned and started hauling her gear down from it.

"Yeah . . . okay," Tommy Lee said, coming after her.

He jerked her gear out of her arms. It was annoying that he could carry it so easily. She hurried ahead and opened the tack door of the trailer. At least she could do that. After he stuck the gear inside, she slammed the door.

"Goodnight," she said.

"Goodnight," he said.

She headed for the cottage, and he headed for the Corvette. She had just reached the back door when he came zipping through the trees and headed away down the drive. Molly went on inside, let the screen door slam behind her, and strode through the cottage to the bedroom, where she tore off her hat and flopped down on the vanity bench.

The image that gazed out at her from the mirror was not an encouraging one.

7
❖❖

Whole Lotta Holes

Early the following morning Molly went riding
again, and when she returned her mother's gleaming
black Lincoln was just pulling around to the back-
yard. Her mother got out—she was wearing her
fuchsia robe—and called to Molly. "Come have
breakfast with me." She lifted two Hardee's paper
bags.

Molly waved and nodded her assent. She dismounted, slowly and stiffly, her legs quivering. Her
pelvis bones were bruised and screaming about it,
too. Over six hours of riding the previous day and
four this morning were about five times more than she
was used to in two days' time. More than Marker was
used to, too. That morning he'd been so annoyed at
the prospect of being ridden again that he'd tried to
buck her off. At least now he'd had the spit and
vinegar worked out of him; he was quiet and obedi-
ent, even appreciative of her care.

"Did you go into Hardee's in your robe?" Molly
asked as she came in her mother's back door and went
to the sink to wash up. Although not quite eleven, the

89

day had become hot, and Molly's clothes stuck to her skin.

"I went through the drive-up," her mother answered, then added, "I have gone into Hardee's in my robe. Not on purpose. I just forgot. No one seemed to pay much attention. There's only a couple of old farts in there this late in the morning, anyway, lingerin' over their coffee. The morning crew are all senior citizens, too—women, thank God. Men are just no good in fast-food restaurants or handlin' grocery checkouts.

"That's quite a sexist view," Molly put in.

Mama gave a dismissing wave. "It's a fact of nature. And that morning crew is the most efficient one J.R. has—J.R. Morehouse runs it now, and you ought to see *him* try to work behind the counter." She rolled her eyes. "J.R. started out with just Geneva Whitefield, and when he saw how efficient she was, he asked her if she knew anyone else her age who might want to work the breakfast shift because he can't hardly get kids to do it. Pretty soon he had a whole Gray Crew— that's what they call themselves because all of them have gray hair. Except Doris Torres. She's black, and she wears her hair cut close, and it is black. She says she doesn't dye it, but I'm not certain that color could be real." She sighed. "I always wanted black hair, and I hated going gray so early. Doris says that as a rule black people don't gray as early as white people. I'll have to research the statistics on that, if there are any. Doris is the one who saves me these cinnamon biscuits, so I can get them even if I don't get up there until after they've quit servin' breakfast."

While she was speaking, Mama was setting the table with festive breakfast plates and cloth napkins and orange juice glasses and small butter knives. She enjoyed her breakfast in the middle of the morning. With the refrigerator open, she poured milk into a dish on the floor for Ace, who came running.

Molly had decided to leave Ace with her mother when she went riding. She felt Ace might get lonely in a strange place, and she had long thought that her mother should consider getting a pet. She thought maybe her mother would be won over by Ace and go out and get her own cat, which would be company for her.

Molly worried sometimes about her mother getting lonely. It saddened her to think of her mother married so many times and ending up alone, although her mother seemed happy with it. Molly wasn't certain she herself would be happy, and it scared her now to think that she was on the brink of being as alone as her mother.

Ace sniffed at the milk. "Mama, that milk isn't ruined, is it?"

"A cat won't eat something that will make him sick," Mama said.

Molly thought of how Ace would throw up hair, but didn't say anything. Ace went to lapping the milk.

Mama said, "I really like this cat."

"You do?" Molly was pleased, but then a little sad, because she liked Ace. Last night he had lain on her belly and soothed her into sleep with his purring. She really didn't want to have to give Ace to her mother.

Her mother nodded. "He never bothers me, and he comes when I give him milk, then goes off again." She spoke as if Ace's behavior was unique. She then brought orange juice from the refrigerator and saw Molly's questioning look. "It's fresh. I bought it just yesterday."

"Thank you, Mama."

Her mother had brought brewed coffee from Hardee's, too. As Molly poured it from the styrofoam cup into the china mug her mother gave her, she inhaled the aroma.

Mama took the opposite chair and motioned at Molly's hat, which she'd forgotten to take off. She'd become used to the tight feeling around her brow and felt a little light-headed when she removed the hat.

"Where have you gone on your rides?" Mama asked.

Molly sipped her orange juice, then replied, "Oh, around the home place—somebody's cut the back fence, by the way. And I've been over onto Salyer's place . . . and down the hole-in-the-rock road to the old schoolhouse."

For some reason, when Molly rode she didn't feel the pressing urge to think. She simply rode, enjoying the feeling of the horse beneath her and the view of the countryside and the quiet all around her. What she liked most about riding a horse was the stark quiet in which it was easy to hear the slightest rustle of the trees and critters moving in the grass.

Mama spooned honey into her coffee. "I forgot about the fence. Loren Settle told me back last winter that he'd cut it one night while he was coon hunting. He said he'd fix it, but I told him to leave it, since we didn't have cattle anymore, and that way he wouldn't have to cut it again."

"You let hunters chase coons on our property?"

Molly didn't like the thought at all. Men with guns running around in the dark seemed a reckless proposition, not to mention that they were after a defenseless little animal. Molly didn't approve of hunting in this day and age, anyway, with meat readily available at any supermarket, and she especially didn't care for it on land that at least in part belonged to her. Or would someday. The Collier land was reduced to only eighty acres now. Half of that was woods and little pastures and the other half was planted in an alfalfa field, which Mama cut and baled herself four or more times a year.

"Well, honey," Mama said in some surprise, "Loren brings his own coons."

There didn't seem to be anything for Molly to say to

that, so she fell quiet, and Mama did, too, each into their own thoughts.

Molly thought of men with guns and dogs chasing coons all over the countryside she had ridden through. She had ridden the miles of dirt roads south and west of Valentine, and through pastures and down canyons on the farms and ranches where she knew the owners wouldn't mind. Most people didn't mind riders coming across their land, as long as the gates that were supposed to be closed were left closed. And thinking of this, she supposed she wasn't much different than a coon hunter, except that she wasn't out killing a defenseless animal.

Just then Mama said, "Loren doesn't kill the coon—not his own in summer anyway. He can only kill a coon in season, which is sometime in the winter. In the summer he has his dogs chase it up a tree. They're trained to do that, and the dogs get points or something for doing it. It's a sport."

Molly heard her, but what she said was, "This is the most riding I've done since that trail ride we went on with Boone when he was in school. There just never seems to be any time to ride, and if I take the time, I usually feel guilty, because Tommy Lee doesn't ride anymore and half the time I end up leaving him with a sandwich for supper. Or the house is a mess, and Tommy Lee is workin' in his shop, and I feel I should be doin' things that need to be done."

"I've always thought Tommy Lee quite intelligent and capable," Mama said, dabbing a chunk of butter on her already oil-rich egg biscuit. "If he wanted a hot supper, I imagine he could cook it, or would know where to go buy it."

"Tommy Lee likes sandwiches," Molly said after a moment. She felt she had made him out in a bad light and needed to correct the impression. "A sandwich is about his favorite thing to eat, next to a hamburger. It isn't that he complains. He isn't one to complain at all. He never says anything about the house being a mess or me riding."

Molly sat there a minute, holding her coffee mug with both hands. "Tommy Lee probably could be described as nearly a perfect husband. He doesn't complain, he works hard to provide a secure home for us, and he never says a word about how much money I spend." She raised her eyes and looked at her mother. "And I am so mad at him, Mama. I'm so mad, and I feel so guilty because he hasn't really done anything wrong at all."

She knotted her napkin in her hand. She felt the guilt falling all over her shoulders in proportion to the anger and confusion welling up in her chest. What did she want from Tommy Lee? He gave her exactly what she told her mother—he was a husband most other women would give their eyeteeth for, and yet she couldn't be content. She wanted his attention, which she had tried, and failed, to gain. Obviously she was the one at fault.

"No one is perfect," Mama pointed out. "Everyone does things that annoy other people."

"Well of course they do," Molly said, now annoyed at Mama. "I didn't say he was perfect. He leaves his clothes around for me to pick up and expects me to know where *everything* is. And he is critical about things I try to do, like painting the house trim—he didn't like the way I held the brush. I used the glue gun in the joints of the old chairs, and he has to tell me the glue won't hold. I use a nail instead of a drill to poke a little hole in the wall and his hair about stands on end. He wants me to watch shows on television that he likes, but he won't watch ones I like, and he never goes riding with me anymore. If we are both in my El Camino, he has to be the one that drives. He doesn't even ask if I want to drive—he asks me for the keys and just gets in." Suddenly Molly heard herself and shut her mouth tight.

"If that is a description of a nearly perfect husband, I wouldn't want to see one who was slightly imperfect," Mama said.

Molly might have laughed, but she suddenly thought she might cry if she made any sound at all. She took her coffee mug and rose, walked to the counter, and sighed deeply.

"None of that amounts to a hill of beans," she said, after she was certain she wasn't going to cry. She felt totally at a loss now and sinking beyond tears. "Most of the time I never notice those things—and heaven knows I have as many annoying little habits as Tommy Lee. But now it's as if every little thing we each do separates us. We are so far apart, Mama, and that's what I'm angry about. I'm blaming Tommy Lee because I'm so mad at him that I can't love him, even though I know good and well I share as much of the blame for us being where we are."

She squeezed her eyes closed and thought how much she wanted to be rid of the pain inside.

"Well, Molly dear, a person can, and usually does, hold certain strong beliefs, while finding it quite difficult to put those beliefs into practice. Take, for example, my firm belief that we should never judge another person. 'Judge not' is a guiding phrase for me. Judging does no one any good, and God knows we all have our weaknesses. Yet, I would have to admit that my opinion of Ella Mae Jolley is that she is a woman of very low character, who wants something for nothing and refuses to own up to the fact that she is poor because she is lazy and graspy and envious and devious, and by that very fact she draws similar ugly things to herself. I have tried to like the woman, but I cannot, because I judge her, and I'm quite put out with her for being the despicable type of woman she is, which leads me to judge her."

Mama gracefully lifted her china cup and drank her coffee.

Molly said, "I think the same thing you do about Ella Mae Jolley."

Mama's eyes sparkled and her lips twitched. "That will remain our secret shame." Then Mama looked at her with tender regard, and Molly felt an easing inside. A certain acceptance.

She set her empty mug on the counter and ran her fingers along the edge of the cool enamel tiles. "Mama, I just couldn't stand the way I was feeling around Tommy Lee. I didn't leave because I couldn't stand to be around him—oh, I have always loved to be with Tommy Lee. But when I'm with him now, I can't stand the hurt and I can't stand me." She brought her fist to her heart, then let it drop.

"I feel like I've failed him and like I'll never be what he needs or wants, and that I'm just so tired of tryin' to be whatever that is." Her voice dropped. "And now he's so angry at me because I left him . . . and maybe he'll want a divorce."

Tears suddenly sprang to her eyes, but she wouldn't let them go in front of her mother. Mama rarely cried and tended to get irritable when anyone else did. As it was, she knew Molly was near tears, and tossing her napkin on the table, she spoke with impatience.

"Of course he is angry with you. You are forcing him to think deeply. To look into himself, and if there's anything men hate, it is havin' to look into themselves. Men avoid deep thinking and looking into themselves the same way they avoid cleaning a bathroom. They prefer to shut the door on anything unpleasant and hope it will go away."

She took a deep breath and let it out in a loud sigh. "It is not a great sin to have taken some time away from your husband, Molly Jean. You haven't run off with another man. Getting angry and leavin' doesn't mean your marriage is over, that you've sunk it with one shot. If you can sink it with this one shot, then there isn't enough left to be called a marriage anyway."

Mama moved her legs from beneath the table, crossed them, and adjusted her robe. "When I lost Al Moss, I was thrown into such pain and to escape it, I ran right straight to your father, without takin' time to truly think and understand my needs and wants. I did this repeatedly, because I was avoiding lookin' into myself. It was quite difficult to face what I saw in myself, so I avoided it, until finally I was alone and there was nothing else to do.

"You are at that point now, Molly, and it is not your nature to run from things. You have always faced them head-on. In fact, you have always raced ahead to meet them," Mama allowed, and not quite in a complimentary tone.

"I've never done anything like this," Molly said, whispering. "I've never felt so . . ." She was at a loss.

"Disappointed," Mama pronounced.

Molly wasn't certain if disappointed was exactly it; she was trying the word on for size, though, and it seemed to fit.

Mama said, "Tommy Lee and marriage and most of all you yourself have not turned out to be all that you'd thought. That is a great disappointment. It happens sooner or later to all of us, honey. You suddenly must face that life isn't ever going to be as you thought and dreamt it would be . . . and that you and Tommy Lee aren't, either. So now comes the time when you begin to appreciate things as they really are."

"Well, I don't know if Tommy Lee can appreciate me as I really am."

"Do you think you can appreciate him as he really is?" Mama asked.

"I don't know," Molly said truthfully.

"You both must find that out," Mama said with

firmness and finality. The next instant she was on her feet and bringing her dishes to the sink. "The best thing you can do is to give you both time to relax a bit, not try to work so hard at the marriage. Just see what happens. In my opinion, you and Tommy Lee have become much too stodgy, anyway."

Then she gave Molly a hug and went off to get dressed, saying she had an afternoon date with the hairdresser.

Molly found her mother's sudden bouyant mood and abrupt departure a little thoughtless. Then she told herself there was no need for her mother's life to be set askew because of her own problems. And Mama had always had swung from low to high, so she was staying right in form.

A few seconds later, Mama poked her head back in the doorway. "I selected a few books you might want to read," she said, wagging her finger at a small stack on the end of the counter. With a little wave, she whirled away again, but Molly called to her.

"Mama." Her mother stopped and looked over her shoulder. Molly said through a tight throat, "I love you very much."

Mama smiled softly. "Me, too, you," and she swept away.

Molly went over and looked at the books; an early one of anecdotes by Erma Bombeck; a mystery novel by Rita Mae Brown; a slim volume of the Book of Psalms; and the essay by Anne Morrow Lindbergh, "Gift from the Sea." Mama liked to cover all the bases, Molly thought.

Suddenly she felt very tired. She plopped her hat on her head, found Ace in the living room, curled on her mother's ottoman, and took him up in one arm, sweeping the books up in the other, and went back across to the cottage. After a shower, she turned on the old black fan and stretched out on the bed. In only a large T-shirt and panties, she thought the breeze from the fan felt delicious. Ace came to lie on her belly, and she stroked his soft fur.

She considered what her mother had said about her and Tommy Lee becoming stodgy. For some reason this statement stood out in her mind—it pricked her like a needle. It annoyed her. It was the truth, but it annoyed her. Why did Mama have to say that one thing, after giving her all that wise and comforting advice?

Her mother had a number of times stated that Molly was being stodgy, and Molly resented the statement. For one thing, "stodgy" was an ugly word. It was hard and unappealing to say or to see. But more to the point, "stodgy" was a critical term. A more positive term, a more accurate term, would have been to say that Molly was "steady," which was as she knew herself to be. "Dependable" would also have been a good word to use. "Steady" and "dependable" were pleasant words, and Molly had always considered herself a rather pleasant person. Other people certainly seemed to find her so.

Molly reflected that she never had taken criticism very well, most especially from certain people, such as Mama or Tommy Lee. Or any of her three children. Kaye could tell her all day long that she was stodgy or bossy or stubborn, and Molly would only laugh at her or tell her to kiss my ass, but when Mama or Tommy Lee or the children criticized her, she was bruised.

It was because she loved them so much, she thought with sudden clarity, and because when they were critical of her, she felt unloved.

Of course that was not true. Simply because a person uttered a criticism did not mean they didn't love you. How many times had she let slip criticism to her children or Mama or Tommy Lee—or been placed in the tricky position of having to criticize them for their own good? And she certainly still loved them completely. Why should she feel they didn't love her?

She didn't know. It was simply the way she felt, and thinking of this made her very depressed. She felt not only stodgy, but crumpled, too.

Then an inner whisper came: *I wasn't so stodgy when I broke those dishes.*

It was this other side of herself who was suddenly demanding to be heard, she thought. A bolder, wilder Molly, who kept getting all emotional and crying and breaking plates. It was this Molly who wanted to break free and do all manner of outrageous things— such as telling someone to fuck off. It was this Molly who was strong and confident, and who shrugged off criticisms.

Molly sighed. She longed to let the bolder side of her nature have free rein. But she worried that maybe she would go too far, and that the other side to her personality might lead her into places she would end up being sorry to have gone. She reflected that Tommy Lee had been horrified at the bolder Molly who had broken their wedding dishes. Although she had gotten his attention when she'd done that.

8

❖ ❖

Life Gets Away From Us All

Tommy Lee found himself feeling perpetually confused. For the better part of twenty-five years Molly had been within shouting distance most of the time; Molly not being near was something he couldn't seem to believe had happened. When he looked up and saw his mother-in-law's black Lincoln pulling up in front of the shop, he felt more confused than ever.

His wife driving out of his life and his mother-in-law driving in, he thought, as he wiped his hands on a shop towel and reached over to lower the volume on the stereo.

"Hello, Tommy Lee," Odessa said.

She came around the front of the car, holding her wide-brimmed hat against the wind. Odessa had always favored big hats that dared the wind. She wore dresses, too, that caught in the breeze and lifted and showed still-beautiful legs. Tommy Lee had always thought Odessa a little bold, especially for a woman who was the mother of five daughters. He thought women who had children should look and behave like mothers. To his mind Odessa never had.

Sometimes Molly didn't appear exactly as he thought a mother should, either. He had tried to tell her what she should do, but she would get annoyed, or hurt, and in any case it never had come out as he'd wished. Molly had been and still was a great mother, however, whereas Odessa never had been too good at the job, in his opinion. He supposed she had tried.

"Hello, Odessa," he said. He tossed the shop towel aside, and they gazed at each other for several seconds.

Odessa's coming to see him was quite a surprise. In all the years he had been acquainted with the woman, the two of them had rarely been called upon to hold a direct conversation. They were inevitably surrounded by Collier women, and they each took care not to be alone together in the same room.

A grin played at Odessa's lips. "There's no need to look at me like I might slap you any minute, Tommy Lee."

Bold, like she always was. She made him feel a little silly, and this irritated him. He wouldn't let her make him look away.

"You're as talkative as ever, I see," she said, moving past him into the shop and out of the wind. Not bothering to be invited, either.

Tommy Lee walked over to the small refrigerator, saying, "I've never felt that you required a great deal of conversation on my part, Odessa."

He pulled a can of Coca-Cola out of the refrigerator and held it up in a silent offering. Odessa shook her head. She stood there, hand on her hip and legs splayed slightly, a decidedly sexual stance that was natural to her . . . and for one sharp instant Tommy Lee saw Molly. The resemblance took him by surprise, and something like pain flashed through him. He popped the tab on the Coke and took a deep drink.

Odessa said, "I suppose you could call our relationship over the years one of mutual evasion. Would you agree?"

Swallowing, Tommy Lee nodded. "If you could say we have a relationship."

"We share disapproval," she said in a teasing tone. "I think that could be called a relationship."

Tommy Lee didn't think there was anything for him to say to that. He noticed Odessa appeared a little nervous. She put her hand to the back of her cheek and then laid it on the tall tool chest, but then she snatched it away and checked for grease. Seeing Odessa nervous made Tommy Lee nervous.

"How's Molly doin'?" he asked before he realized he was going to. He could have kicked himself.

"I think it could be said that Molly is doing along the same way you are—confused, aggravated, hurt. I'll tell her you asked, and maybe that will make her feel better. It might make you feel better to know that we were speakin' of you just this mornin'. She said a lot of good things about you. You are very much in her heart and on her mind."

Tommy Lee breathed deeply. He did feel a little better, hearing Molly was thinking about him. It was funny how a little thing like that could make him feel better.

Odessa said, "I want you to know that I have never spoken of my feelings about you to Molly, and I appreciate that you have never spoken yours about me. I know you haven't, or Molly would have let it slip somewhere. She can't hide her feelings. No matter how she tries, they will come out eventually. I've always thought that her charm . . . and her irritation."

"Molly's honest," Tommy Lee said. "A person always knows where he stands with her."

He didn't think Odessa was quite honest. Maybe few people were as honest as Molly. Tommy Lee didn't want to agree with Odessa, but Molly's honesty at times did get on his nerves. Still, if Molly said she loved you, she meant it, and if she said she was mad, she meant that, too. A person didn't have to wonder if she was saying one thing but thinking another. Of course, sometimes he wasn't certain *why* Molly was mad, and she generally wouldn't tell.

"I've always admired that you haven't said anything to cause trouble between me and Molly," Odessa said. "Only a strong man would control his tongue."

"Well, only a fool would criticize you to Molly's face."

He thought maybe he should add that he admired Odessa for her control, too, but he was uncomfortable with talking about this—whatever *this* was.

"Odessa, I imagine you have a point to this conversation, but—no offense meant—to my mind some things are better left alone." He straightened. "What's goin' on between Molly and me right now is our business."

"Of course it is," Odessa said quickly, and in a way he knew she was going to worm it around to make it hers, which she did in the next breath. "Although I am Molly's mother, and I feel I have a certain right to interfere when her happiness is at stake. What I have to say concerns all three of us. There are some things I have to say, Tommy Lee, and that I feel you must hear, even though you don't want to, and it may not help you at all."

He read what she was talking about in her eyes, and dread shimmied through him. He shook his head.

"It happened almost thirty years ago. It's dead and buried, Odessa," he said, walking to the door.

But even as he spoke, the memory of his father dancing with the woman who stood behind him now came across his mind. The memory had faded with the years, but some things made an indelible impression on a fifteen-year-old boy. After all this time, he could recall his father's strong bare arms sticking out from his white undershirt and how his pot belly pushed his belt buckle against Odessa, whom he held tightly in his arms, his big hand splayed over her rounded bottom, beefy and dark against the shiny satin of her dress.

Tommy Lee asked himself a thousand times afterward why it was that he and Sam had decided the place to hide the quart of vodka was in a cabinet in Molly's cottage. Why hadn't they asked Sam's older brother, who'd bought it, to hold on to it? Sam's mother went through all his things because she was a snoop, and Tommy Lee's mother did the same because she was a neat freak, so their own places were out. It was well known that Odessa didn't hardly go near the kitchen, and Molly agreed to slip it in a bottom cabinet. Later on he wondered why they hadn't simply slipped it under a bush somewhere.

There was no accounting for how young teens think, especially when prodded onward by older teens. The vodka was for the school Christmas dance, to spike the punch, on a dare from Red Stocker, a senior and the toughest guy in school. Tommy Lee took Molly to the dance, of course. She was living at the cottage, only for a couple of months, as he recalled. His dad drove him to pick her up because Odessa wouldn't let Molly go in a car yet with him and Sam Ketchum, who had turned sixteen and gotten his license.

"Well, hello, Mr. Hayes," Odessa had said—Mrs. Stirling she'd been then, although she and Stirling were separated at the time. Her voice was warm as a summer night, like always. "How are you this lovely evenin'?"

"Fine, I guess," his dad answered, his voice clipped, as always.

Tommy Lee had wondered later, despite not wanting to think about it at all, how those two had gotten so far past that inane greeting.

The plan was to let his dad drop him and Molly at the gymnasium, and after the dance had gotten under way good, he and Sam would slip back to Molly's cottage for the vodka. Sam's mother was busy with her Saturday night card game, so they "borrowed" her car. Sam dropped Tommy Lee off up at the driveway to the cottage and drove on to turn around and pick Tommy Lee up on the way back.

Molly's mother was supposedly going out that night, but when Tommy Lee got down to the cottage, he found her Impala station wagon sitting there in the dark. The cottage was dark, except for a light shining from back in the bedroom. He could hear music and faint laughter, too, and he knew Odessa was in there with someone, but he figured he could slip in the kitchen door, get the bottle and get out, and she'd never know. She wouldn't have known, either, if he hadn't been drawn into spying on her. It had been the sound of the male voice; something in the tone had made him go look.

Even as he tiptoed through the living room, he knew what he was going to and told himself not to go look. Then he was standing there and staring into the bedroom, and there was his dad, waltzing Odessa around the room. Another thing he remembered was how Odessa's dress was partway unzipped in the back. He couldn't believe what he saw, but then his dad's head came around, and he was looking straight at Tommy Lee, who stood there with the bottle of vodka in his hand.

Tommy Lee wouldn't ever forget the look on his dad's face, either.

"Oh, my God," he heard Odessa say, but he was already running from the cottage. He didn't hear his dad say anything.

It had been hard to look his dad in the face for a

couple of weeks, but other than that things went on at home as always. He and his dad never discussed the matter. Tommy Lee had never expected his parents to act lovingly toward each other, and they still didn't. Maybe his father was a little more silent.

Tommy Lee couldn't imagine why, after all these years, Odessa felt the need to dredge up the whole thing, but here she was saying, "Your daddy was a lonely man, Tommy Lee. Surely you had to know that. Once—only once—it got too much for him, and he sought some comfort. Was that so horrible a thing?"

"I never said it was." He half turned to look at her. He could have said he understood more than she knew, but he wasn't about to say that. What he knew was his knowledge and didn't belong to this woman.

She said, "I don't know what he said to you, or how . . ."

"He never said anything."

She regarded him. "No, I suppose he wouldn't know what to say. I was surprised when he took me up on my invitation that night. He was such a closed man."

Tommy Lee was amused. He couldn't resist saying, "Once with you—how do you know there weren't others?" As soon as the words were out, he felt like a heel for dishonoring his father . . . and for throwing dirt at this woman he didn't particularly care for but for whom he did hold a measure of respect.

"I knew your daddy enough to know. We grew up here. Oh, he was older than I by a number of years, but Valentine was very small in those days. I also know a bit about men, and he wasn't the type. He was just so sad that night that I prevailed upon him. I did once have a way with men," she said, not at all boasting but as a matter of fact. "That night we were both painfully lonely, both desperately needing comfort. We were both human, Tommy Lee."

"Like I said, that was years ago, Odessa, and none

of it matters now. Dad's gone, and anyway, it had nothin' to do with me."

Odessa shook her head. "Oh, it had a lot to do with you. Your mother and daddy stayed together because they both loved you and neither would give you up."

"How do you know so much about what my parents felt?" Tommy Lee cut in.

"Your daddy told me some that night, and I knew both of them enough—and knew enough of human nature—to piece together the rest. Somewhere a rift developed between your parents, and it got wider and colder, until neither of them could come together again. Yet, neither would break the marriage. Not only did they have you to think of, but a divorce would have meant scandal. It was one thing for me to get divorced as I did—people expected me to act outrageous. But people expected your mother and father to be staunch and upright. Their families would have disowned them, and your father stood to loose half his land, and he wasn't going to do that for anything. So the two of them lived their lives together while loneliness ate at their hearts until there wasn't anything left."

Tommy Lee didn't like Odessa talking about private details of his parents' lives—of his own life—and making it out that they were pitiful, while she had the answers.

"And what about the way you lived, Odessa? Was that so much better for you and your daughters? Don't you think Molly was hurt by your continual marriages and affairs? Why do you think every time I happen to say a cross word to her, she's got to run off and hide?"

He had meant to lash out, but he immediately regretted it when he saw her flinch and draw up straight, as if from a slap.

She said, "I came today because I felt the need to

tell you that I was sorry for what happened back then. Oh, I know it is awfully late to make apologies, but . . . well, I felt the need. I've felt so badly about it for so long, and if you don't need the apology, I certainly need to make it. I'm not apologizin' for what I did with your father," she clarified. "I'm only sorry that you saw what should have remained a private matter for Thomas. That was a cruel thing to have happened, for both of you. And I don't want you to think less of him. Thomas was a fine man, a fine father."

He felt badly about hurting her feelings, but as she went on telling him what a fine man his father was, he began to get annoyed again, so he said quickly, "I know my father was a fine man. I always knew that."

He reflected that he'd had a few doubts after seeing his father with Odessa, but the years of making his own stupid mistakes had erased those doubts.

"Oh, well, good," Odessa said. "I'm glad to know that."

She was looking shaken, and Odessa shook up made him feel very uneasy. They stood there for several awkward moments, and then Odessa came toward him. Her steps and manner were once more firm, and he felt relieved, except that she had something more to say, and there wasn't anything he could do about it, short of stuff a rag in her mouth, which wasn't likely to work for very long.

"Another thing I wanted to tell you today was that I don't disapprove of you. I never did disapprove of you. It only came out that way. I was annoyed with you for so long because you took my Molly from me. I was jealous because instinctively I knew that you could give Molly what I never could. It was selfish of me, and I knew it at the time, but there you have it. I was much more selfish in those days."

"Odessa . . . I didn't mean to . . ."

But she waved him silent. "You have been good for Molly, and I can admit that now, for what it's worth. I would like to see you and Molly work this out." She searched his eyes, questioning.

"I don't know," he said. "I just don't know how I feel right now."

She sighed. "Well, I've been there once or twice myself."

Then she put a hand on his arm; it was soft and cool and in that instant he thought he understood what his father must have felt when she touched him. Odessa Collier could still have a way with men.

She said, "I'm going to give you advice, so brace yourself. Feelin' free to give advice is one of the few things I like about being sixty-four."

"I thought you were only fifty-seven."

She smiled at that, and he felt eased. "You are a good soul . . . and you know, I believe I'm only sixty-three. I've lied about my age for so long, I get confused."

She sighed again and then lifted her chin. "When you get my age, you will see that life is so very short and we should never waste time being cold and lonely. That's what Molly is running from, and well she should. For all my failures, I never raised my daughter to settle for less than all the passion life has to offer. Don't settle for less, either, Tommy Lee. You won't do Molly or yourself any favor if you patch this thing up simply because it is the easiest thing to do. If you can love her, truly love her, then do that and nothing less . . . but if you can't, then have the balls to let her go."

She gave his arm a little pat and stepped out from the shop, immediately putting her hand up to hold her hat on. Odessa always had been abrupt, as if she planned entrances and exits with drumbeats.

He watched her drive away and thought about how

she had said "have the balls." A term like that coming out of her genteel mouth was startling. But she had always done that; shock value, he thought. Odessa always had enjoyed livening things up.

Molly was a lot like her. Molly looked pure and virtuous and refined, but underneath that exterior beat a heart that burned blue flame. He remembered the first time he'd gotten Molly's blouse off—in the backseat of Sam's old Chevy—and discovered that her bra was bright red. The combination of purity and sensuality could be a little confusing . . . and it was a powerful turn-on. Cool, she seemed, and then he would touch her, and she would come at him like a fierce hot wind.

Standing there, staring at the dust Odessa's car had raised, he realized that all Odessa would have had to do was touch his dad's arm, and it certainly would have been enough. He felt very sad for his father . . . and foolishly grateful to Odessa for that one night she had given him.

He turned back to his work, intent on losing himself in it, but after five minutes or so, he realized he was just standing there staring at the engine. He set his socket wrench aside and found the pack of cigarettes he had bought the other night. After about four puffs on one, though, he put it out because he felt a little sick. He got another Coke from the refrigerator and went out the back door of the shop and sat down on the step to drink it. He reflected that he had become as dependent on soft drink as he used to be on cigarettes. Maybe the change was good, though. He'd do soft drinks for another ten or fifteen years and then switch to something else; he might stay healthy by never spending his entire lifetime on one bad habit.

Thinking of his lifetime he suddenly felt very empty. So empty that he thought he might cry. He was alone; there wasn't anyone to see. But he couldn't cry. The only time he could recall crying since he was a small boy was at his father's funeral. The main reason he had cried then was because his mother hadn't, and that had upset him considerably. His mother's stony face had seemed to make all of life seem futile.

His mother lived down in Florida now, in a retirement community. She had left as soon as all the legalities had been taken care of after his father's death. Everything had been settled in only about two weeks, because his father had had his affairs in the same perfect order as he'd always kept the barn. Tommy Lee thought his mother seemed happy now, at least content. He called her once a month. He hadn't called to tell her about him and Molly, though. His mother didn't care to be told of problems, and he didn't see the need, anyway. Anything he and Molly did wasn't going to affect his mother, whose life, like her apartment, was as neat as ever.

The urge to cry faded, leaving him bone-deep discouraged. As near as he could figure it, Odessa had been trying to tell him not to end up like his parents had, but hell, she didn't need to tell him that. He'd been trying not to end up that way all of his life. And look at where he was—alone in the same house they had been alone in.

He thought that maybe he was destined to follow the same course as his parents and be miserable all his life and that maybe Molly was destined to go off on the same course as her mother—she had a late start, but she had left him, as Odessa had done all her husbands.

Maybe it was like it said in the Bible: the sins of the fathers visited on the children. Maybe there was no escaping it, and that thought gave him a sliver of panic.

He thought of calling Molly, but—as his panic gave

over to anger—he decided against it. He'd been the one to call the last time. Now it was her turn. It couldn't be all on his side. And he didn't want to take a chance that she would brush him off. He figured he'd done his part. She knew where to find him if she wanted to make contact. Besides, he thought, sinking, he had no idea what to say to her.

He felt guilty because he had such a difficult time knowing or showing how he felt. It was work to show how he felt. Loving someone took a lot from a person, and the truth at that moment was that Tommy Lee didn't feel he was up to giving whatever it was that Molly needed. He felt used right up.

Rodney Cormac came just before five to pick up his engine. He was a big man in Big Smith overalls, with small eyes set in a fleshy face. "Is it ready?" he asked right off, to the point and acting as if he were in a hurry.

"What are you puttin' it in?" Tommy Lee asked, as he rolled the engine out on the hoist to the bed of Cormac's pickup truck. Normally he wasn't much for chitchat, but this afternoon Woody Wilson had gone fishing instead of coming in to help, which meant the only person Tommy Lee had spoken to all day had been Odessa, and the dog.

"Ain't sure yet," Cormac said, his voice clipped.

"Well, if you have any trouble with it, you don't hesitate to get back to me," Tommy Lee said.

"I won't," the man said, and looked nasty, as if to convey the idea that he might come punch Tommy Lee's face in if the engine let him down.

Tommy Lee had run into that attitude before—not often, because his work was good and there were few failures due to anything he did or didn't do. Sometimes, though, these hot-rod guys could be hotheads and blame him for their own mistakes, and would come looking to take their frustration out of his hide. There'd never been anyone Tommy Lee couldn't make back down. He could appear really tough if it was required. He'd learned a long time ago, back in his teens when he hadn't been so muscular, that he'd do best to appear a cool killer. Guys left him alone that way. He hadn't been in more than three or four fights in his entire life, although he'd been in a lot of arguments.

"My work comes with my own personal guarantee," he told Cormac, assuming his quiet threatening manner. "You have trouble, you come see me."

Cormac's little eyes blinked, disappearing for a second into his fleshy face. "Well, I doubt I'll have trouble," he said. He bobbed his head at Tommy Lee and then hefted himself up into the cab of his pickup. He paused and said, "My son's got a Ranger engine needin' to be rebuilt. Think you could handle it?"

"If he doesn't mind me squeezin' him in. I've got two I'm workin' on for some racin' fellas."

"Well, I'll tell him. Thanks." He gave another nod and drove away.

Tommy Lee stood there, feeling as if he was spending too much time watching people drive off. He went to the telephone and called up Woody Wilson's house to see if he was home yet, but his wife said Woody had called in to say he wouldn't be home until the next day.

Tommy Lee hung up the receiver and felt really alone.

As he was closing up the shop, the dog Jake came running up, wagging his tail. Tommy Lee was absurdly glad to see him. "Where you been all day, fella?" he said, petting the dog, who then followed him over to the house and up onto the back porch, But Tommy Lee couldn't coax him inside.

"Suit yourself," Tommy Lee said, figuring he was being pretty silly trying to get a dog in the house anyway. The dog coming with him wasn't going to make entering the empty house any easier.

This had been the hardest part of the past days, coming into the empty kitchen. He'd cleaned up the broken plates and washed up all the dishes, and now the kitchen was not only empty but perfectly clean, a sure sign of Molly's absence. No supper cooking, no radio going.

He pulled Cormac's check and the copy of the invoice he had given Cormac from his pocket and laid them on the counter. Molly had run up the invoice last week, so it'd been ready. Normally Tommy Lee would lay the checks from customers on the counter, and then Molly would take care of the records and depositing the check. He wasn't quite certain what to do now. He could operate the computer, if he had to, but mostly he avoided it. He decided to leave the check and invoice right there. He thought maybe Molly would return home soon and take care of them, although his hope for that was fading fast.

He went over to the little laundry room and began stripping out of his dirty, greasy clothes, putting them straight into the washer. The telephone rang, and the sound made him jump. He answered it on the second ring, practically holding his breath, wondering if it was Molly and what he would say to her. He wished he had clothes on. He felt a lot more vulnerable standing there buck naked.

"Daddy?"

It was Savannah, and hearing her voice, Tommy Lee was at once glad and disappointed.

"Has Mama come home?" she asked. "I called Grama's house several times, but I can't get anyone."

"No, she isn't here," Tommy Lee said. "You've probably just missed them over there. Try tonight. . . . Your grandmother doesn't drive much at night anymore." He wondered where Molly had gotten to. "Have you called your mother's office?"

"Yes. I got her machine and left a message."

"Well, she'll call you soon."

Savannah said, "I just can't believe you and Mama are separated. What are you going to *do,* Daddy?"

Tommy Lee didn't know what to say to that, but luckily he didn't have to say anything right away because Savannah went on to say that he and Molly couldn't simply throw away twenty-five years. Suddenly she was crying and saying things he could hardly understand, and Tommy Lee was walking around at the end of the telephone cord, wishing Molly were there to deal with their daughter. And wishing he had his clothes on, too. He might have told Savannah that he had to hang up because he was naked, but saying something like that to his daughter was too embarrassing. Besides, he had begun to worry about how Savannah's state of mind might affect her baby. He began to panic, feeling that he had to do something and totally at a loss as to what.

Finally he said, "We're just going through a period of adjustment, honey. It'll be okay. Quit makin' such a big deal out of it."

Tommy Lee thought it was his tone more than what he said that made her quit crying.

She said, "That's true. I think Mama is goin' through a midlife crisis. They've been runnin' a series on the middle years on *Good Morning America.*"

She went on about the changes that happened in middle age, making Tommy Lee feel like he was ready for either the rocking chair or the nut house. Then, at some point while Tommy Lee was thinking about this, she changed the subject to Stephen and chattered on for a bit about her husband's hopes of another promotion. Stephen was an ambitious fellow, and Tommy Lee was satisfied that he would provide well for Savannah, who was a little immature still. He only wished he had more in common with his son-in-law.

Stephen was all retail business and golf and football; he not only didn't know who had won the last Daytona, he didn't know who raced. He even had to take his car to one of those quick-lube places for an oil change.

"I love you, Daddy," Savannah said just before hanging up.

"I love you, too, honey," Tommy Lee managed to get out past the lump in his throat.

Savannah telling him she loved him boosted him considerably. He felt as if he was a pretty good father and had managed the telephone and his daughter's little crisis quite admirably after all. He went up the stairs and into the shower with a lighter step.

But he began to sink again as he pondered Molly's whereabouts. She would have picked up the phone if she was at the cottage or the office, he felt certain. She never could allow a phone to ring and not answer it, like he could.

"It might be one of the kids needing us," she would say.

Years ago, when the telephone company first came out with call waiting, she had been the first to sign up, just in case she might be on the telephone when one of the kids got hurt at school. She used to make certain the kids had quarters tucked in their shoes, so they could call home if an emergency came up.

She was the one who insisted on having her own office, he thought with irritation. *She ought to be in it.* And if she wasn't at the office or at the cottage, *where was she?*

The suspicion as to whether or not there was another man crossed his mind just as he was drying off. The thought struck him so hard that he stopped and stared at himself in the mirror.

He supposed he should have wondered before about another man. It was possibly pretty shortsighted on his part not to have thought of it. Not even to have considered it. Molly would have said that it just went to show how he took her for granted. He had never been a jealous type of man, and this had been some annoyance to Molly.

"You don't think another man might possibly even look at me," she said once.

"Yes I do," he defended himself. Sometimes he found himself under attack and didn't know how or when it started. He thought to say, "You're a very pretty woman."

As if she didn't hear him, she said, "Do you think I'm so undesirable that I couldn't possibly attract someone who might want to have an affair?"

"Of course I don't. I just trust you, that's all." He thought his trust a good thing, but she was acting like it was an insult.

"Sometimes trust is boring," she told him. "Sometimes trust makes a person feel as forgotten as that big old safe in the garage."

Molly liked him to be attentive, and he had come to understand this and tried to remember to be attentive. Recently Molly had said, "I don't want you to *try* to be attentive. If you have to try, I don't want it."

He wondered why trying should make it of less effect. It seemed the results should be what mattered. Sometimes he had to try his best just to get out of bed, but he made it, and that was what counted.

He showered and dressed and went back down to the kitchen, where he stood for several minutes with the refrigerator door open. Disgusted with what little there was in there, he slammed the door closed and grabbed his car keys.

He vaulted over the side of the Corvette, started the engine, and sped it back out of the garage bay. Shifting quick and hard, he spun the tires as he raced up the drive. He had to slow up, though, as the Corvette rode too low to take a chance on speeding on the sandy road, and besides, a couple of Eulalee Harris's chickens were clucking around in the middle.

9

❖ ❖

What Are We Fighting For?

The parking lot of Rodeo Rio's was all but empty at just before seven on Monday night. It being summer, the sun was still bright. Tommy Lee pulled the Corvette to a stop near the door, beside a Jeep Cherokee. He was glad to park so close to the door, since he didn't have the top on his Corvette.

Inside he saw a couple of men playing pool, a man and woman at a booth, and a couple of people at a table in the back near the large television. CNN flickered on the screen, but all Tommy Lee could hear was George Strait singing out from the colorful Wurlitzer. He went to the bar and ordered a steak and a Mexican beer. Rodeo Rio's only offered two things on their food menu: a third-pound hamburger or a T-bone steak.

At the same moment the bartender passed across the foaming glass of Tecate, Winn Ketchum came out the office door nearby.

"Well, hello, Tommy Lee." Winn stuck out his hand as he came forward. "It's been a while."

"Hello, Winn."

Tommy Lee shook the man's hand, and the two of

them traded a bit of b.s. for a minute. Tommy Lee asked after Sam, and Winn said Sam was out in Santa Fe right now.

"He was in overnight last week," Winn said, folding his pudgy arms. "He's met this gal that has her own plane, and she dropped him off on her way to Dallas and picked him back up on her way back."

"That's convenient," Tommy Lee commented.

"You know Sam. Women just about kill themselves to do things for him. I haven't yet figured out why." Winn grinned and tugged at his ear.

The bartender called to Winn, "Carly's on the phone."

Winn waved at him. "Tell her I'm comin'." He looked at Tommy Lee. "Gotta run. . . . The wife's waitin'." He kind of glanced around. "Molly not here with you?"

Tommy Lee shook his head. "Not tonight," was all he said.

"Well, don't be a stranger, hear?" Winn said and clamped a hand on his shoulder as he left.

Tommy Lee ran his gaze over the tables for a moment, then sauntered over to an empty pool table. His game was a little rusty these days, but he knew he'd warm up. He'd once played a lot of pool. He and Sam and sometimes Molly.

Rodeo Rio's had been around since Tommy Lee was a kid, but it was greatly changed. About five years ago Sam and his older brother Winn had bought the place and expanded it with the television area and went to serving hamburgers and steaks and mineral water to those who wanted it. The old small stage remained, with better speakers. The pool tables were fancier, and there was an exhaust system to take care of the cigarette smoke. Rodeo Rio's sat out on the highway to Lawton and was classy enough to get folks coming down on the weekends while retaining a friendly, down-home atmosphere. Tommy Lee stayed too busy these days to come here often. He usually only came when Sam was in town.

Sam Ketchum was still Tommy Lee's best friend, even if they didn't see each other very often. Sam had made a successful career in jewelry design and lived mostly out in Santa Fe, where he had a fancy adobe house and studio.

"My heart's in Valentine," Sam always said, "but my livelihood's in Santa Fe."

He returned to Valentine every few months, staying in an apartment over Winn's garage. He had his interest in Rio's with Winn, and he kept a few pieces of jewelry placed in shops in Lawton and Oklahoma City. Also, Molly was his accountant.

Tommy Lee knew a lot of people, but he thought of them as acquaintances. He never had had a lot of friends; he'd never wanted a lot of friends. He'd had Sam and Molly and that had always been enough.

In thinking of it, Tommy Lee guessed Sam hadn't changed all that much since high school days and was pretty much living the life he had always said he would. He was a free man, having been divorced twice and with no children. Tommy Lee envied him a little.

He looked up and saw a woman bringing his steak. She was immediately familiar—a slim woman with dark hair curling past her shoulders and a sexy rolling way of walking. But what made her name click in his mind were her big breasts bobbing beneath the Rodeo Rio's tight-fitting T-shirt.

Annette Rountree, Gordy Rountree's little sister. Tommy Lee could recall her as a girl with pigtails. Whenever he and Sam went to Gordy's she had always been peeking out from somewhere. Sometimes Tommy Lee would smile at her, and she'd smile back. He used to envy the guys he knew who had sisters and brothers. They all said he was crazy, but they hadn't lived in the silent house he had.

Annette cast him a slow smile as she stopped at the table where he'd sat his beer. "Is right here good?"

"Yeah . . . that's fine. Thanks."

Since Annette was so slender, her big breasts seemed all the more striking, and there was much speculation as to whether or not they were all hers. Molly said that breasts made bigger by implants were hard and tended to stick out. Annette's did tend to stick out. Of course, Tommy Lee only gave them a quick glance. He didn't want to be caught looking.

He forgot to lay down the pool cue and carried it over to the table. That made him feel more foolish than he already did—he was feeling foolish because he didn't often eat alone in a restaurant. Actually, he couldn't remember ever eating alone in a restaurant.

Annette set his plate and silverware in place. Tommy Lee propped the pool cue against the wall and asked her politely how she was and how long she'd been working at Rio's. It seemed he could recall her working at the Main Street Cafe.

"Oh, I've been here about three months now," she said. Suddenly he was looking right into her face, and she was giving him a curious look. "You don't come in here often."

"No . . . usually when Sam's in town, I guess." He thought maybe he imagined how she looked at him. He wouldn't let himself look at her breasts.

"I brought you a glass of water and catsup and steak sauce," she said, pointing at each thing. "That steak sauce is Winn's own recipe. It's real good. Do you want anything else?"

"No . . . no, this is fine. Thanks." He pulled out the chair but remained standing until she walked away.

He scooted his chair in place and looked at his plate a minute and felt dreary. The salad wasn't anything more than a couple of cherry tomatoes sitting in lettuce. The T-bone steak laid across the oblong plate, and a thick piece of buttered toast lay atop part of it. They didn't get fancy here at Rio's.

At least they used cloth napkins; that had been his idea to Sam. Tommy Lee hated paper napkins.

He lifted the fork and shook out the napkin, and suddenly he was recalling what Molly had said to him about eating off forks in restaurants. He gazed at the fork and wondered who had used it before him. He had never thought about it before Molly had said what she did, and he wished she had never put that thought in his head, because now he felt a bit nervous about using it. He wiped it with the napkin, furtively, self-conscious in the action.

He suddenly had a powerful wish that Molly was with him . . . or that Sam was there. It was god-awful eating alone. He almost wished he hadn't come, but the aroma of the steak was enticing. He threw off the thought about the fork and cut into the steak. After the first savory bite, he decided that he was glad he had come. Maybe Rio's didn't get fancy, but the steak was the best to be found anywhere. And he had seen Rio's kitchen, and it was clean.

Tommy Lee considered that he might have to get used to eating alone. The big screen television helped a lot; he could see it easily. He reflected that a lot of people had to eat alone. Maybe a good many people chose to eat alone. Sam surely had to do it all the time. Although, maybe not. Sam tended to be a gregarious sort, and people just seemed to flock around him. Unless he was in a poor mood. Tommy Lee was one of the very few people who ever saw Sam's bad moods; Sam didn't go out of his house when he was in a poor mood. He would sit on the sofa and drink beer and eat pretzels, or he'd stay in bed and stare at the ceiling. Tommy Lee had seen Sam stay in bed for days in one of those moods.

Annette came to refill his water glass from a heavy pitcher and asked, "Do you need anything?"

"I don't believe so." He wiped his mouth with the napkin. "It's all very good."

"Winn gets his steaks from the Hancock place, and he'll only take the best," Annette said, sliding out a chair and setting herself down.

Tommy Lee was a little surprised, but he didn't think he showed it. He was sort of glad, too.

But then Annette went and said, "I heard about you and Molly. I'm sorry. I went through a divorce, and it sure can be tough." Her saying that was embarrassing, but she had a tender look on her face, and Tommy Lee appreciated her trying to be consoling.

He said, "We're not divorced. Molly's just stayin' at the cottage for a while. It's not anything legal."

She looked at him for a moment and then said, "I've been divorced about three years now. I was married to Alvin Osborne."

When she seemed to be waiting, Tommy Lee said he didn't recall the man.

"He was in my class at school. We were four years behind you and Gordy. Alvin and I went together in high school, but after graduation, we went our separate ways. A couple of years later, I moved down to Houston to get away from my parents, and I ran into him. It was like fate, and we got married right off. Alvin was a nice guy for the first year or so, but then he got sour, and one day he was just gone."

Tommy Lee gave a small shake of his head; he didn't know what to say.

"You and Molly have been together for just about ever," she said, and her eyes studied him.

"We've been married almost twenty-five years," he said. He almost mentioned the anniversary party at the VFW hall, but he held that back. There was no need to mention it.

Annette said, "Gosh, it doesn't seem like it's been that long. I can't imagine bein' with a person so long."

"I don't think there's anyway to imagine it," Tommy Lee said. He leaned forward and played with his beer glass. "Years go by and they add up, and they aren't nearly as long as they sound." Then he added, "We're expectin' our first grandchild this summer."

"No kidding? You sure don't look like a grandpa."

She laughed, and he chuckled and rubbed the back of his neck, feeling his face grow warm.

She said, "My aunt and uncle were married thirty years, and then they got a divorce. I guess there's just no guarantees."

"No, I guess not," Tommy Lee said, feeling sadness wash over him, thick and heavy.

"Your kids are all grown, aren't they? Me and Alvin only had one child—my girl. She's twelve now. Of course, by the time her daddy took off, she hardly noticed. He hadn't been home for most of the two years before he left."

There really wasn't anything to say to that. Tommy Lee nodded and took a drink of beer, which had grown lukewarm.

He was both flattered and nervous by the way Annette was looking at him. He kept wondering if he was imagining how she was looking at him. Maybe she looked at all men that way. Some women did— looked at every man as if measuring him and what was in his pants. He couldn't quite believe she would be looking at him in an interested way. But she had been the one to sit herself down, without being asked.

They talked for a bit about this and that. Annette seemed to pick up that he didn't want to talk anymore about him and Molly and divorce. She seemed an intuitive person.

Annette scooted to the edge of her seat, drawing up and poking out her big breasts, saying, "Can I get you another beer?"

He shook his head. "No thanks." He averted his eyes. She rose, and he said, "Thanks for the conversation."

He watched her walk away and imagined himself taking her by the arm and suggesting they have a drink together, then drive . . . where? He certainly wouldn't take her back to his and Molly's house. Maybe they could go to hers, except she had that daughter. A motel . . . up in Lawton . . . and they'd likely run into people they knew.

Even as he thought these thoughts, he knew he wouldn't ask her any of it. He wouldn't know how to go off with Annette, which was bad enough, but the truth was that he didn't *want* to go off with her. He knew that sharply and truly.

Lonesomeness clawed at his insides. He was familiar with the feeling, had learned how to battle it but felt himself losing the fight.

He hadn't quite finished his meal, but his appetite was gone. He dug into his pocket, pulled out several bills and left them on the table. With a second thought, he set the plate on the edge of the bills, so that they wouldn't accidently drift to the floor and to make it more difficult for someone walking by to snatch them up. Tommy Lee had always wondered how many tips left on a table were snatched up by wandering hands.

Annette called good-bye and gave a little wave. He waved back and said thanks.

There was a red line on the western horizon. Rodeo Rio's lights blinked brightly. Tommy Lee jumped over the door into the seat, turned the key, and listened with a measure of satisfaction to the powerful Corvette engine purr. With stars beginning to appear in the darkening sky, he headed down the blacktop, the cooling night breeze whipping at his hair. He circled town and drove past the Collier place. He told himself he was being really stupid.

There were lights on in the big house, but the little cottage was dark. In order to look closely in the darkness, he had to pause at the opening of the drive, and he hoped Molly didn't chance to see him. He saw the dark shadow of Odessa's Lincoln. Molly's El Camino wasn't there.

He pressed the accelerator and drove away, telling himself where Molly was didn't matter. He called himself all kinds of a fool. Hadn't Molly walked out? Didn't that go to show that Molly didn't care what he was doin' right now? She herself had told him to do whatever he wanted.

He was so distracted by his thoughts that when he pulled down his driveway and saw the El Camino sitting there in the lights outside the garage the fact didn't strike him. He simply thought, *Well, Molly's home.*

Then the fact did strike him. *Molly!* He was so surprised, was staring so hard at the El Camino, that he almost ran into it. Then he was out of the Corvette and running up the stairs. He paused in the kitchen. The light was on, but Molly wasn't there. He heard motion upstairs. He took the stairs two at a time and strode down the hall to their bedroom, where light poured from the doorway.

He stopped. At a glance he saw a duffel bag on the bed and Molly stuffing things into it. For an instant the wedding band on her finger caught the light. She still had it on.

Then he and Molly were looking at each other, and it was awkward, neither of them knowing what to say. Oddly in that moment, he noticed how beautiful her eyes were; he'd always thought her eyes the most beautiful thing about her. They were big and green and sensual, and right that minute they were filled with a sensual kind of sadness, which in a perverse way made them even more alluring.

She blinked and looked away, gesturing toward the dresser. "I need some things I forgot. I didn't take hardly any underwear."

"You might need some, I guess," Tommy Lee said.

She looked very sad, and as if she were waiting for him to say something else, but his mind was blank on what that something might be. Anger seeped into his chest with frightening power. He felt she required something of him, but he didn't want to give it, no matter that he didn't exactly know what it was she wanted.

He turned and walked back down the hall and down the stairs.

Molly went over and sat on the bed. She felt as if all her energy had drained right out her feet. She told herself she shouldn't have come. She had simply gotten carried away, the same as she had when she'd left. She'd just been carried along by her emotions, wanting to see Tommy Lee and thinking maybe a few words would wipe out the wall that was between them.

When she felt she could move, she zipped the duffle bag. There was more she might have packed, but she didn't care about any of it anymore. She was having trouble caring about breathing. She didn't want to leave yet, though, so she made the bed. Spread the top sheet that was in a wad like a rag, picked up the summer quilt from the floor and smoothed it, then turned it down in an inviting manner. Maybe Tommy Lee would appreciate finding the bedcovers all smoothed and waiting, she thought, as she fluffed the pillows and put them in place. Then her eyes filled with tears because she thought that now that she was gone, he was sleeping in the bed.

Turning from the bed, she picked up the duffel bag and went downstairs.

Tommy Lee was propped on a stool at the breakfast bar, a bottle of tequila in front of him and a half-filled glass in his hand. That was a somewhat shocking sight.

He glanced at her, then returned his gaze to his

glass. Molly stared at the bottle of tequila. She guessed it was the one from the pantry, which had been in there for about two years. Unless Tommy Lee had drank that one and gotten another.

She was turning this disturbing thought over in her mind, when he said, "Savannah was tryin' to reach you today. She was upset, and not being able to get you made her even more so." He spoke with his back to her.

"I know. Mama and I called her just before I came over here. We called Boone and Colter, too. Boone wasn't in, but Colter is doing fine. He made two twenty-dollar tips Sunday night at that part-time job he has at the Steak and Ale."

Tommy Lee nodded and took a deep drink out of the glass. Molly swallowed, then walked through into the small office and got some forms and a computer disk. When she came out, she said, "I needed to get the tax forms." She paused and added, "I figured I'd go on handlin' your business accounts . . . unless you didn't want me to."

"Why wouldn't I want you to?" He turned and looked at her. "And why do you call it my business? I always thought of it as *our* business."

The questions, thrown at her like that, confused her. "Because it is your business," she said. "You started it, you run it. I do what I can for it because I want to help you do what interests you. I started keepin' the books in the first place because you needed someone to do it. It was something—it *is* something I can do for you. That is my only interest in your business—doing somethin' to help you."

"I can get someone else to do it if you don't want to," Tommy Lee said.

"I know that." Privately Molly thought that he would be in a pretty big mess without her help. He didn't know the half of what she did. "But now I'm all settled in and everything, so I might as well keep doin' it. And anyway, now this part of your business has become my business." She reached over and took the check and receipt from Cormac lying on the counter and tucked them into the folder she held in her hand. "I'll put this in the bank tomorrow."

"But you used to hate it," he said, worrying the subject like a dog with a bone. "You did it, but you hated every minute of doing it, right?"

"I certainly told you that, often enough," Molly said, matching his annoyed tone. "It was hard to like it when I had to learn how to do it in the first place, and I had to do it with kids underfoot. But I don't hate it anymore. I like doing the books now."

He looked downward, and she stood there a long minute, for some reason looking at his hands. There were nicks on the back of them, like always. They were so strong.

Then she said in a softer tone, "I just always think of it as your business, but keepin' the accounts is my part in it. That's how I think of it, so in that sense it is *our* business."

Staring at the glass in his hands, he nodded. Molly wished he wasn't drinking tequila like that. His doing that made her a little scared. He didn't seem like Tommy Lee while he was doing that. She supposed she didn't seem much like herself these days, either.

"Where were you today when Savannah was tryin' to call you?" he asked suddenly, jarring her from her thoughts.

"Out riding."

She wondered why he was looking at her like he was, with his blue eyes so intense as to bore into her.

She said, "I really don't think I have to be by the phone every minute just in case Savannah might call." She felt guilty, though.

"Have you found someone else? Is that what this is all about?"

His question so surprised her that she couldn't say

anything for several seconds. She almost laughed, and then she got annoyed.

"No, of course I haven't found anyone else. And that is not what this is all about. This is about you and me and what's happened between us. And it's about me trying to figure out my feelings. I need space, and I'm givin' you space."

Tommy Lee said, "Maybe I don't want space."

His expression was stubborn and angry. Hateful. Molly gazed at him and her stomach quivered.

She swallowed and then said, "Well, what do you want, Tommy Lee?"

His jawline tightened, and he stared down into the glass he held with both hands. Molly's gaze went over his strong shoulders and slipped down his sinewy arms to his calloused hands holding the glass. She thought that she could stand there as long as he could sit there looking at that stupid glass.

"God, I don't know," he admitted finally.

He raised his gaze to hers. His blue eyes were glistening, despairing.

Molly breathed deeply, then went over and lowered herself into a chair at the table. She was at once relieved and disappointed as she had ever before been.

After a long minute, she said, "I don't know what I want, either. I don't feel like I know who you are, and I certainly don't know who I am. Lord, I hardly know *where* I am these days."

They sat there, Tommy Lee on his stool and Molly over at the table. Molly wished Tommy Lee would say something, but she doubted he was going to. For all of their twenty-five years, it most generally ended up being Molly who talked. Right that moment jumbled words were pushing up from her chest, and she kept swallowing them back down. She wasn't certain they would make any sense, and besides, she felt that all of her talking during the years had not kept them from getting to this strange place. Maybe a change would help. Her not talking would really be a change, and maybe it would give Tommy Lee some of his own medicine.

It occurred to her that her attitude was a poor one, certainly less than positive. But it was what she truly felt. And she really did think she needed to learn to be quiet and to listen. She had tried before to do this, with the result that she had always seemed to end up listening to Tommy Lee's silences.

Tommy Lee remained staring silently at the glass in his hand. Molly had the urge to go over and knock it winding. Then pity fell all over her. He looked so sad, and he couldn't manage to speak of it.

Picking up the duffel bag and files, she quietly left.

She thought to herself that now she had left her husband twice.

Tommy Lee finished the tequila in his glass and then went to drinking out of the bottle. He got choked with the first gulps and took smaller swigs. After a bit, he decided the tequila was starting to taste quite good.

He took the bottle out onto the front porch and sat on the top step. Jake came to join him. It was a bit pleasant at first, just sitting there drinking, and he talked to the dog a bit.

"Where you been, buddy? It must be nice, roamin' around all day and comin' home at night, knowin' you're gonna get fed."

Jake laid his head in Tommy Lee's lap, and Tommy Lee stroked it. "I bet you've been out screwin' the ladies."

Jake looked up at him, and Tommy Lee thought he looked a little guilty.

"You're gettin' pretty old," he told the dog, stroking the dog's white muzzle. "How is it for a dog gettin' old? You probably don't even know it. Well, let me tell you, people know it. One day a man wakes up and sees there's a whole lot of dreams he's never gonna get done. Hell, he wakes up and realizes he forgot all his dreams."

He drank more from the bottle and then said to the dog, "I like talkin' to you, buddy, but it would be better if you could talk back."

Pushing to his feet, Tommy Lee stumbled on the top step but caught himself before falling. His head was spinning. He had apparently lost what little tolerance for liquor he had ever had, which struck him as a money-saving proposition. He could be a cheap drunk.

He decided to call Sam, but he didn't know the number, so he had to find the address book. He found it buried on his desk and took it into the living room, where he sat in his BarcaLounger. He had some difficulty finding Sam's number and then in dialing. He mistakenly got a man who was highly annoyed. Tommy Lee apologized profusely, but the man hung up on him with a loud reverberating click.

Carefully, he dialed again. As the ringing sounded across the line, he wondered if he had dialed incorrectly again and held the phone an inch from his ear, just in case. He tried to figure out what time it would be in Santa Fe. He had scooted up on the edge of the chair, and just as Sam answered, his elbow slid off his knee, and he almost dropped the phone.

"You sound soused," Sam said.

"I think I am," Tommy Lee said. "But not too bad."

"What's happened?"

"How do you know somethin' happened? Maybe I'm just callin' to shoot the shit."

"Not you. You're afraid of phones."

"I am not afraid of phones," Tommy Lee insisted. "I don't like them a lot. I find them annoying. But that doesn't mean I'm afraid of them. Who in the hell would be afraid of a phone?"

"I wasn't insultin' you, buddy. Everyone has fears. I'm afraid of garbage disposals myself—they make my skin crawl, ever since I saw a movie where the bad guys stuck the good guy's hand in one and turned it on. I can't remember the movie or the actors, but I sure never forgot that scene with that guy gettin' his hand chewed up. Geez, it makes my skin crawl just to talk about it. Darlene got real aggravated at me when I wouldn't let her put a garbage disposal in our kitchen. That was one of the things she cited at the divorce."

"I saw that movie. Maybe it was a *Rockford Files* show. Darlene used that in the divorce?"

"She used it as one of my strange idiosyncracies, showin' why I was such a bad husband," Sam said. "So—why are you soused?"

Tommy Lee sighed deeply. "I guess because the tequila is here . . . and Molly isn't."

"What? Has somethin' happened to Molly?" Sam's voice came loud across the line.

"She left me." He was sort of embarrassed to say it, but Sam was his best friend. Sam would understand.

"Geez," Sam said after a few long seconds, "I can't hardly believe that."

"Well, it's true. I wouldn't lie about it."

"I know that," Sam said. "What did you do?"

"I didn't do anything. Why would you think I did something?"

"Because I don't think Molly would just leave you."

"Well, she did. She broke our wedding dishes and said she was goin' to Hestie's cottage and walked out."

"That sure doesn't sound like Molly."

"Well, she's changed," Tommy Lee told him emphatically. He was the wounded party in this, and he wanted Sam to know it.

"The cottage isn't so far," Sam said. "When did this happen?"

"Saturday. We had sort of an argument. . . . Well,

we've been havin' a sort of argument for a while."
Tommy Lee sat back in the chair and rubbed a hand
over his face.

"What have you been arguin' about?"

"God, I don't know." He reached for the tequila
bottle and held it by the neck. "You know—life."

Sam said he was awfully sorry. "I imagine she'll
come back when she calms down."

"Maybe," Tommy Lee said.

"I know this is tough for you buddy," Sam said.
"I've been in that place before, and it's tough."

"I always thought you were glad when you split
with each one of your wives." Tommy Lee halfway
resented Sam saying he had been in the same place.
Sam had never been married longer than two years at
a time, which was nowhere near Tommy Lee's place.

"Well, I was sort of relieved, I guess," Sam said.
"But that doesn't mean it wasn't tough. And Darlene
got a whole hunk of my income. That was tough." He
paused, then added, "Molly isn't like that, though.
You won't have that problem."

Tommy Lee felt sick at the thought of divorce
legalities. How would they possibly split things up?
The attic alone would take five years to go through.

Then Sam said in a low voice, "She didn't find out,
did she . . . about that time when you were in
Charleston?"

Tommy Lee swallowed. "That was a long time ago
and forgotten."

"I'm sorry, T.L. . . . really sorry. Sometimes I say
things before I think. God, things just seem to be goin'
too fast for me these days. It's just hard to
imagine . . . you and Molly not together."

Tommy Lee laid his head back and squeezed his
eyes closed. Tears slipped out and ran down his
cheeks. He was sure glad Sam couldn't see him. He
couldn't talk because he didn't want Sam to know he
was crying.

He choked back the lump in his throat and looked at the tequila bottle he balanced on his leg. Then he told Sam about the macho feeling that came over him when he held a tequila bottle by the neck. Tommy Lee could tell Sam things like that. Sam said he knew that feeling and that it was one of the reasons he liked to drink long-neck beers. Tommy Lee felt a little less lonely. He'd been hesitant to call Sam, afraid he might feel stupid, even with his best friend, but now he was really glad he had called.

He was feeling so close to Sam that he said, "It's sure lonely in this big house."

"I hear that," Sam said. "My place isn't too big, but sometimes it echoes."

"I always sort of thought you preferred being single. At least you don't have to be tryin' to please someone all the time. You can do what you want."

"That gets a little old," Sam said, and something in his voice touched Tommy Lee.

"Maybe I'll come out to see you for a few days," he said, grasping at the idea. "We can cut up. Have it like old times."

"You come on, buddy. You're always welcome here. You know that."

"Well, I might." But the idea was already losing its shine. He was thinking about the two engines he had waiting in the shop, and he really didn't want to go anywhere. It kind of frightened him to think of leaving home. If he left, he may never get back with Molly.

He and Sam talked a little longer—mostly Sam did the talking, about old times and the young woman who had her own plane and Tanya Tucker, who had come into his shop and bought a pair of earrings.

Tommy Lee didn't want to let Sam off the phone, but he couldn't think of a lot to say, and then Sam was gone. Tommy Lee sat totally alone in the Barca-Lounger, holding the tequila bottle, while the memory he didn't want came pushing and shoving itself forward, as if floating up through the layers of the years.

"So you slipped up," Sam had told him back all those years ago. "It didn't mean anything, and the worse thing you can do is tell Molly. You'll be doin' it to ease your conscience, and in the process you'll make Molly have to pay for your mistake with a broken heart. Don't do that to her. You just live with it, and forget it, if you can."

Sam had been pretty put out with him, which had made Tommy Lee feel even worse, if that was possible. He had not expected Sam to condemn him, although Sam was Molly's friend, too, and sometimes pretty protective of her. Tommy Lee had felt so badly, he'd asked Sam to punch him, but Sam had looked shocked and told him not to be crazy.

Tommy Lee had tried to forget, and mostly he had succeeded. Sam had been right. The mistake was his to live with, and there would be no good in making Molly have to live with it, too. But sometimes he suspected she knew.

He'd been out on the circuit for two months with the racing team. Been staying for three days at the Holiday Inn in Charleston, and of all nights for her to call, Molly had called that fateful night he had gone crazy and slept with Josey Hightower. At least that's what he thought her name was; he had so completely blocked the shameful incident from his mind that he was no longer exactly certain of what the woman's name was.

"Tommy Lee?" Molly had said his name in a questioning way, but she hadn't asked the name of the woman who had answered the phone.

Tommy Lee had told her, though. "That was just Josey . . . you know, the woman I told you who manages the payroll and everything." He held the receiver with his shoulder while he slipped into his jeans. "A few of the guys are here . . . you know, havin' a few beers. It's rainin' like crazy outside. Nothin' to do. You know."

As he said that, he went over to turn up the television. On the bed, Josey was propped up on the pillows. She had the sheet tucked up beneath her arms, flattening her little breasts, and was lighting a cigarette. Suddenly Tommy Lee wondered who she was and how she came to be in his bed. She was about fifteen years older than him, and suddenly she really looked it, and hard, too, where only minutes before he'd thought she was really pretty.

After he'd hung up with Molly, he put on his shirt and boots and told Josey that he was going out. He didn't remember now what she had said, if she said anything. He remembered her blowing smoke into the air. He stayed out the rest of the night, sat in a booth at the 76 truck stop across the street, smoking Camels and drinking about a gallon of coffee and wishing some crazed trucker would come in and shoot him. There had recently been an incident like that at a truck stop near Houston, where a trucker had gone crazy on amphetamines and blasted out windows with a shotgun, killing several people in the process. Tommy Lee kept looking out the window for any mean-looking trucker carrying a gun, or even a club, but all he saw were tired faces.

When he finally got up the nerve to go back to his motel room—at dawn, and he figured Josey would be gone—he picked a fight with a trucker coming in the door as he was going out, hoping to get the shit kicked out of himself, but the guy was an easygoing bear of a man and simply laughed and held the door and waved Tommy Lee through. Tommy Lee had thought that incident showed the hand of God intent on making him feel even more guilty.

For the remaining week, until he could cut out for home, he had avoided Josey, had never talked to her again, and had wished with all his might that he hadn't been so stupid. The only reasons he could come up with for his poor behavior had been that he'd been awfully lonely and that he'd slept with only one woman in his life, Molly, and he guessed the curiosity of what another woman would be like had gotten the best of him. Lots of married guys talked of sleeping with other women regularly and apparently with no guilt. Also, it was true that Josey had been pressing him. Not that that was an excuse, but it was a reason.

He supposed the biggest, truest reason was that he had been twenty-one and stupid, and he'd prayed to God that if his lapse could just be covered over and forgotten, he would never be so stupid again. He simply wasn't the kind to sleep around, and that's all there was to it.

The years of deliberately pushing the incident from his mind had made the memory of his foolishness with Josey Hightower no more than a blur, something that seemed to have happened to someone else. The moments on the telephone with Molly were scant at best. His main memory from those moments was of his heart about to beat out of his chest and of being afraid he would have a heart attack and be discovered dead with a naked woman in his motel bed. What he remembered about sitting in the 76 truck stop was that it seemed as if he had sat there for days.

The memory of his arrival home was clear, perhaps because it was exactly like so many before and the few after, when he'd gone away. He remembered Molly coming out the front door, standing there an instant, as if holding her breath, her face bright with expectancy. She wore a flowered dress, and then her long pale hair flew out behind her as she came running, barefoot, across the yard to throw herself into his arms.

Whenever he would come home, he would always find her face all full of eagerness and love so intense that it almost overwhelmed him. He would be so glad to see her love and so pressured at the same time.

Molly's love was a high thing to live up to. Tommy Lee always knew that if he did one thing to let her down, she would be crushed. Her love, at times, was a heavy burden to bear.

But that day when she came running at him, he had grabbed her up and whirled her around in his arms, so glad to have her and promising himself and God that he would never, ever risk losing her love again. He would cherish her because she was his treasure. He promised never to forget that.

That night Molly told him she was pregnant with Boone and cried that she didn't want him to leave again. He told her he would give up the racing circuit. He told her eagerly, and he supposed he jumped at the decision because it was a way to bury what he had done. He sure didn't want to have to see Josey Hightower again. And he had felt so guilty and so grateful that he would have given Molly the moon if he could have.

As the memory of his indiscretion faded, though, he had begun to miss the circuit something awful. But every time he spoke to Molly about the possibility of going back, she got this pinched look on her face. By then there were two children and house payments and doctor bills and he was in too deep to be throwing everything to the winds and following a pipe dream.

Just as the memory of his indiscretion faded, so, too, did his fervent vow to never forget how precious Molly was to him. He loved her, and sometimes he was made sharply aware of how important she was in his life, but more times the burden of her love as well as the struggles of everyday life would overcome him. How was a person supposed to keep in focus the important things when trying to support a wife, raise three kids, get a business going, and keep the wolf from the door?

Somehow romance and love got lost. Sometimes he was doing good to simply hold on to his sanity, much less his treasure.

Too many memories had been forced upon him in one day, he thought and let sleep claim him.

10

❖❖

I Know Better Now

Rennie found the back door of the cottage open and the screen door unlatched. She stepped inside.

"Molly?"

Things were messy, even for Molly. A few cups were scattered across the table, a crumpled loaf of bread and half a peanut butter sandwich. Cups and glasses were stacked in the sink. Several cups on the drain board were half filled with stale coffee. On the little stove sat the jar of generic brand instant coffee, which Molly hated. The kitchen had such a forgotten, used look to it.

Then Rennie saw the black telephone cord snaking across the floor. Her eye followed it to the door of the refrigerator. She opened the door and saw the old black phone sitting inside on the wire shelf. All by itself. The knot in her stomach tightened—a knot she just then realized was there. She closed the refrigerator door.

As she went on through the rooms, hurrying now, feeling urgent and calling to Molly, the scent of the cottage, made stronger by the humid heat of the day, surrounded her. Hardly a breath of air stirred through the opened windows.

She found Molly, wearing only her bra and panties, partially propped on pillows in the rumpled bed—the chenille spread was on the floor and the sheets in a knot, and the whole bed was littered with books, mostly hardbacks, a few paperbacks. And there was Molly, looking like an unclothed rag doll lying in the middle of those books, with a gray tabby cat lying on her bare belly.

When people are depressed they can't get dressed. Mrs. Hinch got like that after her eighth child. After she came out of her house half naked, Mama went down to dress her every morning for weeks. Mrs. Hinch hanged herself with clothesline on her back porch.

The sight of Molly like that shook Rennie. Molly had always been the sane one of all of them. The one Rennie could always run to. It seemed strange to think that Rennie herself had to attempt to boost Molly. Molly was always the one to boost Rennie.

"Why didn't you answer me?" Rennie asked.

"The cottage isn't very big," Molly said. "I knew you'd find me." Her eyes were dull as dishwater.

Rennie breathed deeply. "You are a sight. Don't you think you should keep that back door hooked if you're gonna lie around half naked? I could have been an ax murderer."

"I don't think an ax murderer would care if I wore clothes or not." Molly spoke lazily, her gaze back on the cat, which she continued to pet.

Rennie was a bit reassured that Molly had answered, and so logically, if strangely. But the way she continued to just look at the cat and stroke it made Rennie's skin crawl. The black fan whirred softly from over on the trunk, stirring the curtains and wisps of Molly's hair. There were deep shadows beneath her eyes, and her face was almost as pale as the sheet.

Glancing around for an ashtray, Rennie said, "You still should hook the door. Little boys could get in for a peek."

Molly said, "Little boys wouldn't have to come in the house. They could look through the window."

Rennie went searching for an ashtray and found it beside the sink, with only two butts in it. That was a good sign; it didn't appear that Molly was smoking a lot. Unless she was emptying the ashtray regularly. Rennie looked into the trash can. She didn't see any butts there. She thought maybe she was grasping at good signs. Then she wished Molly were smoking; it would be better than Molly just stroking that cat.

She carried her ashtray and cigarette back into the bedroom. She had to move a pair of jeans and a shirt off the vanity bench in order to sit on it. She gazed into the mirror and raked a hand through her curls, limp from the humid air. Her gaze shifted to Molly in the mirror, and her stomach clenched. She didn't know what to do about handling Molly. She had her own problems right now, too, and this with Molly was simply too much.

Then she looked around, sniffing. "Lordy, it smells in here." She looked down at the jeans and then over at Molly. "Not that usual smell . . . it smells like horse," she said, sniffing in Molly's direction.

Molly gestured, and Rennie looked over to see a saddle setting on the floor behind the opened closet door. The saddle pad was slung over it.

"What's it doin' there?"

"I put it there," Molly answered.

"You have a tack compartment in your trailer." Rennie slung her legs around to the opposite side of the vanity bench. "I thought you kept it in there."

"It leaks." Molly was scratching the cat's forehead, and it was purring. Rennie could hear it from where she sat.

"What are you doing with all these books in the

bed?" Rennie asked. "Isn't it a little uncomfortable when you turn over?"

"I don't turn much."

Rennie stretched over to take up one of the books— *In Tune with the Infinite* by Ralph Waldo Trine. It looked really old. There always had been a lot of books around the cottage, and no doubt their mother had provided some. Colliers were big on books. Especially philosophy-of-life ones. That's what this one was.

Rennie was considered the most illiterate of the Collier women because she read only novels. In her view, she could learn as much about herself and life from novels as from any of those self-improvement books. Besides, she'd had enough philosophy to last her a lifetime, being the daughter of her mother.

Once, after she'd had her miscarriage and had started drinking enough to make her worry that she might end up like her daddy, Rennie had visited a psychologist. After several visits, the whole while watching the psychologist, a thin man with a bad haircut, blink rapidly and pick at his eyebrows, one of which was almost picked out, she had decided she was more mentally stable than he was and quit going.

Later she had visited an Alcoholics Anonymous meeting, where she had felt more at ease, but she never had been much of a joiner. She had, however, cut herself off from alcohol and practiced the twelve steps, which she still did each day. She had also gone on a novel-reading spree. She supposed she could say that for a while she got addicted to novels instead of drinking, most especially crazy novels about crazy people, which made her feel much more sane, or at least that she was no worse off than anyone else.

Another thing she had done at that time was to start eating quite a bit. It had sort of crept up on her—so easy to nibble while she read a novel. When she realized she was eating as much as half a bag of Oreos or a half carton of ice cream at a time, she had gotten very worried that she would turn into an obese person who had to be wheeled around in a wheelchair. This worry, however, only seemed to make her eat more. Time passed, and the worry abated because as it turned out she never did gain a pound. Not one pound, nor did any health problems occur. Rennie attributed this to both a high metabolism rate and God's grace.

Thinking of the Oreos, she tossed aside the Trine book and stubbed out her cigarette, then went to the kitchen and found the remaining half bag of Oreos and brought them back to Molly's bed. Flopping on her side, she ate cookies and looked over all the books, making comments: "I tried to read this"—she held up *Sanctuary* by William Faulkner—"I couldn't understand any of it." She picked up another old hardback, *Where the Red Fern Grows*. "Isn't this great? Remember when Mama read it aloud to us?" She read the inside flap of the Rita Mae Brown mystery and said, "I'd like to read this one when you're done."

Molly didn't have a thing to say. She just kept on petting that stupid cat, and Rennie got really annoyed.

She tossed the book aside. "Don't you need to be countin' people's money or something?"

"I'm on vacation," Molly said, still not looking up.

Rennie started to get scared. She really didn't think she knew what to do. She sat up and closed the bag of Oreos.

"Mama says you won't answer phone calls and haven't been out of the cottage all week."

"I've been riding. And I've talked to you."

Rennie thought it seemed like Molly had been abducted by aliens, who had set this stranger down in her place.

"Well, because you won't talk to Lillybeth and

Season," she said, "I've had to. And you know Season makes me nervous. I never am certain what to say to Season."

"No one is certain what to say to Season."

Rennie waited and stared at Molly, willing her to say more. Molly didn't even look up at her. "Well, I managed with Lillybeth and Season," Rennie said, "but I couldn't help Walter because I'm not the one who counts the town's money. Walter's worried—something about the company hired to repaint the water tower, and Kaye isn't helpin' him at all, because she's busy givin' those Country Interior parties."

Molly just lay there and stroked that dang cat.

Rennie stood up, looked at Molly. The next instant she shoved at Molly's feet. "Get up and get a shower. I'm takin' you to lunch."

The jarring of Molly's body made the cat jump from her belly and cast an annoyed gaze at Rennie. Molly said, "I'm too tired."

Rennie said, "When was the last time you washed your hair?"

Molly looked at her, but almost as if she didn't really see Rennie.

"Don't look at me like that, Sissy," Rennie said.

Molly blinked. "I was just tryin' to remember when I washed my hair."

That sent Rennie practically into a fit. She gave a scream and shoved again at Molly's feet really hard. "Don't do this, Sissy! I can't stand it. Maybe I should be able to, but I can't. You're just bein' selfish, and you aren't supposed to be the one to do that. I'm the one who can do that, but you *can't*!"

Rennie realized she was yelling then, clenching and unclenching her fists.

Molly said in a small voice, "I know. . . . I just don't know how to stop."

Rennie looked at her a long minute, then said, "I

need you, Sissy. Maybe that isn't fair, but it's just the way it is. I need you."

"Oh, Rennie," Molly said.

Rennie gazed at her. Beseeched her with her eyes, and even as she did it, she thought to herself, *I am* beseeching *you,* which was one of those words she would never say.

Then Molly said, "Okay," and slowly, as if it were a very hard thing to do, shoved herself up from the bed.

Rennie jumped ahead to the bathroom to get the water running and lay out a towel. She put the shampoo right into Molly's hand. She started to close the door on her way out, but then left it partially open. She stood there, outside the door, listening for a moment to Molly beginning to wash. There was a tiny fear inside of her that Molly might fall . . . or do something like drown herself. But she would have to look up into the shower spray to do that, which seemed unlikely. Molly never had liked to get her face sprayed.

Satisfied that Molly was truly washing, Rennie was so relieved that she felt like crying. Instead she went into the kitchen, took the telephone out of the refrigerator and dialed Tommy Lee. Of course he was surprised at her call; she heard it in his voice.

She said, "Are you depressed, Tommy Lee?"

"Well . . ." There was a long pause; no doubt he was very surprised by the question, but then he answered, "I guess I am, a little."

"Good," Rennie said and hung up.

She knew it would drive him crazy. She savored that. She had nothing against Tommy Lee, as far as it went, which wasn't very far because she never had gotten to know him well. Since she was a little girl, Tommy Lee had simply been there, at the edge of her life. He had always been Molly's Tommy Lee, as if he never had wanted to belong to the rest of them.

Still, Rennie didn't hold anything personally against him, except that he was a man and at that moment she wasn't at all happy with men. For as long as she could remember, Rennie had wavered between adoring men and hating them, and never did the emotion correctly match the situation she was in with a man. She always adored a man when she should hate him, and hated a man when she should adore him. She really wished she could find a middle ground.

She stuck the telephone back into the refrigerator, then went back to get the bag of Oreos and to pick out some clothes for Molly. She would make Molly fix up, too, put her makeup on her if she had to.

11

❖❖

Halfway Down

Squinting and feeling shaky inside, Molly paused to put on her sunglasses before following Rennie out the door. The air felt heavy, pressing. Her gaze fell on Rennie's back. Wearing a sleeveless shell and jeans, Rennie looked more college student than professor. "What are you doin' down here on a weekday?" Molly asked her.

"I don't have any classes on Thursday or Friday now that it's summer," Rennie said.

Molly paused. "Is this Thursday or Friday?"

Rennie, opening her car door, looked over the roof at her. "It's Thursday."

"Oh."

Molly had lost track of days after Monday evening, when she'd left Tommy Lee again and come back to ride Marker beneath the bright moon. She had ridden half the night. She thought she had ridden Marker again one morning, but she couldn't remember which morning. She thought it was just that morning that she had roused herself enough to consider riding. Then, half dressed, she'd lost heart. Wearing only a denim shirt, panties, and boots, she had trudged out

151

and let Marker into the big grass pasture and brought her saddle and pad inside and gone back to bed.

She had spent most of her days and nights in bed, sleeping and reading and praying. And hiding, from time as well as from everyone else.

In the cottage time didn't matter. There was no clock in the cottage, no way to tell time, unless she turned on the television or radio, which she didn't do. There was nothing in the cottage to tell what day or even what year this was, at least no year after the invention of electricity. While the driveway leading to the highway could be plainly seen from the front windows, the highway itself was obscured by tall weeds and brush. Other windows looked out on the alfalfa field and the pastures. No electric lines were visible, no other houses save Mama's, which was equally old, only Molly's and Mama's vehicles, if she chose to look toward them, which she didn't.

The cottage seemed to comfort and protect her, as if it were enveloping her like a big, warm hug from a grandmother. Both of Molly's grandmothers had died before she was born. Grandpa Harry had remarried Vivian Mae, who had hated children and just about everyone else, but Stirling's mother, Miss Annabelle as they had all called her, had taken them all on as her grandchildren. They had seen Miss Annabelle only rarely, but on those occasions she had always had milk and cookies for them and had told them stories of the "old days" of the Indian nation. Miss Annabelle had been half Cherokee. The cottage seemed now as quietly comforting as Miss Annabelle and her warm cookies and soft voice had been.

Sometimes in the middle of the night, the sweet musky scent of the cottage even woke Molly, and she would lie there thinking about her life. She'd begun to realize that every time she caught the scent, her mind would fill with memories and her heart with feelings she couldn't understand. It was as if the scent brought them. Sometimes she embraced the memories, and sometimes she wished they would leave her alone.

Tommy Lee hasn't called.

Molly thought this as Rennie drove out from beneath the tall elms and up onto the blacktop shimmering in the heat. She couldn't think of why Tommy Lee should call. He didn't want her. She knew that, and that was why she had left him, and since she had left him, he surely wasn't about to call her.

They decided on the Main Street Cafe, but Rennie wanted to drag Main once before stopping. "I want to show off my new car." The day was hotter than blue blazes, but Rennie left the windows down so they could wave at people they knew.

Molly didn't care. She felt sweat beginning to trickle between her breasts and wondered if she would care about anything ever again. Then she sort of picked up because she wondered if she might happen to see Tommy Lee. The thought unnerved her, and she tried to sink back into her nothingness, but that was hard to do, what with riding in a red sports car in the bright sun and Alan Jackson singing "Gone Country" on the radio.

Main Street was about all there was to downtown Valentine. It was the state highway running right through the middle of town. The grain elevator at one end and the gin at the other were bookends for the town in between. The street was wide, a leftover from horse-and-buggy days, and cars parked head-in at an angle up to wide sidewalks along the four-block area of businesses. Beyond this was the Sonic drive-in, the Dairy Freeze, and the Hardee's, which had come in only the past fall, and for which Mama gave daily thanks.

Tommy Lee and Molly used to walk these streets, going to either the Dairy Freeze or the Sonic almost every day for lunch during high school. Of course, that had been the old Sonic; there was a brand-new one now, also built last fall and made to look more like the fifties than the original.

Tommy Lee was the only boyfriend she had ever had.

Molly didn't feel much like waving at people. She felt more like hiding behind her sunglasses, but a person couldn't be with Rennie for more than a few minutes before being dragged along by her playful spirit. Pretty soon Molly was right there waving a hand with Rennie.

"Hi, Mr. Stuart!" Rennie called and waved. "How's the stiff business?" Mr. Stuart was the funeral director. He waved back good-naturedly and called for Rennie to come see him; then he laughed real big.

Rennie called to Mrs. Wood and Mrs. Fellman, seventy-two-year-old twin sisters who still dressed alike. Their clothes were circa 1950, wide-skirted dresses with stiff petticoats and little pillbox hats. Mrs. Wood always carried a black purse and Mrs. Fellman a red purse. They were entering Blaine's Drugstore but paused long enough to give little waves. Then Rennie tooted the horn at young Sonny Hornbuckle in his ranch's one-ton dually coming out from a side street, hauling a load of cattle.

Rennie remarked, "You know, if Sonny don't keep rocks in his pockets, he'll blow away."

"I know, but that boy can eat. When he came over for Colter's graduation party, I saw him put away five country ribs, four fajitas, a big plate of beans, and two pieces of Texas tornado cake, and you know Kaye's Texas tornado cake. Mafia men could use it instead of a cement block."

"Did you hear my speech?" Rennie said. "I said, 'Sonny don't keep.' What is it about comin' back here that makes me slip in my language? I do not speak that way up at school."

Rennie pulled into the lot of the four-bay car wash to turn around. Molly's gaze fell on the brick VFW hall across the road. *We were going to have our twenty-fifth anniversary there.* That they wouldn't be having the party seemed strange. Molly didn't know how she had come to the place where she was.

Molly had never slept with anyone but Tommy Lee. She had never even come close. She had once kissed Sam Ketchum, almost by accident. Once when she was fifteen, she and Tommy Lee had been mad at each other for two weeks, and she had gone to a party and kissed a boy named John. Those two chance kisses were the sum total of her sexual experience with other men. She had never felt the hands of another man, never felt another man inside her. Actually, the only other males she had ever seen naked in her life had been her own sons, and she had not seen them that way since they were eight or nine years old.

My experience is so limited.

Then Rennie was pointing at the water tower back behind the car wash. "Walter said they started, then left. He said why, but I guess I wasn't listenin' too well."

Ropes hung from the top of the tower, and there were rusty patches where some of the peeling silver paint and graffiti had been removed. Molly thought she probably should care about whatever the problem was, but she had trouble doing so.

She was looking again at the VFW hall and thinking that at a family reunion, if their family ever had one, things would be so odd if she and Tommy Lee weren't together. She thought of Tommy Lee, of his blue eyes and his hands. *How would sex be with another man?*

The prospect was more frightening than enticing. She wasn't certain she could have sex with another man. She had run the list of men that she knew through her mind, and none of them were in the least attractive to her, except Sam. Sam was quite attractive, and she could almost see herself naked against him. Maybe. She wasn't certain she could get naked with any man besides Tommy Lee. She wasn't twenty-five anymore. Things had shifted downward. Of course, maybe she didn't have to get naked. A lot of times in the movies people didn't get naked. She wondered if any man would find her attractive.

It occurred to her that she had suddenly started being preoccupied with thoughts of sex.

Then Rennie was heading back through town and the hall was left behind. They passed Ryder's Auto Parts, and Molly tensed, scanning the vehicles out front, checking for the Corvette or the old Chevy pickup Tommy Lee usually drove when getting parts. She didn't see either and was foolishly disappointed.

The next instant Rennie pointed at a tall cowboy type coming out of Longmarch's saddle shop. Crisp straw Resistol, crisp red shirt, crisp Wranglers, carrying a saddle over his shoulder as easily as he would a loaf of bread. "Good golly, he looks like he should be in the movies."

"Rennie . . . don't you stop!"

But Rennie was already stopping and the next instant called, "Hi, cowboy."

The man looked up from throwing his saddle into the back of a beat-up Dodge pickup. Then he gave a slow grin and came toward them.

Rennie was saying, "You sure look familiar to me. I'm Rennie Bennett."

"I might know you," the cowboy said slowly. Molly wasn't looking at him, keeping her arm resting on the open window, but she heard the interest in his voice. It sounded like he said his name was Pete Seeger. Tommy Lee liked the music of Pete Seeger. She rubbed her blouse at the sweat tickling between her breasts and then realized she'd put a wet spot on the silk.

The next moment the cowboy was squatting down and looking right into the car, and Rennie was saying, "This is my sister, Molly."

Molly had to look over at him and say hello, so as not to be rude. He looked a bit like Clint Black.

The cowboy touched the brim of his hat and said, "Nice to meet you."

Molly thought that his mother had taught him manners. Covertly, she pinched Rennie's hip. Rennie did a little flirty chitchatting before she drove on.

Molly shook her head. "Good Lord, Rennie, he was all of twenty-five. And we're women in our forties. We shouldn't be flirtin' out car windows."

"I'm thirty-nine," Rennie said emphatically. "And there's no way he could tell our ages with our sunglasses on." She leaned over and peered in the mirror. "Age has nothin' to do with fun, Molly. We enjoyed it, and he did, too. Probably made his day. If he has a wife, he'll go home and try flirtin' with her." She was quite satisfied with herself. Rennie always could justify anything she ever did.

Molly couldn't recall the last time she had flirted. She was friendly with men she knew, but it wasn't a flirting kind of friendly. She avoided meeting the gazes of strange men. It seemed when she had married, she had shuttered her eyes to everyone but Tommy Lee. That had seemed the correct thing to do, and besides, she'd always had eyes only for Tommy Lee anyway.

The past months she had tried flirting with Tommy Lee, but she didn't seem to know how to flirt anymore.

As Rennie pulled into a space at the curb, Molly said, "A couple of months ago a man I didn't even know bought my Coca-Cola at the 7-Eleven." A warm flush swept her.

Rennie's head swung around, and her eyebrows went way up over her sunglasses.

"I was on my way to the soft drink machine," Molly said, a little hesitantly, "and I happened to meet this man's eyes over the snack isle. They were really blue.

I'd noticed him from the back first, because he was . . . well, sort of Tommy Lee's size, muscular like that and not real tall. He was handsome, a horseman, I think, you know, really short hair and a cowboy hat and starched shirt. He was about my age, too.

"But that second our eyes met . . . well, you know there was that spark between us." She grew embarrassed just remembering. "I said hello to his nod, but something just happened inside me, and I couldn't meet his eyes again. I kept thinking I might know him, but I couldn't think of who he was, and I wasn't gonna stare at him."

At the time she had tried sneaking a better look at him, but he'd been looking at her, and she'd been afraid he'd see her looking at him.

"It was crowded in the store, people gettin' off work, and while we were waitin' to pay, we stood right beside each other, but I wouldn't look at him. I spoke to these guys beside me, and they were perfect strangers . . . but harmless, you know. Then when it was my turn to pay, the clerk told me that the man before me had paid for my drink. I walked out and saw him driving off in this bright red dually pick-up, but he was lookin' back at me and slowing like he was gonna stop. Lord, I didn't know what to do. I was so thrilled and embarrassed—I mean, *me,* some stranger buying *me* a soft drink like that. I think I kind of lifted the soft drink. . . . I wanted to thank him; it'd been a nice thing for him to do, but I just couldn't look at him."

Rennie was shaking her head and grinning. "Molly, lots of men look at you. You just never notice."

"Well, it could have been that he just mistook me for someone else . . . someone he knew."

Since that time, she had indulged in a few fantasies about her gallant stranger. And she had kept an eye out for red pickup trucks. One day she had actually followed a red truck down a street in Lawton, but it had turned out not to be the same one.

"I sure would like to know who he was," she said, speaking her thoughts aloud.

As they got out of the car, Molly remembered how after that encounter she had gone home eager to see Tommy Lee. She guessed it had been how Rennie had said, a bit of flirting had made her more eager for him.

But Tommy Lee had been busy on an engine and hadn't even hardly looked at her, and shortly after, a customer had come and Tommy Lee had spent thirty minutes going over engine specifications with him. Molly hadn't gotten time with Tommy Lee until supper, and then he'd been more interested in talking about the new, powerful air compressor he intended to buy than in paying attention to her.

The cafe was nearly full, but Molly and Rennie found a booth at the back. As they went to it, people called greetings. Molly saw the curious looks and felt self-conscious. It was as if someone had stood up and announced: *There's Molly Hayes, who has been married to Tommy Lee for twenty-five years and took off and left him.* Rennie removed her sunglasses, but Molly left hers on.

"Well, how are you Collier girls today?" Fayrene Gardner said when she brought their silverware and glasses of water. She brought it all without a tray, holding the two sweaty glasses of water in one hand and not spilling a drop. She was older than Molly and had been working a long time at the cafe.

Molly said, "Fine," and Rennie said, "Better than a dog with two tails."

"I heard about you and Tommy Lee," Fayrene said to Molly. "It sure came as a surprise, I'm tellin' you. It seemed like if anyone in the world could hold it together, it sure would be you two."

Molly wasn't certain what to say, but Fayrene

didn't seem to expect an answer. She just asked if they wanted to see menus.

Molly and Rennie had already decided on the barbecue plate, which was the cafe's specialty. As Fayrene walked away, Molly said, "Last winter me and Tommy Lee went through a phase of coming here for the barbecue plate at least once a week. Tommy Lee likes Jud's barbecue better than anyone's. I never can eat all of mine, so I always give half of it to Tommy Lee."

She was looking down at the table and rubbing her hand across the Formica. She wished she hadn't said anything. *Tommy Lee always remarked on how she ate half of things.*

Rennie said, "I'll eat all of mine, but I won't be able to handle yours. I guess we can wrap up what we don't eat and send it to the poor people up in the City."

"I'll take some home to Ace. He eats just about anything."

Fayrene whizzed by and smacked two tall glasses of ice tea down in front of them. Molly sprinkled sugar on top of hers, letting it melt down over the ice. She looked up and saw a woman getting a toddler out of a high chair—a little girl with blond curls. The woman held the child close for a moment, rubbing her cheek against that of the child.

When Molly looked at Rennie, she saw Rennie watching the child, too, with a soft, yearning expression on her face so strong that Molly had too look away. She felt guilty. *How can I want a child? I've had three children, but Rennie hasn't had any. I should be satisfied. . . . I'm beyond children now.* But the yearning remained, taunting her, she thought, even as she said a quick prayer for Rennie. What she thought was, *I'm gonna have a grandchild, Lord, but Rennie needs her own child.*

As she and Rennie chatted about this and that,

Molly felt like she was sort of coming to pieces but
that she was only doing it halfway, which seemed in
some way worse than if she could just give in to it all
the way. She never could seem to go all the way with
anything. She always seemed to have to hold back.
Always fearful of losing control. There seemed to be
some brake deep inside herself that was always on
guard, lest she go too high, too hard, too far.

She wished she could just let loose sometimes, step
over the line and damn the consequences, but those
times when she even went up to the line she scared
herself, she thought, remembering breaking the plates
and Tommy Lee's shocked face.

Fayrene had just brought their dinners when Walter
came rushing over. "Molly."

He didn't say anything more for a minute, just slid
into the booth beside her and seemed to catch his
breath. Then he said hello to Rennie and sat there
another minute, bouncing his legs. Molly didn't press
him about whatever was on his mind; she always felt
Walter pressed himself enough. She asked him if he
wanted to order lunch, or at least a glass of tea.

"No . . . no, I've had lunch," he said, folding his
arms on the table, then straightening again and
smoothing the back of his hair. It was thin and fine.
Everything about Walter was thin and fine. Molly had
always thought he should have been a composer, or a
nurseryman, something that allowed him to be by
himself a lot. She'd seen Walter sitting alone in his
den, and he seemed happy then.

He looked at her and sort of blinked, and Molly
remembered she was still wearing her sunglasses. She
started to take them off, but then Walter went to
talking, so she left them on.

"Orville Gibson and his brother quit work on the
water tower," he said and pulled at his ear. "They got
a job doin' oil tanks, workin' on a whole dang refinery

down in Texas, and Orville says he can't get back to the water tower until fall. He just isn't gonna come back, Molly, and he isn't gonna give back the town's deposit, either. He says he doesn't have it. What are we gonna do? Jaydee thinks we ought to sue. Jaydee told Orville we would, but there just doesn't seem to be any way to scare Orville. We gotta get that water tower painted. There's dirty words on it. We can't let that stay."

"Of course Jaydee wants to sue," Rennie put in. "He went to college to learn how to sue."

Walter glanced at her and seemed to sink down into his shirt. Molly cast Rennie a frown. "The town isn't gonna sue, for heavensakes," she said. "Talk about a waste of taxpayer money. It'd be easier to get blood out of a turnip than money out of Orville Gibson. He has six children. Just call Dave Hawkins and see if he can send a crew over to get started. I'll call Orville and talk to him. He can work out the money on down the road. He'll do that."

"Well, that was grant money the town paid Orville, money meant for the Main Street Project. Gov'ment money," Walter said, as if it came from God. "They could hold us accountable."

"Oh, Walter, the federal government doesn't have time or manpower to go around checkin' every small town to see how the money is spent. They don't really *care* how the money is spent."

"Well, I guess that's so," Walter said, smoothing his hair.

Fayrene set a glass of ice tea in front of him as she whizzed by. Walter's eyes went wide, and he started to call to her. Then Rennie handed him the sugar, and he stirred some into the glass.

Molly touched his arm. "Don't worry about the grant money, Walter. When Orville is out of work, which is bound to happen, we'll get him to paint the swings at the park, and that will mean the money is being spent as it should on improving our downtown. That's all that matters."

"But where do we get the money for a deposit for Dave Hawkins? He wants a lot more to do the job than Orville."

"Don't worry about it, hon," Rennie said. "Molly will take it out of your salary."

Walter looked confused. "Well, I don't really get a salary."

Molly smiled. What she liked about Walter was that he was one of the few truly good and generous souls in the world; he accepted a small expense allowance from the town but not a salary. He said he didn't need the money and the town did. Also, Walter never felt worthy of a salary.

She said, "I'll adjust the capital improvement budget, Walter. Nip here and tuck there. We'll make it."

His fine face softened some. "Okay, if you say so." For some reason Walter had total faith in Molly. Rennie always said that if Molly said it would rain in ten minutes, Walter would go get an umbrella.

Rennie was grinning an amused knowing smile, and then Molly saw her gaze shift and her expression change. Curious, Molly followed Rennie's gaze. She saw Woody Wilson entering the cafe, *with Tommy Lee right behind him.*

Molly jerked her face forward, looked again at Rennie, and then looked back at Tommy Lee, even though she hadn't intended to.

Walter was saying something and Molly had to ask him to repeat it. She tried focusing on him, but her gaze slid past and over to Tommy Lee.

Walter said, "I'd better speak to the other council members and get their okays before I call Dave Hawkins."

Molly watched Tommy Lee remove his Summit Racing Equipment ballcap, saw his dark hair, saw him cast a quick grin and nod to someone who spoke to him. He glanced around the room, and then his eyes lit on hers. *Oh, Lord.* She looked away to her glass of ice tea and took it up. *Would he come over?*

Walter had seen Tommy Lee then, and he cast Molly a furtive glance.

When Molly looked back across the room, she saw Woody and Tommy Lee stopped at a table of men—Jack Prickett and D.W. Leander were two of them. Tommy Lee spoke to them, but his eyes strayed to hers. A number of faces turned her way.

She pushed her plate away, lifted the sugar container and dumped more into her half-empty glass of tea. It occurred to her that Tommy Lee couldn't see her eyes behind her sunglasses.

"You don't have to hire Dave Hawkins," Molly said, facing Walter but with her eyes on Tommy Lee.

"Well, who would I hire then?"

"Oh . . . there's others."

Tommy Lee was looking at her again, standing there with his hand on the back of Jack Prickett's chair and looking across at her. She looked at him. He looked tired. His eyes were hard.

Then Molly turned and snatched up her purse. "Would you excuse us, Walter? Rennie and I need to visit the ladies room. Rennie."

"Well . . . sure," Walter said, rising to let her out of the booth. He had no choice but to move or be shoved onto the floor.

Rennie looked surprised, but she scooted out of the seat, pausing to get a final gulp of ice tea before following. Molly headed on to the ladies room. She had the sensation of Tommy Lee's eyes on her back, which she told herself was just plain silly.

Rennie slipped into the small room behind Molly and closed the door. "Why am I in here with you, Sissy?"

Molly looked at Rennie, and Rennie looked back.

Molly said, "I don't want to go out there with Tommy Lee there."

"Well, we could have left."

Molly shook her head. "I couldn't walk past him and not speak."

"Oh."

Molly sighed and raked back her hair. She leaned close to the oval mirror above the sink. She thought she looked a little wild. Why in the world hadn't she just gone out past Tommy Lee? She was a grown, competent woman. She could speak to him.

"I just don't know what to do, okay, Rennie?" Molly felt tears rising up into her throat. "I just . . . oh, I don't know. It just hurts so bad."

"I wish I'd brought my purse," Rennie said. "I need a cigarette."

"Peek out there and see where Tommy Lee is."

Rennie looked startled but then turned and peeked out the door. "Him and Woody sat down," Rennie said, her eye in the crack of the door. "Tommy Lee took the side where he's facin' this way—and I think he's watchin' me peek out this door."

Molly pushed the door closed and leaned against it. Lord, she felt stupid. "Where are they sittin'?"

"At a booth near the door." Rennie looked at her with concern. "Sissy, if we wait for them to eat and leave, we may get a line forming outside."

After long seconds, Molly's gaze met Rennie's. And then Rennie began to chuckle, and Molly had to, too. Her chuckles were close to tears.

She stepped to the window and put her hand to the lock. She didn't expect it to move; usually the locks on old wooden windows were too coated with paint to move, but this one did. She shoved up the window and felt the heat hit her in the face.

"We can get out this window," she said, pushing her thumbs on the screen hooks.

Rennie's eyes went wide. "You want to climb out the window?" Then her lips twitched into a wry grin. "Why, Sissy . . ."

They turned the metal wastebasket upside down and used it for a stool to get high enough to reach the window. It wasn't a very big window, and they had to squeeze through, then drop to the ground. It was tougher for Molly because she went first. She had to work not to fall on her head in the gravel and weeds of the back alley. It was made even more difficult because she had truly begun to laugh. She thought that what she was doing was right up to the line and quite possibly a little over.

They speculated as to what people would think, should they be caught. Rennie had left her purse in the booth, and they hadn't paid their bill. Rennie kept saying she couldn't believe Molly would do this but that she herself had done it before.

"I went out the bathroom window of Country Joe's Bar and Grill down in Fort Worth . . . and I was gettin' away from a man, just like you are now," Rennie told her. "Only the window was a lot larger and closer to the ground."

"If you have that much experience, you should have gone first," Molly said, as she helped Rennie to turn on the narrow sill.

"This is good for you, Sissy. This sort of thing gets you out of your doldrums. Dang, that hurt my ankle."

Molly reached out to steady her sister, and then they were looking at each other and chuckling.

Molly shook her head and breathed deeply. "Oh, Rennie. I feel so crazy." She gestured at the window. "I mean, climbin' out a window all because I'm terrified of seein' Tommy Lee." The tears came suddenly. "And what I really wanted was to see him. Oh, Rennie, I'm so messed up."

Rennie put an arm around her shoulder. "I know, Sissy. . . . I know." She kissed Molly's warm, sweet-smelling hair and squeezed her close, whispering, "It'll be okay."

But she wondered if it would. Sometimes people just did the silliest things, and some heartaches never did heal. She knew that only too well.

Molly said, "Your purse is still in there . . . and we have to pay the bill."

"My purse isn't goin' anywhere and neither is the bill. Let's go on down to Blaine's and get a Coke. I'm thirsty after that barbecue—and all that climbin'."

Arms around each other's waist, they started down the alleyway. Sprinkles began to fall, and they looked upward to see a cloud right over them while the sun still shone.

12

❖❖

That's As Close As I'll Ever Get
To Loving You

Sam Ketchum slowed as he passed Molly's office on Main Street. He was driving his brother's Bronco, and it kept threatening to die. He shifted into neutral, so he could press on the gas and keep the idle up. Because of the blinds on the big window of Molly's office, he couldn't see if she was in there.

There was no space to park on the block; things were busy on a Friday afternoon. Valentine was the hub of the farming area and growing as a bedroom community for Lawton, for people who worked in the city but wanted to have their country acreages and gentleman farms.

A car honked behind him, and Sam hurried to shift into drive and go on. He felt a nervous itch between his shoulder blades when he thought about Molly catching sight of him stopping; she knew he drove Winn's Bronco when in town.

He proceeded down the block, noting that Blaine's Drugstore had a new sign now proclaiming it as the "hometown choice," and that a Dollar Store had opened in the old Western Auto building.

Sometimes Sam had to ask himself why he continued to be tied to this town where he had never quite felt he fit. To start with, Sam and Winn had been born in New Jersey, his mother's home state. They had come here when Sam and Winn's father had been assigned to the army base in Lawton. Their father had wanted to live in the country. But only a year after getting them settled here, when Sam had been five, he had been working with explosives and gotten blown up.

People here were very friendly, but they'd had trouble understanding a person from New Jersey, an eastern city girl, who had no family here yet chose to stay here after her husband had died. The thing was, his mother'd had no family anywhere, nor any money to go elsewhere.

When Sam had been in high school, he'd had long hair and was one of the first to wear an earring, two things that didn't go over really big in Valentine. His junior and senior years of high school had been his hippie period, when he'd worn sloppy tie-dyed T-shirts and peace signs. He'd been the school's token hippie and added to that was his inclination for art. Teachers in Valentine schools hadn't known what to do with a boy who would rather draw people playing football than play it. When he'd been in Valentine school, art class rated lower than a foreign language with the hierarchy of the school, who lived and breathed for football and basketball and Future Farmers. The art class met and did the best it could in a small portable building out behind the FFA barn. Half the time the music teacher doubled as the art teacher. In his junior year, Sam did most of the teaching. He also started getting into jewelry design then—another thing that hadn't gone over really big in Valentine. Except with the girls. Both his jewelry and Sam had always been a hit with the girls.

After about fifteen years of doing women's hair in

this town, his mother had gained acceptance. His brother, Winn, had become a local business owner and a member of the chamber of commerce, and had been on the school board for the past ten years. Whenever someone disagreed with Winn, it might be pointed out that he wasn't a native, but Winn would just laugh about it. Because of Winn, the school now had fully funded programs in art, music, journalism, and mechanics.

Sam, who had at the start been ostracized because of his art, was now something of a small-town treasure because of his success. When it became known that Robert Redford had bought one of his pen-and-ink drawings and that Reba McEntire wore one of his bracelets, his acceptance was immediate.

Sam supposed he never felt he fit anywhere and that Valentine would always be as much home as any place ever could be. His family and lifelong friends were here. Friends like Tommy Lee and Molly, whom he'd known since grade school.

When he thought of it, which he had on a number of occasions, Sam thought that his friendship with Tommy Lee was an unlikely pairing. He and Tommy Lee were not, on the surface, much alike. Sam was taller and slimmer and more finely made; he had muscles, but not like Tommy Lee's. And Tommy Lee was a steady and straight sort, while Sam tended to be wild and uneven as a dirt road. One thing they did have in common, though, a trait not easily seen and one maybe some people would argue, was that Tommy Lee, although born and raised here, had always been somewhat of an outsider, too. Each of them in their own way, Sam thought, was a person to step to the beat of his own drum.

Turning into the alley, bumping the rear tire on the curb, he drove slowly until he spied the El Camino tucked in near the back door of Molly's building.

He parked, took up the bulging file folder of receipts that was his excuse for coming, and went in the back door, into the hallway that separated Molly's office from the offices of Jaydee Mayall, attorney-at-law. That was the lettering on Jaydee's glass doors and on his plate-glass window, and on his briefcase and the pens he gave out and the billboards at either end of town and even the doors of his Cadillac, all of which seemed a bit much for a town the size of Valentine.

"Are you afraid you might forget who you are, Jaydee?" Tommy Lee had asked the man once.

"Why, no. Why do you say that?" Jaydee had been puzzled, and he certainly couldn't tell by Tommy Lee's tone or expression that Tommy Lee was about to pull his leg. For one thing, Tommy Lee hardly ever spoke out, so no one was ever expecting him to.

"Well, you seem to have your name written everywhere you look. Since we've all known you for some time, I thought maybe you had it for your own benefit, just in case you forgot who you were."

Sam and half a dozen others who had overheard the exchange had gotten a big kick out of it, and what was funnier still was that Jaydee never really had understood that Tommy Lee had pegged him for exactly what he was—a conceited blowhard.

Tommy Lee had always been good at seeing people as they were, and he never was much impressed by anyone. Sam had always envied Tommy Lee's self-assurance. Sam loved Tommy Lee, better than Winn, actually. That was why he had always kept to himself the way he felt about Molly.

Since school days, Sam had loved Molly. But she had always been Tommy Lee's girl.

The door to Molly's office stood open, and he stopped there, hesitant and eager. He saw her sitting at her desk, her back to him. She brought her hand up and tucked her hair behind her ear, setting her earring to swaying. He thought her hair shorter than when he'd last seen her, but it was straight and silky as it always had been. She was talking on the phone. He himself talked at least two or three times a month with Molly on the phone. She did his business records, which was as close as he could keep himself to her.

After a moment of gathering himself, he tapped the file folder against the door frame.

Molly turned and saw him. Surprise widened her eyes, and then pure pleasure filled her face. The light slanting through the blinds made her eyes sparkle like polished turquoise.

She held up a finger, turning her head as she spoke into the telephone receiver. Sam came into the office. It was small, but she had made good use of the space, with a cherry wood wall-unit computer desk, tall cherry filing cabinets, and a lady's writing desk, where she sat now. No carpet, but polished oak floors, with two wool Navaho rugs. The two chairs she had for clients were of a sort that invited people to sit and chat. Molly was a person people felt they could talk to, and she often ended up dispensing consolation and encouragement along with her financial counsel.

Tommy Lee had fought her about the office. Tommy Lee had a controlling streak in him.

Sam's gaze moved around the walls, until it came to the pen-and-ink sketch he had given her—an office-warming gift. She'd been hesitant about accepting it.

"Oh, Sam, I can't take it. . . . It's worth too much."

"Oh, hell, Molly, I have a dozen like it back at the studio."

The only piece of jewelry he had ever given her had been when he'd first started out—a pair of silver feathers. She wore them sometimes still. He would have liked to give her lots of his jewelry now, pieces worth far more than those silver feathers, pieces with turquoise to bring out her eyes and delicate silver and gold to hang against her soft skin. But prudence kept him from it. She and Tommy Lee might have thought something if he tried to give it to her.

Then she was up and coming toward him. "Oh, Sam . . . it's good to see you."

She smiled, but there were shadows in her eyes. She went to reach for his hands, but he opened his arms wide and she came into them, and they hugged. He held her for a moment and inhaled the sweet scent of her, felt her soft cheek against his.

She pulled away, averted her face and tucked her hair behind her ear, nervous like. "Have you spoken to Tommy Lee?"

"I saw him this mornin'."

Her green eyes came to his. Then they were looking at each other. Sam just couldn't help looking at her like he did.

Her face turned pink as a rose, and she glanced through the door—over to where Sophia, Jaydee's secretary, sat across the hall, staring at them. Sam leaned over to give Sophia a good view and waved.

"Hi, Sophia. You want to come on over so's you can hear everything?"

The woman puffed up like a bullfrog, and Molly gave him a little shove and closed the door. Gesturing toward the folder he'd forgotten he held, she said, "I see you brought me some work. I'll get you a cup of coffee and we'll take a look."

As she swept stray hair behind her ear, he saw that she still had on her wedding band.

Molly walked Sam to the back door. Sam smelled really good, a cologne that seemed to burrow down into her senses each time she breathed. He was a tall man; with his hat on he almost scraped the top of the door frame.

For a moment he paused, gazing down at her. His dark eyes were soft as velvet.

"I'd like to see you this weekend. Maybe we can

have dinner together." His accent was distinctive, a drawl but as if it met halfway between Oklahoma and New Jersey. His eyes shifted nervously. "Well, I mean I'm your friend, same as Tommy Lee's. I'd hate to see that change."

"I know. So would I. I'd never put you in the middle, Sam."

"Well, how about lunch Sunday afternoon?"

"I'd like that." She felt defiant and daring, and thought that was really silly.

He nodded and hurried to the Bronco, hunching against the rain that had just that moment started to fall in fat drops. Molly moved forward and put a hand to the door frame and watched him drive away. She gave a little wave, and he did, too. Suddenly the rain came harder, and she looked up into the boiling sky. Thunder rolled, as if echoing the threatening feelings churning inside her.

Sam had looked at her. She tingled with the thought, both thrilled and frightened, guilty, too. She told herself not to be silly. . . . Sam was simply a friendly person. Then she thought that she was *not* mistaken. He had looked at her, and she wasn't sorry she had looked back, either. But of course, she'd known Sam forever . . . and he liked to flirt. Many thought him an incorrigible flirt, but she knew better. Once, a number of years ago, they'd been alone on an early morning on her front porch. Sam had confessed that he wished he could find a woman and have a marriage like she and Tommy Lee had. Sam could be really tender.

Tears came to her eyes. *Why couldn't Tommy Lee look at her like Sam had?*

A panicky feeling came over her. She certainly didn't want to break down in one of her horrible bawling spells there in the office, where Sophia or anyone who happened to walk in could hear. Crossing her arms, taking deep breaths, she walked back to her desk. She felt the fluttery, wild feeling rising up in her chest and spreading through her limbs. She felt off-kilter, as if she were about to run naked in the rain, or at the very least go dance right in the middle of Main Street. As if she just had to do *something*.

She began straightening papers on her desk, tapping them into order, dropped the pencil in the pencil holder, put the coffee cups back on the shelf. Stood there a moment, then reached for the phone and dialed Rennie's number.

"I want to run naked in the rain, but I think it would be better if I went to Rodeo Rio's tonight," she said. "Will you go with me?"

Of course Rennie would go and very eagerly. "Wear that blue chambray dress Lillybeth gave you," she said.

When Molly hung up, she thought that she would go by McMahon's Dry Goods and get those red canvas sandals she'd seen in the window. They had long ribbons that tied up her ankle in a flamboyant, sexy way.

She grabbed her purse and marched to the door. No matter if Tommy Lee still didn't pay her any attention, she wanted to look good. She wanted men to look at her, and she wanted Tommy Lee to see that. She sure hoped he went to Rodeo Rio's that night.

As she opened the door, thundered rolled and rattled the window glass, as if offering warning. Molly looked upward a moment and then slammed the door hard and started purposefully down the sidewalk.

13
❖❖

Going Out Tonight

Molly could ignore the summer storm. Although it made a lot of noise and wind—and Molly listened to the radio for a tornado warning—it cooled everything down, and in all likelihood it would pass over and be gone by the time she and Rennie went out. It was not as easy to ignore Kaye, however, who also made a lot of noise but wasn't as likely to pass over and be gone, and who just seemed to make everything hotter, too.

Kaye telephoned to say she wanted to hold a Collier girls meeting that evening at their mother's house; she wasn't forthcoming as to what she wanted to discuss. "I'll tell you when you get there."

"Rennie and I have plans," Molly said.

"What kind of plans?" Kaye asked.

"We're goin' out."

The line hummed for a long minute, Kaye waiting in a loud silence. Molly let it sit.

Finally Kaye said, "Well, I know this is short notice, but I didn't think I had to make appointments with my sisters. Surely givin' me ten minutes won't hurt anything."

It wouldn't, of course, and the whole time Molly

bathed, dressed, and applied makeup in the spotty
mirror above the bathroom sink, she kept telling
herself that, and that she loved Kaye. She kept trying
to hold a rein on herself. She had the frightening
feeling that she was about to fly off any moment and
be wild and crazy. She felt certain she was about to do
something she would regret.

"Whatever you do can't be more regretful than your
life at the moment," she told her image in the mirror.

She leaned close and applied a bit more blush and a
bit more lipstick. Then she studied her eyes. The low
light of the bathroom was kind to her face. *What will
Tommy Lee think? Will he even pay attention?*

Well, if he didn't pay attention, someone else surely
would, she thought, tossing her makeup back into its
case. She strode into the bedroom, took up the bottle
of Chanel she had purchased that afternoon at
Blaine's—paying full price just to see how it felt—
took out the stopper, and dabbed it between her
breasts and behind her ears, then drew a line slowly
down the hollow of her throat.

Through the kitchen window she watched each of
her sisters—Kaye, then Lillybeth, then Season—
drive up, park in a line behind their mother's Lincoln,
and go in the back door. Rennie was late.

Molly kept waiting for Rennie and thinking that
maybe she wouldn't go over after all, but she simply
couldn't hurt her sisters' feelings—Lillybeth and Season would feel if they had to be there, so did Molly.
And she was having trouble just waiting around for
Rennie.

They were all gathered around the big mahogany
family table in the dining room, and Kaye was serving
sweet rolls on the good Noritake and French roast
coffee, pouring it herself. Right away Molly guessed
that Kaye wanted a big favor from them all.

When Molly came through the swinging door, they

all turned to look at her, all four pairs of eyebrows arching at varying degrees.

"Oh, my," Season said, eyeing Molly with a bright grin. "You look very nice. Where are you goin'?"

"Rennie and I are goin' over to Rodeo Rio's."

Kaye's eyebrows went up further. Mama gave a little smile and commented that she liked Molly's shoes. Lillybeth said her dress looked at lot better on Molly than it had on herself. "I just don't have enough boobs to make that dress hang right."

Season leaned close as Molly sat down. "You're gonna show Tommy Lee a thing or two."

The comment made Molly feel a little silly, but she didn't have to reply or even to think about it, because Kaye said in a raised voice, "Well, Rennie's gonna be late, as usual, so we might as well get started."

Kaye didn't like the attention turned from herself and her plans. She straightened herself up and looked at everyone.

"With the cancellation of Molly's anniversary party, we still have the question of what to do with the VFW hall." She paused. "Well, I've come up with a way to not waste any of our money or our plans. I would like to hold a big Country Interior Design event instead."

"Event" was the term Rennie had applied to Kaye's sales party, and Kaye had readily taken up the term. Kaye had a conniption when anyone used the word "sales." She preferred the term "opportunity-to-own." She had been practicing smaller events—three in the past week and a half alone—and she had proven exceptionally fitted for bestowing Country Interior Designs upon the world. Mama was the one to say that Kaye had found the perfect outlet for her theatrical proclivity, and Kaye was so pleased with herself that she agreed.

"I want to hold a Country Interior Design event

like no one has ever held before," Kaye said, "and I'd like y'all to help me set it up and to hostess." She spoke as if bestowing a great honor upon them.

Molly and Lillybeth and Season looked at each other and then at Mama, who was beaming at Kaye.

"We'll be invitin' all the women who would have come to the anniversary party anyway," Kaye said, "so it won't be like we canceled on them."

Molly thought, *God forbid anyone be inconvenienced*.

Lillybeth, moving so quickly that she startled Molly, set both feet on the floor and leaned forward. "If we do this"—she gestured to Molly and Season— "then are we each off the hook for havin' to host one of your parties at our homes?"

"Well, if that's the way you look at it," Kaye said, bristling.

Molly stared at the table and thought of the brick VFW hall while Kaye went on to say that they could even use the white tablecloths and that each of them could proceed with the refreshment tray they had been assigned for the anniversary party. The silver streamers they had bought could be exchanged at McMahon's Dry Goods for red ones, to go with the red bouquets she planned to have on each table. Oh, Kaye had plans, and all on what was to have been Molly's twenty-fifth anniversary, which no one seemed to notice at all.

Molly took her sunglasses out of her purse and put them on. Season looked at her with a start.

Ten minutes later Rennie drove up, but she went into the cottage instead of coming over to Mama's. Molly, glad for an excuse to escape, went over to get her. When she stepped into the kitchen, she saw Rennie at the sink, popping something into her mouth. Aspirin, from a bottle on the drain board. Rennie's hair was a mess, her skirt was split on the side seam, and there was a rip in her black stockings.

Molly slipped off her sunglasses and took a second look. "What happened to you?"

Rennie was also wearing sunglasses, so Molly couldn't see her eyes.

"It's nothin'. I just stumbled on the steps of my apartment."

Rennie snapped the cap on the aspirin bottle, and the snap was to Molly an exclamation point for a bald-faced lie.

"You have two steps to your front door."

Rennie said nothing to that. Molly put a hand to her hip and stared at her. After long seconds of silence, Rennie, in aggravation, ripped off her sunglasses, and Molly found herself staring a freshly bruised right eye.

"Are you happy now?" Rennie's mascara-smudged eyes glittered with tears and stubbornness. "I ran into my own stupidity with men; that's what happened."

Then she turned and fled into the bathroom and slammed the door.

Molly went to the bathroom door and heard Rennie crying on the other side. She turned and went back and sat on the edge of the couch for several minutes, looked out the window toward her mother's house and then down at the rug.

Whenever Rennie was upset, she would run and lock herself in the bathroom. Once, when she was nine, she had locked herself in and the lock jammed, and Mama had to take the knob off the door to get it open and Rennie set free. When Rennie had had her miscarriage, she might have died in the bathroom if she hadn't unlocked the door before she passed out.

Molly wondered why everyone had to keep pulling and tugging her into their lives.

She rose and went to the bathroom door and rattled it. "Rennie, open the door."

Rennie made no sound now.

"Rennie, I'll kiss it and make it better."

Rennie said nothing. Rennie could be more stubborn than a herd of mules.

Just then the telephone rang, somewhere in the living room. Molly's first inclination was to ignore it, but then she got worried that it was Kay, and surely if ignored Kaye would come storming over. Molly had to follow the cord to find the phone setting on the far side of the sofa.

It was Kaye, and Molly told her, "Not now, Kaye, Rennie has diarrhea," and hung up.

Turning, she saw light pouring into the hall from the bathroom. She went to the open door. Rennie was at the mirror with Molly's makeup spread out around the edge of the sink.

"That was Kaye, wasn't it?" Rennie said, sponging makeup over the bruise beneath her eye. "What did you tell her?" She paused but kept her gaze on the mirror.

"That you had diarrhea."

It was the old standby excuse, one they had used since childhood; the subject was rarely questioned and never open for discussion.

"Well, I want to get out of here before any of them come over," Rennie said, once more dabbing makeup high on her cheekbone. She turned and faced Molly. "I think it's better now."

Molly looked from the bruise to Rennie's muddy-green eyes.

"You need ice."

She went to the kitchen, wrapped three ice cubes in a cloth, and broke them with a hammer. She did not need this, she thought as she whacked the ice a good one. *It's my turn.*

"Come sit in the kitchen and hold this on it for about twenty minutes." She smacked the ice packet into Rennie's hand. "I'll make us some coffee."

Molly turned her back and returned to the kitchen

and put the kettle on to boil. *Why couldn't she be allowed to focus on her own crisis?*

They sat at the table, beneath the single light above. Rennie set aside the ice pack while she lit a cigarette. Molly saw that Rennie's hand shook. Molly felt shaky herself, felt the panic rising up in her chest. She shoved up the window and opened the door to have a draft to suck out the cigarette smoke. Ace appeared, and she let him outside.

"It's quit raining," she said, inhaling the fresh earth scent and thinking of how Tommy Lee always liked to go out on the porch and watch it rain.

Behind her, Rennie got up and rifled through the cabinets, looking for food. When Molly told her the Oreos were all gone, that all she had were generic crackers, Rennie about bit her head off. Rennie got the crackers and peanut butter and began to eat the peanut butter right out of the jar, scooping it out with a cracker. She would use both hands to scoop, then hold the ice to her bruise while she chewed.

It was hard for Molly to believe that someone had beat on Rennie. There had always been something about Rennie that made people step lightly around her. She could have a dagger look and an even sharper tongue. Who would dare to raise a hand to her?

Molly realized that in her mind beatings by men were something that happened to other women, women who were weak and foolish, certainly not to a Collier girl, who was of a good family and education. She had to laugh at herself. Undoubtedly every spectrum of weakness and foolishness could be found within the Collier family.

But not violence. The Colliers were against physical violence. Her own mother had never raised a hand to her girls; Mama did not believe in spanking. Molly thought her mother far too permissive—a very avant-garde liberal—and had been determined to be more firm with her own children. Once, when Savannah had been four, Molly had hauled off and spanked her for some infraction—back-talking. Oh, Savannah had had such a smart mouth. Molly had smacked her thigh. But Savannah's thigh had been bare, and suddenly Molly had seen the white imprint of her own hand. It had raised a welt, and Molly had faced that she had hit her child. No matter the reason, nor the term, she had hit her child, and she found it unacceptable. After that she had never again spanked any of her children. Sitting Savannah on her bed for fifteen minutes had worked much better anyway. To have to sit still and be ignored was for Savannah almost too horrible to be endured.

Tommy Lee had honored Molly's feelings in this matter, despite his belief that sometimes a boy needed the threat of violence to keep him in hand. They'd disagreed over this, although once Molly had let Tommy Lee have his way with Colter, when Colter had taken the car, without benefit of driver's license or permission, and driven all the way to Oklahoma City and was not inclined at all to remorse. She'd given thanks that Colter had backed down; she didn't believe Tommy Lee would ever have forgiven himself had he come to blows with his son.

Molly spooned the instant coffee into two cups. She really was going to have to buy a coffeemaker. Instant coffee simply did not provide in crisis.

"Who is this guy?" she asked.

Rennie breathed deeply and shifted her gaze to the peanut butter jar. "A guy that was in one of my night classes this past spring. He got out of the army last year and started back to school."

"Well . . . what's his name, and why does he want to use you for a punching bag? Did you give him a bad grade?"

Rennie shook her head, a sad grin playing on her pale lips. She looked so pale, Molly thought. So pale and fragile. So unlike Rennie.

"His name is Eddie Pendarvis, and we dated for a few weeks. When I tried to break it off, he didn't want to. He's been pesterin' me."

Molly poured the hot water into the cups. She was so unnerved by what Rennie told her that she splashed the steaming water onto the table and had to reach for a cloth.

Rennie pushed away the crackers and peanut butter and reached for her cigarette. "He caught me as I was leavin' the apartment. He has a really bad temper and just sort of goes berserk."

"We need to go to the police and press charges." Molly gripped the dishcloth. "You can get a restraining order."

But Rennie was already shaking her head. "No."

"Rennie, you can't just let this go."

"No," Rennie said firmly. She looked at Molly. "I think it will be settled now that he's seen I really mean business. I kicked him really good, Sissy." She jabbed her cigarette out in the ashtray. "I've been once to the police, and I won't go again." She raked her fingers through her hair. "They asked, and I had to admit that I slept with Eddie. So in their view I pretty much asked for what I'm gettin'. I don't need any more of that." She stared into her coffee and drank deeply.

"You've been to the police once already." That's all Molly was thinking. That it had been bad enough for Rennie to go to the police, and yet she hadn't said a word to Molly.

Rennie glanced at her, only then realizing she'd let the cat out of the bag.

"Oh, Rennie." Molly reached for her sister's hand, squeezing it. She thought that she might be capable of killing this man who had dared to hurt her Rennie, one of the kindest spirits on earth. *Oh, Lord, what if he gets her again and does worse harm?*

"You'll have to be more careful," she told Rennie.

At that, Rennie snatched her hand away and stood up. "Thanks for the advice, dear sister."

"What did I say?"

Rennie jabbed her hand to her hip. "You tell me to be careful, like what happened was my fault. Like I wasn't careful enough, so I got hit. It wasn't my fault, Molly. I didn't do anything but be nice to a guy, try to have a good relationship, and he ends up smacking me for it."

"I didn't mean it like that. You know I didn't. It wasn't your fault, no, but Rennie you cannot continue to take men you hardly know into an intimate relationship. It's dangerous. You don't know enough about a man before you're having sex with him, for heavensakes!"

"Okay, so it's my fault." Rennie gestured wildly, then let her hand drop.

"No. No one should be hit, ever. And your sweetness and giving spirit shouldn't be so rewarded. But the fact is that this world is a mean place with mean people. None of that is your fault, and it isn't your fault that you need to be more careful, either. I think, though, that *you* think it's your fault."

Molly realized she was up and leaning over the table and poking her finger at Rennie in exactly the same annoying way Tommy Lee poked his when he got carried away. She jerked her hand back and behind her, as if to hide it.

Rennie looked down at the floor. "Eddie was really sweet at first." She lifted her gaze, and her sad eyes hit Molly like a blow. "He was so kind, and we seemed, well . . . oh, Molly, I thought: Maybe this time. I keep thinking that, Molly . . . that maybe this time I'll meet the right guy. But I just keep choosin' the wrong ones."

Molly came swiftly to put her arms around Rennie. "Oh, Rennie, you'll meet somebody someday. You will."

She held her sister close, knowing she was lying, knowing love is never quite like it is made out to be and that some never find it. Or when they do, somehow it slips away.

"I love you, Rennie."

She and Rennie held each other tight for several minutes, and Rennie said, "I know," into Molly's neck.

When they broke apart, they gave each other hesitant, self-conscious smiles. Molly wiped her eyes and then wiped Rennie's eyes.

"I'm okay, Sissy," Rennie said. "Now, let's get out of here, before we get waylaid by Miss Righteous Kaye. Let's go out and howl."

14
❖❖

A Woman's Got A Right

Rodeo Rio's was rocking on a Friday night, with a local country band and a good crowd. The noise level irritated Tommy Lee, and he would have gone else-where to play pool, if he could have thought of somewhere else to go.

He had become somewhat addicted to the game of pool during the past week. Each evening he had divided his time between pool and driving the Cor-vette. He would come to Rio's to have either a steak or a hamburger and to play pool on one of the big tables beneath one of the long stained-glass lamps. When he was so full of pool that he could not stand it, he would go out driving around in the Corvette. He drove with the top off and the wind battering his hair and ears. He drove all the roads of the county and into the next. He drove down to the river valley road, where the kids still drag raced, and watched. Once he even succumbed to participation, racing a young fellow in a brand-new 240Z. The teen having a car like that annoyed him; when he was in his teens half the kids couldn't even afford a car, much less a brand-new sports model. Tommy Lee beat him simply for the principle of the thing.

He would play pool and then drive and drive until he reached a zombie state, where pool balls and the black road leading off into the blackness took up his entire mind, body, and soul and kept him safe from thoughts of Molly.

Just then he sunk the seven ball and the eight ball with one shot, causing Sam to throw up his hands. "You're ruthless, buddy. I'm quittin' and takin' away what pride I have left."

"You're the one who invited me here," Tommy Lee said.

Sam's wanting to quit annoyed him. He could recall when he and Sam would play pool half the night, and besides, he felt the need to go on playing. He felt comfortable at the pool table, whereas he didn't at the bar or out at the tables. And if he went to the bar, Annette Rountree came and stood close to him.

As it was, Annette Rountree sat nearby, bouncing her crossed leg. She wore a really short skirt that seemed to inch upward with every bounce. She had been nearby all evening. She had the night off, something which she had to keep reminding Winn, who kept calling to her to serve someone. She would still get up and go serve, though. She brought Sam and Tommy Lee their beers, and she had even played a game of pool with Tommy Lee. She had played a number of times with him that week. It had become obvious to him that Annette was just waiting for him to make a move on her. Actually, he thought that any minute she might jump his bones. She made him feel excited and guilty and nervous as hell.

"Double or nothin'," he told Sam, racking the balls.

Sam grinned, shook his head, and then pulled out three tens. "Triple or nothin'."

Sam broke and sunk a ball right off and was on his second shot when Tommy Lee glanced up and saw

Molly and Rennie standing at the edge of the table area.

For a moment he told himself the two women wearing sunglasses in a dimly lit club were not Molly and Rennie. That blond woman with a dress that showed her curves was *not* his wife.

He jerked his attention back to the pool table and downed his beer while his mind kept seeing the two women in dark glasses. Sam missed his shot, and Tommy Lee got into position for his. As he and Sam played, he kept glancing out across the room, keeping an eye on the women, seeing when they took a table and when they spoke to the waitress. Ordering soft drinks, he guessed; Molly never drank much, and Rennie had given it up. But when he next looked at their table, he saw the waitress delivering two glasses of wine. He watched Molly lift her glass to her lips. Just then he saw Sam cast him a curious look.

Tommy Lee put his attention back on the pool table, but he missed his next shot. Then when it was his turn again, he forgot his were the solid balls and hit one of Sam's striped ones into the pocket by mistake. He didn't want to go on playing pool, didn't want to go to the bar or sit at a table, but he did not intend to leave, either. And there was Sam watching him with worried eyes.

Molly and Rennie tapped their wineglasses together. "To sisters," Rennie said.

"To dark glasses," Molly said, and Rennie laughed. Then Molly sat back in a deliberately lazy fashion. She knew Tommy Lee had seen her. She felt his focus. Her own eyes kept moving to him. She could watch him, or anyone, from behind her dark glasses and not appear to be watching.

More people recognized Rennie with her sunglasses on than they did Molly. A couple of men said hello to Molly without knowing who she was and were surprised when she called them by name.

Corey Jessup, passing as she and Rennie stood looking for a table, bent close enough to Molly to brush her breasts, gave her a leering grin, and said, "Hello, beautiful. Where have you been all my life?"

"Hello, Corey."

The man looked startled and peered closer. "Molly?"

"Yes. How's Velma? Is she here tonight?"

"Uh, no. She's at her sister's this week." He touched the brim of his hat, "Nice seein' ya'," and hurried away.

One great drawback to the dark glasses, however, was eye strain. Molly had a great deal of trouble seeing her way through the maze of tables, and once she mistook a stranger for Tommy Lee when she got confused and watched the wrong pool table. The stranger had the general shape of Tommy Lee's back end, but not his muscular arms at all. Another time she returned from a trip to the ladies room and almost sat down with a strange woman. By then she was feeling tipsy.

Rennie had ordered 7Up served in a wineglass, saying, "I'm the designated driver," but Molly ordered wine. When the waitress asked, "Sweet or dry?" Molly looked at Rennie, and Rennie said, "Red or white?"

"Red," Molly told the waitress. The wine her mother usually kept in her refrigerator was red; Mama had taken up having a glass of red wine before bed each night. She said it was to purify her blood.

After her first sips, Molly decided the wine not only tasted good but it must do something good for the blood because she felt a very pleasant sensation spreading throughout her body. When she finished her first glass, she ordered a second, and halfway through it she removed her dark glasses. She crossed her legs and let the folds of the calf-length dress fall open from far above her knee, and she experimented with not averting her eyes when a man looked at her, and she accepted the first man who asked her to dance. And the whole time she was thinking, *See this Tommy Lee.*

Tommy Lee watched Molly. He didn't want to, but he couldn't help himself. He watched her lift the wineglass to her lips and drink, watched her laughing with people who stopped and spoke, watched her dance with different men. He couldn't believe she would be here, acting like this.

He knew Sam saw her, too, caught Sam looking out across the crowded room. Finally Sam leaned close and said, "Aren't you gonna go speak to her?"

"Nope." Tommy Lee drank deeply from a fresh mug of beer, then pointed his stick, saying, "Number three ball in the side pocket."

He told himself to ignore Molly, but every time he looked at Sam, he found Sam watching her. Sam's watching her pricked Tommy Lee. He did not find it appropriate for Sam to watch his wife like that.

Then Sam said, "You're bein' a stubborn fool, you know. Can't you see that Molly's wantin' you to go pay her attention?"

"Seem's to me that she's gettin' plenty of attention. It's your turn."

Sam frowned. "Molly is still my friend. I'm not just gonna ignore her, T.L."

"Fine," Tommy Lee said.

The next instant he was startled when Sam called to Loren Settle, "Finish my game for me," and threw Loren his pool cue.

Tommy Lee watched Sam walk away toward Molly, watched him speak to her, saw her rising and Sam leading her out onto the dance floor, whirling her into his arms. Tommy Lee gripped his pool cue and for an instant felt like breaking it over the table.

Then he caught Annette watching him. Self-conscious, he proceeded to beat the socks off Loren in two games. Loren never had been very good at pool; he was just killing time until he went to train his hounds on coons.

Still, the whole time he played, Tommy Lee watched Molly dancing with Sam or Pinky Miller—who was at least ten years younger than her—or some guy he didn't even know. He watched as one guy cut in on the dance floor and took her away from another guy. He watched these men put their hands on her, and hold her, and make her laugh.

Taking careful aim, he popped the four and six and eight balls into pockets at the same time, straightened, and laid down his stick.

"Will you dance with me, Annette?" He didn't wait for her to answer before taking her by the hand.

He had a moment's confusion when he reached the dance floor. "I'm pretty rusty at this."

He hadn't danced in years. He didn't take hold of Annette so much as she took hold of him. He was suddenly staring at her big breasts pointing right at him.

"All we have to do is hold on to each other and move," Annette said, putting her lips right up to his ear and pressing her body right on him.

For an instant his gaze met hers. Her eyes were dark and hot. And then she and he were moving out among the other dancers. Thankfully it was a slow tune. Tommy Lee could manage a slow tune. Annette put her head up near his shoulder.

Tommy Lee danced the slow tunes with Annette and sat out the fast ones up at the bar, where he switched to tequila shooters. It didn't take long for the drinks to have an effect. When Annette's hand smoothed up and down his back, he didn't move away from her. When he danced with Annette, he held her close, felt her breasts press against his chest and her thighs brush his.

His eyes met Molly's before she was whirled away.

Molly looked over her shoulder and saw Tommy Lee following Annette Rountree from the dance floor. His hand was pressed low on Annette's back. Molly felt sick and murmured an apology to her partner—a young man who said his name was Gene—and headed for the table. The young man gallantly followed, holding her elbow.

The table was crowded now, and all the faces seemed to blur in front of her. She couldn't locate Rennie, but then Sam was there, saying that Rennie was out dancing.

He took her arm. "Are you okay, Molly?"

"I feel sick."

Her gaze, searching the room despite she didn't want to, caught sight of Tommy Lee standing with Annette.

"Tell Rennie I'm goin' to the car."

She bumped into a shoulder and murmured an apology as she started through the maze of tables and people, music and voices pounding inside her ears. When she reached the door, Sam was beside her, his hand pushing the door handle. She burst outside and gulped in the fresh night air.

She headed for Rennie's Mustang. The image of Tommy Lee and young Annette kept spinning inside her head, and she thought she might throw up. She reached the car, put her hand on the door to steady herself. Sam followed her, and he hovered at her back.

"Molly." His voice floated over her, and then his hand touched her shoulder tentatively. "You can use my shirttail to wipe your eyes."

She shook her head, fearful that if she said anything she would break out in horrible wracking sobs. *Oh, Lord, it was embarrassing, having him see her like this.* Little sobs slipped out.

Sam moved nervously. "Molly?"

"I'm okay." She sucked in a breath. "I j-just need the air. And a tissue . . . I need a tissue." She fumbled for the door handle, opened the door and slid down into the passenger seat, located the box of tissues and blew her nose, and pinched it tight to press down the sobs.

"Feel better now?" Sam's voice was concerned. He crouched at her knees.

Molly nodded. She wished she could hide. She wished there was a hole she could crawl into. She wanted to throw herself down and cry until there was nothing left of her at all.

The next instant Sam's face was blocking out light and his hands had cupped her face, and he was kissing her. Prying open her lips with his own, and kissing her deeply and seductively and completely.

Molly was too shocked to respond or to stop him. But then she did not want to stop him. She needed to be kissed and to be held, and the next instant Sam had pulled her against his chest. She clutched his shirt and buried her head against his warm chest and sucked in the sensual scent of cologne and male body. She wanted to hold on to Sam forever, while at the same time she wondered how they could possibly part without embarrassing each other. She actually thought that maybe they could stay so entangled forever.

Then a voice penetrated her fuzzy brain—Rennie, saying, "Ouch . . . ooh . . . oooch."

Sam's arms fell away, and he moved back. Rennie, carrying her shoes because she had developed blisters and removed them, came tiptoeing and ouching across the gravel parking lot. Sam hurried over and scooped her up into his arms. Rennie laughed and called him her knight in shining armor. Molly watched them, feeling strangely unable to move.

A hand jerked Tommy Lee around, and he found Sam glaring at him.

"I hope you got what you wanted, shovin' Annette

in Molly's face. Geez, T.L., what in the hell is the matter with you?"

"With me? I'm not doin' anything Molly isn't doin'—if it is any of your business."

He had seen Molly and Sam go out the front door, and he had the powerful urge to punch Sam in the face. Seeing Sam now confused him, though, because he wondered where Molly had gone. He wasn't going to ask. He was having trouble keeping up with the conversation as it was, with his head all full of tequila.

Sam shifted his stance. "You just don't get it. Molly was dancin' with a lot of guys, flirtin' with a bunch, meanin' none of it counted for anything. But you, oh, no . . . you had to go and carry on with Annette."

A heat popped inside Tommy Lee's chest and spread upward. "I don't remember askin' your opinion of any of it."

Sam regarded him. "No, but I'm givin' it just the same. You better make up your mind whether or not you want to keep Molly, because you're both headin' for a big wreck. I know, man. I've been there."

"Aw, don't give me that. You haven't been there. You can't call what you've done hardly bein' married at all. You can't stay with a woman long enough to understand."

"Maybe I could have, if I'd had Molly," Sam said.

Tommy Lee stared at him, feeling as if his feet were lifting right off the ground. Then Annette came up, saying that she had her stuff and was ready to go. She slipped her arm through his.

Stepping around Sam, Tommy Lee left with her. It was mostly that he suddenly found himself walking outside with her while his mind kept seeing the way Sam had looked at him and said "if I'd had Molly."

And then Annette was saying, "You want to come to my place?"

Tommy realized they'd stopped beside a white Camaro, yellowish in the lights from Rio's.

"I have my own car," he said, his head spinning and tequila in the back of his throat.

"You can follow me," Annette said, "or I can bring you back for it."

He looked down at her hand lying on his chest and then into her face, into her dark, sensual eyes. A chill prickled up his back, and suddenly he felt all desire shrivel up and die right then and there.

"No . . ." and because he didn't want to hurt her feelings, "Thanks a lot, for tonight, but I'm not ready to take on more." He felt like a dirty dog for the way he'd used her.

She looked disappointed. But then she patted his chest and said, "You just remember, Tommy Lee Hayes—you can park your boots under my bed anytime."

She slipped into the seat, and he closed the door. Shoving his fingers into his pockets, he stood back and watched as she drove away. Her red taillights and the hum of her engine faded quickly, leaving the loud chirping of crickets and katydids coming from the grass and the muffled beat of music coming from the building.

He looked around the parking lot for Molly's El Camino; it seemed it ought to be there, but he didn't see it. He wasn't seeing very well anyway. Another car left, tires crunching in gravel. He started for the Corvette, thinking that what he wanted was to be out on the open road. He had certainly had enough of crowds.

He felt confused and reflected that he'd felt this way ever since Molly had broken those dishes. He had trouble digging his keys out of his pocket and finding the ignition, so he didn't think he should drive. He sank down in the seat of the Corvette, leaned his head back, and looked up at the stars. They spun, so he closed his eyes. He thought how crazy it was that he hadn't taken Annette up on her offer. If only to get a look at those breasts. But when he'd looked into her eyes, he'd felt totally empty, as if he didn't even have a reason to breathe.

He wasn't going to make a right by doing wrong. And it was Molly he wanted. *It was Molly.*

15

❖❖

The Woman In Me

The Mustang headlights played upon the rutted driveway and then upon the cottage, and the bouncing light made Molly's head pound harder. She had left her dark glasses somewhere back at Rio's. With Tommy Lee and Annette, and Sam, who had kissed her.

"Mama's still up," Molly said. "She probably has a bottle of red wine in her refrigerator."

"Drinking is not going to help the situation," Rennie said in that tone of voice she always took on when speaking of alcohol. After her bout with the demon, she believed the shadow of the same hung over her sisters, just waiting to grab them at their weakest moment. "But maybe a hot fudge sundae would help."

"And just where in Valentine would we get a hot fudge sundae at this time of night?" Molly tried to slam the car door, but her hand slipped.

She still felt a bit of wine spinning around her head and through her blood. It seemed the beating of her heart made a rhythm to the scenes in her mind: Tommy Lee and Annette's bodies moving together, and then Sam's lips upon her own. The images and emotions twirled in her mind like a cyclone, making it hard for her to breathe.

"I could get a package of brownies and a pint of ice cream down at the Texaco," Rennie said.

"I hate that cheap ice cream."

Molly went into the kitchen, where the light had been left on and almost blinded her, no matter that it was a single sixty-watt bulb. She went over and opened the cupboard door and stood there a minute, staring at the old mismatched plates. She took one out and broke it over the sink divider. Behind her, Rennie gave a little yelp. Molly got another plate and broke it, squeezing her eyes shut and smacking it a little harder.

"Oh, Sissy." Rennie's arm came around her from behind, and Rennie leaned her head against hers. "You're scarin' me."

"Well . . ." Molly turned from the sink, pulling away from Rennie, too. "It didn't help, either."

She twisted her wedding ring, but it still wouldn't come off. She thought vaguely of using cream on it, but something made her drop the entire idea, and then she was sliding downward into a deep, dark pit. She thought she might cry, but then she realized she felt too low for crying.

She said, "Don't come through here barefooted."

"Tommy Lee was just usin' that tramp to make you jealous, Molly." Rennie had already said this in the car. She added, "Annette isn't his type at all. She's just too sexy."

"Well, thank you, Rennie."

"Oh, I didn't mean it like that. I mean bold—tacky, that's what I mean. Tommy Lee likes class, and Annette isn't. Lordy, there never was a classy woman with breasts the size of watermelons."

Molly said, "You're just jealous."

"That could be," Rennie admitted, lighting a cigarette. "But that doesn't change that she's tacky. There's a line between trashy and tacky, and Annette crosses it."

Mama and all of them felt like that. A bit of trashy was fun, but tacky was simply in poor taste. Kaye had trouble riding the line and usually ended up on the tacky side, but Mama, even at her age, was a master at appearing classy and trashy at the same time.

"We ought to go back to Rio's and beat the crap out of her," Rennie said, so suddenly and fiercely that she startled Molly.

Then Molly said, "Wouldn't that be more on the tacky side?"

"I think it could be safely trashy."

"Well, Rennie, you lost the last time you got in a fight." Molly was wondering what she could do—she felt she had to *do* something.

Rennie touched her bruised eye. "I suppose so— but that was against a man. I think I can take Annette. She may be younger, but I'm tougher—and I don't have those watermelons holding me down." She appeared intrigued with the prospect of violence.

Molly lit up one of Rennie's cigarettes. "I do believe I have made enough of a fool out of myself for one evening."

"Why do you say that? Because you had a little wine and danced and flirted a little? You didn't sin, Molly."

"It wasn't me, Rennie."

"It seemed to be you. And you seemed to be havin' a darn good time, too."

Molly shook her head. She felt the cottage closing around her, the musky scent of it becoming thick. The scent of all the lonely women who had spent lonely hours here. She watched Rennie's blue cigarette smoke trail out toward the dark living room, growing narrower and fainter as it went. Just like her life, Molly thought.

She jabbed out the partially smoked cigarette, saying, "I'm goin' ridin'," and headed for the bedroom to change.

When Molly came back through the kitchen, Rennie was sweeping the floor. "You're stayin' the night, aren't you?" Molly asked.

"I thought I would."

They gazed at each other. Molly said hoarsely, "Thank you. I just need to know you're here."

She also needed to know Rennie was safe from Eddie Pendarvis, who might still be lurking in wait. She thought it best not to mention that, though. Fears given thought were strong enough.

She had a tussle with Marker, who didn't want to leave the corral, but once headed away he kept going, as if eager to reach a destination. The moon was no longer full, but it gave enough light to see when out in the open. Only after she was riding away did she remember the bottle of wine in her mother's refrigerator. She could have snuck in the back door and got it. Of course, she had not done well drinking at Rio's, and she didn't think she had any business drinking while riding a horse at night.

She didn't have any business doing what all she was doing, and she didn't know *what* she was doing. She did not know how she had come to this place in her life, where she was going off to Rio's and flaunting herself in front of her husband and all kinds of strangers . . . and failing miserably, she added. A further disappointment was that she seemed incapable of going over the line. She could only go halfway, that's about as far as she had gone at Rio's, and she had messed up with even that halfway by running away.

Tommy Lee had not said a thing to her. Sam had kissed her.

She wondered if Tommy Lee had taken Annette home to their house, into their bed. The prospect haunted her and filled her mind with all kinds of weird imaginings. Shocking imaginings. The entire idea was shocking. Somehow she simply couldn't believe that her husband would make love to another woman in their bed, that something like that would happen in her life, although she reminded herself she had not heretofore believed that any of her family could get knocked around by a man. She had been mistaken in her assessment of things all the way around.

Her knowledge of one of Tommy Lee's idiosyncracies, however, made her doubt that he had brought Annette into their house. Tommy Lee had an aversion to strangers in the house. He was a very private person. He used to have a hard time when Savannah or the boys brought home friends to stay the night.

Tommy Lee might have gone home to Annette's, though. He might have done that. Although he was awfully funny about being in other people's homes, too. He was never comfortable.

Molly reflected that after twenty-five years of marriage, she really only knew a few hard and fast things about Tommy Lee. Was it because people were always changing? She sighed and thought that at that moment she knew herself even less than she knew Tommy Lee. She never would have thought she would kiss Sam.

In thinking of the kiss, she supposed that technically she had not kissed Sam. She had simply not stopped him from kissing her. She might have kissed him, however, if she hadn't been so surprised. And she *had* thrown herself on his chest and into his arms.

She kept on riding, keeping to open pastures and wide dirt roads. She startled a young couple out parking at a pasture gate, and Marker almost threw her when he spied three coyotes running across a ridge. It occurred to her that a nearly middle-aged modern woman out riding a horse all over the countryside in the middle of the night was a crazy thing. She might come across clandestine operations, such as drug dealers harvesting a hidden marijuana field, or a meeting of drug smugglers, or perhaps cattle rustlers, who could be every bit as ruthless as drug smugglers. Her imagination began to run wild, fed by stories she had heard.

In fact, not having before considered the hazards of her situation was positively and totally crazy. Realization of this made her feel a measure of satisfaction at doing something other than halfway.

That bit of satisfaction soon evaporated, however, and whatever desperation had driven her out riding went with it, leaving her too weary to feel anything other than a nagging worry that Marker might throw her and she would lie broken for days, without anyone ever knowing. She turned Marker back to the cottage, and the trip seemed so long. She had a sudden desire to close herself into the cottage now, and when she and Marker reached the corral, she unsaddled him and let him go and simply threw her tack atop the corral fence and left it, starting to run for the cottage, as eager to be there as she had earlier been eager to leave.

Shucking her boots and jeans, she threw herself onto the couch in the living room and wrapped a cotton blanket tight around her like a cocoon. Rennie was snoring in the bedroom, and Molly couldn't stand the thought of sharing a bed with anyone, because it made her long for Tommy Lee, long to say to him, "Hold me."

The following morning Rennie slipped out of the cottage and went down to Swanda's hardware store and purchased a Mr. Coffee machine. Eugene happened to have a can of coffee for the store, and Rennie talked him out of it, so she didn't have to go to the IGA. As she walked back out to her Mustang, she reflected that it probably wouldn't have been hard to talk Eugene into giving her the coffee machine itself. Eugene looked at her; he had always looked at her, so hard he almost drooled. He got so flustered that he made three mistakes in ringing up her purchase.

It was probably being full of herself with this power she had over Eugene that encouraged her to drive past Annette Rountree's house on her way back to the cottage, to stop and warn Annette to stay away from Tommy Lee.

"Hey, look, I didn't twist Tommy Lee's arm last night. He's a big boy. He can decide what he wants to do."

Annette, obviously pulled from bed, crossed her arms, squeezing her enormous boobs inside a sleep shirt with Mickey Mouse on the front of it. The Mickey Mouse shirt led Rennie to the conclusion Annette certainly hadn't had a man in bed with her last night.

Rennie said, "You and I both know that half the time a man doesn't know what in this world or out of it he wants. You and I are very much alike." Rennie gave a pregnant pause, and then, "Molly's my sister. I'm tellin' you to stay away from her husband, or I'm gonna make certain you regret it. I'm speakin' for myself, not my tender sister. You don't want to get on my wrong side." Another pregnant pause and she added, "Think about it."

She had her eyes bore a hole in Annette. Although she wore sunglasses, which she didn't want to remove and reveal her bruise—which would not aid in her threat—the force went through them. Annette paled slightly. Rennie, moving with perfect timing, turned and strode boldly away.

Dealing with Annette in such a way gave Rennie confidence that she could deal with Eddie Pendarvis, should he show up to bother her again. And Tommy Lee had better watch his step. Right that moment she wasn't very happy with him. She might have stopped by his place, too, but she figured Molly would find out about it and be upset with her. *Poo, she was on such a good roll.*

Molly was sitting up on the couch when Rennie walked in. Just sitting there, staring, her hair all tangled and her shirt all wrinkled. The sight made Rennie's high mood fall.

Gathering herself, she smiled and said, "Look. I got us a coffeemaker."

She was convinced that drinking all that god-awful generic instant coffee was one thing that was straining Molly.

16
❖❖

Keep Walkin' On

Molly thought that she needed to figure out what she was going to do with the mess of her life. The conviction grew on her as she sat drinking coffee with Rennie and Mama, who came over to join them. The three of them sat around the maple kitchen table, drinking coffee, with the hot breeze blowing in the back screen door. Rennie was dressed, but Mama was wearing her fuchsia robe and appeared as cool as always, and Molly was wearing her blue robe, letting it fall off one shoulder in trying to be cooler. Rennie alternately smoked cigarettes and ate powdered sugar doughnuts, and Mama, her reading glasses halfway down her nose, worked on the electric plug to the black fan, which had burnt up that morning. Molly simply sat with her coffee.

Molly reflected that when she had walked away from Tommy Lee, she had not thought anything out. She had been reacting to heartache and frustration, and she had been reacting ever since. This is what she tried to explain to her mother and sister, the two people she felt might know something about this sort of predicament, as they each had certainly had their share of emotions wrapped around a man.

Rennie said, "Did you want to walk out when you did it?"

"Well, at that minute I did, but I really didn't want to. I simply couldn't stand another minute of things as they were."

Rennie pointed out that Molly had decided to stay here at the cottage and had decided to escape Tommy Lee at the cafe, via the bathroom window—and then she had to tell that story to Mama, who found the whole thing very funny—and to flaunt herself at Rio's, in an effort to scratch Tommy Lee. Mama had to be brought up on that, too. In hearing the way Rennie told the story, Molly got freshly embarrassed at her foolish behavior and then annoyed with Rennie for telling. Maybe she hadn't really done anything wrong, but it had been wrong for her, and she didn't care to be reminded of it.

Then Rennie said, "You chose to do all those things, Molly, regardless of the reason—reaction as you say—so I really think you are deciding to do a number of things."

In Rennie's view, people only thought they were deciding courses in their lives, while in reality what they were doing was reacting to their circumstances, whether good or bad. Put in this light, Molly had to agree, although she didn't aloud because a thick desperation fell over her and made her lose the urge to converse. Remembering her various activities of the past week did nothing to bolster her confidence. She felt she had made a great many mistakes.

She became aware of the scent of the cottage, above the scents of the coffee and Rennie's cigarettes—it was that strong and seemed to grow with the heat of the day. She felt as if the cottage were sucking her into its very plaster and wood.

Maybe it was something to do with her female

Collier blood, she mused as she looked at her mother and sister. Maybe each of them could only be drawn away by a man for a time before they had to come back to their own. And here she sat among them.

For much of her married years, Molly had felt somewhat as if she were split between her mother and sisters and Tommy Lee, as if she stood with one foot in Tommy Lee's life and the other in the lives of her mother and sisters. She didn't suppose it was so much their lives as *a way of life.* Her way of living was vastly different than Tommy Lee's. For one thing, Tommy Lee ignored any ripples in his life and went about his way, working, always working. Molly had trouble ignoring the ripples, and she got darn tired of working. At times she needed fun and frivolity—Tommy Lee pretty much looked upon frivolity as he would an engine missing a piston, which was to say useless, while to Molly frivolity was at times the very breath of life. She had always thought of herself as a blessing to Tommy Lee in this regard, for she saved him from a stark existence.

Rennie left to go back to her own apartment, saying, when Molly tried to caution her, "I'm not goin' to hide from Eddie Pendarvis, Molly. I do have to have some fresh clothes."

They whispered these things out beside the Mustang because they had told Mama none of it.

Rennie drove off with her gay little wave, leaving Molly staring after the red Mustang, worrying about her, yet thinking that Rennie had had a choice and made it and wishing her own choices were as clearcut.

She went back inside and sat at the table and watched her mother working over the old fan plug. Peering up over her half-glasses, Mama said, "What you have to do is figure out what you want, Molly. Do you know what you want?"

"I want things to be like they were years ago, when

Tommy Lee and I were in love and all of life was ahead of us with no mistakes cluttering it up."

Molly said this at first slowly but ended up with a suddenness of clarity. Even as she spoke, she knew she wanted what she could not have. That she wanted it easy, and that it would never be easy.

Mama smiled softly. "Honey, I wish I could be as clean and fresh of mistakes as I was at thirty-five, too."

Molly felt herself sinking, as if she were melting down and becoming part of the linoleum and the cottage.

"Mama, I feel like I'm fading. I don't want to, but I can't seem to help it."

Mama said, in that firm voice she used whenever she sensed panic, "Sometimes, honey, the only thing you can do is walk on through it, not knowing where you're goin' but having the grit to keep walkin' on. Such is life."

That was not at all what Molly wanted to hear. She wanted sweet, heartfelt sympathy, some "poor darling" would be nice. But Mama never had been very good at sympathy; sympathy just made her too nervous.

After her mother left, Molly took to her bed and books again, with Ace upon her belly and the now fixed fan blowing air softly over her body as the heat and despair grew. She read and slept or just lay there, drinking the delicious coffee from the maker and smelling the lonely old woman scent of the cottage and thinking dark thoughts.

Her thoughts were not straight. They were a whirl of images: past to present, Tommy Lee and the children, the mistakes made time and time again, no matter how she had tried. Mistakes that caused wounds that caused scar tissue that would always be there and made the heart vulnerable and tough at once.

Sam was in her thoughts, too, and every time she thought of him, she felt guilty and excited.

At one point she had a really crazy moment and reached for the phone to call Tommy Lee. *Get ahold of yourself!* Which she did for about three seconds and put the telephone down, but then picked it back up and dialed.

Her mouth went dry when Tommy Lee's deep, soft voice answered. "Hello?"

It was so familiar, the way he said a hello that was curious and hesitant at the same time. Molly immediately thought of putting her hand on his bare, hard chest.

She asked, "Are you sleepin' with Annette Rountree?"

Shocked silence. Then he said gruffly, "No."

"Okay."

She hung up, quickly, as if the receiver was on fire. Terribly embarrassed. But she was also satisfied to have given Tommy Lee a jolt, which she felt he had coming.

She sat staring at the telephone, expecting it to ring, but it did not, and that made her angry. She had just made a fool of herself. The least Tommy Lee could do was call back and act interested.

Molly was asleep when Boone and Colter came. It was embarrassing and awkward for all of them. Her sons had never seen her like this, wearing nothing but a big shirt and panties—and thank goodness she had at one point slipped into the shirt—her hair on end and face all puffy from compulsive reading and sporadic crying. She quickly went into the bathroom and put a cool, wet cloth on her face for two full minutes, but there was not much help for it. She slipped into her jeans and straightened herself up as best she could, though, because there were proprieties to be observed. She was the mother and they her children, no matter they were grown.

In the kitchen, both sons stood with their backsides resting against the sink cabinet, their hands stuffed into their front jeans' pockets. Molly sat at the table, first drawing her legs up, then self-conscious for some silly reason about showing her bare feet, she tucked them beneath the table. She wished for one of Rennie's cigarettes. But she wouldn't smoke, not in front of the children, not even when Boone had had his wreck. Then she'd gone into the hospital rest room to smoke, and she'd had to quickly put out the cigarette when Savannah had come in. Savannah had noticed the smoke smell and said indignantly, "Somebody's been smoking in here," and Molly had baldly lied and said there was a woman in there before her smoking like a chimney stack.

No matter that her sons didn't say it, she could hear the questions: "Why, Mom? Can't you fix this? Don't you know what this does to us?"

The closest they came to speaking of it was when Molly jumped up and got them Coca-Colas from the refrigerator.

"Hey . . . the little Coke bottles," Colter said. "Man, I haven't seen these in aeons."

"Your Aunt Rennie bought them. She says they taste better than the cans or big liter bottles." Chatter, something to fill the wide crack she had made in their relationship.

Colter held his bottle up, looking at it. "Remember when we were kids and you would leave the lid on and punch a hole in it with an ice pick, so we could suck the Coke out?" His dark eyes lit on her and shifted away.

And then Boone said, "Dad used to put peanuts in it for us, and you'd get all worried and say we might get one stuck in our throats."

His pale eyes rested on her, long and hard and demanding, which annoyed her because she didn't think he had room to demand. Then she felt guilty.

What could she say to any of it? How could she explain when she didn't understand and no explanation on God's green earth would serve anyway?

What occurred to her was that her sons had driven home together, something they had never before done. They had never done much of anything together. They were so different, Boone as fair and wild as the Collier side of the family, and Colter dark and steady as the Hayeses. But here they both were, looking at her with the same hesitant and uncertain expression and moving from one foot to the other, while still making an effort to say without words: I love you.

Then, right with her boys there, Sam called.

"I'm down in Dallas," he said when she didn't say a word.

She couldn't say his name with her sons staring at her and couldn't think of anything to say anyway. She was thinking, *He called!*

"I have a meeting with a shop that might carry my designs, and I'll be stayin' the night, but I plan to come by and pick you up at one tomorrow, if our date's still on?"

"Yes, of course," Molly said, as if speaking to the appointment clerk at the doctor's office.

Sam said, "Well, see you tomorrow."

And Molly said, "Uh-huh," and hung up.

Minutes later Colter and Boone edged their way out the door, which they had pretty much been doing since arriving. Molly followed them out and made her arms stay at her sides when they kept straining to reach out and hold her sons to her. Since they were little boys, whenever they would leave her, going off on the school bus, or leaving for a sleep-over at a friend's, or off to work and college, she would have this crazy sensation that her arms, if not contained, would stretch out and grab her sons and hold on. Today the sensation was so strong that her arms actually did come up, moving ever so slowly, and she pushed them back down, and then up they came again.

The boys had driven in Colter's dandelion yellow '65 Ford pickup truck. At the front of it, they paused, looking sheepish, saying they were sorry the visit was so short; Colter had to be back to work by tomorrow afternoon, and Boone had a big horse sale at Fort Worth. They each needed to get some sleep before heading back.

Molly allowed herself to reach upward and muss Colter's hair. He grinned at her, but it was a sad uncertain grin, and his "Awe, Mom" was uncertain, too. She gave way and reached out and hugged him, stretching out for Boone, too, giving relief to her aching arms and ignoring Boone's initial reluctance. Boone had never been one to hug. He did hug her this time, though, and tightly.

"I'm sorry, boys. . . . I'm sorry," she whispered.

"Mom, what in the hell is goin' on with you and Dad?" Boone asked, his eyes once more sharp and intense.

"We're tryin' to work it out, honey. That's all I can tell you."

Boone jerked from her, smacked his fist on the yellow hood. She reached for him, but he kept on walking away. Colter kissed her forehead. "It's all right, Mom," and then he, too, was walking away, opening the truck door.

"Come again when your grandmother is home and can get to visit with you." And, "Take your vitamins . . . drive carefully." Then she called, "God Bless," something she hadn't said since they were children.

And then she was standing there, at the edge of the

tall trees, waving as they drove off, going home. Where she wished to be.

Why didn't she just go?

Because she could no longer convince herself that she and Tommy Lee shared a love, and she couldn't live with that anymore.

The rest of weekend, during which Tommy Lee never once called, Molly forced herself to straighten up, clean the cottage, call Savannah, do her hair and nails. She decided that what she had to do was take one day at a time. Keep walking on, as her mother had said. She wasn't ready to say her marriage was over, but she supposed she would have to consider the possibility, since Tommy Lee did not approach her.

Her anger over this pulled her up from her desperate depression. What she thought was that Tommy Lee should at least call her so she could hang up on him, and she knew this was crazy, but feeling a bit crazy was preferable to feeling desperate. There never had been anything appealing about a desperate woman.

By Sunday morning, she began to be terribly excited about Sam coming. The weekend had been stretching so long, with her mother and sisters all busy with their own lives—of all times for her family to have their own lives. She was tired of reading and of petting Ace and of drinking coffee all alone. She was *so* lonely. She needed to talk to someone about everyday things.

She tried on darn near everything she owned in choosing an outfit. Threw the clothes all over the bedroom, tried her hair in a dozen different ways, and finally settled on how she always wore it. It was crazy to get so overwrought about the thing.

Date. That's what Sam had called it on the telephone. But sometimes Molly said "I have a lunch date with Rennie," so it really was just a figure of speech.

She and Sam were old friends getting together, just as they had forever.

Except now Sam had kissed her.

She was ready and waiting by twelve-thirty, looking out the window every three minutes. Sam came in his brother's Bronco, and she went out to meet him. Her heart was beating fast. She kept thinking of how he had kissed her and thinking that she was making too much of it and that she should act natural, but she didn't feel very natural.

"Hi there, darlin'."

Oh, my. If Sam felt awkward, he certainly didn't show it. He smiled his ever-charming smile and was easy, just as he always had been.

"Little Joe's sound good to you?" he asked, his dark eyes sparkling, giving her a wink as he started the Bronco.

There wouldn't be another thing in the world to say to his words or his wink besides, "Yes . . . fine," and she had a feeling she was getting close to the line again, and she started hearing the tune, "Heaven's Just a Sin Away" playing through her mind.

He looked at her as a man looked at a woman, and everything inside Molly that was a woman responded. She sat there feeling a sort of glowing excitement as he drove along, past houses and pastures and fence rows. Then she got ahold of herself and told herself firmly that Sam was a friend and that she still wore a wedding band on her finger. She wasn't going to go off on a silly pipe dream just because she was lonely.

It was a little hard to do, though, when every time she looked his way, he smiled at her and seemed so very glad to be with her. How could a woman not respond to that?

Little Joe's was known for the biggest and best hamburgers in half the state, and pecan pie, too. It was a rustic sort of place but had a nice covered patio outside, with lots of potted ferns and hanging baskets of geraniums. Molly wondered if Sam thought the same as she did—that they weren't likely to run into a lot of people they knew here, but that they weren't really hiding, either.

They started conversing about everyday things: the weather, the styles of the sixties and seventies returning, new movies they had seen or wanted to see. They went on to talk about their mothers, both of whom were growing older and wilder. Molly talked of her mother fixing electrical appliances and going to Hardee's in her robe, and Sam spoke of his mother getting speeding tickets and having her hair teased up so high that sometimes she had trouble getting into her car. The way he told the stories had Molly laughing so hard she had to wipe her eyes.

When Molly saw a young pregnant woman, it reminded her of Savannah, and she spoke of her anticipation of her first grandchild.

"I'm not certain I'm ready to be a grandmother," she said, "but I'm a lot more used to the idea than when she first told me."

"You sure don't look like a grandmother," Sam said.

"Thank you," Molly said. There wasn't anything else to say, although she was thinking, *Do you really think that? . . . Tell me again.*

They lingered over soft drinks and kept on talking, going on now to likes and dislikes. Sam had taken up riding horses, kept a gelding at a stable, and he found he enjoyed naps now, and he had just gotten a CD-ROM for his computer—did she have one? Yes, she did and she loved it, most especially a CD of quotes.

After Little Joe's, they went to an art gallery managed by a friend of Sam's, and then, since they were up near the Kmart, Molly said she wanted to pick up a few things. It was fun going through the store with Sam, who kept cutting up, trying on hats and picking up things and making outrageous comments. Sam could be really funny at times. And he looked at her, really *looked* at her, as if he enjoyed what he saw. He looked at her and made her feel so much a woman. It was odd how this seemed to make her feel very sad.

Throughout the afternoon, neither of them mentioned Tommy Lee. They walked around his name and the subject of marriage as they would have a snake coiled on the sidewalk.

It had always been Molly with Tommy Lee, and Sam joining them. This time now with Sam was almost as if she and Sam were alone simply because Tommy Lee was just off getting gas in the car or something. It was easy to think of it like that, yet thought of like that, Molly continually felt that Tommy Lee was looking on, or perhaps about to return just any moment.

She would think how beautiful Sam's brown eyes were, how they were so dark that she couldn't even see a pupil at times, and then she would think of Tommy Lee's blue ones, how when a shaft of light hit them just so they would have gold flecks in them and be bluer because of it. She would remember Sam's kiss, how startled she had felt and how warm his lips had been, and then think of a time Tommy Lee had kissed her, how he would smile at her afterward, as if the kiss lingered in his smile. She would catch the muskiness of Sam's cologne and think of how Tommy Lee smelled . . . and for some reason she kept remembering how she liked to hold one of Tommy Lee's T-shirts to her nose before she put it in the washer.

She began to be aroused but found herself thinking lewd thoughts of *both* men, which made her feel very guilty, although the guilt didn't stop her from having the thoughts. She began to realize for the first time that her body was at times stronger than her mind. Such was an exciting and fearful realization.

It was after six o'clock when they turned down the driveway to the cottage and saw the red-and-white Corvette sitting there at the end and Tommy Lee leaning against the front fender.

17

❖❖

It Matters To Me

Somehow Tommy Lee had known Molly was with
Sam. The two of them stared through the windshield
at him, and Tommy Lee, arms crossed, stared back.

As the Bronco stopped, he straightened and went
over to open the passenger door for Molly. She looked
at him a second, then lowered her gaze and hopped
out. He thought to lift a hand to help her, but she was
out before he touched her, and then he felt like he
shouldn't touch her. She had on a soft cotton dress. It
fell over her curves and was so thin that it gave the
appearance of seeing the skin through the fabric. This
startled him, to think not only he but Sam could be
seeing her flesh, but then he realized the fabric was
cream colored. It was thin, though. The familiarity of
it came to him with a suddenness. He'd seen the dress
a dozen times before but had never noticed how it fell
over her breasts and hips.

Sam came around the front of the Bronco, putting
his straw Stetson on his head. Since moving out to
New Mexico, he had taken to wearing a cowboy hat.
Tommy Lee thought that if it came down to it, he
himself was more cowboy than Sam, who could better

ride a Harley than a horse and who never had done more than see a cow from the far side of the fence. Sam had on a light sport coat over a T-shirt, a real macho-male look these days. Tommy Lee was glad he had worn a crisp shirt and shined boots.

"Hello, Tommy Lee," Sam said.

"Hello."

Molly didn't say anything; she just looked at him with her big green eyes.

"I came to speak with my wife," Tommy Lee said.

Sam blinked and shot Molly a questioning look, then said, "Of course."

"I had a really nice time, Sam," Molly said. "Thanks so much. Oh, I'd better get my things."

Sam pulled plastic shopping bags from the Bronco and started to take them into the cottage for her, but Tommy Lee stepped in front of him. "I'll take care of them."

He walked off with the bags to the cottage, leaving them alone to say good-bye. In the kitchen, he quickly stepped to the window to watch. He didn't want to watch, but he couldn't help himself. He wondered if Molly still had on her wedding ring, cursed himself that he hadn't thought to look. He couldn't see now.

He saw Molly speak to Sam, saw her uplifted face and the slope of her neck. His pulse pounded in his throat as he watched for Sam to sneak a kiss. But Sam didn't. He backed the Bronco, and Molly stepped away. The breeze fluttered the hem of her dress and the wisps of hair around her face. When she shifted her eyes to the cottage, Tommy Lee quickly backed away from the window.

He stood there a moment, wondering what he would say to her. Then he ran his gaze around the kitchen. A crawling feeling came over him. He never had cared for the cottage and always felt it hated him. He always had the odd feeling that something, a picture or some piece of molding, was about to come flying across the room and hit him upside the head.

Propelled along by the feeling, he stepped to the back door and out of it, then stood waiting for Molly. It was a minute before she came around the corner of the house, and then she stood looking at him, her arms dangling by her sides. She wore her ring.

"Let's walk out back," he said.

They walked side by side out to the wooden fence. There Tommy Lee leaned his forearms on the top rail. The fence needed painting. So did the little horse barn. He toed his boot in the dirt and the image of Molly and Sam together came across his mind. He pushed the thought away. Words wouldn't come, at least none he thought prudent to speak. He just never had been any good at deep conversation. He kept hoping Molly would start the ball rolling, which was what always happened. This time, however, Molly was apparently set to be stubborn and not help at all.

He cut his gaze to her and saw her eyes were a deep turquoise in the light of the setting sun. His gaze followed the slope of her neck down to where the pale swell of her breasts showed above the cut of the dress. It came to him suddenly what that skin felt like, all warm and like satin. A desperation welled up inside of him. He felt as if he was holding on for dear life but his grip was slipping and a big wind was going to blow him right away from her.

Then she said, "Do you remember the horse barn?"

He was relieved she had spoken but confused at the same time because his thoughts had been far from that horse barn. Her warm tone and the look in her eyes told him she was saying something specific, but he didn't know what. He said noncommittally, "It needs paintin'."

She regarded him intently. "I was talkin' about us in the horse barn. When we made love for the first time."

"I know that," he said quickly. He looked at the barn again. The memory was fuzzy. The barn in memory had looked a lot bigger and more substantial. And the two people in his memory were distant strangers from the past.

Molly went to staring off into space again, and he looked down at his boot and toed the ground again. There they were, trapped in the fruitless silence.

"I thought you came to speak to me," Molly said and in a tone that brought Tommy Lee's head snapping up.

He said, "I am talkin' to you. Are you in a hurry? . . . Have some place to go?"

"No. I just thought you ought to talk, if you came to talk."

"Maybe I just came to stand here with you. Is that some sort of crime?"

"No. Except you did say you came to talk."

He toed his boot, and Molly leaned against the fence, staring at the barn again. Then she said, "You didn't remember the barn."

"I remembered."

She looked at him. "No, you didn't. Would you just admit things? Just say things straight out? I never know where I stand with you because you won't say things straight out."

"When I say things straight out, you get mad at me. You ask a question and then you don't like the answer. I don't remember much of that time in the barn, okay? Geez, Molly, we'd necked hot and heavy a thousand times before, only that time it got out of hand. It happened twenty-five years ago and was over in about five seconds, and I was so horny and dizzy what memory I have is all fuzzy. I don't count what happened in that barn all that much, not to times that came after."

"Well . . . I'm glad you finally said exactly what you think." She was righteous now.

He took a breath, raked a hand through his hair, and said, "Have you figured out anything yet—about us?"

She shook her head. "Not really. Have you?"

"I guess not." He looked at her. "Do you want a divorce?"

"No," Molly said breathlessly. "Do you?"

"No," he said hoarsely, and fell back into a steaming kind of silence, his mind casting around, having strange but powerful thoughts of grabbing Molly and shutting her up with his own lips and body, right there on the grass. Emotion tumbled and rolled inside him, like storm clouds trying to decide whether to erupt or blow over.

Molly felt the words coming and tried to hold them back—she shouldn't do all the talking, she should listen, but her feelings were welling up, no matter that they didn't seem coherent. She simply felt as if *she* were welling up.

"We used to talk," she said. "We used to not be so afraid of what we said."

Tommy Lee looked at her with a pained expression.

"I guess we don't have much in common to talk about anymore."

"Yes, we do. We have a lot in common."

"What?"

He frowned. "I don't know . . . lots of things. We both like to eat Mexican food."

"*You* like to eat Mexican food. *I* like to eat fajitas without hot sauce and sour cream, which you like a lot of. You like cars, I like horses. You like to work half the night, and I like to watch old movies."

"So what?" he said. "We've been like that for twenty-five years, and it worked all that time."

She looked sad. "It worked when we had the kids tying us together, but we don't have them anymore."

He shut his mouth tight and looked away from her. She wanted to reach for him and pull him to her. But she couldn't, and she couldn't stop her heart from pouring out, either.

"It just seems to me that I'm always trying to approach you," she said, "and you back up from me. Oh, you give me anything I could want, the house, the El Camino . . . any amount of money . . . as much as we have, anyway. But when I reach for you, you back up. Then, when I find something else to fill my time and interest, you come after me, like you want me . . . but if I turn to you, back you go again."

Her voice was rising, and she gestured. "Oh, I can't put it into words. It's like you want me, to have me around, but not too close. Like you don't want me to need you . . . not the things you can do for me, like taking care of me, you don't mind that, too much, but you don't want me to need *you*."

Tommy Lee felt a rope wrapping around him. He heard truth in her words and turned from it. Women sure could make a lot out of nothing, he thought, but he knew darn well he'd better not say it. That was honesty she sure wouldn't want to hear, and sometimes honesty wasn't the entire truth. But he couldn't explain that, and he knew he'd better not say any of it, either. She was looking so forlorn, and any sense of power he had felt was turning into confusion. He wanted to have answers, and at the same time he wanted to run from it all.

"I've tried, Molly."

"I know that," she said quickly. "I think we've both tried. You're a very good husband, Tommy Lee." She looked about to cry, and he sure hoped she wouldn't. "It just seems like we don't have anything in common anymore, and I . . . well, I can't go on feeling like I'm tyin' you down."

"You aren't tyin' me down, Molly." He felt her slipping away and himself blowing away.

She shook her head and chipped paint off the fence with her fingernail. "You had to marry me, and I know you had lots of hopes and dreams that never came to light because of that."

"That isn't the way it was." But he felt guilt and a voice saying, *That is the way it was.* "I never felt like that, Molly—like I had to marry you." Mostly he hadn't.

"Yes you did." Her eyes were steady.

"Okay, we had to get married. I've thought about it like that—that we both had to do that, and not only because of you gettin' pregnant, but because it always seemed like we were supposed to get married. Maybe there have been times when I've wanted to go off and do somethin' else, but that doesn't mean I didn't want to be married to you. I've always loved you, Molly."

He saw doubt in her eyes, and it made him feel helpless . . . and like smashing the fence.

She said, "We have loved each other, but that hasn't prevented us from growin' apart."

"Okay . . . so we've grown apart." Tommy Lee gestured wildly. "You comin' over here to Hestie's cottage sure hasn't helped that."

"Well, me stayin' at home wasn't helpin' it either."

Her words flashed through him, and Tommy Lee hit back with, "Well, even when you were at the house, you weren't all that available to me, between the kids and your horse."

To which she said, "Who do you think picked up after you, if it wasn't me bein' there for you?"

He couldn't see that that had anything to do with the argument, or with anything at all, and he told her that and a lot more. Tommy Lee couldn't recall ever being so angry in all his life, and he found himself dragging out every little thing he had held back for all the months, and in a couple of cases, years.

"You say I back away from you? Well, you don't exactly step toward me, Molly. You want it all your way. You want us to be together, but you get your own office off in town, and you get a separate checking account. I guess that's okay, as long as *you* decide to do it. Do you think I don't feel left behind when you and your mother and sisters take off for Oklahoma City or somewhere? I don't say anything then! I like my time alone, and so do you, so don't be makin' me out to be a fault because of it."

He realized he was poking his finger at her, and she was staring at him, and suddenly his high emotions scared him. He clamped his mouth shut, and then Molly turned away from him.

He stared at her stiff back, then said, "I just don't know what in the hell you want from me, Molly. Why don't you just tell me that—*what do you want?*"

She whirled on him. "I have told you. And what good is it when I have to tell you—to ask you? I want you to think of it on your own. I'm tired of beggin' for you."

"You're drivin' me crazy. You know that?" And he shoved from the fence and stalked away to his Corvette.

Molly stood there and watched him go. She gripped the top plank of the wooden fence, and when the Corvette went up the hill onto the road, she turned and kicked the bottom plank with all her might, and the darn old thing splintered and fell in two.

She stalked into the cottage, changed her clothes, and without pause stalked out again to the garden shed for tools to fix the fence. She patched the break with an old piece of two-by-four, and when she finished hammering the last nail she went to hammering on the ground until her arm gave out.

Then her mother was there, bending over her. "Molly . . . Molly Jean, honey."

"Oh, Mama, I'm just so stupid. I want Tommy Lee more than anything, and I just keep pushin' him away. I can't stop. What's wrong with me? . . . Oh, Mama . . . what's wrong with me?"

"Oh, baby, you're just a woman." Mama gathered her close. "A woman in love with a man."

In Mama's estimation there was no harder place on earth for a woman to be to be than in love with a man.

As Tommy Lee drove, fast, over to beat up Sam, he reflected that he might not be thinking straight. He rebuked this thought. He was thinking straight and knew, for a change, exactly what he wanted to do.

It seemed to him that all of life was one big confusion, and that too many times he had not acted on those rare times when he knew exactly what he wanted to do. He had had the brief inclination to toss Molly to the ground and screw her so that she had to shut up. That had seemed one way to drag her past all this crap she kept throwing in the way. But the certainty of that course had passed before he could make up his mind to act on it. He knew now he should have done exactly that. He felt certain now, deep in his bones, that no matter what the experts said, sex could melt a lot of resentments.

He wished he could make up his mind more easily and stick to it. His poor inability to make up his mind struck him, in that moment, as a great failing. And it was simply one more reason for him to beat the shit out of Sam. At least he had made up his mind on that score. Sam deserved it, and Tommy Lee wanted to do it.

Sam answered, barefoot and shirt open, threw the door wide and told Tommy Lee to come on in, which seemed a really stupid thing to do for a man who had been flirting with another man's wife.

Tommy Lee said, "You asshole," and sprang at him, giving release to the ball of frustration in his gut. Sam managed to block his punch but went stumbling backward, over a counter stool. Tommy Lee jumped on him, and they went grunting, grappling, and punching around the small living room, knocking over lamps and vases and books, collapsing a drawing table.

At last, spent, they broke apart. Sam's nose was bleeding. Tommy Lee tasted blood and tongued a crack in his bottom lip. He hauled himself to his feet.

"It's a low thing to do," he said, his swelling lip causing the words to sound strange, "goin' after a best friend's wife."

Sam, rising up on his knees, said, "You threw her away, man, so don't go blamin' me for your own mistakes." Sniffing, he got to his feet and wiped his nose with his T-shirt. Then he lifted his eyes to Tommy Lee. "I've loved Molly for a long time, but you never did see it. Why? Damn, T.L., I'm your best friend, and you know everything else about me. Why didn't you see how I felt about Molly?" He shook his head. "I guess you never could believe that she might look at someone else besides you. I guess you thought she'd be there whenever you decided to look her way. Well, I feel for you, buddy, but I think I have a chance now, and I'm not givin' it up. I think I can make her happy."

"I saw it all along," Tommy Lee said flatly. "I just ignored it because I figured our friendship was more important than bein' jealous. I thought our friendship was . . . ah, hell . . ."

Going for the door, he caught sight of a picture hanging there beside it. It was a drawing Sam had done of the old Chevy Tommy Lee had had when they were teens. Lifting it off its hook, Tommy Lee smashed it on the floor and then walked out.

18

❖❖

What I Meant To Say

When Sam called, Molly was across the hall in the tiny storage room–kitchen, at the coffeemaker that she shared with Jaydee and his secretary, Sophia. Even while she poured herself a cup of coffee, she had one foot turned toward the door, one ear listening for the telephone in her office.

Molly had been expecting Tommy Lee to call ever since their awful quarrel. Hoping, feeling foolish, grasping at expectation, she had carried the telephone around the cottage with her. She had taken it into the bathroom with her and as far out the door as it would go when she'd given Marker his grain, and then into bed with her. Ace got into such a fit over it being in the bed, he wouldn't come lie with her.

Rennie had called to chat. Walter had called, wanting to know the possibility of all the new clothes Kaye was buying being a tax deduction, since she had started selling Country Interior Designs. When Molly said no, Kaye had to take over and argue the point for ten minutes, until Molly said, "I don't make the laws, Kaye. Call the IRS," which infuriated Kaye so much she hung up. Shortly afterward, Season had called to simply give her love and Lillybeth's, too. First thing in the morning, before eight o'clock, a man had called selling lightbulbs guaranteed to last ten years.

Tommy Lee had not called, after they had had the worst fight of all their years together.

"Why don't you call him?" Mama suggested when she came over bright and early that moring, dressed this time, bringing cinnamon-raisin biscuits she'd gotten up at Hardee's.

"Well, because," Molly said. She had tried to get herself to call Tommy Lee, but each time she got no further than lifting the receiver before she quickly hung up. "He should call me. He's the one who never cared enough to stop me from leaving, and he hasn't asked me to come home, and he is the one who stalked away mad yesterday. I don't think he wants to hear from me."

"That's pride talking."

Molly gave her a look that said: You are stepping on dangerous ground.

Of course that didn't faze Mama, who went right on with, "You should just call him up and tell him how you feel. How you *really* feel, which is that you want to make up."

"I can't," Molly said.

"Can't and won't are about the same thing," Mama said and got up and left.

Molly called after her, "You're one to be talkin'," but that really was a weak retort, and really childish, too, which did nothing to help Molly's poor mood.

Then, at the office, when the phone did ring, it was like a fire alarm, because Molly had switched it to the loudest setting to make certain she would hear it should she be in the bathroom when it rang. At her desk in Jaydee's offices, Sophia yelped. Molly started for the phone and realized she was carrying the pot in one hand and the cup in the other, hot coffee sloshing all over her hand. Phone ringing, Molly crying, "Yeow!" and shoving pot and cup onto the counter, patting a napkin on her hand as she sprinted across the hall and to her desk, tripping on the chair she'd left pushed out and answering breathlessly.

Hearing Sam's voice, it took her a moment to bring her mind around that it wasn't Tommy Lee.

"Oh, hello, Sam." Then Molly lowered her voice and carried the telephone as far as the cord would reach across to the door. Sophia was watching from her desk with a stretched-out ear. Molly pushed the door closed with her hip.

Sam asked her to lunch, and when she declined, he asked her to supper. Slowly lowering herself into her chair, Molly gripped the receiver and told him she didn't think it was a good idea for them to go on seeing each other.

"The truth of it is that it's more than friendship between us, and there just isn't room for that right now."

It occurred to her that she sounded overly dramatic, and she had an instant of feeling silly. It was possible that she had misconstrued Sam's kindness to her as something more.

But he said, "I'm in this, Molly. I don't see how you can ignore that."

His voice was sexy, like he could make it when he wanted to. Molly realized she was damp between her breasts—Sam's tone was the sort that made a woman realize she had breasts.

She got ahold of herself. "Oh, Sam, I'm tryin' to be honest with you. I'm confused enough with my marriage right now, without adding . . . well, whatever it is we would be adding. I have nothin' to offer you. It wouldn't be fair to you. . . . I'd just be usin' you."

"So, use me. I'm beggin' for it."

She swallowed, smiling and teary at the same time.
"I can't, Sam . . . and I don't want to cause an argument between you and Tommy Lee." Although she
wasn't certain Tommy Lee would argue over her.

"Too late," Sam said.

"Too late?"

"Tommy Lee and I already had our fight, so you
don't need to worry about that."

"You had a fight?" She shouldn't feel excited. That
was awful of her, she thought, trying to shove the
emotion aside, even as she held her breath to hear
details.

All Sam said was, "Just a bit of an argument.
Nothin' serious."

"Oh, Sam." She rubbed her forehead. "I still can't
see you," she said, the words squeezing out her throat.

"Okay. I can accept that . . . but I'm still here," he
said and hung up.

Molly replaced the receiver and sat there at her
desk, staring at papers in front of her, hearing Sam's
voice. It was true, she thought. She could say no to
Sam all the day long, but the fact was that he was still
there, offering his warm eyes and strong hands and
just about anything she may want from him. And her
lonely heart knew it.

Her body began to melt with the thought, to seem
to buzz and jingle and seep out her toes. She did not
think she could stand to go on this way, *needing*
something but uncertain as to the exact nature of the
need. A yearning, that's what it was.

Then, as she pondered this and tried to find a way
to pacify the awful yearing, the telephone rang again.

Molly stared at it, actually doubting she had heard
the ring. But it came again, and she jumped. Was it
Sam again? What would she say to him? Maybe it was
Tommy Lee.

She snatched up the receiver. "Hello?"

"Molly, this is JoEllen Bloom, and Tommy Lee's

lost a bunch of accounts on his computer, and he's drivin' me crazy."

JoEllen's speech pattern was to string all of her sentences together with hardly a breath. She was always in a hurry. As the owner, installer, and maintenance person for the local computer store, which she'd opened after she'd retired from the air force, she was kept busy. She said it was working all of her life with computers that made her go racing through her days.

Molly, gripping the receiver, listened as JoEllen said that she couldn't get out to help Tommy Lee today because she was in the midst of putting in a new system for Dr. Greene, who dealt with life and death and so of course had to come first.

"Tommy Lee has called me at least half a dozen times, and the last time he hollered so loud that standing next to me Eugenia jumped and threw files for three different patients all up in the air, and now their records are all screwed up, so I just hope none of them needed a heart transplant."

Tommy Lee did get crazy over a computer. For someone so smart about any intricate mechanical thing, he was awfully dumb about using a computer. He'd taken lessons JoEllen offered when she set their system up, but he had never gotten very far. When working at the computer, he tended to get so wrought up that every muscle in his body got locked, except his knees, which he bounced at racing speed. He had ended up turning all computer operation over to Molly, who appeared to have an innate ability for working a computer. She talked to it, as if it were a human intelligence at her disposal. This drove Tommy Lee wild. He would walk out of the room when she did that.

"I know about you two," JoEllen said in a low tone, as if it were a secret, "but, Lord, Molly, he's drivin' me crazy, so do you suppose you could go help him?"

Molly cleared her throat. "I'll go see what I can do."

She went to the rest room and freshened her makeup, combed her hair. She started to dab on Chanel, told herself to stop it, then dabbed quickly down her bosom. Out on the road she turned the El Camino's air-conditioning on full blast and willed herself not to sweat.

She made herself slow down for Eulalee Harris's chickens wandering all over the road. At the entry to her own drive, she stopped, the memory of her and Tommy Lee's fight coming back and causing her to sink. She checked herself in the mirror and applied fresh lipstick. Her hand was shaking. Then she went on down the drive and pulled the El Camino to a stop in front of the garage doors, beside Tommy Lee's old green pickup. Jake came to greet Molly as she went to the back steps. "Hello, fella." She let her fingers linger in the thick fur at his neck.

Tommy Lee was in the office. She heard his cursing as she entered the house. Suddenly he came storming out and almost knocked her down. Upon seeing her, his eyes went wide.

Molly said, "JoEllen called. She said you're havin' computer problems."

He stared at her. His bottom lip had a small scab—and there was a bruise by his eye!

Had he and Sam come to blows? Sam hadn't said that. Molly wasn't going to ask. She dropped her gaze. "I'll go in and take a look at it," she said and slipped around him, hurrying through to the office.

She sat in the chair, heard Tommy Lee's footsteps, the swish of his jeans as he came behind her. She smelled the scent of him. Her pulse beat hard, and all of her body listened for his touch. *Just touch me, Tommy Lee.*

The computer blinked at her: bad or missing command interpreter.

Molly said, "What happened?"

"Hell, I don't know. If I knew what happened, I would have corrected it."

Tommy Lee guessed reading the instruction manual was his first mistake. Using the damn machine at all was his first mistake. Pencil and paper didn't have to be plugged in, and he'd long ago mastered the use of them. He shifted from foot to foot and looked downward at Molly's shiny, silky hair. At the creamy skin of her softly rounded shoulders showing below the curve of the sleeveless dress. He imagined putting his hand there, slipping his thumb beneath the fabric of the dress.

"Well, what accounts were you workin' with?" Molly asked. "I sort of need a place to start."

He shifted his stance again. "Uh . . ."

He pulled over the invoices he'd been working with. His arm brushed her shoulder, and he jumped slightly. Maybe she wouldn't want him touching her. He didn't want to show he cared. He wasn't the one who had walked out.

"These. I thought I'd just post 'em up, but I saved them in the wrong place. I found 'em, but, well, hell, I don't know what happened."

There was no way he could explain what he'd done. He felt foolish. The entire situation, Molly right there under his nose after all they had said to each other yesterday, acting like nothing was wrong, was confusing. He had no idea what he should do, *what he should feel*.

Molly started typing. "I told you I would go on takin' care of the business records."

He didn't have anything to say to that. Her saying that annoyed him, as did her being able to get the machine to work. As he watched, she typed as if she knew exactly what to type, and the screen changed. He turned and went into the kitchen and got a can of Coca-Cola from the refrigerator, wandered around the kitchen for a minute. He didn't want to watch her work the computer when he had such trouble with it. That did not seem the correct nature of things.

It struck him that he was glad she was there. Almost glad enough to cry, which shook him considerably.

Then suddenly Molly cried, "Oh! Tommy Lee . . . oh!"

He sprinted for the office. Molly was dancing around and hollering, "Fire! Fire!" in front of the computer, where a veil of smoke wafted out from the disk drive. "Oh, God—get the fire extinguisher," she yelled and dashed through the door.

One long stride, and Tommy Lee pulled the desk away from the wall, reached down, and jerked the computer's plug out of the receptacle. Then he had to grab the extinguisher from Molly before she soaked foam all over everything. "It's okay now." The smoke had faded to a dying spiral slithering out of the disk drive.

"Oh, my goodness," Molly said, shaking.

"It was just a little smoke," Tommy Lee said, feeling on firm ground once more. Mechanical breakdowns he could handle. He took her hand. "Here . . . sit down. Are you okay?" Molly had gone white as the wall.

"It just surprised me is all. Whoever thought a computer would catch fire?"

"It's electrical. Anything electrical can catch fire. But you never spray it with anything wet, at least not until it's unplugged."

"I know . . . you've told me. I just got so jangled. Fire just scares me."

"Bein' scared is better than bein' unprepared," Tommy Lee allowed. People who lived as far as they did from a fire department were trained by circumstances to have a healthy fear of fire. They kept fire extinguishers handy and taught the kids early how to use them.

For a few minutes they both stared at the now

innocent-looking disk drive. Tommy Lee wondered aloud if he'd done it, but Molly said she didn't think so.

"I really don't think you can get a computer to start on fire by getting the software all messed up. Maybe it was having problems and that's why you got all messed up."

Then they were gazing at each other. Her eyes were very green in the light of the office, her skin soft looking, her lips moist.

The next instant, so quickly Tommy Lee took a half step backward, Molly got to her feet and started gathering up the invoices and files, saying she would take it all down and update everything on her office computer. "If you'll carry it out to my car, I'll take the computer in for JoEllen to repair."

The wall between them had crumbled for an instant, but it was firmly in place once again, Tommy Lee thought as he lifted the machine and carried it out to the El Camino. He had just shut the car door when Molly came out of the house. They stood looking at each other, squinting in the hot sun.

Then Molly said, "I'm sorry about the other day, Tommy Lee. I said things that I didn't really mean." Her eyes looked sad and earnest.

"I know. I did, too." That seemed too little to offer, so he added, "Thanks for comin' out to try to help me today."

There, with his hands stuffed into his pockets, gazing into her luminous green eyes, his entire body sort of leaned toward her, without moving a fraction. Then she was tucking her hair behind her ear and moving away from him, murmuring, "Well, I'd better get back. I have the monthly taxes to take care of." He watched her earring sway as she ducked into the car seat.

He let her go, stood there and watched the El Camino disappear into the road dust, feeling his heart

sort of settle like the dust did, all parched and
desolate.

Tommy Lee didn't know why he didn't ask her to
stay.

A big part of him was afraid she would say no. He
thought that if she had wanted to stay, she would
have. Maybe she wanted him to ask her to stay, but he
didn't think he ought to have to ask.

Turning, he swung his fist down hard on the hood of
his old green pickup.

Molly told herself that her marriage was over. She
told herself to be practical. To look the thing in the
face and accept it. There was no way to revive the
marriage, so the quicker she let it go, the quicker she
would be over the pain.

At the office, she turned the telephone ringer back
to low and let the answering machine pick up. At the
cottage, she put the telephone in the refrigerator. She
told herself she wouldn't speak to Tommy Lee if he
begged her. They were simply too far apart now. They
had not been able to scale the wall that afternoon, and
she didn't see that they ever would. She was going to
put him behind her and walk on.

Yet, she never could bring herself to take her
wedding ring off her finger, and stubborn, painful,
annoying hope simply would not die. Hope appeared
to be like the flu virus and would simply have to run
its course, she told herself. *Hope springs eternal.* Who
was it to first say that? Whoever did say it probably
meant it more as a threat than a positive point.

And then flowers came. Roses.

Fitch Grace delivered them, in the bright yellow
Grace Florist van that he parked in the yard, in the
fork where the driveway split between her mother's
big house and the cottage, as if he hadn't been able to
decide which driveway to take.

Molly was coming home from the office, and when

she saw the van, the first thought to tumble through her mind was: Maybe Tommy Lee had sent flowers. Then she dampened that silly notion by thinking realistically that Mama had probably gotten flowers. Fitch Grace, the original owner of the flower shop who still worked in it part-time, said that it was Mama's beaus who had kept him in business during his first twenty years. Mama still got a lot of flowers. Sometimes she would have a bouquet delivered to herself.

Nevertheless, Molly found herself holding her breath, the virus of foolish hope running rampant through her veins as she removed her sunglasses and got out of the El Camino. Fitch, carrying an *enormous* bouquet of red roses, came from around the back of Mama's house. He peered around the big bouquet, as if through jungle ferns. He must not have remembered her because he said, "Are ya' Molly Hayes?" as he came toward her with a rickety gait. The bouquet got bigger and bigger.

"Yes . . . yes, I am." Molly stared at the mass of roses, crimson, just ready to bloom against the green leaves. *For me? Oh, my God.*

"Nobody to home at either place, and I wadn't sure where t' leave 'em. Here they are, fer Mol-ly Hayes."

"Thank you." She reached out and took the vase. Almost dropped it, and he helped her.

"Got it now? Want me to take it inside fer ya'?"

Molly shook her head. "No . . . I have it . . . thank you."

"Well, you'd better add a bit of water to 'em. It's a scorcher, ain't it?"

"Yes . . . I will."

The vase was cool to her hands; the fragrance of roses filled her nostrils. She went straight for the cottage, set the vase on the kitchen table. It was big. The entire arrangement was big. Grand. Roses. *Oh-mygod.* Through the window she saw the van leave.

Then she was gazing at the flowers again, heart beating like a wild thing. From Tommy Lee? Oh, my mercy.

She looked long at the note card sticking up on the plastic spear. Her name written there, but not in Tommy Lee's hand. It might have been written by whoever had taken the order at the florist. She inhaled deeply, held her breath a second, opened the card.

> *Just want you to know I'm here.*
> *Love, Sam*

Written in his own hand, quite a jerky scrawl for someone who could draw beautiful pictures. *Love, Sam.*

Molly sank slowly into the maple chair, dropped the hand holding the card into her lap, and gazed at the roses.

Oh . . . *oh!* Disappointment thick and heavy, but gladness poking at her, too. Flattered. Flattery could always be counted on.

The roses were beautiful . . . they really were. There was no way she could send them back. Florists didn't take back flowers, and the scandal should she try! She couldn't take them to Sam, either, because his feelings would be so hurt. It was wonderful that he had sent them. . . . It really was. She loved flowers. Wasn't a woman on the earth who couldn't be touched by flowers. Sam knew it. But Tommy Lee didn't. Tommy Lee didn't send them. Tommy Lee didn't want to touch her.

"What happened to us, Molly?"

The roses reached out to her with their scent. She sat there staring at the mass of sweet fragrant crimson while the warm summer breeze stirred through the back door.

Rennie came and found her like that, sitting in the

kitchen as the sun set and cast golden patches of light
where it slanted through the back screen door. With
her hand on the worn door pull, Rennie looked
through the grayness of the screen and immediately
her heart hit her shoes. She needed Molly now; she
really did. Then she gathered herself and tried to find
good sense.

"Hi, Sissy," she said, opening the screen door with
a shaking hand. She had been having too many
cigarettes and too little food for the past few days. She
made her voice light and gay, hoping she had been
wrong about Molly's mood.

Molly turned and gave a wan smile, and Rennie
thought that at least it was a smile.

Then Rennie got a full view of the flowers. "Well,
my gosh, roses! Aren't you the lucky lady. Who sent
them?" She leaned forward, inhaled their fragrance
and felt their scent seep sweetly through her body.

Molly handed her the card. Rennie read it, looked
at Molly, and raised and eyebrow. "So?" It all seemed
awfully romantic to Rennie.

"So, I don't know." Molly pushed herself up and
moved to the sink, began to make coffee.

Rennie said, "Well, it is wonderful to get roses."

Rennie had received three bouquets of roses in her
life. For a woman, at least an ordinary woman, not a
movie star or some such rich celebrity who likely got
bouquets every day of the week, each bouquet she
received remained embedded in memory—and roses!
Well, a woman held the count of the rose bouquets she
received in her heart and each detail about them in
her soul. Again Rennie was drawn to putting her nose
to a blossom and inhaling. Ah . . . their scent was
heady in the warm room.

The memories came: her first bouquet of roses from
sweet Lyle Jennings, her beau in the tenth grade. Her
second bouquet of roses Mama had given her upon
graduating college. Her third bouquet, the grandest

thing, thirty roses for her thirtieth birthday, from
Jonathan Hart, the only man she had ever truly loved,
and had let slip away. In between those times she had
received a number of single roses, or roses with
carnations, but those a woman didn't keep as close a
count on.

Rennie straightened and looked around at Molly,
who was looking so sad that she made Rennie shake.
"You haven't heard from Tommy Lee yet, have you?"

Molly shook her head.

"But these came from Sam," Rennie said encouragingly.

"Yes."

Rennie was at a loss. If roses from a man could put
Molly into such gloom, there didn't seem to be
anything puny words could say to help.

Then Molly was shaking her head. "It's all my own
fault with Tommy Lee."

"Oh, please," Rennie said, irritated. "Women always take the blame. Why can't it be on him? Any
relationship is fifty-fifty, Molly. You can't take it all."

Molly pressed back against the sink and looked at
the flowers. "No, Rennie . . . relationships are rarely
fifty-fifty. Sometimes they're sixty-forty, and sometimes twenty-eighty, and sometimes one in the relationship has to give a lot more than one hundred
percent. I was better equipped to understand and deal
with our problem simply because I am a woman.
Men . . . oh, Rennie, they have such a hard time with
it all."

She looked at Rennie. "Isn't it funny how when
you're doin' something, it's really hard to see why
you're doin' it? All you know is that you have to do it.
That's how I felt when I left Tommy Lee. . . . That's
how I've felt all these days. I told myself that I was
setting us both free. Tommy Lee just didn't seem to
care about me anymore, so I was setting him free.

"I think now, deep down in my heart, I was

countin' that he'd miss me and realize how much he needed me and loved me. I wanted him to find that out on his own, because that's the only way it's really worth anything." She spoke earnestly, knotting her fist.

Rennie went over and again put her arm around Molly. "It isn't too late yet, Sissy. It's only been just over a week. Men can be really slow, you know."

"I don't think so," Molly said, shaking her head vehemently. "I think he found out something all right. He found out that he doesn't need me, doesn't want me. Oh, Rennie, I never should have left. That was a big mistake. It was just runnin' away and leavin' him wide open to be carried away by the part of him that really did want to break away . . . and by someone like Annette. Oh, Rennie, men can be so stupid about women. They just can't see! I should have stayed and made myself indispensable to him . . . made myself someone he did love."

"You can't make people love you, Sissy. Either they do or they don't. You can't be turnin' yourself inside out, trying to be someone you're not. But I do know that Tommy Lee has been crazy about you all these years. *You,* just as you are. And if you feel you've made a mistake, nothin' is stoppin' you from gettin' in that car and drivin' out there and movin' right back in."

"No," Molly said, shaking her head, her face all filled with despair. "No. I just can't. I can't go, knowin' he doesn't want me."

Rennie felt helpless. She wished Molly would get straightened out because she had her own problems, and she needed Molly to help her have courage. Rennie felt really badly for feeling all of this. And she felt Molly sinking and herself going after her.

"Let's go up to the cafe and get some fried chicken and onion rings," she said.

*   *   *

Tommy Lee lined up and hit the two and three and seven balls into pockets on the same shot. The two and three balls went into the same corner pocket, while the seven went into the side.

He had gotten so good at pool now that he could earn a living at it. He had returned to playing pool at Rodeo Rio's every day around four o'clock, when the place was all but deserted. He did this partly because he was truly addicted to the game now. It was the only thing that seemed to fill his mind too full to think of Molly. And he did it partly because he wasn't going to let the possible presence of Sam run him off. He figured he had as much right to be at Rio's as Sam did—more, he guessed, because he hadn't been the one to betray a best friend. The way Tommy Lee saw it, it was his duty to come into Rio's and be an annoyance to Sam.

Sam had only shown up twice, though, and each time he hadn't lingered. He'd spoken to Winn and gone back out again, never saying a word to Tommy Lee, which Tommy Lee considered remarkably intelligent on Sam's part. It was a comfort to think he was keeping Sam from Rio's.

Annette arrived for her night shift and came right over to him. "Do you want another beer?"

Tommy Lee pointed to his glass, said he still had some, and began racking the balls again. He didn't look at Annette, but he knew that she looked at him before she went away and busied herself with whatever it was she had to do to get ready for later in the evening.

The one real complication with coming to Rio's to enjoy pool and annoy Sam was Annette. She would push her big breasts out in front of his nose and touch him whenever she had the chance and simply just waft around him like a hot Gulf breeze. Tommy Lee would have had to admit to being a little flattered, but he was mostly nervous as a buck deer at hunting season. Being nervous struck him as being childish, so he set himself to ignore it.

After a while, Annette came over again, lit up a cigarette, and used the ashtray setting on the table with his beer. She asked him if he wanted a steak, and he said he wasn't too hungry and kept his eyes on the table.

Then she said, "Sam sent Molly two dozen red roses today."

That made Tommy Lee look at her, in spite of himself. He quickly put his gaze back on the pool table and tried to figure out which ball he'd been thinking of shooting, while the words "Sam bought Molly roses" kept echoing around in his head.

Annette just stood there smoking and looking at him. Tommy Lee didn't intend to enter into the conversation with her, but her saying something like that irritated him so much that he found himself saying, "You're a wealth of information." He hit the five ball with his cue; it missed the pocket.

"I just thought you ought to know," Annette said. "My friend, Leanne, works at Grace Florist, and she told me. Mr. Grace only had half a dozen roses left when Sam ordered them, and Sam thought those were poor anyway, so he had Mr. Grace send a special truck to the market in Dallas and get what he wanted fresh. It cost a bundle, too."

Tommy Lee couldn't think of a thing to say to any of it and came to the conclusion he'd rather be silent. For about five minutes, Annette stood there, as if expecting something from him, and then she finally walked off, her hips swaying like a clock pendulum.

Tommy Lee kept hitting balls, kept lining up his shots and hitting the balls into the pockets. He moved with rhythm, like a machine, *crack crack* as the balls hit each other and *kerplunk kerplunk* as they fell into the pockets, never taking his gaze off the green felt of the table. When the table was empty, he fished out the balls, set them up, and went at it again, all with an economy of motion.

All of a sudden he looked up and saw that at least six people had gathered round to watch. "Man, you're good," one man said.

Tommy Lee put down his pool cue and walked away. Annette was at the cash register. He threw a ten-dollar bill on the counter as he passed.

"Tommy Lee."

He stopped and turned. She leaned forward, giving him a good look.

"I'm sorry about you and Molly," she said. "If you want company, I can get off . . . now, or any time. We don't have to talk. Sometimes a person just needs another warm body around. No strings, either."

Tommy Lee just shook his head. "Thanks anyway."

He went out, jumped into the Corvette, threw gravel as he peeled out of the lot, shifted hard, and went flying down the highway.

He drove and drove, and then he found himself driving past Aunt Hestie's cottage and then back by it again. Molly's El Camino wasn't there the first time and was there the second time. He slowed down, gazing at the cottage with the faint glow of light showing in the windows. Then he pressed the accelerator and roared away.

Molly would have to get straight about Sam on her own, he thought. He wasn't going to interfere. Molly was the one making her own choices. Besides, what could he do to top two dozen of the finest roses brought up from Dallas? Nothing. He wasn't even going to try. He'd look foolish if he tried. He didn't think he ought to have to try.

"Wait a minute, Rennie!"

Molly took up the big vase of roses and hurried out the screen door after her sister. Her wrapped robe fell open and off one shoulder. It wasn't yet seven in the morning. Rennie had stayed the night and was leaving early in order to get to her own home, shower, and change before she had to teach class.

"Take these, Rennie. You'll enjoy them a lot more than I will."

Rennie looked surprised. "Oh, Sissy, don't do this."

Molly ignored her and went right on around to the passenger side. "Open the door for me."

Rennie followed, protesting, "Maybe these aren't from Tommy Lee, but you can still enjoy them. They can still comfort you." She opened the door.

"They are beautiful, and I have enjoyed them," Molly said. "Now I want you to enjoy them. They came from a dear friend, and I'm passing them on to my dearest friend—they suit you much more than they do me, anyway. Think of them as my thank-you for stayin' with me last night. *You* comforted me." Molly set them in the passenger seat, propped between Rennie's big bag of a purse and her briefcase. "You'll have to be careful on the turns."

Rennie stood there a moment longer and watched Molly pull her robe back around herself. She felt guilty. She still hadn't told Molly that the real reason she had stayed all night was that she had been frightened of going home. She didn't think it would help to confess that now. She kissed Molly's cheek, then got behind the wheel and started slowly away, intent on protecting the roses. She wasn't as foolish as Molly to give up two dozen roses, no matter who they came from. One of Rennie's fantasies was to soak in a sunken tub surrounded by masses of roses whose petals fell into the water to scent it.

Molly stood back, one hand across her middle while waving with the other. Then, feeling suddenly bereft, she walked back inside the cottage.

The table looked strangely empty without the huge bouquet.

For a moment Molly thought she might have cour-

age enough to call Tommy Lee, but her courage
deserted her as soon as she lifted the telephone
receiver. She did take the telephone into the bathroom with her, though, and set it on the floor while
she showered.

She paused, gazing at herself in the mirror. She had
decided on a course, she thought. She hadn't really
decided what she should do, but she had decided what
she was *not* going to do.

19

❖ ❖

Early Summer Rain

Light rain sprinkled the windshield. Rennie found herself crying, and when she saw the rain, she cried harder, which made absolutely no sense. She wasn't the one who was estranged from her husband and who had just turned away a lover's advance.

Rennie knew then what she was crying over—she wished there was a man crazy enough over her to send her two dozen roses. Having two dozen roses now riding along beside her, given to her by her sister, simply served to point up the fact that the only man in her life at the moment wanted to knock her teeth out. And the only man who had ever given her an enormous bouquet of roses she had turned away from because she'd been so afraid of having her heart broken. Being afraid of having a broken heart had made her jump ahead and make certain she had one.

With a blurred windshield and blurred vision, she pulled into the Texaco station. Intent on caring for the roses, a few of which were rubbing on the seat back, she drove so slowly that a car behind her honked angrily. This made her jump and glance in the rear-

249

view mirror, and in doing that, she then bounced the rear tire up over the curb. The vase of roses wobbled precariously, and she reached out to grab them and almost ran into the gas pump island before she got stopped.

Heart beating fast and tears startled away, Rennie sat there a moment to catch her breath. Then she pulled up to the front pump, filled her tank, since she was right there, and went in and paid and got the cigarettes, bottle of juice, and two packages of peanuts she had stopped for in the first place. When she came out, there was Sam Ketchum, just getting out of a brown Bronco parked right behind Rennie's Mustang.

Rennie stood there a moment, in the humid, after-rain air, with the sudden thought that it was like something out of the movies. There was Sam, standing on the wet blacktop, looking at her. Tall, lean, every inch a man to grab a woman's eye and make her long for his touch.

And here she had his roses—roses he had given another woman—in her car. Here he was smiling at her and saying hello in that sexy way of his. Of all the people she would happen to run into, here he was, coming over to speak to her, holding the door for her as she slipped into the seat. Surely he'd see the roses through the windshield.

"We need this rain," he said.

"I suppose," Rennie answered. "I still don't like it. It makes everything sticky." He was looking down at her, not through the windshield.

Then he asked about Molly, casually but with an intent look in his eye.

Rennie said, "She's okay, I guess."

Just then he crouched down, and his gaze went past her and right to the roses. Rennie watched his dark eyes focus on the flowers and saw the shadows of confusion and pain there. Her heart squeezed. Then he looked questioningly at her.

"She loved the flowers, Sam. She took them as a comfort from a friend, but they can't be anything else to her. Her heart's crowded right now."

It was the best Rennie could do. She bit back saying she was sorry, which she didn't think would do anything but add to hurt pride. He was the saddest-looking thing, and she ached to take him into her arms and nestle him against her breasts.

A dismal crooked smile crossed his lips and he kind of shook his head. "Some things just aren't meant to be, I guess."

"Seems like it," Rennie said with a large sigh, thinking of how many times she'd said that to herself. She had felt the same pain and wished so very much that there was something she could do to ease him.

Then they were looking at each other, sharing, frankly and sorrowfully, and then curiously.

Rennie said, "My heart isn't crowded at all, Sam, just in case you'd like to know."

His dark eyes sort of jumped, as if she'd startled him. Then he said, "I appreciate the information."

She thought she saw possible interest. She really did think so, maybe.

"If you get at loose ends, you call me, Sam. I'm in the book."

He gave a little nod. "I'll remember that."

They said good-bye, and as she drove away, Rennie found sight of him in her side-view mirror. He was gazing after her. She smiled, remembered his words: "I appreciate the information." Not many men would have come back with such a turn of words.

When she got well out of town, she pulled over, flipped open her cellular phone and dialed Molly.

Molly answered breathlessly, expectantly, making Rennie say, "It's me, Molly, I'm sorry."

Rennie told her about running into Sam and him seeing the flowers.

"How did he seem about it?" Molly asked, intense and melancholy at the same time.

"He took it okay. Disappointed, but okay."

Rennie didn't tell Molly that she had told Sam to call her sometime. Maybe she was afraid that despite everything, Molly wouldn't like it. Or maybe she didn't want to seem silly about the hope that had suddenly begun to grow again in her heart. She'd been so long without hope.

20

❖❖

Wild Angels

After being so stubborn about having her own office, Molly could not get herself together to get to it. She awoke before the alarm went off and lay there, thinking that she had to get dressed and off to work. But there seemed to be little point to it, or even to breathing. Why breathe? Tommy Lee didn't want her, so why want herself? There was a part of her spirit that got very impatient with this selfish attitude, but that part of her spirit still couldn't seem to get her to the office. She was yet wandering around the cottage in her robe when a car came down the drive, horn blaring like a tornado siren.

Peering out the window, Molly saw that it was her mother driving her black Lincoln, and Kaye was on the passenger side. Startled, Molly clutched her robe around herself and raced out to see what the matter was.

Mama poked her head out the car window. "Get in."

"What is it? What's wrong?" Bending, she looked across at Kaye, who was frowning darkly.

"Why aren't you dressed?" Kaye said. She gestured

at Mama, who was in her fuchsia robe. "Good Lord, am I the only one in this family who believes it is necessary to get dressed in the morning? It's after ten, for heavensakes. Maybe you're self-employed, Molly, but you need a routine."

While Kaye was going on, Molly glanced down in the seat and saw the Hardee's bags. "Mama . . ." Molly started, but Mama gestured.

"Just get in. I have somethin' to show you."

Molly got in the backseat. "What is it?"

"You'll see," Mama said mysteriously.

"Oh, Lordy, yes, you'll see," Kaye said. "It's important enough for Mama to race back home and get you but not take time to put on clothes. You both should put clothes on, Mama."

"A robe is classified as clothes," Mama said.

She was backing at breakneck speed, turning and making marks in the lawn. Molly braced herself in the seat and hoped that her mother didn't intend to show her something where she had to get out of the car. It was one thing for stately and eccentric Odessa Collier to go around town in a fuchsia robe that went from neck to feet and quite another for Molly, not nearly so stately and, until now anyway, not known as eccentric and whose robe was thin cotton and only came just below her knees anyway.

She wished very much for her sunglasses as Mama drove down Main Street toward the end of town and pulled to a stop in the parking lot of the VFW hall.

"Look," Mama said, and at first Molly thought she meant the VFW hall, which Molly didn't want to look at because looking at it made her feel nauseous. But then she saw Mama pointing in the opposite direction.

Highly curious, Molly followed the line of her mother's finger, which pointed across the street and upward . . . at the water tower. Men working, sanders going, half of the tower down to metal.

Then . . . there in faint red lettering were the words TOMMY LEE LOVES MOLLY.

Molly peered harder, making certain she did see what she thought she saw. The words were faint, uncovered from the years and layers of paint but readable, just like the memory now floating up from the deep recesses of her mind.

She recalled the girls at school: "Did you see?" "We saw on the way to school." "Gosh, Tommy Lee must really be wild for you." Tommy Lee never said a word. He would only grin.

When Molly could get away at lunch, she had raced the two blocks east, where she had a good view of the water tower. Even when Tommy Lee would not say the words to her, he had painted them up there, for all to see. She had cried over it.

Kaye's voice broke through Molly's thoughts, ". . . terrible, havin' words like that up where little children and old ladies can see. It would have gone faster if they could have sandblasted, but Walter said Dave Hawkins advised against it."

The four-letter words had been painted in black, while the TOMMY LEE LOVES MOLLY and the GARY LOVES PATTY and the GO TIGERS had been in red, green, and orange respectively.

"I imagine most kids and old ladies are familiar with those words," Mama said, then added, "Tommy Lee sure used good paint. He always was a man to know quality."

It had been lead paint in those days, and Tommy Lee had put it on with a brush, not a spray can like kids used today. Molly's heartbeat raced, and her eyes teared, and she kept on staring even after Mama began to pull back onto the street.

Tommy Lee was coming out of Ryder's Auto Parts when he passed Walter going in. This was a surprise, because Tommy Lee had never known Walter to have any need of an auto part. Tommy Lee would not have thought that Walter could identify an auto part.

"Hello, Walter."

Walter's eyes met Tommy Lee's briefly, then skittered shyly away. "Hi, Tommy Lee." He bobbed his head, rubbed his finger aside his nose. "How you been?" He took the door Tommy Lee held for him.

"Okay, I guess. Are you havin' trouble with one of your cars?"

Tommy Lee was about to offer to fix it. He always felt like he wanted to be nice to Walter. It seemed like Walter being married to Kaye should be enough for any man to take. In fact, that Walter could hold up under Kaye made Tommy Lee have a great deal of respect for the man.

"No . . . no," Walter gestured, "Ryder's on the town council."

"Oh, yeah . . . well, have a good one." Tommy Lee continued on down the steps, but at Walter's call, he stopped, turned, and looked upward. He really hoped Walter wasn't going to say anything about him and Molly, but seeing the way Walter pulled vigorously at his ear, he figured it was going to be some sort of condolence.

But Walter said, "Uh, have you seen the water tower recently?"

"No . . ." Tommy Lee answered, curious.

"Well, you might want to drive down that way and take a look at it. There's somethin' there you might want to see. Uh . . . you might better do it right away."

"Okay, Walter," Tommy Lee said, puzzled. He started to ask just what it was he was supposed to see when Walter bobbed his head and slipped quickly inside the store, as if he suddenly felt the need to run.

Curiosity tugged at Tommy Lee. What could Walter think was interesting about the water tower? Walter was somewhat of an odd and simple fellow, he thought as he headed his old pickup out onto the street. Maybe the water tower simply being there was enough to captivate Walter. Sometimes at gatherings with Molly's family, Tommy Lee and Walter would chat a bit—Walter was about the only one Tommy Lee ever really did talk to—but even that wasn't a lot of conversation, because most of Walter's interests in life seemed to center around fruit trees and classical music, and Tommy Lee didn't know much nor care about either.

He spied the water tower through the Chevy's old dirty windshield. Men were working on it, which he had seen before. Maybe that's what Walter had wanted him to see.

Then he saw it. TOMMY LEE LOVES MOLLY.

He leaned forward and peered hard through the glare and film of the glass. The lettering was patchy and faded, but still readable.

The next instant he saw the rear end of a station wagon approaching at a fast rate of speed. He jammed on the brakes, then sat there gripping the wheel with sweaty palms and berating himself for poor driving.

Keeping his eyes on the road, he drove past the water tower and pulled off onto the shoulder. He twisted and looked through the back window . . . up at the water tower, hazy in the sun and with old paint whizzing off it.

He had been fifteen, almost sixteen. The days of his invincible youth. He had climbed up the tower ladder with a half-filled gallon of paint, and the wire handle had cut into his hand. It had been just after midnight, in the summer like now, although he didn't recall the date. Man, how sweaty his hand had gotten on the rungs of that ladder. If he had thought at all of the possibility that he might fall to his death, the thought had been a fleeting thing. He had been intent on impressing Molly. He could still remember the look of surprise and awe on her face when she had seen what he had done. The way she had looked at him, like he was next to God. After all these years, covered over by several layers of paint, the words remained: TOMMY LEE LOVES MOLLY.

As he watched, a workman began sanding away the *T*.

Turning forward, he shifted into gear and headed back out on the road. The next thing he knew, he was turning the Chevy into the gravel lot of Smith's Fruit Stand and Nursery. He had gone four miles and not remembered anything along the way.

He came to a stop in front of the stand's red-and-white awnings flapping in the wind and found himself staring at lines of flowering plants. He got out, went over, and walked down a row of tiny bushes, until he came to some with small yellow flowers. Really pretty delicate flowers. Molly liked yellow flowers.

"You wantin' some roses?"

Tommy Lee looked up. A withered old woman almost hidden beneath a straw hat came toward him. She looked more like a man, dressed in overalls and with a mustache, but he decided she was a woman because of her voice and the pink shirt.

"Is that what these are?" he asked. He'd thought so, but he wasn't certain. They looked so small.

"Yes, siree. Miniatures. Keep 'em on the porch or in the house, or most anywhere." That she could lift the pot so easily amazed him. "These's my favorite. Ain't they the prettiest thing? Dainty and refined, yep, my favorite. Hello, there, little honey." The old woman tilted her head, talking to the plant now, telling it how beautiful it was and how she loved it.

Tommy Lee bent and snatched up a plant. "I'll take this one."

He drove off with the little thing on the floorboard. Every now and then he looked down at it. It shimmied with the motion of the old truck. It had cost him under eight dollars, another eight for the fancy basket

he'd had the woman stick it in, all of which was a far
sight less than the cost of two dozen big red beauties.
But this bush was a living thing. When those big red
beauties wilted, this would still be blooming. Molly
liked living plants.

He took the plant in and sat it on the workbench in
his shop. He turned on the radio, but the plant
seemed to quiver, so he turned down the sound and
moved the plant away from the speakers. Debating
the wisdom of giving the little bush to Molly, he went
to work on the engine for which he'd bought the parts.
The plant sat there and seemed to keep waving to
him. He got worried about it dying in the heat, so he
closed the shop up and turned on the air-
conditioning.

He couldn't see himself simply going up to Molly
and giving her the plant. That certainly wasn't much,
after she'd received two dozen red roses, delivered.
The memory of how he'd climbed up to paint the
water tower all to impress Molly kept playing at the
edges of his mind.

It occurred to him that he had not set out to
impress Molly in a long time. Impressing her had
gotten covered over by a lot of living, he guessed. And
the truth be known, he didn't see that a man should
have to keep impressing the woman he married.
Apparently, however, these things were important to
a woman.

Maybe they were important to a man, too, he
thought. Maybe it was all these crazy little things in
life that kept the life in a person.

Finally he threw down his tools and wiped his
hands and went into the house to shower and change.
Then he got the little rose plant and set it on the
floorboard of the Corvette. When he drove past her
office and saw she wasn't there, he was at first relieved
because he didn't want to try to give the plant to her
in so public a place, in case she threw it at him or

something. Molly never had been one to throw things, but then she never had been known to break dishes, either. He simply didn't know where he stood with her.

As he drove on out to the cottage, he began to get worried that she wouldn't be there. Maybe she was out with Sam. He might have to shoot Sam, he thought.

This worry about her being with Sam was relieved, however, when he reached the cottage and saw the El Camino sitting beside it. He stopped at the entry to the drive and debated what to do. It appeared to him that his options were limited, since he couldn't drop out of the sky or anything, so he continued on down the driveway. On impulse he cut the engine and let the car coast, having the hope Molly wouldn't hear him coming. He thought it would be best to simply appear at her door. It seemed to him that would be a little impressive.

Taking up the rose bush, he got out of the Corvette and stood gazing at the cottage. The windows were all up, and he heard music playing. He suddenly thought he could smell the scent of Molly. And just as suddenly he knew what he had come for. *What he had to have.*

He went to the back door and peered through the screen. For an instant he had a strange feeling of having been in a similar predicament on the night he had caught his father and Odessa in the cottage, which should have been a lesson to him about sneaking and spying through open doors.

The kitchen was dim. Late afternoon sunlight made patterns on the refrigerator and cabinets. He didn't see Molly or the two dozen roses, and he didn't hear any voices. He did have the distinct impression the cottage was telling him to go away.

Ace the cat suddenly appeared at the door and meowed, and Tommy Lee about jumped out of his skin. Quickly he set the little rose plant on the bottom step, scratched on the screen to get Ace to meow again, and then strode quickly back to the shade of the big elm trees. He leaned against the trunk of one, propped himself, and gazed toward the cottage. His blood was running warm and he thought of touching Molly.

The next instant he was startled when he saw an image shimmering behind the black window screen, not Molly's face, but the face of an old woman looking angrily at him. Then it was gone, as the evening sunlight shifted through the trees and made moving patterns across the cottage walls and windows.

Molly's voice: "Oh, Ace . . . I'll let you out."

Her shadow appeared behind the screen, and it swung open. Molly stood there, looking downward at the little bush. The yellow sunlight turned her hair to gold and played warmly over her face, down her body, down her legs that were bare beneath a big denim shirt.

Tommy Lee stared at her legs.

His gaze drifted down her pale thighs and to her bare feet. He felt his blood run harder as she came slowly down the steps and bent over the little bush. The shirttail rode up high on her creamy thigh.

Then she was lifting the pot, reverently, as if it were a golden chalice. Her face came up and she looked straight at him.

He straightened and took hold of his courage. "Hello, Molly."

"Hello."

Molly held the pot hard against her fluttering heart, feeling as if she needed to hold on to something. She felt, too, that she held a treasure to be protected. She stood there and watched him saunter toward her, his muscles firm, his movement fluid, his eyes intent upon her.

He stopped when still ten feet from her, cocked his head slightly, and perused her with a gaze that made her tingle all over. His eyes were dark blue, blue as summer evening sky.

Molly had the sensation of glass walls cracking around her and fresh breezes beginning to blow. Suddenly, in a hot flush all over, she knew exactly what she wanted, and she knew as clearly as if he'd yelled it at her what Tommy Lee had come for.

She looked downward at the little flowers of the bush because right that instant it was much easier to look at the plant. Her heart was pounding and she grew warm in intimate places.

"You like the plant then?" Tommy Lee asked, a silly question like he could ask.

"I love it," she said, raising her eyes to his.

"The old woman said it was a miniature rose bush. That it could be kept anywhere. I thought you might like that . . . that it was a living thing and would keep on blooming."

She thought then that he knew about the flowers Sam had sent her. She said, "Yes, I do. . . . I love it."

His eyes were intent on her. Searching her.

"Would you like to come inside?"

His gaze shifted to the cottage for an instant. He shook his head. "Walk out back with me."

Her heart caught. "Well, okay. I have to get pants and shoes on first."

She raced back inside the cottage, pulse pounding. She feared he wouldn't wait. She jerked on her jeans, slipped into her shoes. *Silly to be so flustered.* She stopped to dab Chanel down her breast. Another dab for good measure, and all the while she was thinking about Tommy Lee and how he felt against her.

Back through the kitchen she grabbed up the little rose bush from the table where she'd set it. She didn't even realize she had taken it up, until she stood once more on the stoop, holding it close to her breast.

There was strain on his face. But it eased when she walked toward him. Without a word they walked together out to the wooden fence. They stood there, and Molly, heart pounding and every cell in her body screaming for his touch, began to wonder if Tommy Lee was going to say anything. Was he going to *do* anything?

She began to get impatient, and panicky, thinking maybe nothing would come of it, and that she was likely to die if she didn't get to have him. The sun was a red ball far in the west, painting things golden. It really was pretty, and here they were standing in it, getting hotter and hotter. Longing so much for him that she thought she might cry.

She was to the point of just telling him what she wanted, when Tommy Lee moved and slipped through the fence. She could not imagine why he did that. He turned back to her, took the rose bush from her and set it on the ground, took her hand and tugged her through, then led her over to the barn.

"Tommy Lee . . . what . . ."

He stopped her there, in the bright red-gold light pouring over the barn front. "Just don't say anything, okay, Molly?"

He took her face between his calloused palms. The wanting he saw jump into her eyes startled him. Gratified him.

He kissed her.

Instantly he was on fire, hauling her tight against him, pressing her against his groin. He went at her hard, and she came back at him just as hard. He was somewhat startled by her passion, but then he fell deeper into her moist eager lips and trembling hands. He fell deeper into her sweet perfume and sweet woman scent and hot muskiness of mating humans and ripe summer earth. *Good Lord Almighty,* and it was a prayer.

He shoved her against the wood planks of the barn

gate and went at her, kissed her again and again and again, until they were both feverish and out of breath, and he was about to burst right through his jeans.

It was Molly who took his hand, opened the gate that kept the horse out of the hay, slipped through, and led Tommy Lee with her. He sat on stacked bales, spread his legs, and pulled her between them. The pressure of her gave him a brief ease. He lifted her shirt and kissed the warm, silky skin. She moaned and pushed her belly at him. He fumbled with the button of her jeans. She quivered. He paused to savor the quiver with his hands, and his lips. He went lower with his lips.

"Tommy Lee . . . *please* . . ."

"Oh, Molly . . ."

He jerked his shirt off and spread it for her, spread his jeans and hers, but never got beyond getting her shirt unbuttoned.

She was beneath him, coming to him with with a luxurious sigh that made him glad to be a man. Her scent surrounded him, and her skin slid sweaty beneath him. Her breath caressed his ear as she moaned urgently. She spread her legs for him and pushed at him. She was ready. He felt the golden beams of sun on his back, and his blood burned in his groin.

There was no going sweet, no going easy. It was hot and sweaty and earthy, the sun setting the barn and the hay and him and Molly on fire. They had both come a long way since the first time in this very barn. They both knew the notes of pleasure in each other's body and how to play them. It came to him, as he shoved into her whimpering, quivering, eager body that this was what he had been needing for months.

"Molly . . . I can't hold . . ."

She covered his mouth with her own and wrapped her legs around his hips. The last thing he heard was her calling his name in conjunction with God's, before he heard only the roar of blood and heat and pounding need.

Molly felt thoroughly, deliciously wrung out. She stretched languidly and cracked her eyes to see that the setting sun cast a rosy glow into the barn. It was as if the rosy glow came from her and Tommy Lee. She kept her nose turned against him, inhaling his virile scent, and kept her body pressed tight against his, savoring the heat and the sweat and the memory of what he'd just done to her.

Had it ever been like this? Oh, Lord, thank you! Oh, maybe now I can go on living a while longer.

But passion cannot, no matter how magical the moment, be sustained indefinitely. There always came valleys after mountain tops. Marker came peeking in at them, and as soon as he awoke from dozing, Tommy Lee began to twitch and rub his feet together. Shortly he began kissing her shoulder and a bit after that he was on his feet, slapping at his back. "Geez, the mosquitoes are comin' out."

Molly lay there and watched him in the light of the setting sun. He was naked, except for his socks. He grinned at her, blushing as he reached for his jeans. She sat up and pulled her shirt together, began buttoning it.

"We should make a shrine out of this place," he said as he zipped up his jeans.

He spoke low and huskily, and she looked over to see him cast her a shy smile. She smiled back at him.

And then she went to him, pressed herself tight against his chest. "Thank you, Tommy Lee."

His arms tightened around her. "Thank you, darlin'."

He hadn't called her darlin' in so long. He held her and kissed the top of her head.

Molly wished they could hold on to each other

forever and was annoyed when Tommy Lee pulled away. How long could a couple hold each other? How much heat could they endure? How long before their legs gave out and mosquitoes ate them up? Molly didn't care at all for reality, which seemed to be crashing down on her.

While Tommy Lee put on his shirt, she tugged on her jeans and slipped into her shoes. She left him searching for his boots from where he'd thrown them and went out the barn gate, hurrying. She picked up her rose bush at the fence and walked quickly across the shadowy ground beneath the elms and in the back door of the dark cottage, where music still played softly.

Tommy Lee wondered at Molly's abrupt departure, as he stomped his left foot into his boot. He couldn't think of what he had done to anger her . . . but maybe she wasn't angry. Maybe she was simply being practical and getting away from the heat and mosquitoes.

He straightened, looked down at the strewn hay and then up at the orange horizon. He tried to imprint the past moments into his memory, having a feeling that he would need the memory, not wanting it to get away, as had the one so long ago.

It had been somewhat barbaric, he thought, a little awed at the passion that had taken hold of him. He thought that it was a good thing such passion didn't take hold of a man every day, because like as not, he'd be dead quite quickly. Sweet death, he supposed, as he walked slowly toward the cottage.

He searched the window screens, black squares in the cottage walls now, but he didn't see any old women's faces. A soft light fell out the back door, and faint music came with it. He stood there a moment, gathering himself to go inside, thinking of how Molly had raced away from the barn.

Inside he found her watering the little rose bush. His gaze slipped down the neckline of her shirt, where it hung loose and he could see her pale flesh. He remembered how her skin had looked in the glow of the setting sun. How it had felt beneath his hand . . . beneath his body.

Then he glanced back into the living room and wondered where Sam's roses were, if they weren't anywhere in the cottage. He wasn't going to ask. She offered him some ice tea, and he said that would be nice. It seemed strange to be talking about ice tea with her scent and sweat still clinging to him.

When her gaze met his, he knew she was remembering how they had been only a few minutes earlier.

"Let's take it out on the front porch," he suggested, experiencing again that peculiar sensation that something was about to fly off the cottage wall and hit him.

He had assumed that, after what had just happened between them, Molly would quickly pack herself up and come home, but he began to fear that he had been jumping to conclusions. She didn't seem as if she was going to pack.

Instead, the two of them sat on the small wicker settee—so old and fine that Tommy Lee was careful when he sat and didn't move much either—on the screened porch of the cottage where Molly now resided, having cold glasses of sweet tea and watching the sky shift from red to coral to purple and saying stupid things like: "The sky is beautiful . . . mosquitoes are thick this year . . . cicadas are loud," while the heat of passion was still whispering around them.

Tommy Lee decided he was absolutely not going to ask Molly to come home. He sure hoped she said something. He laid his arm along the back of the settee and made circles on her shoulder with his thumb, while he thought up a dozen ideas of what to say but couldn't get any of it to his tongue.

After what seemed an eternity, she said softly, "Maybe we can love each other but not live together."

"I thought we were doin' okay a few minutes ago," he said. "In fact, I thought we were livin' together mighty well."

"We were"—and she smiled a smile she tried to hold back—"but that isn't everything, Tommy Lee."

"It's a hell of a lot." He felt her blush, felt the heat in her eyes. He knew she was thinking about it and still feeling him inside her and thinking about doing it again, just as he was. He kept circling his thumb on her shoulder, needing to keep touching her.

She said, "You thought that we had sex, so everything was going to be okay."

"It seems logical, Molly." He started to get mad, mad enough to say, "Especially the kind of sex we just had. God, Molly, I know you felt what I did." He drew his arm from around her then and leaned forward.

"I did," she said in a hoarse whisper.

They sat there, each falling into taut silence. He was glad she had admitted it. He'd begun to worry that maybe he'd been mistaken. He felt more confused than ever, however, and he thought hard, trying to figure out what he was leaving undone. "Molly, what do you want me to do?"

She didn't know what to tell him. She had begged him often in the past year to spend more time with her. She had tried to explain that she needed him. Each time he would get angry at her, then would end up promising to give her more of his time, and she knew he tried, he really did, but it was his having to try that hurt most of all. She didn't want him to have to *try* to be attentive. And somehow whatever he gave her wasn't enough. How could she say that to him?

"I don't think there is anything you can do," she said. "It's me, Tommy Lee."

After a long minute he said, "You've been like this since Colter went off to college."

"It was before . . . only I just never had time to think of it. The kids kept me busy." Then she added, "They filled the hole."

She sat very still, waiting for him to leave, because she knew he was going to.

Tommy Lee got up and went to the screen door. When it simply fell off in his hand, he was momentarily startled away from his anger.

"We haven't gotten it fixed," Molly said. "Rennie and I just propped it up there. It still more or less keeps out flies and mosquitoes."

Tommy Lee shifted the door aside, tossed the melted ice from his glass outside, and set the glass on the plant stand. He didn't know what to do then. He had intended to just leave, but the broken screen door had somehow distracted him from a grand exit.

Finally he said, "It's been fun," and left, striding out and around to his Corvette.

Molly watched his back disappear into the darkness. Then she put her head down on her arms. She felt as if all life were leaving her. She thought of running after him, but that just didn't seem right. She had to let him go. She could not try to change him for her needs. That wasn't fair, and it would never work anyway. Good Lord, they were entering middle age. Neither of them could change.

A limb snapped, and she jerked upward. Tommy Lee came striding back into the faint light.

He gazed down at her, and then his hand came up and he pointed a finger at her.

"Okay," he said. "We'll just do it your way. You know where I am, when you're ready to come home. I'll *wait*."

The next instant he crouched in front of her, grabbed her head, and kissed her soundly, taking her breath and her senses.

"You know where to find more of that any time you want it." Then he stalked off again.

Molly started crying. Jumping to her feet, she pushed out the doorway and called after him, "You know where to find it, too!"

21

Life's A Dance

The next morning Tommy Lee called Molly and woke her before the sun was fully up. She had to roll out of bed, sending Ace flying with a loud meow, and find the telephone.

"You awake?" Tommy Lee said, laughter in his voice.

"I am now." But maybe she wasn't, she thought as she wandered with the phone. Maybe she was dreaming. Was that really Tommy Lee?

"Well, I'm awake. I'm havin' breakfast . . . sausage and eggs and biscuits. And I'm naked, darlin' . . . and willin'."

His voice held all the memories from the previous evening, and they came through the telephone line and down Molly's spine, making her begin to throb.

"Where would you get biscuits?" She lowered herself to the sofa edge, her legs feeling weak. Her legs suddenly feeling Tommy Lee's hands upon them.

"It is amazin' what they can do with frozen food. Heat 'em up, put butter on 'em . . . umm, good."

"You are actually heatin' yourself biscuits?"

"A man can do a lot of things, with the correct

motivation. I think yesterday was a prime example of that."

Molly didn't know what to say. This was Tommy Lee, talking to her like this?

"Well, I just called to wish you good mornin'," he said. "And to let you know what you are missin'. You have a good day."

"You, too, Tommy Lee," she said at first faintly, ending ardently.

Molly slowly replaced the receiver. Her heart beat rapidly. She went into the kitchen, got a glass of water, and dribbled it onto the tiny rose bush. With the tip of one finger, she touched the edge of a blossom and gazed at it.

He had called her. Her heart swelled and she felt a tremendous smile all over. *Oh, my, he had called her.*

She had to wonder why he had never done this when she had been home . . . never gotten her breakfast or suggested sex first thing in the morning. She had. She had worn a sexy nightgown and asked him to have breakfast with her, and he was always too busy.

Mama used to say that it was up to a woman to make a man chase her. Molly never had understood that, never had cared for the attitude. Why would people need to play games? Also, she had been with Tommy Lee since way before the age of chasing; he never had had to go looking for her. She had always been hanging on to him.

She thought all this as she set the rose bush into the morning sunlight on the back step. She stood there, looking out over the trees and pasture.

Was she making Tommy Lee chase her now? she wondered. Was that all this was? She didn't like the idea. Well, maybe she did, a little bit. It made her feel vibrant, powerful. So much a woman.

She didn't have much faith in it, though. What would happen once the chasing stopped? That was the trouble with playing games. It was much better all around to be open and know exactly where one stood. But this was fun. And maybe it was good for Tommy Lee, too. Was that what Mama had meant?

Mama knew! She had not even been home when Tommy Lee had come the evening before, but she knew that Molly had had sex with him.

"It shows," Mama said airily. "After a woman has had a wondrous affair, the emotion makes her glow. For you to glow like that, it had to be Tommy Lee, because he is the man you want so badly." Her eyes twinkled, and she added, "Besides, I came home from Wichita Falls and saw Tommy Lee's Corvette here. I left, so I wouldn't inhibit you two. Still, it shows on you, always does after a woman has been . . ."

Molly jolted up straight. "Mama, I really don't want to talk basic with you."

Mama shrugged. "I know all about it, Molly. You won't shock me."

Molly knew virtually nothing would shock her mother; her mother had long ago perfected not being shocked.

They were having breakfast in Mama's kitchen. Molly had brought over her brewed coffee, and together they made toast, neither feeling like running up to Hardee's. The days were growing so warm that even the mornings dawned sticky and lazy.

"I could go home now," Molly said. "Tommy Lee would like me to."

Her mother raised an eyebrow and waited.

"He's payin' me attention now, but after I was home a few days, everything would fall back into the same pattern. I don't want that. I want to get an understanding."

"It's been my experience that the ground for understanding between men and women is poor," Mama said dryly. "The best way for us to go is accepting.

Then one doesn't wear oneself out tryin' to understand. One has more energy left over for accommodating accepted facts."

Molly thought about that. "I don't know if I can
accommodate. I have tried, and I really want to. It
just doesn't seem like either Tommy Lee or I can, and
in tryin' we seem to be makin' both of our lives
miserable. Maybe it's best that Tommy Lee and I live
apart."

In truth, Molly had been giving the idea more and
more serious thought. She rather liked not having to
pick up after anyone but herself, and not even that if
she didn't want to, and doing what she liked when she
liked.

Mama shook her head. "Not you two."

"Mama, all my life I've looked to Tommy Lee to
make me happy. And I've spent most of my life
thinkin' that if Tommy Lee leaves me, I'll *die*. That's a
burden for any man . . . and it isn't how I want to live
the remainder of my life."

She looked at her mother, trying to understand her
own confusion. It was like opening a cabinet door and
searching inside on dim, crowded shelves.

"Mama, I have spent all my life twisting myself
around, trying to be what I thought Tommy Lee
wanted me to be. He has never asked me to do that—I
have just done it automatically, for whatever reason.
Well, I can't do that any longer, and I can't go on
thinkin' he's all that will make me happy, either. I
have to find what I need inside myself. Tommy Lee
can't give it to me. And for some reason I can't find it
when I'm livin' with him, because I keep expectin'
him to provide it, and he keeps tryin, because he
thinks he should provide everything for me." Then
she added, "And when I'm alone, I'm sort of content.
I'm not expecting things from him and continually
bein' disappointed."

Mama sighed, a deep, sad sigh. "Molly, I did this very thing with Stirling."

She shut her mouth tight and looked past Molly's shoulder, and Molly was startled to see regret in her mother's face. She wasn't certain she had ever seen regret in her mother's face. At least not so profoundly.

Mama's hand laid softly over Molly's. "Honey, men leave us sooner or later, because we usually outlive them. Until then the best we can do is give what we can and enjoy it and take what a man can give and enjoy that. The sad times, well, honey you just have to let them fly away."

She averted her eyes and rose. "Molly, I'm content living alone, but I'm often lonely. Sometimes I'm *so* lonely." Her voice shook, and Molly stared at her profile as her mother gazed out the window.

"Is it better to be lonely alone, Mama . . . or lonely with the person you love livin' right in the house with you?"

Molly searched her mother's pale eyes. Her mother breathed deeply and shook her head.

"I don't know, honey. I really have no answer to that. Except to say that both times come into a life. And with someone you love, with a good man—and Tommy Lee is a good man—there will be times you are not only *not* lonely, but are *filled* to the *brim*."

She gestured with her graceful hand, and her face lit with ardent memories. Then she focused an eye on Molly. "When you are alone, there are few of those times. At least for we mortal women. I don't know about saints," she added offhandedly, bringing her coffee cup to her lips.

Molly had known her mother was a woman of passion, but she had never known it so deeply as she did right then. It was a little disconcerting, as was seeing the longing in her mother's eyes when she said Stirling's name. After all these years.

That afternoon, Molly drove out to the house to see Tommy Lee. She wore a soft rayon dress that she had not worn much, so it wouldn't be too familiar to him, piled her hair up off her neck, and wore her shoes with the ribbons tied up the ankle. It was easy to use updating the accounts on the computer that JoEllen had returned and set up two days earlier as an excuse.

Tommy Lee was busy with a customer, who had just brought in an engine. The *customer* looked at Molly. She wasn't certain about Tommy Lee. She very casually waved a file of papers at him and went on inside. It was really silly to be disappointed. Silly to have visions of flirting and falling into mad love on the workbench. She was the one who wanted to learn to live without him. Maybe she wanted to live by herself and have mad love on the workbench occasionally.

She stood for a second just inside the door. She hadn't noticed that her own house had a scent. It closed around her, making her almost start crying. She went to the counter and ran her hand along it. Tommy Lee had always been neat, but a man rarely wiped the counter when it needed it.

The office chair seemed to have a giant spring on it that popped her up every five or ten minutes to go look out the window and see if Tommy Lee's customer had left. The man stayed long enough to be charged rent. Finally he was gone, but Tommy Lee didn't come in. When he didn't come and didn't come, Molly went out to find him.

He was changing a rear tire on the El Camino. "You almost had a flat," he said, straightening and setting aside his tools. "And I added a quart of oil, too."

He looked at her, and she looked at him.

She said, "Thank you."

"I don't mind doin' it."

"I don't mind doin' the records."

"I know." His eyes were asking her if she wanted to have sex. He was *flirting* with her.

Molly fumbled for the door handle. "I've got to get back. Gib Henderson wants to see me when he gets off work. He's bein' audited."

"Okay." Tommy Lee wiped his hands on a rag.

Molly let herself be carried away with her emotions and went over, wrapped her arms around his neck, and kissed him. His arms came to her waist, and he returned the kiss ardently.

They drew apart and gazed at each other.

"I like takin' care of you, Molly," Tommy Lee said, and she saw the words coming from deep inside him, as if he'd had to wring them out of himself. "Maybe I need to do that. Maybe that's my need, and I don't care to analyze it the way you do."

She caressed the hair at the back of his neck. "I like for you to take care of me, Tommy Lee. . . . I need it. I always have. Just because I have an office in town or a separate checking account doesn't change that."

His eyes held her for a long minute, and then he nodded. They broke slowly apart, their eyes lingering on each other. Questioning and promising at the same time.

As Molly backed out of the drive, she saw Tommy Lee through the glare of the windshield. He stood there, strong arms hanging at his side, staring after her.

Well, that was something.

While Tommy Lee thought he was catching on to what was going on between him and Molly, he still found himself feeling as if he were hanging out in the wind. Who he wished he could talk to about it all was Sam.

He'd never been one to stay mad long, and now Tommy Lee really missed Sam. Obviously Molly wasn't sleeping with Sam, and she didn't appear to be in love with him, either, so there seemed to be little point in Tommy Lee staying mad at him.

It seemed odd to miss a man who desired his wife. He'd known all these years that Sam was attracted to Molly, and he'd ignored it, just as he'd said, because Sam meant so much to him. Sam had always been the brother Tommy Lee never had. Since his anger had cooled, Tommy Lee had even begun to feel vaguely guilty about keeping Molly from Sam. He knew Sam hurt because of it. Not that he would hand Molly over to Sam, even if he could, but he felt badly for Sam. There was no way he could speak of any of this to Sam, but he still did want to make up with his best friend.

Tommy Lee decided to go to Rodeo Rio's and take a chance on running into Sam. That way he could approach him casually. As things turned out, this worked quite well; it appeared Sam was of the same mind because he came in and stood staring at Tommy Lee.

Tommy Lee said, "I'll bet you a beer on a game of pool," and Sam said, "I'll bet you two beers," and took up a cue, and it was all settled. Tommy Lee was greatly relieved.

After they each had had a couple of beers and run through a couple of games, Sam said, "Have you talked to Molly the past couple of days?"

"Yes, I have. She was out at the house this afternoon, as a matter of fact." Tommy Lee wanted to let Sam know that he and Molly were no longer quite so split. He knocked two of his balls into pockets and cocked an eyebrow at Sam. "Have you?"

"Not since Monday," Sam said. "She told me she didn't want to see me."

Tommy Lee paused, then knocked a ball in the corner pocket. He straightened and said, "So you sent her roses?" He had forgiven Sam, but he found he was still a bit annoyed.

Sam gave a small grin. "Can't blame a guy for tryin'. Especially for Molly."

Tommy Lee thought Sam should not be frank about it all and didn't respond to the comment. He still wondered what had happened to the roses but decided not to speak of it. After all, he was the one winning with Molly.

"So, what are you gonna do?" Sam asked. "She loves you, you horse's ass."

"We're workin' on it," Tommy Lee said and chalked his cue.

Sam said, "The problem for you two is that you never had to court each other. You've simply always been together. You always had Molly hangin' on your every word, and you had a kid before you even got out of your teens. Molly's woke up and is missin' what she never had."

"I said I'm workin' on it." Tommy Lee missed his shot and gave the table over to Sam. He was annoyed at Sam now for acting as if he understood what was going on between him and Molly. He might have thought of getting advice from Sam, but he hadn't *asked* for any.

Sam said that Tommy Lee had to be more romantic. "Get her some perfume. Expensive. And go up to the mall and buy her a sexy nightgown. Better yet—go down to one of those exclusive stores in Dallas and get her one."

Tommy Lee thought how he could count on one hand the number of times he had been to a mall. He did not see the lure. Too many people to suit him. Molly used to ask him to go, but she gave that up and went with her mother or sisters. She hadn't asked him to go with her in a long time.

"You've got to work at it, Tommy Lee. You can't just let romance go. That's the main mistake of the human race. People just let themselves get bored."

"Sam, you've been divorced twice."

"And believe me, I learned from my mistakes."

Annette, holding up the telephone, called to Tommy Lee from the bar. "Sounds like Molly."

Startled, Tommy Lee hurried over. It wasn't like Molly to call after him. She had always said to call around after him appeared tacky.

"Tommy Lee?" The line crackled with static, as it did sometimes when she was calling on her cellular, and her voice was strained. "I'm drivin' up to Rennie's. I'm afraid somethin' awful's happened to her. She called me, cryin'. . . . Some guy's been botherin' her. Stalking her and threatenin' her. God, I don't know what all has happened. Can you come?"

"Are you drivin' by yourself?" His mind was filling with pictures of some lunatic who might be after Rennie and get Molly.

"Well, *yes!*" As if he were idiotic. "I've got to get to Rennie."

"Wait for me," he said.

"I *can't*. Rennie . . ."

"I'm comin'." He dropped the receiver.

Sam was right beside him. "What's wrong?"

"Molly said some guy is harassin' Rennie, and she's already on her way up there." He was striding for the door as he spoke.

Sam came, too, of course. He didn't ask, just came. It seemed natural, as natural as them both jumping over the doors and into the seats and roaring down the road in the Corvette, heedless of speed limits and not paying a lot of attention to stop signs, either.

22

❖ ❖

If I Needed You

Seeing the condition Rennie was in upset Molly as much as she had ever been upset in her life. Rennie, who was the very epitome of audaciousness, was cowering and peeking out the windows of her own home. It was a garden apartment in a small, exclusive complex; the kind with specialized front door treatments, private backyards, athletic club, hot tub, and no children allowed. It wasn't the type of apartment where one should be cowering behind walls.

Following her, Molly peered, too, but didn't see anyone.

"When you came up, he ran off," Rennie said, "but he was there. He's there every time I look around."

Molly was highly incensed that things had gotten this out of hand without Rennie's telling her any of it. Suddenly perceiving her error, Rennie stubbornly shut her mouth on further explaining, and Molly had to extract information out of her by ruthless questioning.

Eddie Pendarvis had been following Rennie for almost a month, and during the past week things had accelerated. The man had begun showing up each day when she came out of school, and later pulling his car into the parking lot of the apartment complex and sitting there. He had also been calling her, saying lewd things. He left threatening messages on her answering machine, speaking in a high-pitched voice, or sometimes he would call and simply breathe into her answering machine. Molly listened to the latest recording. There was someone breathing on it.

"He says if I don't come back to him, he's gonna shoot me." Rennie put out her cigarette and immediately reached for the pack.

"We're callin' the police," Molly said, and took up the phone. Rennie ran out the room, and a second later Molly heard a door slam. She knew it was the bathroom door. That did not deter her from calling the police. The questions of the woman who answered the telephone annoyed her no end, however, and she finally yelled into the phone for an officer to get him or herself over and question her in person. "This is an emergency!" She hung up, shaking, telling herself losing her temper was not going to be of help.

Tommy Lee and Sam arrived, and eventually the police came, but Rennie wouldn't come out of the bathroom. It was probably just as well, because in Molly's opinion the police did not take a serious enough view of the situation. For one thing, they did not arrive for nearly twenty-five minutes, and they did not come with lights flashing and sirens blaring and then dash off immediately to take Eddie Pendarvis into custody, preferably in handcuffs and leg irons. That was what Molly felt should be done, but the policemen, two young men who looked so much alike she couldn't tell them apart, said that they would go and talk to Mr. Pendarvis.

"Talk to him?" Molly said, her voice rising. "He needs to be taken off the street. He has already assaulted my sister. He has threatened to shoot her."

The policeman said, "Yes, Ma'am . . . but we have no witnesses." He had a curious way of appearing apologetic and skeptical at the same time.

"My sister has reported his harassing her before. She told me. You should have a record."

"Yes, Ma'am." He checked his little notebook. "Approximately three weeks ago, your sister reported that Mr. Pendarvis was following her and calling her. She didn't swear out a complaint, though, and since that time we have had no further reports of any problems. We do not have a report of an assault, and we have no witnesses to what you are saying. We'll also need your sister to press charges, Ma'am." He glanced toward the hallway.

"*I'll* press charges," Molly said, jabbing her chest with her finger. "I saw her with her ripped skirt and black eye. I made an ice pack for it."

"Yes, Ma'am, but we need to have a witness who saw Mr. Pendarvis assault your sister. We need someone who has seen and heard him threaten her. We'll talk to him, and we'll investigate to see if there are any witnesses that your sister may not know of."

That set Molly right on fire. "The entire aim of a stalker is to not *let* anyone see or hear him. It is a secret, single activity . . . not a group activity!" she said, very close to yelling.

In Molly's estimation, these men, who were sworn to protect and to serve, were not doing either very well. And she was also not really happy with the way Tommy Lee didn't say a word in support of her. He propped himself on the back of one of Rennie's expensive overstuffed chairs and seemed preoccupied. And Sam did nothing more than sit uneasily on the sofa.

Molly was so wrought up that she told the policemen, "You are next to useless, aren't you? This has been going on for two months, has escalated to the point he is threatening to shoot her, and you are still asking questions. Perhaps my sister should just plan on stayin' in the bathroom for the rest of her life. She is *safe* there!"

"Molly." Tommy Lee, who had been dividing his attention between Molly and the policemen and the enormous bouquet of red roses setting on the dining table, stepped forward and put his arm around her. She had a wild look, and he thought she might hit the man. "They'll handle it. They have to follow procedures . . . investigate first. They can't just go up and arrest a man."

The young policeman looked grateful. He bobbed his head. "Yes, sir. We'll investigate and we'll talk to Mr. Pendarvis. Someone will be in touch. Please feel free to contact us if anything else comes up." Both men were easing themselves toward the door.

"What? You mean if anything comes up like my sister's body riddled with bullets? Stalkers do kill, you know."

Somewhat afraid she would pounce on the policemen and end up arrested, Tommy Lee kept his arm tight around her until the door closed behind them.

Only a few times in their lives had he seen Molly this worked up, and always it was brought on when there was a threat to the happiness and well-being of one of her own. She had once sat in the back of Savannah's English class to monitor a teacher whom she believed did not like Savannah and was being ugly to her. Savannah had been mortified, but within two weeks of Molly's scrutiny the teacher had quit and gone to another school in another state and Savannah had ended up finishing the year a happy child excelling in English. When Tommy Lee asked Molly if she didn't feel a mite guilty for driving the woman off, Molly said, "No. Not only was she spiteful but she was no good at teaching. Children at the school where she went had better have parents as alert as I."

The doctor who had treated Boone when he

wrecked his car suffered similar treatment. Molly followed the doctor around, making certain he did all he should for Boone and was unfazed by the doctor's threats to have her banned from the hospital. God help the man who did not do right by those Molly loved.

. Molly swung around and glared. "Well, you two were a lot of help."

Tommy Lee glanced at Sam, and both of them remained silent.

"Do you think she's makin' this up?" Molly demanded. "Rennie doesn't make things up . . . and I did see her black eye. It was the night she and I went to Rio's."

"No, I don't think she's making it up," Tommy Lee said. Although now that she had said it, he did wonder. He certainly wasn't going to give voice to that thought. "It's just that the police have to abide by laws, Molly. They can't just go haulin' people off the street."

"Well, they have, you know," she said, intent on getting in the last word, which Tommy Lee prudently allowed.

Molly stalked off to the kitchen. Tommy Lee shared an uncertain look with Sam. It made him feel a little better to see Sam felt uncertain, too. Then Tommy Lee's gaze again fell on the enormous bouquet of roses, and he glanced back at Sam. Sam just looked at him. Tommy Lee went off to the kitchen.

Molly stood with the coffeepot in hand, and as he watched, her head slumped downward. Going to her, he took the coffeepot and set it on the counter and pulled her into his arms. She resisted, but then gave way and sank against him.

"It'll be okay, honey. Rennie's safe, you're safe. . . . It'll be okay."

He was glad to hold her. When he and Sam had come racing up to the apartment, he'd been really scared that something may have happened to Molly. Seeing her fuming around Rennie's living room had brought him great relief. He had been equally relieved about Rennie, too, because as long as Rennie was okay, Molly would be okay. Since they were both okay, he'd calmed down considerably and had begun to wonder if the women weren't blowing everything out of proportion.

"Oh, Tommy Lee"—she spoke in a hoarse whisper and pounded a fist on his chest—"I'm sorry I was so ugly a minute ago. I'm just so upset." She raised teary eyes to him. "How dare that man do this to her. How dare he!" Then she cried against him, and he did the only thing he knew, which was to hold her until she could calm down.

When she did finally stop, it seemed her tears shut off like a faucet. She lifted her head. "Something has to be done. This cannot go on."

She turned from his arms, and he sensed her gearing up again. Thinking to divert her, he said, "The first thing is that we need to get Rennie out of the bathroom. Find something to heat up. The smell of food will bring her out."

She cast him a dark look but went to the freezer, pulled out a box of honey buns, and put them on a plate for the microwave.

Sam was just walking into the living room when Tommy Lee appeared again. "She's still in the bathroom," Sam said. "How's Molly?"

"Better," Tommy Lee said. He went and looked out the front window.

Sam sat again on the edge of the sofa. He couldn't help but admire the room, nicely put together, comfortable and pleasing to the eye. He always noticed things like that. Then he fell back to thinking about the reason he was there. He felt totally out of his depth, as experienced as he was with women. He wondered if perhaps that was because he had never experienced a crisis with anyone he truly cared about. Seeing Molly so upset really upset him. He had never seen her this distraught, and then there was Rennie in the bathroom. That upset him, too. He really wanted to do something, but he wasn't certain what to do.

Rennie took a shower before she came out of the bathroom. She wasn't coming out until the policemen were gone, and when she heard Sam's voice with Tommy Lee, she decided she had to get a hold of herself. She did not want Sam to see her as some weak wacko. As a matter of fact, while she washed and made up, thoughts of Sam became more numerous than thoughts of Eddie Pendarvis. By the time she did emerge, she had clean, shiny hair and fresh makeup on and was thinking about and anticipating Sam. She noticed he looked appreciatively at her.

Molly had made honey buns, and Rennie ate one and started to take another but refrained, not wanting to look like a pig. Finally, her nerves getting the best of her, she took half of it. It took a lot of energy to appear calm in the face of a threat from one man and possible attention from another.

Molly came up with the wild proposal that they all go over and beat Eddie Pendarvis up. When Rennie laughed and tried to make light of everything, Molly pointed out that Rennie had proposed beating up Annette Rountree only the week before and for much smaller infractions than Eddie Pendarvis had committed.

Tommy Lee's and Sam's eyebrows went up, and Rennie was immediately embarrassed. "I was only kidding," she said.

"No you weren't," Molly said. "And something's got to be done. You cannot remain at the mercy of this man, Rennie. It's too dangerous."

Molly saying that brought Eddie Pendarvis back into sharp focus in Rennie's mind. She had made wrong decisions and now she was going to have to pay for them. The trouble was, she tried so hard to make the right decisions. Depressed, she looked at Sam and wished things would straighten out. It seemed in that moment that her life had never been straightened out.

Molly said, "I've seen features about this sort of thing on television, and the consensus is there is no dealing with people like Eddie Pendarvis. The only thing that works is what they understand—force. Maybe we could hire someone to go over and threaten this horrible man, make him leave town. Can't people be hired for that sort of thing, even around here?" She was looking at Sam.

"I imagine so, Molly," he said. "But *I* don't know anyone."

Tommy Lee didn't like that Molly looked at Sam for a solution. "It's late," he said, getting to his feet, "and the best thing to do now is get Rennie on back to Valentine for a few days."

The women went off to pack, and Tommy Lee felt relieved to have set them on a course that kept them occupied and not crying or hiding in the bathroom. It was also fortunate that Molly drove an El Camino because of the amount of stuff Rennie insisted on bringing. She insisted, too, on bringing the enormous bouquet of roses, although she decided that she could cut the bouquet down a bit. Some had died, so the rest would fit in a smaller vase.

While Sam and Tommy Lee were loading the bags and trunks into the back of the El Camino, the telephone rang. Tommy Lee paid little attention to it, until he saw Molly's face. She had answered the telephone. Rennie was staring from the kitchen doorway. Molly said, "You bastard," and threw the receiver and sent the telephone to the floor.

"It was him," she breathed. Her terrified eyes caused Tommy Lee to drop the bag he carried and race across to pick up the phone.

But he heard only a dial tone.

Molly said, "He thought I was Rennie. He said the police had been to see him, but he didn't use his own phone and that he could call her anytime he wanted. He just laughed this awful laugh."

This shook Tommy Lee up considerably. Until that instant he'd had a lot of doubts about the true seriousness of the situation. On occasion a woman could get wrought up about next to nothing. Now it came to him sharply that there was peril, and that it was as much for Molly as for Rennie. Molly could never stand for anything to happen to Rennie.

"Let's get goin'," he said quietly. "Rennie, leave your cellular phone here."

When Tommy Lee declared that Sam would drive Rennie in the El Camino, and Molly would ride with him in the Corvette, Rennie worried about her car. Molly gave her a look that conveyed: We're going with the men. Rennie shut up and got into the El Camino, all the while carefully holding her precious bouquet of roses.

Each of them riding with a man made Molly feel safer all the way around, although she saw no need to admit the fact aloud. She also had a hard time looking at the rose bouquet and meeting Sam's eyes. There was nothing to be done about *that,* so it was best to ignore it.

Speeding down the state highway, the Corvette's headlights illuminated the El Camino ahead of them, and the soft summer night blew around the windshield. Molly relaxed, feeling they were leaving the danger behind. Rennie had never taken Eddie Pendarvis to Valentine, nor spoken of where her family lived there; it would take a while for him to find them. And should Eddie Pendarvis come down to Valentine, Molly would be ready with Kaye's ladies' shotgun. That she had never used Kaye's shotgun was a small matter.

In the back of her mind she was considering hunting down Eddie Pendarvis and putting a stop to him herself. Her mind filled with an image of herself in black leather with a big gun confronting Eddie Pendarvis, whom she had never seen but pictured with greasy hair. No one would suspect her, she thought, good mother and upstanding citizen and lifelong member of the Free Methodist Church that she was. The fantasies comforted her, made her feel less helpless.

She told herself that for now Rennie was safe and they were all going home. Mama would be waiting because they had called her. With a deep sigh, she leaned her head back against the seat. She looked over at Tommy Lee, at his profile lit by the silvery-green dash lights and his thick hair buffeted by the wind.

She suddenly thought, *He has been with me through every crisis in my life.*

Tears filled her eyes, and a panic came over her. What would she have done without him tonight? Oh, granted, he hadn't done all that much—he hadn't backed her with those policemen, which still irritated her. But he had kept her from smacking one of them, and she *might* have regretted that.

He had been calm when she was losing it. That's the way they had always played things. When one of them lost control, the other kept it. It was almost like an unspoken agreement: Only one of them allowed out of control at a time—and usually it was Molly out of control and Tommy Lee holding calm. She felt guilty because so often she was angry at Tommy Lee's calmness. Sometimes the way he remained *so* steady made her grit her teeth. But more often it got them through. Oh, yes, Tommy Lee's steady calmness had gotten them through so much.

Quite suddenly, Tommy Lee glanced at her. He reached out and took her hand and squeezed it. An electric warmth swept up her arm and into her chest.

Molly averted her eyes, not wanting him to see her tears. But she held on to him, even when he had to shift gears.

Rennie chose to stay at their mother's house, up in the room that had once been her own. Molly had not lived in the house but a year before marrying Tommy Lee, so it had never been home to her the way it had been to Rennie. The men brought in the bags but didn't linger.

"Don't you want some coffee?" Molly asked, surprised when Tommy Lee and Sam headed for the back door. "We've got a coffeemaker over at the cottage now—I'll go get it."

His hand on the doorknob, Tommy Lee shook his head. "No, thanks. It's late, and I need to get Sam back out to Rio's for the Bronco. You women keep the doors locked, just to be on the safe side." He opened the door and started out.

Sam said, "Goodnight, ladies," and his gaze lingered on Rennie.

"Thank you for all you did tonight," Rennie said, then called to Tommy Lee, "Thanks for comin', Tommy Lee," but her gaze was still straight on Sam.

Molly was somewhat startled by the manner in which Rennie looked at Sam. And the manner in which Sam looked back. Molly wondered exactly what had gone on between the two during the drive from Rennie's apartment.

She followed the men out the door. She met Tommy Lee's gaze in the glow of the porch light. He slipped his arm around her shoulders as he started away for the Corvette. She wound hers around his waist. She couldn't seem to let go of him, and she felt torn because she didn't want to leave Rennie and Mama right now, either.

"I thank you both for coming," she said.

Tommy Lee squeezed her shoulders. Sam said

goodnight and walked on off to the Corvette. Tommy Lee stopped and looked down at her. She couldn't see his eyes in the dimness, but she felt his warmth.

"I think everything's fine, but make certain you lock the doors anyway," Tommy Lee said.

"I will. I promise."

Molly's heart swelled at his attentiveness. She looked at him, then laid her head against his shoulder.

"I don't know what I would have done without you tonight."

Tommy Lee said, "You're my wife, and she's your sister." But he said more by putting his hand into her hair at her neck and pressing her against him.

There were so many emotions swirling inside her. Molly held on to Tommy Lee and willed herself to savor the bond that burned bright and shining between them in that moment. In that moment she experienced a feeling of total rightness, so pure and precious she wanted to stay in it forever.

Then Tommy Lee put his hand beneath her chin and lifted her face and kissed her, sweetly and seductively. Her head was spinning when he drew back. They gazed at each other for a long minute.

"You'll be okay here," Tommy Lee said. "Just lock the doors like I said. I'll see you tomorrow."

He slipped away from her. She reached for his hand. "Tommy Lee . . ." The words were confused inside her. She didn't truly know what it was she wanted to say.

He bent and kissed her cheek. She felt his smile in the darkness. "Me, too," he said. "Now get on inside. Get some sleep."

She let him go reluctantly, squeezing his hand one last time before he broke away. She watched as he got into the Corvette and turned it around. Before the taillights disappeared, she walked back to the house. Mama was making them all hot chocolate. She had turned the air conditioner up, "So we can really enjoy this cocoa," she said. Then, at Molly's look, she added, "These packages have been in the freezer. I'm sure they are fine."

The way Tommy Lee saw it, he had little choice but to go up and do what he could to take care of Eddie Pendarvis, and the sooner the better. He didn't think going the legal way was going to produce quick, satisfying results.

His main worry was that Molly might take it into her head to go after Eddie Pendarvis. He knew Molly; once she got wrought up there was almost no limit to what she might do to protect her own. Also, if Pendarvis came after Rennie, he was likely to get Molly, too, because Molly was certain to stick to Rennie like stink on a skunk. Molly's life was tied to Rennie's; whatever harm came to Rennie would come double to Molly . . . and would turn Tommy Lee's life more inside out than it already was. The more Tommy Lee thought about this, the angrier he got at Eddie Pendarvis for wrecking his life.

Sam came with Tommy Lee. They didn't really have to talk about it. Tommy Lee said he was going, and Sam said he thought he would, too, and came right along while Tommy Lee went to his own house, parked the Corvette, and got his old Chevy pickup. Sam smeared mud on the license plate.

"What did you do that for?" Tommy Lee asked, getting uneasy. Sam doing that made Tommy Lee begin to feel like a criminal. Just because what he was fixing to do could be construed as a criminal act, he didn't think he needed to start acting like one.

Sam said, "So no one can read it and identify us. Saw it on *Matlock*—you know that murder mystery show with Andy Griffith."

The mention of murder startled Tommy Lee. "I wasn't thinkin' of killin' Pendarvis."

"Oh, I didn't think you were," Sam said quickly,

and a little relieved. After a minute, he added, "I figure you just plan on goin' in and scaring him real good."

"Me? I thought you were comin' along."

"I am. I'll be right behind you, backin' you up. I hope you don't plan to beat him up, though. I can't risk ruinin' my hands."

"I'm not certain what we should do," Tommy Lee said.

He kept thinking about facing Pendarvis. He didn't like the idea. For one thing, he was afraid he might get shot. And it was funny, but he would really be embarrassed, dead or alive, when Molly found out he got shot trying to face Pendarvis.

Tommy Lee didn't say it, but he was relieved that Sam was going along. Tommy Lee would have gone alone, but it would be easier with Sam. Just then it occurred to him that only five short days ago, he and Sam had come to blows over Sam's going after his wife. Now here they were together, Tommy Lee relying on Sam, as if their fight had never happened. It didn't really seem as if it had ever happened.

After a bit more mulling, Tommy Lee had to say, "I don't want to get you into trouble, buddy. We aren't kids anymore. You're an artist, Sam."

"And you're a . . . well, what are you Tommy Lee? Are you a mechanic? Does a mechanic build engines, or just repair them?"

"Both, I guess. But neither of us go around bustin' heads."

"I told you, I'm not busting a head." He held up his hands. "We have to convince. This takes brain-power."

When they reached Lawton, it was well after midnight and the streets were almost bare of cars. They went to the all-night Wal-Mart Supercenter, where they bought a package of emergency flares, a Louisville Slugger baseball bat, two big, rather soft cantaloupes, two fried chicken dinners, a couple of containers of yogurt, and two soft drinks. Sam remembered they might want to leave a note, so he got a drawing tablet because he could always use one. Tommy Lee's stomach started bothering him, so he ate a container of yogurt, using the fork from the chicken dinner, before he left the parking lot. Sam had started sketching on the tablet and kept it up as they drove down the street.

Finding where Rennie said Eddie Pendarvis lived in a bungalow in an old neighborhood wasn't hard. Rennie said Pendarvis drove an eighties dark blue Thunderbird, and by golly one sat right in the drive, beneath an enormous elm tree. The dim, flickering glow showing through the front window indicated Pendarvis had a television going.

Tommy Lee pulled the Chevy to the curb several yards down and across the street from Pendarvis's house. It fit right in with all the other cars and trucks parked up and down the street. From his rolled tool pouch behind the seat, Tommy Lee took out a modified table knife and a bent wire, which he unwound. He always had to be prepared because Molly had a habit of locking her keys in her car. He got a Bic lighter from the glove box, snugged one of the flares into his back pocket, and took up the other one. Sam got the two cantaloupes and the baseball bat.

They walked quickly, and their boots sounded loud on the pavement. A dog started barking, and then another, and Tommy Lee's heart started to beat out of his chest. The Thunderbird was locked. Using the table knife and bent wire, Tommy Lee had it open in ten seconds. Sam peeked in the window of the house and sprinted over close enough to whisper that Pendarvis seemed to be asleep in a chair. Tommy Lee lit the flare, tossed it into the seat of the Thunderbird, pushed the door closed. Then he hopped up on the porch from the far side while Sam came from his.

They looked at each other and listened. There was a good glow going in the Thunderbird and the dogs were barking. A murmuring from inside, the television.

Tommy Lee knocked on the door. "Hey, Pendarvis, your car's on fire." He tried to sound frantic but not too loud.

Noise from inside, the door was flung open. A big man filled the doorway, and Tommy Lee thought, *Oh, no.* He and Sam pushed themselves at Pendarvis's. They had the advantage of surprise and of Pendarvis just coming awake. They shoved him into the middle of the room, and Sam closed the door. The man croaked, "My car . . . my car!" Then he was looking wildly at Tommy Lee and Sam. And the baseball bat Sam held high.

Tommy Lee advanced on the man, who to his relief did step backward and looked fearful. Having taken the advantage, Tommy Lee kept on going, as if he were going to walk right over the bigger man. Pendarvis fell back across the arm of a chair. "I'm tellin' you to lay off Rennie Bennett," Tommy Lee said. "If you don't, this is what will happen to your head."

Sam tossed up a cantaloupe, swung hard with the bat, and smashed the cantaloupe with a sickening thud, sending cantaloupe flesh and seeds flying. Then, grinning wickedly, he did it again, and the entire time, Pendarvis stared, wide-eyed.

"Got the picture?" Tommy Lee said.

Pendarvis nodded.

"It might be good if you went somewhere else to live," Tommy Lee added, feeling quite full of himself.

Then Tommy Lee and Sam got out of there. Glancing in the rearview mirror to see Pendarvis jerking opened the door to his Thunderbird, Tommy Lee pressed the accelerator and headed the Chevy away.

Sam said, "Whooee. I can't believe we did that."

Tommy Lee eased the spare flare out of his back pocket and grinned. He felt suddenly light-headed. "We didn't do that—that was two knuckleheaded fools who forgot how old they are."

"We're older, but we're smarter, too," Sam said, his grin as wide as Tommy Lee's. He popped the tabs on two of the Coca-Colas and handed Tommy Lee one. "Do you think it worked?"

"God, I hope so," Tommy Lee answered. "It felt pretty good while we were in the midst of it, but I'm clean out of breath now."

A little way out of town, Tommy Lee pulled over at a roadside park. He needed to unwind, and he had suddenly gotten really hungry.

Sam said, "Me, too. Threatening a guy really leads to an appetite."

They ate their chicken dinners and recounted the events, bolstering themselves.

"You know you scared me, buddy," Sam said. "God, you looked to me like you were gonna kill him."

Tommy Lee said, "Your grin was an artful touch."

"It was, wasn't it," Sam agreed proudly.

Tommy Lee couldn't quite believe he had done something like he had done. So few times in his life had he done dangerous and outlandish things. His dangerous acts had generally revolved around driving fast and doing stunts with cars, and for him that wasn't all that dangerous. As for outlandish, well, he couldn't really say he'd done anything outlandish. He wasn't an outlandish kind of guy. He supposed the most outlandish thing he had ever done was hiding that bottle of vodka in Molly's cottage, an act that had nothing to recommend it.

He sure hoped Pendarvis left Rennie alone now. He sure hoped it was over and that he and Molly could get back to the problems of their own lives. He began

to feel deflated, as if what he wanted was never going
to come about.

Later, as they drove on to Valentine, they discussed
telling Molly and Rennie and decided not to. They
needed to see how everything came out first.

23
❖❖

Deep Down

Mama called Kaye first thing the following morning. Rennie had asked her not to, but Mama had said, "Of course I'm calling your sister. She'll want to give her support."

And Kaye did! She came bursting into their mother's kitchen, voicing righteous indignation as only Kaye could, damning the perpetrator to everlasting hell and Rennie, if not to sainthood, up near an innocent and misused angel.

"We won't let this man get away with this, Rennie," Kaye said. "We'll sue him, that's what we'll do. You can hit a person hardest in the pocketbook. I've already spoken to Jaydee, and he's goin' to get started on a civil suit. We'll teach this pervert that he can't treat our Rennie like this. Here, let me get you another cup of coffee. . . . You are wrung out."

Good Lord, would wonders never cease? Watching Kaye's solicitous expression, hearing her righteous words, Molly felt great surprise and even greater relief.

Lillybeth and Season were called and came straight down, and then there they all were in Mama's kitchen, and Rennie was basking in their attentions. The more of a fuss they made over her, the more she came out from beneath her guilt and shame. Molly hadn't seen it before, but she saw it now, how Rennie's shoulders had been drooping and how now she was like a flower hit by sunshine after rain, straightening and opening up.

"A suit is just the thing," Lillybeth said, agreeing with Kaye for the first time this century. "We can get him for mental anguish like he's never been gotten before. We'll teach him he can't play around with the Collier girls."

"But court cases take money," Rennie said, looking worried again. "And can you sue without evidence?"

"A person can start a suit for anything," Lillybeth said airily. "Don't worry about the money. I have a lawyer friend who will do it for little or nothin'."

Kaye put in, "Walter and I will handle the cost, Rennie. I am not going to let this thug get away with terrifyin' my little sister."

"What if he just runs away and starts stalkin' Rennie from a hidden place?" Season said, her eyes wide and round and worried. "What if he stops on Rennie and starts on some other unfortunate woman?"

Molly hadn't thought of that, and in looking at her sisters, she saw neither had they. Rennie began to hunch over again.

Season continued with her dire scenario. "Starting a lawsuit against him may just set him off and make him come right after Rennie. It won't be hard to find her down here. Everyone knows us and . . ."

"Season," Molly broke in, "we're not helpless. We'll deal with him, one step at a time."

Then Kaye said, "Well, we'll just have to go after him. There's five of us, and only one of him."

Kaye saying that, and in the tone she used, was

surprise enough, but then Mama said, "I know someone." They all turned to her. "Well, I don't *know* this person, and it *was* years ago, too, but I know someone who knows a person who can be engaged to handle unpleasant people."

"Mama?" they all said at once, but, gazing at her mother, Molly wasn't really surprised. Mama had led a wide and varied life.

And the important thing was that they were for once in agreement, all of them together. Molly glanced around the room, at all of them around the table, Season on the high stool she always preferred, the table covered with china breakfast dishes and the leavings of breakfast Kaye had brought from Hardee's.

There had been a threat, Molly thought, and they had circled the wagons, and now Rennie was being drawn tight into the circle. Molly hadn't realized until that moment how much Rennie had been hurting, feeling the odd one out. It was seeing her sister being drawn in and glowing that made her see how it had been. Rennie had been dying on the vine!

Was that why she had kept after all those men? Was feeling the black sheep of the family what made her continually sink her own chances for happiness— because she felt unworthy? Why would Rennie feel unworthy? Why would she feel any less than the rest of them? They'd all had it tough. . . . Look at Kaye, she didn't feel unworthy. She thought she was God's gift to the world, no matter the evidence to the contrary. Then there was Season, with her depressions . . . and Lillybeth didn't trust men. Actually she hated men. And there was Molly herself, who so much of the time felt a heavy dread that she never quite understood. Finding out the why of any of it would take a lifetime, and probably wouldn't be of much help, either. Walk on, Mama said. Mama was an example that doing so worked.

Oh, I love you, Rennie. Molly looked around the table. *Oh, I love you all.*

It was one of those moments that struck a person, one that brought with it no particular understanding and yet an understanding beyond words. Molly got up and began clearing dishes, moving in and out between the chairs, refreshing coffee, touching each one, feeling glad for the moment and tucking it away in her heart.

Later, when she got a moment alone in the kitchen with Kaye—the others were upstairs in Rennie's bedroom looking through old photographs—she said, "I want to thank you for what you've given Rennie today, Kaye. You might not realize it, but she was terrified you were going to criticize her, blame this thing with Eddie Pendarvis all on her. She has been blaming herself, you know."

Kaye looked surprised. "Why would I do that? Good Lord, you both must think me an ogre." Her bottom lip sort of quivered.

"No!" Molly said quickly, startled at seeing that bottom lip. "It's just that you and Rennie often clash . . . and well, she needed you so much right now, and you came through. I just wanted you to know what it means to her. It means the world, Kaye."

"Oh." Kaye turned abruptly away, went and shut the back door, saying, "Mama keeps this house too darn hot. I'm turnin' on the cooler."

Then she was just standing there, looking at Molly. "I know I can be harsh sometimes," she said, and right in front of Molly's eyes she seemed to wilt. "I know I criticize. It's just that I have standards, you know, and it seems like no one keeps standards anymore. Look at the *world,* Molly!" Then, eyes straight on Molly's, she said coolly, "Walter is havin' an affair."

Molly could not have been more surprised if Kaye herself had said she was having an affair.

"Oh, Kaye." She didn't think she wanted to hear this. Oh, *why* did everyone insist upon confiding in her? Kaye's bottom lip had begun to quiver again.

"I know I criticize him," Kaye said, "and he's found someone who hangs on his every word." She kept her chin up, but her bottom lip continued to quiver dangerously.

"Maybe you're mistaken. Not Walter. I don't believe it." Now that she thought of it, Molly could not believe it. "I imagine you saw something that looked suspicious but is truly nothin' at all. Have you asked him about it?"

"I heard it, Molly. I picked up the extension in the bedroom to call Murlene, and Walter was on the telephone with Fayrene Gardner. They didn't hear me because Fayrene's voice—you know how it is."

"Fayrene Gardner from the cafe?" She simply could not believe it.

"Yes. She was complimenting him on what a man he is and how he made her feel so much a woman. She said she couldn't wait to see him again."

Ohmygod, Molly thought. A shocking image of Walter in bed with a woman flashed through her mind and she chased it out. Before her face Kaye was holding on and crumbling at the same time. "Oh, Kaye." Molly stepped forward to embrace her sister, but Kaye's stance caused her to drop her arms. "What are you goin' to do?" she asked.

Kaye's bottom lip quit quivering. "I went to Fayrene and I told her that I was not about to throw twenty-one years of marriage down the drain. That I would tell her husband and would broadcast her indiscretion all over town, and when I saw her out anywhere I would attack her and snatch her bald and that she would never know a moment's peace from me."

"Oh, Kaye." Molly could imagine all of it. Kaye was like everyone, weak in some areas, strong in others, and where she was strong, she was granite.

"I know a lot of people may not think that Walter is much."

"Oh, Kaye . . . Walter is a fine man."

"I know that people think I henpeck him and that he is weak, and in a way, in the *world's* way, maybe that is so. But we are not of this world, Molly. The Bible says so. Walter has loved me, and he is my world. And Fayrene is right—he is so much more a man than anyone realizes. He's strong enough to love me. Only brave people can love, Molly."

"Oh, Kaye." Molly felt reduced to that one phrase. She did think, as she hadn't before, that it would take a strong man to love Kaye. She began to see in Walter someone she had never seen before.

"Well," Kaye said, quite matter-of-factly, "I'm going to hang on to him and *make* him glad to have me."

Molly gave herself over and went to embrace her sister, but Kaye stood woodenly and after a minute, Molly let go.

"I will hold my head high, no matter who knows, but I would prefer that you didn't tell the others," Kaye said and left the room, head still high.

When Molly thought about it, she couldn't recall a time she had ever seen Kaye cry. And thinking about that, Molly began to cry, feeling both despair and a strange happiness. She went home to the cottage so no one would hear her cry, and when she had stopped, she called Tommy Lee and chatted with him about almost nothing.

"I just wanted to hear your voice," she told him.

After she hung up with him she called each of her children and told them about Rennie and asked them what was going on in their lives. After that she was too exhausted to think and fell asleep with Ace on her stomach.

Sometime later Tommy Lee called and woke her and asked if she wanted to go to supper and a movie. Of course she said yes.

"No pressure," Tommy Lee said. "Let's just forget everything for a while and have a nice time."

And of course she said yes to that, too. Tommy Lee didn't know it, but she was in the mood to say yes to everything he said.

She hung up and sat with her hand still on the receiver, wondering why in the world she wasn't at home with him. Kaye had said that she was going to *make* Walter glad to have her. How did she propose to do that, and why didn't Molly see things in that light? Was it her pride? Why couldn't she get herself straightened out?

She was certainly confused, but she did know one thing: If she been at home with Tommy Lee, he wouldn't have called her for a date.

24

❖❖

Then Again

Molly was startled to realize she had gotten so preoccupied thinking about her date with Tommy Lee that she had clean forgotten about the horrible threat of Eddie Pendarvis. The sound of a car driving into the yard reminded her. Visions of a man jumping out of a vehicle with a gun made her leave her makeup spread all over the bathroom sink and run to go look out the window.

Why, it was Sam, and he had parked on Mama's side of the drive.

Gazing at him, Molly thought she should speak. That she was disheveled didn't matter. She *had* to speak to him, and wondering exactly what she would say, she hurried out the back door to catch him.

At her call, he turned. Barefoot, she stayed on the back step, arms wrapped around herself, while he came toward her, a cautious look on his face. She thought of how he used to come toward her with a happy, expectant look on his face.

"I can't thank you enough for what you did for us last night, Sam." His eyes jumped, an odd look. "It was very kind of you to come with Tommy Lee and help bring us home."

"Oh . . . it wasn't anything." He was looking in the vicinity of her chin.

"I'm glad you and Tommy Lee worked things out," she said earnestly. She was so very glad; she didn't want to carry the guilt of having broken up a rare, lifelong friendship.

"We never have stayed mad long, I guess."

His eyes seemed to drift up and meet hers. They were sad, yet intent. She found herself saying, "I loved your roses. I really did."

He didn't say anything.

Molly said, "I . . . well, if things weren't as they are, I would have kept them."

His sad eyes gazed at her intently, and the understanding passed between them. She hadn't taken his heart for granted. She cared, he cared . . . *another time, another place.*

"Do you think we can get back to bein' the friends that we were?" Molly asked. Searching his eyes, she thought maybe she shouldn't have asked that. Maybe there wasn't an answer for that.

Then suddenly Sam bent and brushed his lips across hers in a kiss that was light yet intimate.

Trembling, Molly made a smile for him. When he smiled in return, hers became real, smiles to let go and accept.

"You're goin' in to see Rennie?"

"Thought I might."

They looked at each other again.

"Well . . . I'm glad." She told herself that she really was.

He went off, and she watched him a moment and felt a little peculiar. Rather like closing a door and wondering if she had forgotten something just on the other side.

* * *

Molly decided on the chambray dress Lillybeth had
given her, a bra but *no* panties—ohmygosh, but it was
her little intimate secret fun!—her new shoes with the
ribbons tied up around her legs, hair pulled back
loosely because she would be riding in the Corvette,
silver earrings, Chanel dabbed between her breasts.
The perfume sort of dribbled with the perspiration
there. Molly stood in front of the fan to dry herself. At
the last minute, when she heard the unmistakable
sound of Tommy Lee's Corvette coming down the
drive, she slipped on the bangle bracelets Rennie had
left on the dresser. In the past Molly never had felt she
could wear bangle bracelets, but she really thought she
could now.

From the kitchen window, she saw Tommy Lee stop
the Corvette, saw him smooth his hair with both
hands and then unfold himself out of the car. He wore
his azure blue sport shirt, long sleeves, cuffs turned up
like he preferred, showing his strong wrists. For him,
it was dressed up. He was so handsome in that shirt!

Molly pushed from the sink, grabbed her small
purse, and ran to the back door to meet him. His eyes
jumped when he saw her, and then he told her she
looked nice. His blue eyes were shining and all for her.
She told him he looked nice and let her eyes shine all
for him.

He had brought her a present!

It was in a small box with a red satin ribbon. The
way the ribbon was tied, she knew he had done it. She
opened it, there, on the step. A set of wind chimes.
They were brass pipes and calibrated for certain
tones, so beautiful that Molly kept looking at them
and saying, "Thank you, oh, *thank* you."

Here she had ran off from him and he was having to
make his own meals and pick up after himself, and he
had given her a rose bush and wind chimes. She held
up the chimes and jiggled them, delighting in the
sound.

"They're door chimes," Tommy Lee said. "You hang them where they jingle when you open the door."

He was gazing at her . . . as if she was a desirable woman. She looked back at him. No pressure, he had said. *"Just forget everything for a while and have a nice time."* What a relief to do that, to not think that she *had* to know what to do, *had* to make a decision. She could let herself look at him, flirt with him . . . let decisions and doubt and fear just blow away.

Tommy Lee was driving down the road before they even settled on where to go for supper. He always did that. He couldn't just sit behind the wheel of the car and wait until they decided where they were going. He had to *drive*.

"Where are we goin'?" Molly asked.

"I don't know. Where do you want to eat?"

"You're drivin'."

"What would you like to eat?"

He had no idea where he was going, but he was heading right on through town like he did.

"You're drivin'," Molly said. "You choose. You just drive, until we come to some place."

He sort of slowed down. "I don't know where," he said.

"We'll come to someplace."

Forget everything . . . have a nice time. Molly felt herself drifting upward on a beautiful balloon, cracking right through the clouds of dread. Tommy Lee kept glancing over at her, grinning, his eyes sparkling. As if he was glad to be with her. She felt so glad to be with him. Happiness just seemed to be wafting up around them. It was like in an old romantic movie, that's what it was like.

So he kept driving, and they went all the way to the lake, where there was a little restaurant. Neither of them had been to the lake in years, and the restaurant had changed.

"What do you think?" Tommy Lee asked, looking doubtfully at the new restaurant. It was a strange place, and he didn't much care for strange places.

"We should try it," Molly said. She didn't usually care for strange restaurants, either, but she thought she needed to get beyond that. She needed to get beyond a lot of things. "I'm really starving."

The place turned out not to be a real restaurant but more or less a take-out place that served fried catfish and barbecue and hamburger baskets, with soft drinks in styrofoam cups. There were nice tables, though, out on a wooden deck at the edge of the lake. Molly wondered at the few people there, and when they began to eat, they discovered why. The food was awful, just awful.

"So much for trying a new restaurant," Molly said, dumping their baskets into the trash; she wouldn't even feed it to the ducks. She was still starving, and when she got hungry, her mood generally turned poor.

"I guess," Tommy Lee said, and he looked so dejected that Molly tried to think of something to praise.

"It's nice to sit out here . . . nice it isn't crowded, either."

"Are you still hungry?" Tommy Lee asked.

"A little."

"I saw a freezer in there with packaged ice cream. I'll go check it out."

He came back grinning triumphantly. "Ice cream sandwiches, Madam?" He brought her two; he knew she loved ice cream sandwiches.

"My hero," she said.

Just forget everything for a while and have a nice time. They were, but maybe they didn't forget *everything,* Molly thought. Maybe memories of how things had once been lingered deep in their minds, and in their eyes, too.

As time wore on, however, Molly felt herself grow-

ing more and more relaxed, and she sensed that
Tommy Lee did, too. The two of them seemed to get a
lot better at forgetting everything and having a nice
time. They decided not to go to a show but to drive
and walk around the lake. They watched people
fishing, watched ducks, watched a man start a big pile
of brush on fire, which Tommy Lee said was a really
stupid thing to do with the breeze blowing as it was.
They watched to see if the brush pile would ignite a
grass fire, but thankfully and miraculously it did not.
They came by a bait shop–convenience store and
bought Coca-Colas in little bottles and snack cakes,
not the most nutritious food, but they were forgetting
everything and having a really nice time now.

Tommy Lee gave Molly a bite of his brownie, and
Molly gave him a bite of her oatmeal cream cookie.
Then she leaned over and licked cream from the
corner of his mouth with the tip of her tongue. He
looked startled, and she knew he was self-conscious
because they were right out in public—no matter that
no one was around. Still, she gave his lips another
lick, and then Tommy Lee started laughing and almost fell off the retaining wall where they sat.

When they got back into the Corvette, Tommy Lee
took her hand and kept hold of it even as he shifted
the stick of the Corvette, like he used to do back in
high school.

Following a rutted road off from the lake, they came
to a fenced pasture. Two horses were inside the fence.
They were well-cared-for horses, muscular and tame
and obviously well used. They came right up to the
fence when Molly smooched to them. Delighted, she
blew in their noses and petted and talked to them.
The two were amusing in their attempts to gain
attention.

Tommy Lee touched one, then got bored and went
off, looking at an old falling-down cabin. Next thing,
he gave a shout. He had found an old truck. A Ford,

he said, but how he knew it was beyond Molly; she didn't see an emblem when she finally picked her way, in her new shoes and slim-fitting dress, through the tall weeds to have a look at what had once been a truck. Tommy Lee was inspecting every rusty part.

"It's hot," Molly said after several minutes, and went to sit in the Corvette parked in the shade and wait for Tommy Lee to get through his enthusiasm for a hunk of metal with rotted tires.

Waiting, trying not to sweat, Molly began to get sad. She told herself it was silly, especially when he came back so excited and talking about finding out who owned the old truck and buying it and how he could put a four-sixty into it, which was apparently some great motor. How could she be sad when his eyes were dancing like that? When he took her hand like that? Did it really matter that he didn't have one iota of interest in horses and she didn't care one whit about that truck? What she cared about was being with him. And what he truly seemed to care about was being with her.

Tommy Lee drove around the lake until he came to a small beach area with no one in sight. He lolled on the grass while Molly took off her shoes and went wading, holding her skirt up and feeling very seductive. She felt Tommy Lee's eyes on her. She looked over her shoulder at him. Slowly she turned and, her eyes on his, walked toward him. She sat beside him and kissed him, and he propped her against his chest while they watched the sun getting really low in the sky.

"We both like to look at the sunset," Tommy Lee said suddenly.

"Yes . . ." Molly said, ". . . and to drive around and do nothin'."

"We like Cokes," he said and kissed her neck.

"Ah . . . we like summer." He was kissing down her neck now, and she was starting to tingle.

The grass was summer brown and prickly and they had no blanket or even a towel, so they got into the Corvette to neck. It wasn't the most comfortable place, but they tried forgetting that, too. Molly couldn't help thinking how silly, when they had beds back in Valentine. Even if a person was young, could a body possibly be able to bend to the extent needed to enjoy passion in a two-seated sports car?

But there was something about it all—about the youthfulness of it, about reliving the memories it evoked, the daringness of it. There was just something wild and wonderful about it, causing them to not only disregard the uncomfortableness but to slip right beyond it to boiling blood and forgotten reason.

Then suddenly headlights and the sound of vehicles jerked them out of the depths of passion.

"Oh, my Lord," Molly said. Tommy Lee said something stronger under his breath. Molly, blinking, only just then realized the sun was gone and dark had all but come. The headlights bounced over the grass and trees—a carload of teens, and a pickup truck followed them.

"Hey, man, cool car!" Teens pouring out of the car and out of the truck, coming across to admire the Corvette while Molly tried to pull her dress back down over her bottom and get it buttoned over her breasts.

Then Tommy Lee got out and showed the boys the engine. Five boys and one girl. Several other girls waited over in the car and truck, the same as Molly did, withered and hot and sweaty in the seat of the Corvette.

Maybe it was the teens making them suddenly aware of their foolish actions, or perhaps it was simply being interrupted, but whatever the reason, their romantic night appeared to have ended. On the drive back to Valentine, Molly began to worry whether Tommy Lee would go to their house or to the cottage. He had fallen back into his usually quiet self, and she remained unusually quiet.

She didn't think she was ready to return to their house. The more she thought of it, the more she concluded that she had reached her limit for forgetting everything for a while and just having a nice time. All the fears and doubts about her life and their marriage seemed to be falling right out of the sky and landing on her. She couldn't explain it to herself, much less to Tommy Lee, so she couldn't tell him *not* to go to the house. She grew more and more nervous, waiting to see what he would do and hoping they didn't end up in a big fight.

The closer they came to Valentine, the more tense she became. Then, when Tommy Lee drove past the turnoff for their house and kept on, heading for the cottage, Molly suddenly got very depressed. He hadn't even asked her if she wanted to go to the house. She told herself she was being really unfair and erratic, and realizing this made her grow even more blue.

When Tommy Lee pulled into the drive and Molly saw the soft glow from her mother's living room windows, she realized she had once more forgotten all about the threat of Eddie Pendarvis.

"Oh, gosh, I didn't call and check on Mama and Rennie."

"They're okay. Sam's still here."

He was; there was the Bronco patterned in the thin moonlight. Apparently he was staying the night; it was after midnight.

Molly wondered where Sam slept. To her mind it would be poor taste for Rennie and Sam to carry on right in Mama's house. But then Mama was quite liberal about these things, and in this Molly agreed with Kaye.

"I still should have called," Molly said, feeling guilty. Then she realized Rennie's car sat on the far side of the Bronco. In the few seconds it took her to realize it was Rennie's car, she was struck with alarm, thinking someone else was at her mother's house and that that someone could be Eddie Pendarvis. The recognition of Rennie's car came with great relief. "I guess Sam took Rennie to get her car."

"He said he was going to," Tommy Lee said absently.

Molly thought about that. "You might have told me."

"Why?"

"I would have liked to know about my sister goin' up in the vicinity of that madman. And I might have worried if I hadn't been able to reach Rennie."

She felt his surprise at her attack, and she realized it had been sort of an attack, although she hadn't meant it to be. Or maybe she had. He was being way too calm again.

"I would have told you then," he said. She could tell he was wondering at her; she could hear it in his voice.

But she continued right on. "Maybe you wouldn't be with me, and I'd call, and she wouldn't be at Mama's and maybe Mama wouldn't be there to tell me where they were."

"Well, none of that happened," Tommy Lee said, which pretty much shut her mouth.

He had stopped in the deep darkness beside the cottage and cut the engine. They sat there a few minutes. Molly realized she was taken by the strong reluctance to leave him, an emotion that seemed quite strange, considering how tense she also felt.

Apparently Tommy Lee didn't want to leave her either, however, because he didn't shove her out and zoom away. He was just sitting there, staring straight ahead, his profile a shadow in the darkness.

"Do you want to come inside?" she asked.

He shook his head. "No, I guess not."

After a minute, Molly said, "Okay." Still, she sat there. "I had a nice time this evening, Tommy Lee. A really nice time."

"I did, too."

She felt around for her purse. Tommy Lee hopped out of the car and came around to open the door for her. He took her hand and walked her the few feet to the back door. Then with suddenness and strength, he pulled her into his arms and against his hard body.

Thin moonlight shone down upon them. She looked up into his face, into his eyes, before he lowered his head and kissed her. A hard kiss, seductive and deep, deeper and deeper, entering her and drawing her to him, until she lost her breath and just about everything else.

"Come inside, Tommy Lee," she whispered hoarsely.

"No," he replied, thick and firm.

Molly was somewhat stunned. Tommy Lee was gazing down at her. He brought his hand to her cheek, rubbed his calloused thumb over her lips.

"I can wait for you, Molly. Until you're ready."

He left her there.

She watched him stride away, then turned and fumbled for the handle of the screen door, hurrying inside so as not to stand there and watch him leave. She stood in the middle of the dark kitchen and listened to the Corvette engine disappear down the road. She knew that a part of her heart went with Tommy Lee, and a part of his stayed with her. They were each searching for the whole.

25
❖❖

Diamonds To Dust

Molly slept so late the following morning that the sun was high and the black fan blowing hot air over her. She wandered into the front room and over to the window. Sam's Bronco was gone, and Kaye was just leaving from her Sunday visit with Mama. Molly watched her sadly, praying things were better between Kaye and Walter.

She stood there a moment, looking at the driveway, recalling how she had stood in this very spot and watched Tommy Lee drive up the day before. Memories and feelings from that afternoon and evening stole over her. Memories of Tommy Lee's warm eyes and his hand reaching for hers.

Turning, she went to shower and get dressed and get herself over to her mother's. She had a confusing mixture of emotions and felt the need to be with Rennie and her mother. Perhaps she wanted one of them to be able to answer the telephone should Tommy Lee call. The prospect of having to talk to him unnerved her.

Molly had an odd feeling, as if time was at hand, for what she was not quite certain. Maybe it was the weather, she thought, as she walked across the lawn to her mother's house. The air was heavy and still, as it often was before a weather change. And that was how Molly felt inside herself, too.

When she stepped into her mother's kitchen, Rennie was on the telephone. "The *police*," Mama said, for some reason whispering.

On her end Rennie said little more than yes and no and thank you. After she hung up, she said simply, "Eddie's left town," causing Molly to have to request a more thorough explanation of the conversation.

In an oddly bored and distracted manner, Rennie related that the policeman had called to inquire whether she had heard from Eddie Pendarvis. When she said no, the policeman informed her that it appeared sometime late Saturday Eddie Pendarvis had taken all of his worldly belongings and left town. Rennie, who had quite quickly returned to her old audacious self in the security of her family, now painted Eddie Pendarvis in a ridiculously stupid light and gave no credence to the possibility that the man might stalk her from an unknown, hidden place. She appeared to have put all fear of Eddie Pendarvis behind her.

Her attitude both relieved and perturbed Molly. Molly thought it at least within the realm of possibility that they had not heard the last from Eddie Pendarvis. Still, she had to admit that ignoring all thought of the man might be a good course. Rennie was happy, happier and more upbeat than Molly had seen her in a long time. She even began to speak of moving down to Valentine permanently.

"Let's face it," Rennie said, "How many stalkers and muggings do we get in Valentine? And it's time I thought of *buying* a house." She went on to talk about a house being an investment and how much fun it would be to have one of those Victorian places up on

Church Street, with a wide porch and flowing hedges of yellow forsythia. "I've always dreamed of having a place like that."

This dream came as news to Molly, as she couldn't recall Rennie ever mentioning it. A house like that certainly was a far cry from the adults-only, modern living community where she now resided. In fact, Rennie had at one time said she had to shake the dust of Valentine off her feet and not look back. Molly suspected Rennie's not only looking back but running back had much less to do with practical investment and safety and a lot more to do with desire for Sam Ketchum.

"Well, maybe . . . I guess so," Rennie admitted when Molly said this to her.

They had moved up to Rennie's old room—Mama had waved them away because she wanted to watch the television show *Home Repair,* which was featuring electrical wiring repair. Rennie, clutching the silk blouse she had been about to hang in her old bedroom closet, threw herself across the bed and gazed earnestly at Molly, who was propped against the pile of feather pillows. It appeared Rennie had slept on those pillows alone, that Sam had slept in the bed in what had once been Lillybeth's and Season's room and what was now the official guest room. Molly had seen the rumpled covers. But it was a short walk down the hall from that bed to Rennie's. Molly was ashamed of her curiosity and refused to be so bold as to ask. It was not her business and right now she didn't really think she wanted to know.

Rennie said, "Do you mind a whole lot about me and Sam, Sissy?"

"Of course not," Molly answered quickly, and once she had said it, she had made it so.

Rennie said, "I guess it wouldn't matter if you did mind."

She didn't say it without care, only matter-of-factly, and Molly knew it anyway. Then Rennie sat up, still clutching the silk blouse, rather wringing it, and Molly thought that the thing was going to be ruined.

"I know that I'm second place," Rennie said, averting her eyes. "I imagine Sam looks at me and sees you. I'm not fooling myself about that, Sissy. I've seen for years how he looks at you, and a guy doesn't stop yearning for a woman like that one day and start yearning for her sister the next. But there is *something* between us. We've both been knocked around a lot, and we know what that feels like. And Molly, I am about to be forty and I want a husband and children. And maybe being your sister, being so much like you, will make it so Sam will really fall for me after a while."

Molly sat up, put her feet on the floor. "Rennie, you are making excuses as to why Sam could not look at you for yourself."

Rennie began shaking her head.

"Yes, you are. I don't know why you are. . . . Maybe you're scared to think it could work out because then an awful lot will be required of you. You will have to *sustain* a relationship. Now, I will grant you that you and I are a lot alike. So what? So we are *both* his type. I'm sure there are a lot of his type around. What I think is that Sam has finally reached the point where you're at. He's wantin' a home and family, too. He's finally just got a good look at you when the time is right."

Getting up, she took the blouse out of Rennie's hand. "Let me hang this up. You are about to turn it into a rag."

Oh, Lord, she thought, as she wriggled the blouse onto a hanger. She did not know what she would do if this romance did not work out for Rennie. The entire situation made Molly feel tense and as though she should start paying some sort of penance, because she felt surely that if it did not work out, it would somehow be all her fault.

She looked at Rennie. "I cannot advise you, Rennie. I certainly have not proven to be a shining example of relationship wisdom lately. But what I guess I'm saying is don't be too scared to take this opportunity and don't discount Sam's feelings. I know him enough to say that. He is not the type of man not to know exactly which woman he is lookin' at."

Molly felt better for having said that, and Rennie seemed to brighten, too.

"Oh, Sissy, will you go with me to look at houses?"

Molly said she would, and Rennie went off to take a shower, humming happily the way a woman does who has just sunk into a new love. Molly went down the hall, intending to return downstairs and see if her mother had finished watching television. Passing the guest room, she glanced in and saw the rumpled bed where Sam had slept. At least supposedly. She could not seem to help wondering, and she put it down to her romantic streak.

Turning into the room, feeling the sudden need for straightening things, she pulled the sheets off the rumpled bed, wadded them on the floor and respread the coverlet. She gathered the bundle of sheets, and when she stood up, she found herself staring straight at the array of framed photographs across the bureau.

As if drawn by a cord, Molly went over and stared at the photo of her and Tommy Lee. Their wedding photograph. She had not seen this picture in a long time, she thought, as she took it up and peered closer. Softly, she touched her fingertips to Tommy Lee's image. So young, children almost, the two people gazing back at her looked more scared than in love. They stood so close, pressing against each other, holding hands. Holding on to each other, she thought.

She set the photograph back in place and left the

room. At the bathroom door, she called to Rennie through the door, "Hurry up, Rennie. We don't have all day. It's already afternoon."

Molly drove the Mustang because Rennie said she couldn't really look at houses and drive, too, but she insisted on taking her car.

"My car is so much nicer, Molly, and you know *you* won't drive the El Camino around with the air conditioner going and the windows down."

That was true; Molly couldn't stand to waste gas and cold air like that. She could do so in Rennie's car.

They went all over town, looking at prospective houses for Rennie, but then Molly got sidetracked and began visiting places she and Tommy Lee had lived. Her reminiscing started when they happened to pass by Montgomery's garage, the first place she and Tommy Lee had lived together. She found the old building quite a shock. It was boarded up.

"It's at least fifty years old," Rennie said, "and it didn't start out as much to begin with."

"Gosh, how could I not know it was all boarded up?" Molly wondered aloud, her mind tumbling back with the years.

The Montgomery garage had been her and Tommy Lee's first home together. They had rented the apartment on the top, and Tommy Lee had helped old Mr. Montgomery repair brakes in the garage below. Gazing at it, memories and feelings tumbled over Molly, how they had put a fan in the window in order to survive the heat at night and later had to stuff towels around the same window, trying not to freeze. She remembered their first night after coming home from their New Orleans honeymoon trip.

"I had a bad dream about a man in the room," she told Rennie, "and when I woke up, Tommy Lee was vaulting over the end of the bed, yelling *'Grrr.'* I went screamin' after him, and we both ended up in the kitchen before we got fully awake. Tommy Lee said I had woke him up, whispering, 'There's somebody in here.' I guess he was after whoever it was."

He had held her so tight, even as they laughed and laughed about it. "Are you okay, Molly?" he'd asked repeatedly, worried about her and the baby she carried. She guessed he had had to worry about the baby she carried for most of those early years.

After Montgomery's garage, Molly went to each of the places where she and Tommy Lee had lived. They had moved often, each time Tommy Lee made a little more money, each time they had another child.

This harking back annoyed Rennie, who was interested in houses to buy for herself, *now,* not old places for Molly to wax nostalgic over. While she kept pointing out houses, Molly was preoccupied with trying to remember the locales of where she and Tommy Lee had lived, even speaking her thoughts aloud—"Now, was it 1113 or 1013?"—and driving to each address in the order in which she had lived there, a further annoyance to Rennie.

"You are wastin' time and gas goin' from one end of town to the other," Rennie said. "Why don't you drive by them as you *come* to them?"

"I can't remember them that way," Molly said.

With each place she would stop right in the middle of the street and tell Rennie a little something about when she and Tommy Lee had lived there, but pretty soon it was almost as if Rennie weren't there with her, as if she were taking the tour through memory all by herself. It didn't matter that the duplex, into which they had moved after Montgomery's garage, had been bulldozed and a double-wide trailer with chain-link fence stood in place of the white clapboard building and picket fence. She remembered the double apartments and how lonely Beatrice Lessing had lived in the adjacent apartment with a dog she dressed in the baby clothes Savannah outgrew. Beatrice was company while Tommy Lee was out on the racing circuit as a mechanic for Jack Kemp. Sometimes Beatrice would watch Savannah for them so Tommy Lee and Molly could go out to eat or to a movie.

She and Tommy Lee had had a fight in that duplex apartment that Molly had never forgotten. Actually the fight didn't begin at the apartment. It began over at a friend's house, where Tommy Lee and some other men were working on a racing car. They left the women waiting in the house nearly all night while the men alternately worked on the car and chased around getting beer. At nearly one o'clock and Tommy Lee gone somewhere in their car, Molly took Savannah and walked home and locked the door against Tommy Lee and wouldn't let him in for a day. She would have gone home to Mama, but Mama was back with Stirling then.

Molly sat and thought of all this until Rennie prodded her. "Would you please drive on? The air conditioner can't hardly work with the engine just idlin'."

Next Molly drove to see the first true house she and Tommy Lee had rented. It happened to be right down the street from Annette Rountree—Rennie pointed that out.

"I got pregnant with Boone in that house," Molly said, staring at the small house. "Me and Tommy Lee had a big fight about him being out on the circuit, and then we made up and I was pregnant." The house really needed painting now.

Their second house had been older but bigger and right across the street from the elementary school. Molly would stand in the yard and watch Savannah cross the street. Tommy Lee had come off the circuit then and was working up in Lawton for the Ford dealer; they had moved to this house because it had a huge garage, and Tommy Lee could work on cars back there to make extra money. He had caught the garage on fire, but he had saved the car inside. The house looked exactly the same, except the tricycle in the yard was one of the big plastic kind, not one of the little red metal ones Savannah and then Boone had shared. Tommy Lee used to wheel each one of the children up and down the sidewalk.

The next house was up in Lawton, but Rennie put her foot down about driving up there, so Molly drove out to the last house they had lived in before they moved to the Hayeses' farm. It was out at the edge of town, closer to Tommy Lee's parents. He had been helping his daddy farm then, in addition to working at a machine shop. This house she and Tommy Lee had bought. They had brought Colter home to this house. He had been a wakeful baby, and it got to where Molly would nurse him, and then Tommy Lee would walk the floor with him to get him to sleep.

By now Molly was crying, which made Rennie really irritated. "You don't need to go around and see all these old haunts if you're gonna cry about it," Rennie said. "Would you please pull off the road before we get rear-ended."

Molly pulled the car over, and Rennie insisted on taking over the driving. "I don't want you wreckin' my car and maybe gettin' us killed just when I may have found the man of my dreams," she said, shoving at Molly to get out of the seat.

Molly thought it just as well. She was overrun with memories, times past that she could not get back and in some cases would not want to get back. Although she could not get them back, however, they seemed to be clinging to her, bringing all their joys and difficulties and regrets down upon her at once. As she came around to the passenger side, the heat radiated up off the blacktop and gravel, and it seemed to shimmer up around the house. Molly stared at it, feeling as if she was any moment going to hear the kids' laughter and Tommy Lee call out that he wanted a Coca-Cola.

It was Rennie's voice that hollered, "Get in, Molly."

Molly got in the car, and Rennie handed her a tissue and told her to wipe the mascara from under her eyes.

"Why don't you just go back home to Tommy Lee?" Rennie said and pulled back out on the road.

"I can't," Molly said.

"Well, why not? You are plainly still mooning over him."

Molly stared out the windshield. "That isn't the whole of it, Rennie," she said. "It takes a lot more than loving. It takes believing."

26

❖❖

Can't Keep A Good Man Down

When Rennie and Molly pulled down the driveway, they saw Tommy Lee's Corvette sitting beside their mother's house. Seeing the car surprised Molly, but what was curious was that it was parked on her mother's side of the driveway. And then the back door to her mother's house opened and people poured out.

"Savannah?"

Her daughter, pudgy and round, came hurrying across the grass, and Tommy Lee and Mama came behind her.

Molly and Savannah hugged, and then Rennie and Savannah hugged, and then Savannah went back into Molly's arms, clinging like a child. Molly looked over her daughter's shoulder at Tommy Lee and Mama. Mama had that speculative expression, and Tommy Lee definitely looked pained and confused. Molly noticed then that Stephen was nowhere in sight.

Savannah said, "Oh, Mama . . ." and buried her face against Molly's neck.

*   *   *

Savannah had driven all the way from Arkansas by herself. Molly's mouth went dry as she looked at her daughter, who was huge with child, and thought of her driving all that way alone. Molly had been up to see Savannah three months earlier, and she remembered some of the roads were through lonely hills.

Savannah said, "I want to have my baby down here, with you and Grama with me, Mama."

As she spoke, she nibbled on crackers and peanut butter that Rennie had brought from over at the cottage, Mama's peanut butter being in the refrigerator and suspicious. They were around the kitchen table—Molly and Savannah, Mama and Rennie. Tommy Lee had been with them for a while, until he'd managed to slip himself out to the living room, where he had turned the television to a car race on the sports channel. Rennie was nibbling away on crackers and peanut butter, too, especially since Savannah had asked her to please not smoke in the room with a pregnant woman.

"Stephen just refuses to understand," Savannah said between bites. "He told me it was too late, and that we lived up in Arkansas now, and that I was bein' a childish Mama's baby."

Molly glanced up to see her mother's face register the thought: *That was the boy's first mistake.*

Savannah laid a hand on her rounded abdomen and leaned forward. "I know I waited late to decide this, but I don't see that it is *too* late. The baby isn't born yet. As for livin' in Arkansas, I guess we do, but we also have transportation for wherever we want to go. And I don't know why it should be considered childish to want to be with those people you love at the most momentous time in your life. I'll tell you, Stephen has told me just once too often that I was bein' childish."

She stuck her chin out and looked stubborn, as if she expected more criticism.

Molly couldn't keep herself from saying, "Honey, you should have told me you wanted to come back home. I would have come up and gotten you."

Inwardly she kept thinking of Stephen and wanting to smack his face, but she didn't think this would be a helpful attitude.

Savannah said in a very practical tone, "I was just so mad. And it isn't the same at all to get mad and call your mother to come get you. That is childish, Mama."

They all had to chuckle at that. Mama commented that she didn't know why people were always pointing at other people and calling them childish. "There's none of us that ever grow up. We just get older." She patted Savannah's arm.

Thus far Mama and Rennie were restraining themselves from many comments, obviously believing, and rightly so, that this was a time between mother and daughter, but they had to be in on it. It didn't matter what Savannah's attitude was, either. They were so *for* her. This struck Molly, made her feel a surge of thankfulness.

"My car is new and it is only a six-hour drive, Mama," Savannah was saying. "Well, it took me more like seven hours, because I got out and walked every hour or so, like the doctor told me to do, and I had to keep peein'. But I didn't have any trouble at all on the trip, and if I would have, I had the cellular. Now, what is the problem with any of that, I ask you?"

Molly said Savannah had done remarkably well. "But, honey, why didn't you say anything about wantin' to come down here? We would have arranged everything weeks ago."

Savannah looked defiant for a moment more, and then she seemed to sink. "I guess I kept thinking that I should have the baby where Stephen wanted me to. I mean we do live up there now, and he just seems to think it so important. But the closer the time got, I just didn't want to, and I don't see that it is all that big a deal. All I wanted was to come home for a few weeks. Stephen just refused. He never wanted to come for you and Daddy's anniversary, and when it was called off, he told me I was not going to come down here and that's all there was to it. He told me that."

Molly thought that Stephen was the foolish one for using that tactic. She met Rennie's and Mama's eyes and they silently agreed.

Savannah continued, "We got in this horrible fight last night, and Stephen slept in the guest room. When I got up this mornin', I just got my stuff and came home."

"You didn't tell Stephen you were leaving?"

"I didn't see the need in gettin' into another fight. I left him a note."

"Well, have you called him at all?"

Savannah shook her head and bit her bottom lip. "I guess I should have. I guess that is childish, not callin' him, even if he deserves it."

Molly said, "Call," and Mama brought the telephone. When Savannah got no answer at her home number, she dialed Stephen's cellular number, too, but she got no answer there, either.

"He's on his way down," Mama said.

"Oh, Grama, do you really think so?" Savannah said, looking from her grandmother to her mother and then to Rennie, too.

Molly said that of course Stephen was coming down, and Rennie said, "Well, if he isn't, you don't want him."

Savannah began to get agitated and to stuff peanut butter and crackers into her mouth at an alarming rate. Molly suggested that Savanna needed to lie down. Savannah agreed that she was tired, but she didn't want to lie down at her grandmother's. She wanted to go home to her own bed. She did not mean Arkansas.

"You'll come home, won't you, Mama? At least for a little while?"

Molly said she would, and she went to get Tommy Lee from the living room. In the few minutes they were alone, Tommy Lee said, "How is she?"

"Well, she's pregnant," Molly said. "Really pregnant."

Tommy Lee just looked at her and nodded. Then they were both gazing at each other and without speaking they knew exactly what the other was thinking: *What about us?*

"She's our daughter, Tommy Lee," Molly said.

He gave a tired grin, and he put an arm around her as they returned to the kitchen.

They had been home no more than fifteen minutes and Savannah had gotten settled into bed, Molly massaging her feet, when Stephen arrived. Savannah, who had excellent hearing, recognized the sound of his car.

"That's Stephen!"

She jump up and hurried down the hall. Molly was amazed that Savannah could move as fast as she did. The weight of her abdomen made her do this curious waddle in which she seemed to keep a precarious balance. Molly worried that her daughter would either fall over backward or pitch over forward. She couldn't recall how she had managed in such a state, but that had been years ago.

Molly followed Savannah to the window in her and Tommy Lee's bedroom, where there was a view of the driveway below. It was dusk now, the driveway illuminated by the lights. Tommy Lee, who had gone directly to the shop, was striding toward Stephen. Molly recognized that walk; it meant Tommy Lee was mad.

She and Savannah pressed their foreheads against the screen, straining to see and hear, but the men's words were indistinct. It did appear that they were arguing, however, and in minutes their voices rose.

"What do you think you were doin', lettin' her drive off by herself like that?"

"I didn't know. . . . She didn't *tell* me."

"You should have known," Tommy Lee said. "You are responsible for her." He went to pointing that finger at Stephen like he did when he got upset.

They tossed a few more angry accusations back and forth, Tommy Lee more or less faulting Stephen for lack of attentiveness to his responsibilities, and Stephen saying Tommy Lee hadn't known how to raise a daughter with any sense, and then Stephen came stomping inside saying, "I want a word with my *wife!*"

Savannah looked wildly at Molly for a moment and then turned and headed out of the room in that curious waddle again. Molly hurried after her, determined to catch her if she fell, whether forward or backward.

At the top of the stairs, Savannah looked down and said in that righteous way she could have, "You do not need to come in here, disrupting everyone, Stephen."

Stephen looked upward in surprise. "Me disrupting? What do you think you're doin'? You ran off, Savannah!"

"I came home. I made it home without your assistance, so you can just go back to your precious job that you couldn't possibly take time away from."

At that Savannah huffed off to her bedroom and slammed the door while Stephen called, "This is not your home!" and came up the stairs, taking them two at a time, casting Molly a look that was somewhere between a glare and uncertainty as he passed.

Savannah wouldn't let Stephen into her room. He banged on the door and frowned at Molly, but she refused to budge. She felt the need to stay right where she was, in case Savannah came out and took it in her head to go down the stairs. Savannah had come up the

stairs quite well, but Molly worried that if upset, she
might not handle going down too well.

Stephen was leaning up against the door now, and
her anger at him eased. He was hunched over, as if
hunched against the world. The back of his shirt was
sweat stained after the long hours of riding in the car.
He looked at Molly for a minute, and then he knocked
on the door and said more calmly, "Savannah, I have
to talk to you."

Molly went down the stairs then. She told herself
she should not be interfering, and she prayed Savannah would not fall down the stairs.

When she came around the corner, she almost
bumped into Tommy Lee, who had obviously been
standing there, listening. For a moment, both of them
stood there together, trying to hear. Stephen was still
knocking on the door and talking to Savannah
through it, speaking too low for them to hear what he
said.

Tommy Lee slipped his hand to the back of Molly's
neck. "Do you want a Coke?" He moved away to the
refrigerator.

Molly took the can he handed her and poured half
the contents into a glass with ice and gave Tommy Lee
the rest. Taking their cold drinks, they went out the
back door and to the driveway now crowded with
cars. Molly sat on the fender of her El Camino and
Tommy Lee leaned against it.

Tommy Lee said, "She isn't gonna let him in."

"No, I don't think she will. She might come out to
go to the bathroom, though."

Savannah took a long time to get mad, but once she
did, she burned for quite a while.

Tommy Lee said, "She'll wet her pants first."

After several long minutes Molly said, "Those two
remind me of us."

"No." Tommy Lee shook his head. "We were never
that stupid."

"Oh, Tommy Lee. Remember the fight we had over the television? You said it was *your* television because your parents had given it to you when you were fifteen, and so it was your right to take it into the bathroom to watch television while you shaved, never mind that I was watching it."

Tommy Lee started laughing. "So you poured a glass of water in the back of it and blew it up."

Molly remembered how she had cried and thought their marriage was over after only two weeks, and how since they had no television for a number of months, while they saved to buy one, she and Tommy Lee spent many evenings talking on the back steps and afterward they would make wonderful love with the summer breeze blowing in the window. Thinking of it now, she realized the loss of the television had been a very fortunate thing.

She looked over at Tommy Lee. He was gazing downward, lost in thought. Was he thinking the same thoughts? She noticed his hair curled down on his neck. Without her reminding him it was time to get a haircut, his hair had gotten longer than he normally let it, and it curled behind his ear. Molly raised her hand to stroke him there, then let her hand drop without touching him.

"Stephen is not totally responsible for Savannah," she said. "She's a woman grown, and he isn't her father, he's her husband."

"He married her. He should take care of her."

"He can't take care of her if she won't let him. And she shares the responsibility for herself. She can and should take care of herself."

Tommy Lee gave a little derisive snort.

"She did okay comin' down here."

"Only because nothin' happened. If anything had happened, she wouldn't have known anything to do but panic."

"You don't know that."

"I do know that. She isn't the woman you were when you got married. She's six years older than you were when you had her, and she's ten years behind you then. Our daughter is still pretty much of a spoiled little girl. But be that as it may, Stephen married her, and he should be able to take care of her." Even though he held the Coke can, he still pointed his finger.

Molly herself thought Savannah might have panicked, but she didn't care for Tommy Lee thinking that. Then what he had said about Molly herself struck her. It was pleasant that he spoke of her in a rather glowing way.

She said, "Stephen is not the man you were, either. He doesn't know at all when to keep his mouth shut. You always knew how to at least pretend to understand me, and how to maneuver me, but Stephen keeps trying to order Savannah. For a young man who graduated top in his class at college and who thinks he knows everything, he doesn't know anything that matters."

That all sat there between them for a long minute, and then Molly said, "Oh, Tommy Lee . . . I should have seen this comin'. I know Savannah. I should have known how much she wanted to come home. I *did* know it . . . but I was just so distracted by myself and me and you. I haven't talked to her hardly at all these past weeks. She's needed me, and I just haven't been there for her." Molly felt so tired and wished to go to bed and pull the covers over her head.

"Molly, you have a right to your own life. And Savannah is twenty-four years old. She has to start facing her own choices and mistakes. And she has to quit thinkin' that whenever she's scared, she can come runnin' back to you. That way, she'll never face what she needs to."

"I suppose that's so," Molly said.

She mused on this, finding Tommy Lee's attitude a

bit contradictory. She didn't think she should call him on it, though. She said instead what she had been thinking for the past weeks.

"I've often thought that one of the reasons you and I made it over the years is that we never had anywhere to run to whenever we got angry at each other. We only had each other."

Tommy Lee looked up at her. Then he moved and shoved in between her legs, encircling his arms around her waist.

"Honey, you've always been there for the kids. What I said the other day, actin' like I resented that— I don't. I've always admired that you put them first, before yourself and me and even God himself. They're my children, too, and one of the things I love most about you is how you have cared for them. I guess I took advantage of that. Knowin' you were so vigilant, I didn't have to pay as close attention. I could go on about whatever I wanted or needed to be doin' and leave the kids to you."

"Oh, Tommy Lee . . ." She stroked the hair behind his ears and gazed into his eyes and felt tears welling into her throat. "You have always been a good father. You were even a father to me, and sometimes I fought that, but the plain fact is, I've needed you to be that for me. I guess it wasn't fair to you . . . but I couldn't help it. I've grown up now . . . at least some, and I know that's hard on you. But it's you who have helped me to grow."

He looked long at her, and she at him. He pressed his hand against her back, and she stroked the hair behind his ear. She blinked tears from her eyes and kept on looking at him and holding on to him.

The next moment the back screen door smacked and the back porch stairs creaked, drawing Tommy Lee around. Stephen came into view, shoulders slumped so that Molly's heart tugged for him.

"Tommy Lee . . . speak to him."

"No. I can't stand him. You do it," and he shoved from her and started away for his shop.

After a moment of absorbing that, Molly hopped down and walked over to where Stephen stood with his car door open, waiting for her. It struck her that Stephen's car was a Mercedes sitting alongside the El Camino, Tommy Lee's old Chevy pickup, and Savannah's Taurus, which Tommy Lee had picked out for her. Stephen was as different from them all as Molly had been from Tommy Lee's parents.

"Give her time to cool off, Stephen. You both need time to cool down."

"She had no right to run off like that."

"No more right than you have dictating to her," Molly said.

Stephen got into his car and slammed the door. "I'll be back tomorrow. Maybe. Until then, I'll be stayin' at my sister's."

Molly watched him drive away and thought, *I guess I handled that poorly.* She went back into the house to check on Savannah. Savannah's door was closed but not locked. Molly simply twisted the knob and went in.

Savannah was propped up in the bed. She said, "Stephen never tried the knob. I never did lock it, and he never did try it."

Molly couldn't tell if Savannah was amazed or annoyed; perhaps a little of each. Molly thought that both Stephen and Tommy Lee underestimated Savannah.

She went about seeing to her daughter's comfort, enjoying the hovering and comforting and protecting. She got Savannah another pillow, brewed her some chamomile tea, lowered the thermostat a notch.

"Mama, Stephen tells me everything to do . . . just like Daddy always has done you. But I can't do what he says, like you always have done just exactly what Daddy says."

Molly raised an eyebrow. "Oh, have I?"
Savannah nodded.
"Have I?" Molly said once more.
Savannah blinked, then frowned, thinking.

"Savannah, you are gonna have to learn to pay attention to what your husband says, and then do what you want, without making a big ruckus out of it, or you're gonna either be divorced or wrung out in short order." Then she conceded, "I have often done as your father said, but your father is *right* so very much of the time." And it was always easier, she thought.

"I don't want to play games."

Molly breathed deeply. "I never did either, but maybe doing so comes natural to human beings. I'm coming to think that it isn't so much playing games as being diplomatic and keeping life smooth and enjoyable all the way around. It's like manners. Some people don't see the point in them, but manners enable humans to live together in a civilized manner."

"I've hurt his feelings," Savannah said, looking pensive and slipping down further into the bed. "I wish I could feel more sorry."

"I wish I could say that you and Stephen will never have another fight . . . but you will."

Molly decided she needed to go then because she wasn't being very positive. "You'll feel better after you get a good night's sleep." Savannah's eyes had already drooped shut.

Molly turned out the hall and stairway lights as she went through the house. She paused in the kitchen and looked around before taking up her purse.

Tommy Lee was standing beside the El Camino when she came out. He asked how Savannah was, and Molly said fine and sleeping. He opened the car door for her, closed it after she got inside, and stuck his head in the window to kiss her lightly.

Then she drove away, back to the cottage. She didn't really ask herself why she had come back, until she walked into the kitchen and the heat and the scents closed around her.

She found her cellular phone and called across to talk to her mother.

"Well, hello honey," Mama said. "What's the story?"

Molly told her all of it, in the same manner that Savannah had come telling.

Ruthann Johnson, Savannah's childhood friend, came out early the next morning, and soon after she arrived, Stephen showed up. Savannah did speak to him this time, but she refused to return to Arkansas with him. She intended to have her baby in the bosom of her family. Tommy Lee heard her yelling that at Stephen all the way from outside: "I'm havin' my baby in the bosom of my family!"

Savannah had the strength of her home behind her now, and she was standing firm. Tommy Lee felt Stephen was being run over, and this made him start to have sympathy for the boy.

"You can't be forcing a Collier woman to do anything, you know," he told Stephen, breaking down and offering the boy a Coca-Cola and trying to help by explaining some of the facts of the family.

But Stephen said, "Savannah is now Savannah Locke—and she never has even carried the Collier name."

Tommy Lee shut his mouth on further advice as to how Stephen should progress. If the young man would not listen to the facts of the case, he wasn't about to listen to how Tommy Lee had learned to go about bending those facts. Tommy Lee figured there was no profit in trying to help a fool. He began to think it best that Savannah stay home and that he had been mistaken in giving her hand in matrimony to this senseless boy who didn't know enough to admit what he didn't know.

Savannah was causing Tommy Lee considerable consternation. He worried about how she waddled around.

"Should she be going up and down those stairs?" he asked Molly.

"The doctor says she is in very good health and that a little bit of exertion is good for her."

"I don't recall you gettin' that big. Isn't she gettin' too big?"

"She has gained too much—she's been unhappy and just kept eating. And Mama says she was too thin before and that her body is making up for that in order to provide for the baby."

Whatever was the cause, it was hard for Tommy Lee to watch his daughter struggle to get up from a chair and sigh in relief when she sat down and to keep holding her back all the time. Savannah was his firstborn, his only girl, and he began to get even more irritated at Stephen for getting her into this shape.

That afternoon Molly and Odessa and Savannah and Ruthann held a powwow on the front porch, discussing prospective doctors and getting an appointment set up for Savannah for the following day. Stephen returned that night but left a bent young man. A young man who was trying to make a dent in a brick wall with his head, instead of a decent tool. Tommy wondered if there would be a decent tool for the matter.

Most of that day and those that followed Tommy Lee kept to himself in his shop, kept his music turned up and his attention focused on building one engine and rebuilding another. He thought how Molly thought he kept himself separated out in the shop, and quite often he would have to admit to the truth of that. This time, however, he was keeping to himself and observing, too. He observed everyone coming and going and that Savannah appeared just fine where she was. He observed that Molly was totally taken up with her daughter and appeared to have all but forgotten him. He observed that he was, for the moment, somewhat content with that, although not totally.

By Wednesday, Tommy Lee had grown decidedly discontented with the entire situation. It seemed to him that there were a lot of people at his house and that not one of them was the one person who was supposed to be there, which was his wife.

Ruthann Johnson was now residing in the guest room, and Stephen had taken it upon himself to move into the boys' room. Tommy Lee's estimation of the young man rose with that happening, although it meant he had to keep running into Stephen, and this worked on his nerves. Also, friends of all three of the young people were coming and going. Molly herself came and went several times a day, and her mother and each one of her sisters paid a visit, too. Kaye came, bringing Country Interior Designs for the baby that wasn't even here yet. Hard rock music played through the house, and at least once a day Stephen and Savannah got into a fight.

Then, one evening after a hard day's work, Tommy Lee came in hot and tired and thirsty for a cold Coca-Cola, only to discover that the case of soft drink he had purchased only three days before had been drunk up. Right that minute five people—three of them whom he didn't know and who kept calling him "sir"—were drinking the last of *his* Cokes right then in his living room.

Tommy Lee slammed the refrigerator closed. Twenty minutes later, showered and shaved and carrying a small bag, he left the house of people he barely knew. He hopped in the Corvette and took off down the road, letting the wind blow his damp hair. By feel, he pulled out a tape and stuck it in the cassette player, turned the volume up loud. Country music, sultry songs, Molly's favorites, and he hummed along and drove faster.

27

❖❖

Once Upon A Lifetime

When Tommy Lee came driving in, Molly was over in her mother's dining room, with Kaye and Rennie and Mama, planning the baby shower for Savannah. Kaye had insisted she needed to be in charge, since she specialized in events of such a nature, as she put it. Rennie was so intent on being in on the plans that she had told Sam she would have to meet him later.

"Molly, that's Tommy Lee who just drove up." Mama had the sheers pulled back and was peering out the window.

"Hummm . . ." Molly was working on the list of people to invite to the shower. "Tommy Lee?" She realized then that she had heard a car. The faint sound of music came to her.

She stood beside her mother and looked out. The sun had dropped but there was enough light to see the dust the Corvette stirred. Tommy Lee went clear to the end of the drive out beneath the tall elms. The engine noise stopped, but the music continued.

Molly's heartbeat fluttered. She hadn't been thinking a lot about Tommy Lee lately. She had been so taken up with Savannah. Well, she had thought of

343

Tommy Lee, but it was to think they would have to put their difficulties off for the time being, although several nights she had wished for him.

"Oh!" she said now, whirling from the window, "maybe somethin' happened with Savannah."

"Nothing has happened with Savannah," Mama said, letting the sheer curtain fall back in place.

Molly looked into Mama's eyes. Then she put a hand to her hair and turned to Rennie.

"Do I look okay? Oh, gosh, Rennie, can I use your lipstick?" She was glad she was freshly showered and wore a dress. *Why* was she so nervous? Was it some special knowledge in Mama's eyes? Mama *knew* about these things.

Rennie said, "You don't want lipstick. . . . It'll just get all smeared," laughed, and waved Molly away. "Go see what he's come for."

"Well, I don't know why Tommy Lee can't come to the door and ask for Molly," Kaye said, digging into her purse. "That's the gentlemanly thing. But wait a minute. Here . . ."

Somewhat to Molly's amazement, Kaye handed across a small spray of White Diamonds cologne. Molly spritzed several times on her neck, and Kaye, saying, "Oh, here, let me do it," sprayed a bunch more and then made Molly lift her dress so she could spray the backs of Molly's knees, "just in case." Apparently Kaye had been doing some investigation in the seduction department.

Then Molly was going out through the kitchen, out the back door and into the night, thinking that by the time she got over there Tommy Lee would be gone.

He wasn't. The Corvette sat in the deepening shadows beneath the trees, music coming from it, and Tommy Lee leaned against the front fender, waiting. Seeing him there, watching her come like he did, caused a warmth to shimmer up through Molly and burn on her cheeks. Her steps faltered, but Tommy Lee just kept on watching her, and she couldn't quit looking at him. It was as if he drew her to him. Without one word, while she was about to say hello, he stretched out an arm, took hold of her and pulled her against him.

He turned her, pressed her backside against him, and pointed. "Look there."

"Oh!"

It was the moon. Big and round, just like God had polished a gold coin and placed it in the sky.

Then Tommy Lee shifted, pulled her face around and kissed her.

"Oh!" she said again when he lifted his head.

He didn't let go of her, though. He pressed himself against her, and he had grown hard, and Molly was growing damp.

"They're watchin' from the window," she said, feeling her mind sort of melting.

"I don't suppose they'll see anything they haven't seen before," he said and kissed her again, a soft, seductive kiss.

Molly trembled, and eagerness took hold of her. She truly hoped, however, that Tommy Lee did not intend to retire to the barn because as romantic as that was, she would so much rather have him in a soft bed, without sticky grasses or mosquitoes. These thoughts were very jumbled and frayed, positioned as she was, feeling the hardness of his body and inhaling the male scent of him.

The next instant Tommy Lee straightened, took hold of her, and waltzed her out into the deeper darkness beneath the trees.

Molly was so surprised that she stumbled, but only for an instant, and then there she was, dancing with Tommy Lee in the sultry night over the cooling ground. Around and around they went, flowing to their own steps, laughing and savoring the silliness. The song ended, and they fell together, gasping for breath.

Then the music began again, the tones filtering to them through the darkness. A familiar, favorite song.

"Once upon a lifetime . . ."

Molly and Tommy Lee gazed at each other, as if each was judging whether to take hold, or even to breathe. Their hands met at the same instant. Again, this time with sureness and grace, they waltzed across the cooling earth, letting the music have its way with them.

The song floated out into the night, as golden as the moon, coming over them like the moon did, flickering down through the elm leaves. Tommy Lee's hand was warm upon her back, his breath caressing her ear, his scent and that of the sweet summer earth filling her. She saw the moonlight flicker in his eyes, saw the strong line of his jaw. She listened to the music and recalled the two frightened children staring out from their wedding photograph.

Then Molly closed her eyes and gave herself over to the music, the moon, and the man who now held her in his arms. When the music coming from the car stopped, it went on and on inside her.

Tommy Lee whispered in her ear, "I'm runnin' away, and the only one I have to run to is you, Molly."

"Then I think you had better come inside."

They gazed at each other, Molly holding her breath. The cicadas took over for the music, and so did the night birds and the moonlight, all of it wrapping around them. Tommy Lee stepped out, and they walked hand in hand toward the cottage and into it. The moon shone so brightly through the kitchen window that Molly didn't need to turn on the light.

Tommy Lee pulled her into his arms and kissed her. Pushed her against the sink, held her there with his hard body and kissed her again, hard and demanding.

She took his hand and led the way through the dim cottage. At the bedroom door, Tommy Lee kissed her again, and again in the middle of the almost black room, where he fumbled with the buttons of her dress and she with the buttons of his shirt.

They tumbled across the bed, finding it and each other mostly by feel. She opened her eyes and saw thin moonlight patterns on the wall, thinner moonlight on Tommy Lee's face. His features were gripped by a desire so fierce that seeing it set Molly on fire.

The sounds of the bed creaking, of their breathing and grasping, drowned out the cicadas. They made love, knowing and giving and taking as only two people can when they know each and every sensitive spot of their bodies. The warm summer breeze blowing soft and silky on her skin, the sheet rubbing cool and smooth on her back, and Tommy Lee pounding hot and hard between her legs, taking her right up there to the moon and beyond.

Clean out of breath, Tommy Lee rolled to his back and pulled Molly tight against him, felt her sweat slipping with his and her scent filling his nostrils. He breathed deeply, listened to his heartbeat try to slow back down. The pillow was heaven behind his head, and he held heaven in his arms, and tiny beams of heaven pierced the window screen and sprinkled over their bodies.

Although he would never have given voice to any of those thoughts, he did think they were quite poetic. He thought he was maturing into a very deep thinker and that such thinking seemed to take hold of him at particular times. Molly stretched against him and gave a tremendous sigh of contentment that echoed all the way through him.

"Amen," he whispered, light enough that she couldn't hear.

The next instant he thought he heard another sigh

out of the darkness. He lay very still, thinking that there couldn't possibly be anyone else in the room. Peering into the darkness, he saw the faint, tiny patterns of moonlight on the walls. Then, for a heart-stopping instant, he thought he saw the old woman's face there on the wallpaper . . . and *another* . . . And it seemed the faces *smiled*. He blinked, and they were gone.

He stared at the walls, and then he ran his gaze around the room.

Suddenly music came floating through the window. This startled Tommy Lee, taken as he was by seeing things appear and disappear on the wallpaper. It took him a few seconds to realize the music had been started again out in the Corvette.

Molly giggled into his neck and murmured, "Mama or Rennie is bein' helpful."

Embarrassment sliced through Tommy Lee when he thought of his mother-in-law knowing what he was doing, but Molly sliding halfway atop him and kissing him and putting her hands all over him pretty much pushed coherent thought aside.

She said huskily, "Oh, Lordy, that music turns me on."

She was all the way atop him now, and he began to have fearful doubts about his capabilities. "Ah . . . Molly . . ."

Her kiss stopped his words. A few moments later he discovered to his amazement that he could after all, and he did it until Molly lay limp beside him and was crying and saying, "I love you, Tommy Lee. . . ."

"I love you, Molly." The words came thickly. He'd very rarely said them aloud, but he felt very good for doing so now. "I do, Molly."

With that she cried a little more.

Afterward, as they lay tangled and drifting into sleep, Tommy Lee again heard that strange satisfied sigh from around them. He was certain he heard it. It was as if the *cottage* sighed. It occurred to him that, sounds or no sounds, he no longer felt like something was going to fly across the room and hit him. He felt something of a conqueror. He had a strange but profound feeling that he had done a lot more than he realized.

28
❖❖

Heaven In My Woman's Eyes

When Molly discovered that she had done the amazing thing of waking before Tommy Lee, she carefully slipped out of the bed and into Tommy Lee's shirt and tiptoed to the kitchen, where she hurriedly put together a breakfast tray. If he awoke before she got it done, like as not, he wasn't going to stay in bed. In twenty-five years, she had never known him to loll in bed once he'd gotten his eyes open. He might loll in his BarcaLounger or out around a car, but not in bed.

It was a good thing Tommy Lee wasn't much for having a big breakfast, because all she had was toast and coffee, but she thought it looked very pretty on the old wooden breakfast tray. She sat the tray beside the bed on the vanity stool. When she went to slip back into bed, she found Ace had come and stolen her place, so she moved him to the foot.

Once more stretched out beside him, she lay there and let herself gaze at Tommy Lee. She took note of his face in repose, how even in sleep his strength was apparent. He had a light stubble of a beard; he never had had a thick growth, and she was just as glad. He slept on his stomach, and the tanned skin of his back and shoulders glowed in the early morning sunlight.

A flood of love washed over Molly, making her heart feel as if it swelled to take up her entire chest. It struck her that she could recall the sweet feeling from long ago. She thought that maybe by giving thanks for it and taking careful note of it, she could hold on to the feeling.

She watched through blurred vision as Tommy Lee started digging his feet in the sheet as he came awake. Then he opened his eyes and looked at her. He smiled and reached for her, pulled her over to him and held her for about five seconds before he started stretching and sitting up and saying he smelled coffee.

"I've missed your coffee, Molly," Tommy Lee said, holding the cup appreciatively.

"Is that all?" She gave him a saucy look and took a bite of toast.

"Don't go fishin' for compliments."

"Why not?" She had never felt quite so bold.

Tommy Lee just smiled. Then he looked around the room. "Is this place always this bright?"

She looked, too. "In the early mornings, before the sun gets up over the trees, I guess it is."

The expression on his face made her look around for something she may have missed. The room did seem different, although she couldn't see how.

She got up to adjust the blinds, saying, "The breeze is up. I guess that kind of makes the room feel more open . . . takes away the old scent."

The room seemed to feel lighter, and Molly realized that she felt lighter, too. As if a weight of sadness had been lifted from her heart. She didn't feel the need to think about tomorrow or even that night. She was too caught up in enjoying this time with Tommy Lee, eating breakfast in bed, smiling at him and sharing silent secrets of what was between them.

Tommy Lee had never been one to linger in bed, though, and no sooner had he finished his coffee than he was ready to be up and taking a shower. Molly sat and watched him pad naked out of the room. She sat and listened to the water running in the bathroom sink. She felt a sad fluttering in her chest that she tried to ignore but that kept growing.

"I forgot my shavin' kit in the car," Tommy Lee called. "Would you get it, Molly?"

She padded out in bare feet and Tommy Lee's shirt, got the kit from the car, brought it into the bathroom, and sat it on the shelf. Then she stopped, looked at the kit, and quietly opened it. Listening to the shower spray behind her, she pulled out Tommy Lee's shaver, shaving cream, and aftershave lotion and sat them out on the sink for him. From the medicine cabinet, she got her toothbrush and paste, put the paste on the brush, and laid it alongside Tommy Lee's things.

Then she slipped out of his shirt, let it drop on the floor, and stepped into the shower with him. Tommy Lee's eyes popped wide, and then he grinned and caught her to him. They kissed with the water running in rivulets over their bodies. They washed each other's backs and then some. Leaving her to finish washing her hair, Tommy Lee got out, and Molly heard him humming as he shaved. Peering around the shower curtain, she saw he was brushing his teeth, with her toothbrush.

He was in the bedroom, looking for his socks, when she came in wrapped in a towel. Molly threw herself over him and began to pester him. He was surprised, but then he kissed her.

"I do have a job . . . and so do you," he said when he lifted his head.

"Oh, Tommy Lee, I'm not suggesting we should let our *responsibilities* go—heaven forbid—even for one full day." She dared to boldly caress his chest and willed away the sad, desperate fluttering in her chest.

"But the world certainly will not come to an end if we spent a few hours, or even the entire morning in the bed."

She looked up at him. "I just want time with you, Tommy Lee."

Immediately she ducked her head, wishing to hide, feeling that she was asking Tommy Lee for intimacy he wasn't prepared to give—feeling the familiar sickening terror of need of him and that she was about to fall into the empty abyss.

She turned to push away from him, but he grabbed her and held her and forced her look at him. His eyes were deep blue and intent. Then he kissed her long and hard, and he kissed her again.

"I love you, Molly."

"Oh, Tommy Lee . . . I don't want you to feel you have to. . . ."

"I don't feel like I *have* to. I want you, Molly. I just have trouble sometimes lettin' go of all that I know needs to be done. Maybe that isn't romantic . . . but that's me. Don't pull away from me, Molly."

The panic in his voice caught her. She gazed at him and saw the earnestness on his face. She reached up and stroked his cheek. He ran his hand up her thigh and over her hip. Together they sank across the bed. Tommy Lee held her gaze and caressed her belly. The intent in his eyes and in his touch took her breath.

Then his eyes twinkled. "Are old married people supposed to do this?" He whispered a lewd suggestion in her ear.

"Oh, Tommy Lee!"

"Well, we're married."

Then he was kissing her and she was kissing him, and they were having a wonderful time, when into it all the telephone rang.

"Leave it," he said.

Thinking her mother or Rennie would get the phone, Molly tried to ignore the incessant ringing and let Tommy Lee's sweet touch take her away. But . . . "It could be Savannah."

"Your mother will get it."

But the telephone kept ringing, so now it was Molly turning away from Tommy Lee in order to answer the telephone. He gave her an annoyed look, and she wondered if either of them would ever get it right.

She followed the cord to find the phone and answer. Stephen's voice came across the line. "Savannah's started with contractions."

Molly and Tommy Lee raced around the room, trying to find clothes.

"Oh, this is your sock."

"Give me my shirt."

"It's in the bathroom. Tommy Lee, do you see Mama's car out there? What about Rennie's?"

"No. Neither one. Why did Stephen call here? Shouldn't he call the doctor? Did that idiot say they called the doctor?"

"I didn't ask. I do think they should handle it."

"You don't look like you're lettin' them handle it." Then he added under his breath, "Lettin' them handle things is how they got at our house, and we got over here."

"Not at all, Tommy Lee, don't blow it all out of proportion. You always do that. You exaggerate to make things just how you want them."

"I'm the calm one, remember?"

He did look calm. He looked calm and annoyed at Molly, who kept telling him to hurry up. "I don't really know why I'm goin'," he said.

"To drive, Tommy Lee . . . you'll have to drive."

The entire time they were dressing they were making their way to the Corvette. Molly was slipping on her Keds while Tommy Lee turned the car around. She had the sudden thought that it was a strange how-do-you-do that their daughter had started into labor just as the future grandparents were enjoying sex. She wondered oddly if it showed and looked down at herself.

"Do I look all right?" She brought sunglasses out of her purse.

Tommy Lee cast her a puzzled frown as he shifted and pressed the accelerator. "You look like you just got out of the shower. I have to say that." He shifted and sent them forward.

"Oh, dear." She stuck on her sunglasses and hoped they helped.

"What is it?"

"Well, do we look like we've just been havin' sex?"

She thought he did. There was a look about him, his hair on end and just a look, until he looked totally shocked at her question.

Then he frowned. "We didn't get that far."

Molly's thoughts had gone on way ahead by then, though, and she told him to forget it and to honk when he passed the Hardee's, because she was willing to bet that's where Mama was.

"See . . . there's her car." She waved and called, "Come on, Mama," just as if her mother could hear her.

They found Savannah perfectly composed and Stephen only slightly less so. Savannah was so confident that she was in the bathroom, fixing her hair. Yes, Stephen said to Tommy Lee's terse question, they had called the doctor.

"I'm not a complete idiot," Stephen stated, as if reading Tommy Lee's mind.

Savannah said, "My contractions are twelve minutes apart—there's plenty of time."

She had a contraction shortly after speaking, stood and held her belly, and breathed to Stephen, who counted. When the contraction passed, she took a deep, confident breath and told them all she was doing just fine. Then she focused Molly and Tommy

Lee with a look and said, "Just where were you two last night, and why didn't you tell us you were leavin', Daddy?" She was totally pleased with her proper attitude. Tommy Lee blushed and told her not to be smart.

Molly didn't think Savannah was paying enough attention to just what was at hand. "Honey, this is your first baby. You can't tell how things might go. I think we should hurry along here."

"We *know,* Mama. We've had classes." So, in other words: Get out of our life. Savannah returned to curling her hair.

Tommy Lee gave Molly a skeptical glance and then headed without a word back down the stairs, probably to get a Coca-Cola. Molly vaguely considered finding a cigarette from somewhere. Stephen went to put Savannah's bags in his car, promising to return within the prescribed twelve minutes to meet her next contraction.

In the face of all that calmness, Molly felt a little deflated. She wandered down to her and Tommy Lee's bedroom, thinking about the night that she had awakened Tommy Lee and they had hurried to the hospital for Savannah's delivery. The hurrying had been premature; Molly had been in labor twenty-four hours before Savannah decided to make an appearance. Savannah had been one to tary all through her life, Molly thought, going on to remember how Tommy Lee had stood beside her the entire time. She wouldn't let go of his hand. He'd been so long on his feet in one place that his knees had swollen to the size of cantaloupes.

When Boone had been born, Tommy Lee had missed it because Boone had come in twenty horrible minutes in which Molly had barely made it to the hospital, and Tommy Lee had not made it at all. Colter had settled on having a nice predictable labor of four hours, and Tommy Lee had helped the doctor "catch," as Tommy Lee had called it. Molly said she had had headaches worse than Colter's delivery.

In their bedroom, Molly went over and ran a finger across the dust atop the dresser. The photograph of herself and Tommy Lee was once again sitting in place, and seeing it brought a strong feeling to her chest. She ran her gaze around the room and then went over to make the bed, which appeared not to have been made since she had last done it. Finished, she ran her hand over the solid cherry wood bedpost, then looked at each of the pieces—furniture she and Tommy Lee had saved for and bought one at a time. It was all solid cherry wood, and someday the set would be handed down to one of the kids and on to the grandkids.

Grandchildren . . . oh, my. With this thought, she lowered herself to the edge of the bed. It felt strange to think she was going to be a grandmother.

Tommy Lee, holding a can of Coca-Cola, appeared in the doorway. Their eyes met and held. Slowly he came across the room, propped himself up on the pillows. Molly moved to lean against him. He handed her his Coke, and she took a swallow and handed it back. She felt his warmth through her clothes and caught his scent, so familiar, that of cologne and cotton and sunshine and male skin.

"So, how are you with the grandmother thing?" he asked.

"Oh, I'm gettin' use to it. I've figured out I'm not gonna be gettin' a cane the minute the child pops out. How about you?"

Tommy Lee gave a wry grin. "I guess I'm gettin' use to it, too. I don't think it would do any good to *not* get used to it."

They chuckled together at that. The sounds of Stephen and Savannah down the hall came to them, and they both stilled and listened. Then Tommy Lee's arm came around Molly, and he pulled her back against him and nuzzled her neck. She savored the feeling.

"Molly," Tommy Lee whispered hoarsely into her ear, "I know I've taken you for granted . . . but you've always been there. I guess I just always feel like you will be. I can't imagine my life without you, Molly. That's how it is. Not neglect, but that you're so much a part of my life that I just don't even consider what it would be like without you there."

For an instant, her heartbeat stopped. Then she grabbed his hand and entwined her fingers into his calloused ones. His grip tightened on hers, holding her, willing her to him.

"Sometimes . . . ," she said, her voice thick, ". . . sometimes I need you so much that it scares me. And I know that my need scares you, and then I feel that something's wrong with me."

In the silence that followed, she heard her heartbeat in her ears and felt his breathing against her back. She tried to hold her tears. She didn't want to upset him, or make him feel obligated.

Then he said, "I do get scared . . . because I'm afraid I can't be what you need. That I'll let you down. And I guess I get mad at you for putting me in that position."

"Oh, Tommy Lee." She twisted and laid her face on his chest, rubbed her cheek against the smooth cotton of his shirt. "We're goin' to be married twenty-five years, and I would not trade a single day of those years. I wouldn't even trade away the days we argued or the days we let each other down, either. Those times are what have made us grow into where we are today."

"Where are we, Molly?"

"Well . . . I guess we're here . . . with each other."

She lifted her head and gazed into his blue, blue eyes, and he gazed back.

They each began to grin, and no words were necessary.

An alarming cry from down the hall rent the moment. Molly and Tommy Lee looked at each other, and then jumped to their feet and raced down the hallway, Molly calling, "Savannah?"

Savannah was bent over and gripping the side of the sink and sucking in great breaths. Molly went over and rubbed on her back, saying, "You're doin' fine, honey."

Tommy Lee hovered in the doorway, and Stephen came clamoring up the stairs and crowding beside him. Both of them looked in with helpless faces.

"Oh. That was a surprise." Still stunned, Savannah gave a shaky smile. "Gosh, I guess we'd better get goin'."

Stephen took her gingerly, helping her down the steps, while they said to each other, "We're about to have our baby. . . . Oh, I love you, honey."

Molly told Tommy Lee, "Get out there and get the car goin'."

He looked startled, then hurried around Stephen and Savannah down the stairs.

Molly pulled two sheets out of the linen closet and grabbed one of the baby blankets Rennie had bought, too.

Savannah had another contraction on the back porch, one so strong that she cried out and sank to the floor. Stephen urged her to breathe, and she tried, then smiled weakly at him and said, "I'm okay," and struggled to her feet.

Molly's mother, in her fuchsia robe, was just getting out of her car. Seeing her, Savannah perked up. "Oh, Grama! I'm havin' the baby!" as if she were about to climb on a carousel horse and go for a ride.

Tommy Lee ordered Stephen to put Savannah in the back of Mama's Lincoln, which had just neatly

blocked in all the other vehicles. Stephen balked for
an instant, then gave in. As she got into the car,
another great contraction took hold of Savannah, one
so great that she groaned through gritted teeth until
she could tell Stephen to shut up about breathing.

Mama suggested that it might be a better idea to get
Savannah back inside the house, but Stephen and
Tommy Lee and Savannah, too, all said, "No!"

Savannah added, "Get me to the hospital. . . . Oh,
get me there, Daddy."

Her words were like the on button for Tommy Lee,
who jumped in behind the wheel and started the
engine, even while Molly was still helping Stephen
and Mama to settle Savannah in with them in the
backseat. Before Molly got her own door closed,
Tommy Lee raced away up the drive, sending dust and
gravel flying. He plowed right through the chickens in
front of Eulalee Harris's house, sending them every
which way. He slowed only enough so as to not throw
everyone around when he turned onto the state highway, and then he floored the accelerator. It seemed as
if they were a plane zooming over the blacktop,
passing every car they approached. Glancing over at
him, Molly was startled to see Tommy Lee sitting
relaxed, one elbow propped on the arm rest, while his
fingers maneuvered the wheel.

In the backseat, between some lighter contractions,
Savannah told Stephen she was sorry for yelling at
him and that she was doing fine, and then she
immediately went into another hard contraction and
alternately groaned and tried to breathe. Then she
said, "Oh!"

"Her water just broke," Mama said, in the same
tone that she would have said the sky is blue.

And Stephen said, "Oh, God," as if he might be
sick.

Molly stretched over into the backseat, passing one
of the sheets to Mama and stroking Savannah's head

helplessly. She started to tell Tommy Lee to drive faster, but she thought they could not possibly go any faster. Savannah began having contractions one right after another, alternately groaning and praying.

"How did I get into this?" she asked, whimpering. "Oh, Daddy, hurry. . . . Oh here comes another pain."

Stephen made a valiant effort at trying to get back on track with their birth training. "Breathe, honey, see, now pant. You can handle this contraction. Think contraction, honey, not pain."

Savannah yelled, "These are pains, Stephen! Why don't you have a few and see?" The next minute, with panic, "It's comin'. . . . The baby is comin'."

"Pull over, Tommy Lee," Molly ordered.

"No!" Stephen said, and he put his hands on Savannah's stomach. "She isn't. We'll make it."

"Pull over," Mama said in that tone and began tugging Savannah's underpants off.

Tommy Lee pulled over, and Stephen was saying, "Oh, God, oh, God," and Mama told him to keep praying and told Savannah not to be frightened, in the same manner she would tell her not to comb her hair at the table.

Molly looked over at Tommy Lee and said, "We've had three children, and Mama has had five. We should be able to handle this."

Tommy Lee clamped his jaw tight while Mama said from the backseat, "I was asleep during all my deliveries, Molly. But hasn't Tommy Lee delivered cows?"

Stephen said, "Cows?"

Tommy Lee said, "Call the hospital emergency, Molly."

Until that moment, Molly had forgotten all about the cellular phone Mama always kept lying in her front seat. While she dialed the emergency number, there was a quick debate about whether Savannah should lie on the backseat or get out of the car. Mama cut into it, saying she had a quilt in the trunk and for Tommy Lee to get it. With the phone to her ear, Molly instructed as to just where on the grass to spread the quilt.

They got Savannah laid down and draped the remaining clean sheet over her bent knees. Stephen had another moment's panic, where he stood back and almost fainted, but after one look at Tommy Lee, he came around and propped Savannah's head in his lap and gripped her hand and tried to get her to remember her breathing. Mama produced bottled water and a handkerchief and went to wiping Savannah's face while Tommy Lee and Molly crouched down to see what was going on with the baby. By then a medic had answered on the other end of the line, and Molly began telling her what was going on.

"Oh . . . the head is showing," Molly said. "Tommy Lee—there's the head! Savannah, honey, your baby's almost here."

Everything started going so fast. Savannah's urge to push intensified, and the baby's head got bigger and bigger. Excited, Molly told the voice on the phone to just hang on, and barely even realizing her actions, she tossed the telephone aside and reached for Savannah's hand.

Seeing the phone fly three feet, Tommy Lee felt fear grab him by the throat. This was *his* baby about to deliver a baby, and he was a bit embarrassed all the way around, too, but he didn't have time to consider any of it because his daughter went to groaning and straining and Molly went to telling her to push all she wanted, and Tommy Lee saw the dark head getting bigger. The contraction ended, and the dark head receded. Tommy Lee told Stephen to hold Savannah up and help her with the next push, which came immediately, and the head came popping right out, which thoroughly shook Tommy Lee. *The cord was looped at the baby's neck.*

"Get that damn medic back on the phone," Tommy Lee hissed to Molly.

She gave him a blank look, then scrambled to get the phone. Tommy Lee bent close to inspect the baby. He murmured soothing words to Savannah, although he had no idea of what he said. He was busy assessing the situation. He did not think he could wait for the medic's instruction. Moving by instinct, he took his finger and eased the cord from around the baby's neck, even as the baby began to slip right out into his hands.

"Molly! Molly, It's comin', it's comin'!"

Molly's hands were suddenly with his, and the baby slipped right out into them. For a moment suspended in time, Tommy Lee and Molly, side by side, held their squirming little grandchild.

Molly could hardly see through her tears. "Oh, Tommy Lee." She turned her gaze to him and saw he had a stunned expression on his face. She made certain he held the child firmly, and then she sat back and gazed at him, with his grandchild in his hands. It was a girl, who, after a few heart-stopping silent seconds, let out an enormous angry squall. That jarred them all out of the magical moment. While Tommy Lee gave his granddaughter over to her mother's waiting arms, Molly searched around for the baby blanket they had brought. Then she knelt beside Tommy Lee and watched as Savannah and Stephen, heads together, cuddled their brand-new child.

Tommy Lee's arm came up and he pulled Molly against him. She saw tears flowing down his cheeks, and the sight made her begin to cry again.

"Oh, Tommy Lee . . . you did it," she said through sobs against his neck.

"*We* did it, Grandma," he said hoarsely.

"Yes, we did, Grandpa."

The baby let out another good wail, and Odessa said, "Another Collier girl. They have good lungs."

Stephen came up straight. "She is a Locke. That's her mother's name and my name. Locke," he said, casting each of them a firm look.

Mama raised an eyebrow but didn't say a word.

Molly and Tommy Lee looked at each other, and then they kissed, deeply and passionately.

29
❖❖

Here We Are

Everyone came to the hospital, Rennie, Kaye and Walter, Season and Lillybeth, and Ruthann, who was supremely disappointed to learn all the excitement had started ten minutes after she had left for work.

Sam even came. "I was there with your mom and dad when you were born," he told Savannah. He looked somewhat startled. "I didn't think I was that old," he said.

Then a strangely familiar man was coming down the hall toward them, a tall, well-built man with thick white hair dressed in expensive-looking casual clothes and shiny shoes.

"Good Lord, it is *Stirling*," Molly said as she watched her mother greet him.

Mama was still in her robe, of course, which Kaye had had a fit about. But as if she wore a fine evening gown, she took Stirling's arm and came toward Molly and Tommy Lee.

Stirling kissed Molly's cheek, shook Tommy Lee's hand, congratulated them, and said, "Now, I'd like to see that new mother and baby. This is sort of my great-granddaughter, isn't it?" He went on into Savan-

nah's room and was met with stunned but happy
greetings. A few minutes later Molly heard him say,
"Ah . . . another Collier girl, Odessa."

There in the hall, Tommy Lee laughed and laughed,
and put a hand to Molly's neck and drew her against
him. Molly held on, savoring being able to do so.

By noon, the head nurse came with all her authority
and ordered everyone out and the mother to sleep.
Stephen could rest in the reclining chair. As everyone
started to group in the hall, the nurse told them they
had to "leave!"

"I guess I'll hitch a ride home with Sam," Tommy
Lee told Molly. He had his hands stuffed into his
jeans pockets. Molly thought he looked tired but not
much like a grandfather. "Are you gonna wait and go
with your mother?"

His eyes were anxious, questioning, although he did
not voice the questions that Molly was asking herself.

She nodded. "We're gonna go and buy Savannah a
few things she needs. That'll be easier than runnin'
home for her bags we left in Stephen's car."

His eyes searched hers for long seconds and then he
gave her a quick kiss, turned, and walked away down
the corridor. Molly watched him, watched his familiar saunter and the way his shoulder muscles moved
beneath his shirt and the way his jeans fit over his slim
hips, until he disappeared through the double doors.

She kept having the sensation of shifting time, of
yesterdays mingling with todays, until she couldn't
recall what had happened when, or if it even mattered.

It was late afternoon when Molly and her mother
drove back through Valentine. Mama waved at people
and called out about her new great-granddaughter.
She caught Jaydee Mayall walking down the sidewalk
and hollered to him to put new Molly Lynn down in

her will. Then they were pulling into the driveway, and Mama said, "Safe home again," with a big sigh.

Molly gazed at the cottage once more from behind sunglasses.

Mama started gathering her purse and packages. She now wore a tunic and big pants in crinkled cotton, very expensive because Kaye had bought the outfit for her, insisting she must get dressed. Molly helped her mother with the packages, and then, slowly, she opened the car door, got out, and stood there, gazing at the cottage.

Mama said quietly, "You can come back for your things later, Molly."

"No." Molly shook her head. "I think I'll take them now."

She went to the cottage, changed into jeans and a sleeveless cotton shirt and her boots, and began throwing clothes into her suitcases. Mama brought a box and began emptying the refrigerator, and shortly Rennie arrived to help. The entire time Rennie chattered about a house she thought she might buy up on Church Street.

Before Molly left she made certain to replace all the books onto their shelves, stack those that didn't fit, strip the bedsheets for washing, and respread the coverlet. Making everything ready for the next occupant.

Finished, she stroked her hand one last time over the pillow and looked around the room. The scent was different, she thought. The entire cottage seemed lighter, even though the day was heavy with heat.

Then Molly had the horse trailer hooked up, Marker inside it, and Ace in his carrier in the back of the El Camino.

She hugged Mama. "Oh, thank you, Mama."

"I do my best, honey," Mama said.

"I'll help with your house, Rennie."

"Tomorrow. I want to show it to you tomorrow. Oh, good luck, Sissy."

Molly got behind the wheel and waved as she drove away. Heading home. She didn't look back, didn't even think to.

The sun was a golden ball in the west when Tommy Lee heard Molly's El Camino coming down the road. He was out on the back step, feeding Jake. He walked to where he could see the El Camino turn into the driveway. He saw that the horse trailer was hooked behind, that Molly's bags were in the back. His throat got all tight.

She stopped and looked at him, but he couldn't see her eyes through the dark glasses. He didn't need to; he could feel them. She smiled, and he smiled, and then she drove on down to the pasture gate.

When he reached her, she already had Marker out of the trailer. He couldn't see her eyes because she was still wearing her sunglasses. Tommy Lee opened the pasture gate for her and Marker and turned on the spigot to fill the water trough. When they walked out, he checked the gate to make certain it was secure. Then he helped her unhook the trailer. All the time neither of them said more than thank you to each other. As Molly headed back for the house, he jumped into the back of the El Camino, like he was a young fella, instead of a grandpa. He didn't think he was so old. He'd just started young.

He'd started good, too, he thought, despite all his mistakes.

Molly came to a stop behind Savannah's car. Tommy Lee opened the car door for her, and she looked up at him. Slowly, she removed her sunglasses, unfolded herself from the seat, closed the door and leaned against it, gazing at him. Her eyes were like polished turquoise.

With deliberate slowness, he placed a hand on either side of her, against the top of the door. He looked long and deep into her eyes. They were achingly sad and sensuous and warm. Welcoming.

"Did you find what you went after?" he asked, his heart beating rapidly.

"I think so. Well"—her lips twitched wryly—"if I even know what I went after."

For a moment they shared knowing amusement, and Tommy Lee felt his life going around a bend, straight open highway ahead.

Molly tucked her hair behind her ear, and he watched her search for words.

Her eyes came back to his, and she said, "I've gone from thinkin' that we have lost anything that was ever there, to knowin' that we have an awful lot together. I don't want to live without you, Tommy Lee. Not that I *can't* . . . that I *don't want to*."

Tommy Lee took her words in as she said them, slowly and deliberately. What he saw in her green eyes made him have the urge to stand a little straighter, a little taller. What he saw in her eyes was something a man could take hold of and know deep inside that it was true.

He swallowed and looked off in the distance. Tears filling his eyes startled him. He had to get ahold of himself before he could speak, for fear he was going to out-and-out cry.

Finally he looked at her. "I guess I found a lot when you went lookin', too," he admitted in a hoarse voice.

He felt his words not quite adequate, but Molly's eyes softened and warmed, and the next thing she had wrapped her hands behind his neck and brought his lips to hers in a soft, seductive kiss.

Then he took her hand, entwining his fingers tightly in hers. He managed to get out, "How 'bout we get a couple of Cokes and go watch the sun finish settin'?"

As they walked toward the house, Molly slipped her arm around him and rubbed her face against his shoulder. She was home.

30
❖ ❖

Time Marches On

On Saturday the anniversary party was back on at the VFW hall. Lillybeth and Season and Rennie insisted. Molly felt so guilty about taking the party back from Kaye that she let Kaye do everything she wished, from hiring a live band that played ballroom music, Kaye's favorite, to laying out Country Interior Design brochures all over the tables. Lillybeth had a fit about this and went around picking them all back up again. Kaye threw her own fit when she discovered what her sister was doing.

"I don't see anything wrong with givin' out my Country Interior brochures," she said, shaking one in Lillybeth's face. "There are goin' to be a lot of disappointed people since I postponed my party."

"It is an *anniversary* party now," Lillybeth maintained. "You are not going to be so tacky as to *sell* at it."

Molly settled it by telling Kaye to leave the brochures on the entry table for anyone who was interested. A few minutes later she saw that Lillybeth had gone and set an enormous bouquet on the table, almost obscuring the brochures.

Then Season and Rennie came hurrying in the side door and behind them came Sam and Winn, rolling in the Wurlitzer jukebox from Rio's, which was loaded with country music tunes.

"We'll take turns," Rennie said. "Kaye's music for an hour, ours for two."

Mama appeared in the doorway. "Molly!" She motioned for Molly to come. Her voice and manner drew Lillybeth and Kaye from nearby in the kitchen.

"What is it? Well, hello, Stirling."

Mama had admitted to seeing Stirling since Christmas, but she would not tell how serious it was. It looked serious. Stirling's car had been seen early mornings at the big brown Collier home.

People were arriving in the parking lot. Here came Colter and Boone driving in, Boone coming in his own pickup truck behind Colter's yellow one. Boone had said that one trip with his brother had been enough. Stephen was helping Savannah out of the car with the baby. Just out of the hospital that morning, Savannah and the baby would only stay an hour, but Savannah had been determined to come. "We are here," she kept telling Stephen.

Drawn by sight of the baby, Molly started off that way, but then Mama said, "Molly!" and tugged at her arm, pulling back her attention. "Look up there." She pointed across the street, upward at the water tower.

Shielding her eyes from the bright afternoon sun, Molly gazed up at the gleaming, newly painted tower. Walter was awfully proud of that water tower. Mama's manner already had Molly's heart beating faster with curiosity, and when she saw the familiar figure up near the top, on the thin ladder, her heart just about leaped right out of her chest.

Tommy Lee? She peered harder and recognized his shirt and the shape of him.

"Oh, my God." He kept going upward . . . and he

had something in his hand. A can. *He was going to paint the water tower.*

Lots of people were looking now, and a collective "Ohhh" went across the parking lot.

"Oh, my gosh, Mama. He shouldn't be up there. Oh!" Molly stepped forward, thinking of helping in some way, tears coming to her eyes with a rush of excitement and joy and fear. What if he fell? She would be made a widow right there on her twenty-fifth anniversary. She had to *do* something. The only thing she could think of was going right up there with him.

Mama grabbed her arm. "You can't go up there, Molly," she said. "He's a capable man. He'll be okay, but you'll kill yourself."

Kaye's voice came loudly, hollering for Walter to get Tommy Lee back down. "I don't care if it is Tommy Lee, we have a fence around it just to stop this sort of vandalism. He's settin' a bad example. Walter, tell him there is a fine for what he's doin'."

"Might make him fall if I yell," Walter said.

Molly, with her hands shielding her eyes from the glare, watched as Tommy Lee reached the top and came around the narrow platform circling the tower. A cheer went up, and it was quite loud, as not only was the parking lot full, but people were watching from the car wash and the nearby laundry. Tommy Lee waved down.

Oh, so full of himself, like he could be at those rare, shining times.

Still gazing upward, shielding her eyes, Molly began to cry. Boone and Colter came beside her, both of them grinning, looking from her up to Tommy Lee. Molly kept blinking, trying to clear her vision, watching Tommy Lee using red spray paint this time, writing TOMMY LEE LOVES MOLLY, STILL.

Molly began to sob, and Kaye came over and hissed, "Molly . . . you're embarrassin' everybody."

The party was a great success and was talked about for weeks. People got teary-eyed watching Tommy Lee dance alone on the big dance floor with his firstborn granddaughter.

Someone—Kaye swore it wasn't her—called the police, and Micky Oakes came over and gave Tommy Lee a ticket for painting on the water tower. Boone and Colter wouldn't let their daddy pay. They scraped together the money and gave it to Mickey right then.

Lillybeth became a little tipsy and actually flirted with the bass player of the dance band. Sam came and asked Molly to dance, and soon afterward he and Rennie took a bottle of champagne and a big plate of food and left. Murlene and Eugene Swanda got Kaye and Walter line dancing to country music; that was something of a sight, Kaye in her flowing chiffon and Walter in his polyester trousers.

Loren Settle, who met Season for the first time, was so totally struck by her that he dared to make advances to her. Amazingly Season saw something in tall, skinny Loren, too. Loren, however, didn't know of Season's animal rights commitments and in trying to impress her, spoke of his dogs and went further to make the mistake of bragging about their coon-hunting abilities. Season was horrified and spent the rest of the evening trying to convince him of the error of his ways while he stared forlornly and adoringly into her eyes.

Molly and Tommy Lee didn't go home that night, where all their children and their granchild were. They took a bottle of champagne and drove out to the lake in the Corvette, played music and danced in the grass and watched the sun come up . . . among other things.

* * *

Two weeks after the party, another vandal hit the water tower and WALTER LOVES KAYE appeared in blue on the fresh silver paint. Walter admitted his action and paid his fine, which had been increased to $500, and Kaye walked around with a dazed expression for days.

Mama and Stirling ran off and got remarried, and Stirling moved into the big Collier home, which Mama refused to leave. Stirling traveled a lot now, anyway, looking after a chain of dry cleaners that he had going. He would be gone for a week at a time, and the arrangement seemed to suit them both.

Rennie bought a house on Church Street. She and Sam got married in August. They had to; Rennie was pregnant. They were both scared but very excited and acting like teens. Rennie agreed that she would move out to Sam's house in Santa Fe, but only after the baby was born, because she had to be with Mama and Molly for that. Sam never argued.

Loren gave up coon hunting for Season and even moved up to Oklahoma City after they got married. Together they began to raise and train dogs to help the handicapped. Loren did keep one coon dog, though, and Season said she felt so guilty that she broke down and encouraged him to visit with his coon-hunting friends once in awhile. She said she saved a lot of animals and was not going to worry over a couple little racoons.

Lillybeth began working with a famous divorce attorney and adamantly said she would never marry. She seemed to take particular care, however, to remain beautiful and attractive, if unattainable.

In the spring of the following year, two weeks after Rennie's baby girl was born, Aunt Hestie's cottage burned to the ground. A short in the electrical box was deemed the cause. The insurance inspector found a penny had been wedged in the fuse box.

A week after that, on a warm, sunny morning, a

crew arrived to clean away the rubble for rebuilding. Seeing how Molly and Odessa and the other Collier women stood and stared at the ruin compelled Tommy Lee to have the place rebuilt. He simply knew that it had to be, and he had learned to pay attention to such feelings.

Walter and Sam and Stirling and Loren agreed to join him in the endeavor. It seemed like they understood, although none of them spoke of it. Tommy Lee called Stephen to see if the young man wanted to join them, and Stephen thought the idea was stupid, but he didn't want to be left out, so he would send a check to help with expenses. Sam, talking to Rennie, came up with plans as close as possible to the original structure.

Over the following weeks, the men oversaw the construction and the cottage went up. The women were happy, and Tommy Lee had a sense that he had done a very good thing. Especially when he looked into Molly's eyes.

❖❖

If you are a fan of country music, you probably realized the chapter titles are actually song titles. Many thanks to the singers of these songs that bring pleasure, comfort, and inspiration. I couldn't write without your music.

—CAM

Discover Contemporary Romances
at Their Sizzling Hot Best
from Avon Books

JONATHAN'S WIFE   *by Dee Holmes*
78368-1/$5.99 US/$7.99 Can

DANIEL'S GIFT   *by Barbara Freethy*
78189-1/$5.99 US/$7.99 Can

FAIRYTALE   *by Maggie Shayne*
78300-2/$5.99 US/$7.99 Can

WISHES COME TRUE   *by Patti Berg*
78338-X/$5.99 US/$7.99 Can

**ONCE MORE
WITH FEELING**   *by Emilie Richards*
78363-0/$5.99 US/$7.99 Can

HEAVEN COMES HOME   *by Nikki Holiday*
78456-4/$5.99 US/$7.99 Can

RYAN'S RETURN   *by Barbara Freethy*
78531-5/$5.99 US/$7.99 Can